Comhairle Contae Fhine Gall

Fingal County Council

Items should be returned on or before the last date shown below. Items may be renewed by personal application, writing, telephone or by accessing the online Catalogue Service on Fingal Libraries' website. To renew give date due, borrower ticket number and PIN number if using online catalogue. Fines are charged on overdue items and will include postage incurred in recovery. Damage to, or loss of items will be charged to the borrower.

Date Due	Date Due	Date Due

D1139021

SEEKING
MR HARE

Also by Maurice Leitch

Novels

The Liberty Lad
Poor Lazarus (Guardian Fiction Prize)
Stamping Ground
Silver's City (Whitbread Prize)
Chinese Whispers
Burning Bridges
Gilchrist
The Smoke King
The Eggman's Apprentice

Short stories

The Hands of Cheryl Boyd
Dining at the Dunbar

Audio book

Tell Me About It

Television plays and screenplays

Rifleman
Guests of the Nation
Gates of Gold
Chinese Whispers

SEEKING MR HARE

Maurice Leitch

THE CLERKENWELL PRESS

Copyright © Maurice Leitch, 2013

1 3 5 7 9 10 8 6 4 2

Printed and bound in Great Britain by
Clays, Bungay, Suffolk

A CIP catalogue record for this book is available from the
British Library.

ISBN 978 1 84668 9376
eISBN 978 184765 9507

The paper this book is printed on is certified by the © 1996 Forest
Stewardship Council A.C. (FSC). It is ancient-forest friendly.
The printer holds FSC chain of custody SGS-COC-2061

For Louis Andrew Leitch
Born 31 August 2011

By the way, gentlemen, has anyone heard lately of Hare? I understand he is comfortably settled in Ireland, considerably to the west, and does a little business now and then, but only as a retailer, nothing like the fine thriving wholesale business so carelessly blown up in Edinburgh.

On Murder Considered as One of the Fine Arts,
Thomas De Quincey

J ohn Fisher, the head jailer and best of a rotten lot for his colleagues would dearly love to do me in and save the hangman a job, says there's a gentleman who needs to take a likeness of me, one of the other turnkeys having brought a broadside in with a picture of Willie Burke on it and didn't they get him to the life, the neat, dapper little figure of him like somebody you'd willingly marry your daughter off to instead of Beelzebub's nephew. Not that I claim any such dispensation in that department myself, him with the cut of a lay preacher in his frock coat and cravat and me a slovenly-looking blackguard by comparison, but still and all the pair of us ran neck and neck, shoulder to shoulder, ending up in here together facing the consequence of our misdeeds.

And so this other turnkey, who hates the Irish as much as the rest of them do, knowing I've not been blessed with the benefit of schooling like my partner lodged in the other part of Calton Jail, says he'd be happy to read the piece out to me, and so off he goes: *'Come all ye resurrection men, I pray you beware, you see what has happened Willie Burke, and likewise William Hare,'* and it's odd listening to our history sold in the street to people who never heard tell of us a month previous and now are of the opinion they're privy to all concerning us, except we never did dig any bodies up, a malicious story put about by certain folk for their own ends and lying satisfaction.

It being the first I've set foot outside my cage for near on a month, led along the corridor a barrage of insults and spittle comes my way, one of my abusers withdrawing to his dark hole sucking his knuckles, for Fisher carries an ebony club and is not backward about using it. But finally I'm brought to a large chamber with raised seats all around, a reek of something chemical in the air making me think this might well be the very place they dissect the bodies, even those the pair of us delivered up to Dr Knox and his young jackals hungry for fresh entrails to dabble in, and sure wouldn't it be the grand jest entirely if yours truly ended up on a slab himself like the one in the middle of the room.

Motioning me to sit on a chair alongside it, Fisher stands nearby until some gentlemen start taking their places on the high benches all around as if at a show, and me the object of their entertainment, this Irish savage shackled and in his shirt, same garment sticking to his back for want of a change or a wash like its owner since getting lifted by the Watch in the early part of October.

And so there I remain until an elderly, foreign-looking gent in a long doctor's coat makes his appearance along with another man, only younger, with the look of a lackey about him, bearing a basin of white stuff, and without a word of by your leave doesn't this same fellow start rolling back the neck of my shirt as though intent on barber's work, but instead of which he starts rubbing some manner of oily substance on my head and into my scalp.

Now how such a procedure might prepare one for a drawn likeness is a mystery to me, but I endure it nonetheless, for lying on damp straw with an empty belly hardens a man's resolve to escape the noose by fair means or foul and if that entails playing the model prisoner, fair enough, for this Irish neck is still precious even if some youth is anointing it with oil from a vial without excuse or explanation, until finally our young friend finishes his business with me, his superior motioning him to stand aside, then addressing those up in the gallery.

'Gentlemen,' says he in a strange sort of an accent, 'we are ready now to apply the first layer of plaster of Paris, and you should be aware a life mask demands more skill and expertise than one taken after the subject's demise, as working with the living, breathing flesh requires a fine and delicate touch so as to cause as little discomfort to the sitter as possible.'

Well, on hearing this, Fisher went pale, as if the intended 'subject' was himself and not his prisoner, noticeably so, for normally he has a high colour due to a fondness for the whiskey, which I smelt on his breath when he came to fetch me, setting off a craving for a dram myself, not having enjoyed a taste or even a sniff of the *cratur*, since getting lifted from my house in Tanner's Close in the early hours, Burke as well, I'd wager, having heard reports of him taking near half a pint of laudanum on account of him getting neither his rest nor sleep at night.

But then the nightmares always were a torment for Willie, his woman, Helen MacDougal, complaining of it, as in the grip of whatever was afflicting him he would sometimes near throttle her before regaining his senses with her lying alongside him in the bed. And many's the time, too, haven't I heard him cry out in the next room, convinced it must be the murders preying on his mind, which still may be the case even if he has no longer cause or opportunity to suffocate and strangle others.

Having been made to lie flat on my back on the table, a pair of quills inserted in both nostrils to allow me to breathe after the plaster is lathered on my face, the Professor, as now I will name him, explains the next stage in the procedure, a thread to be laid across the forehead, bridge of the nose, mouth and chin, before a second layer of the stuff is put in place so as to make the final separation easier.

Lying there at his mercy, yet determined to display no sign of weakness, I concentrated on the twin channels of my breathing while the stuff dried and tightened like a second skin before a fresh coat was buttered on, but pulpy this time, more like mortar, and then all those present adjourned, for I could hear them leave, until it seemed I was the only one left in that place, mummified from the Adam's apple up, when to my surprise Fisher's voice sounded nearby.

'Never in all my born days have I seen the like of what these people have done to you. Like a graven image you are, although the mould, they say, will come off in one piece, your friend Mr Burke having one rendered as well.'

Which turned out to be the case, but only after the rope had been cut from off his neck, and before Knox opened up the rest of him for public display.

After that I heard nothing further and so it came to me, the jailer must have left like the rest of them. But if my vision was impaired my smell was not, for detecting a blast of liquor breath, I heard him sigh, 'Willie, Willie, it's still not too late, you know,' thinking he meant for me to rise up like Lazarus and tear the mask away.

But then the notion of repentance coming from Fisher was a surprise, him with the drink and all, although many's the time I've seen others in the Lawnmarket just like him condemning the 'devil's buttermilk' whilst barely able to stand upright.

'No one, no matter how awful their sins might be, should face their Maker without first purging the purple stain of transgression. Already your own friend has bared his soul to certain gentlemen of the cloth, although being a Roman like yourself his first call was to the Reverend Father Reid.'

Aye, and someone who'd come sniffing around me as well like a dog smelling a bone to suck and slaver over. But didn't I give him the short shrift with a thank ye kindly, monsignor, but not today, nor any other day behind your little lattice screen, except we were in the cell at the time, him with his fine lawn handkerchief pressed to his nose, regretting, no doubt, the absence of incense to cloak the stink of piss and sweat and other foul stuff, and sure I haven't seen hide nor hair of him since, giving me up as a bad job, unlike Willie down on his knees fingering his rosary beads every chance he got.

But Fisher was not the one to be put off, babbling on about everlasting mercy and heavenly forgiveness when, if I'd had the power of reply, I might have told him time enough for that after I had got out of having my neck stretched. Still, like all the rest of them with their broadsides and ballads, let him go on believing what he wants to believe, and those other fine judicial gentry, too, for I've had my fill of *them* these past weeks, picking over our comings and goings like crows on a dunghill.

And so then this other flock of scientific scavengers filed back in again, the Professor directing his young helper to test the plaster, when I could have told him, that's if I was able to, it was near as hot and hard as the hobs of hell itself with a raging itch beneath, which maybe was the desired intention, putting me through this form of correction.

Lying there, I felt the thread drawn clear, followed by the outer mask coming off, then, 'Observe, gentlemen, the negative mould from which an accurate positive can now be made!', a sigh going up as if those present had witnessed some kind of a miracle.

Still all that concerned me was how long it might be before I could open my eyes and mouth and have the straws taken from my nose, also if I'd be afforded the opportunity of seeing my own likeness when complete, for not too many men are given the privilege of having their features faithfully rendered in plaster in company with the likes of Julius Caesar and Napoleon Bonaparte, even the great Sir Walter Scott, who, I'm given to understand, attended some of our trial days in person himself.

Suddenly, I felt someone take a tight grip on my skull followed by a sharp tug, then a dry cracking sound like the breaking of the shell of an egg, and finally I was free of my restraints. The straws were plucked clear, a wetted cloth passed across my face, my eyes and mouth wiped clean, and I could see once more, with the Professor holding up his handiwork, and even though the thing itself was rougher than expected I half-recognised myself, eyes closed as though in a deep sleep.

'This, gentlemen, concludes our demonstration. The mould you see before you will now be taken to my studio to be finished and replicas made for those desiring to make private use of them.'

And, bowing low before an outburst of clapping, the little man in his white coat took his leave, followed by his young assistant bearing the plaster head. *My* head, I kept reminding myself, not entirely enamoured of the notion, let it be said, though others might relish being preserved for posterity in that fashion, even someone with a reputation as bad as my own. But then I had neither desire nor appetite for any further notoriety, vowing if fortune smiled on me I would vanish from the public gaze as if the earth had swallowed me whole.

In the meantime I decided to present a more agreeable face to my jailer, even if it meant swallowing some of his religiosity. So, meek and mild, I climbed down from the table to be escorted back to my underground hole where raging and throwing yourself against stone walls and iron bars was for the likes of those others I could hear crying out in the small hours without a plan or purpose, or the likelihood of another drink.

Returning to the lock-up, no angry outcry greeted my appearance, Fisher's truncheon having something to do with it. Yet I still could smell resentment seep from each cell, as if I'd received some form of preferential treatment instead of a sound beating while away, some white stuff on my hair and cheeks only adding to the mystery and a desire to find out more, for 'Hare, Hare, what did they do to you?' one of them called out after I was locked up, 'Did you get a dram at all?' as he was on a charge of public drunkenness and so his thoughts ran on no other topic.

Fisher had left me a small pocket testament, telling me it would provide comfort from its mere touch and presence, and putting on a show of gratitude I took it from him and off he went content he'd opened heaven's door a crack, letting yet another poor sinner creep through. And from that moment on I kept it on display, for he couldn't stay away, peering in at me with his wee leather-bound book in my hand every chance he got. The sight seemed to gratify him and every so often he would slip the odd morsel through the bars, a heel of bread, a bit of cold mutton one time, even though it was forbidden by those in authority, who preferred seeing me gaunt and drawn in the dock when ordered to appear there.

Strangely enough, after a time I grew attached to that little book, it being the sole article remaining in my possession, having been stripped of everything save the clothes I stood up in, or, more truthfully, lay down in. Opening it, I would sniff its pages even though they had no proper odour, running a finger along the edges, blood-red in hue, becoming darker when pressed together. The cover was of some stiff stuff like buckram, the title imprinted in gilt, or maybe gold. *Holy Bible*, I think it said, for even if the art of reading had escaped me I could still make out the odd word, and it came to me if I'd had the benefit of schooling like Burke I might have passed the time rightly, delving into some of those Old Testament tales I used to hear back home in Killeen chapel.

The turnkey who read out my ballad that time brought in another piece of writing, from the *Evening Courant* on this occasion, labelling me 'a rude ruffian, drunken, ferocious and profligate', and I don't know what was expected of me, outrage at being slandered, maybe, even though most of the words were accurate save the word 'profligate', which evaded me.

When he was gone, taking his newspaper with him, I repeated the words over and over, wondering what they might look like on the page, for being able to read them for myself would have been a fine thing instead of hearing them in his low Scottish accent, and staring at Fisher's wee Holy Book gave me call for thought, for a world of knowledge was contained there, and so I toyed with the notion of asking Fisher for some tutoring in the matter. But the fancy died as quick as it arose, telling myself I was missing nothing I hadn't experienced in that other classroom of hard knocks outside these four prison walls. Within, as well, even though I endeavoured to keep myself to myself throughout my sojourn there.

Still I preferred it that way, the hours slipping past in dreams and fancies, mostly about growing up in Down before I crossed the sea, recalling faces, hearing voices I thought had long vanished from memory for good.

One day followed on from the next, for I think our trial was one of the longest in legal history, many witnesses called to speak against us, some I had never seen or heard tell of, and there were times when I longed for the thing to be over and done with, even if it meant suffering the same fate as I had set in train for poor Burke by testifying against him.

Every so often I would be brought to the court and made to stand in the dock to face the public crammed in the gallery, and if they couldn't gain access they clambered on to the windowsills outside, for I could see their faces pressed to the glass mouthing insults, grimacing like monkeys.

Inside the courtroom itself, it became wearisome listening to our crimes pecked over by the same pair of learned game-cocks in gowns and wigs, so if the intention was to make us feel remorseful, the strategy was a misguided one, Willie, of course, being another matter, for from what Fisher informed me he was beating his breast and weeping tears of repentance every chance he got.

But if I imagined my own top knot was of no further interest to the scientific fraternity, now they had a cast of it, I was to be proved wrong, for once more I was returned to the same place for the scrutiny of yet another crowd of eager onlookers, and even though not made to lie flat on a table this time, it still became obvious no other part of me intrigued them, for another man, but without the white coat, started prodding and fondling my scalp as if uncovering something fresh and fascinating there.

Later I was to learn this person was a Mr George Combe, the renowned phrenologist, which I also discovered was someone who read people's personalities by the bumps and ridges on their skulls, and presently didn't he air his theories concerning my own particular outcrop for the benefit of the members of his famous Edinburgh Society gathered there.

'As might be expected the faculty of Benevolence appears severely restricted, whereas Destructiveness on the other hand is strongly positive. In the Perceptive faculties, Idealism and Sublimity are both deficient, while Mirthfulness is in the ascendant, giving rise to ridicule and sport of the infirmities of others, with Veneration also deficient, signifying a disregard for all things sacred ...'

And a lot more of the same. But, to make a jest of it, most of it went over my head, which the same gentleman continued fondling with eyes closed the better to carry out his work, all the while Fisher having an expression of dread on his face at what he must have considered the devil's work, this stranger gauging my character so accurately. But then anyone with a grain of sense might have provided a similar reading given the widespread public record of my offences. And the more I listened to this gentleman preening himself in front of his enlightened friends the more I dismissed him as some form of jumped-up gobshite overfond of the sound of his own voice.

'What you see before you is a typical example of the Celtic sub-race. Ireland, indeed, has the largest head size of any equal land area in Europe, the cranial vault low and domed, nose long, large and high-bridged, the lips thin to medium and a little everted, skin colour pale white, sometimes ruddy, often freckled, hair dark brown, or medium brown, red, rarely black.

'Sadly what we also observe is yet another living illustration of the gulf separating our own indigenous Scottish Lowland population and a degenerate foreign importation, for as the late John Pinkerton once wrote, "what a lion is to an ass, a Goth is to a Celt". And so in all sincerity, gentlemen, I tell you we must rid ourselves of this criminal underclass and the canker on the fair flower of our own proud nation, otherwise outrages of a similarly brutal nature must surely occur.'

Gazing up at the faces in the gallery, I thought I caught the same expression I had seen in the court, for despite their fine clothes and manners, given half a chance these same people would willingly despatch me on the spot, and hearing them stir and murmur I began to fear Fisher might not be able to get me out of there in the same state as I had arrived.

But raising a hand, Combe calmed his audience.

'Gentlemen, gentlemen, we are here purely in a spirit of scientific endeavour. It's not for the likes of us to pass judgement on this wretch seated here despite our revulsion at his inhuman and brutal acts. Take comfort from the fact that shortly he will be made to pay, and pay dearly, the ultimate price for his misdeeds along with his fellow assassin Mr Burke,' and at the mention of Willie's name there arose an even greater outcry until Combe silenced them once more.

'A little over a week ago in this very chamber a cast was taken of our subject's head by the renowned sculptor Giuseppe Fontanello and copies made of it, one of which has been generously donated for the Society's future use. And so with the aid of such a replica, at our next meeting I intend to conduct and carry out yet another even more detailed phrenological study of this particular felon's personality.'

So, finally, it seemed, they were done with me, Fisher escorting me back to the lock-up in Calton Jail where I served time for another wee while.

I have no wish to linger over the remaining days of my

captivity there. Compared to the events taking place in the court they are of little significance, for in the small hours of Christmas Eve Burke was found guilty and sentenced, the news brought to me by Fisher, prayer-book in hand, carried, too, on the cries of glee from the other prisoners, one of them calling out to ready myself, as I was next to be measured for the hempen necklace.

Yet they were all to be proved wrong, as a month later on a dark Thursday evening I was privately informed I was to be set free to go where I pleased, although the land of my birth it was assumed would be my destination, well away from the wrath of the mob still intent on seeing me dangle in the Lawnmarket like poor Willie.

Fisher brought the news of my release, his demeanour a sorrowful one, for I do believe he still had hopes of gathering me into the Heavenly Fold, and regarding me with that reproachful Presbyterian expression of his, he said, 'I trust you will heed how Providence has smiled on you this day. In the matter of the murder of that poor simple lad of theirs, the Wilson family did their utmost to have you arraigned, but have dropped the case on the advice of their counsel,' the boy referred to being the one called Daft Jamie, the smothering of whom still bothers me more than any of the rest, even the old woman Docherty from Inishowen, although it was Burke who ended her life while I sat on the chair looking on while he did it.

However, going down on my knees to please someone, even John Fisher, or resorting to the laudanum bottle like poor Willie, is something I will not do. Let them do their damnedest, say I, for thus far I have bested them, and when I felt the pure air of freedom on my face I rejoiced, not in the name of the Almighty, as my jailer might have hoped, but at my own hard-wrought victory.

As the authorities had no wish for any further disturbance on the streets, my final exit was accomplished discreetly. Fisher put me in a hackney carriage, and the pair of us travelled to the outskirts of the city to await the arrival of the mail coach going south, and when it arrived, Fisher, careful to the last, bade me farewell with the words, 'Goodbye, Mr Black, I wish you a pleasant journey,' as if we were two business associates instead of jailer and prisoner, while providing me with a name conjured up out of his own head, although I suppose it had the right ring to it for someone with the taint of murder hanging about him.

Travelling on the outside of the coach was a raw and bitterly cold experience, and when we reached a place called Noblehouse to break our journey I went into the inn there and seeing the state of me a man bade me warm myself by the fire. But putting off my hat I saw a gentleman present take a hard look at me, as if recognising my face. And so there my luck ran out, or maybe I had used up my ration, having had more than my fair share of it until then. To cheat the gallows, then be granted free passage to a destination of my own choosing might seem to some the lottery of a lifetime, and I should have been content to leave it like that, but not wishing to brave the weather a second time I asked if I might take a seat inside the coach as one had become vacant there.

Looking forward to dozing in a corner with my cloak pulled over my head, I was already in place along with three other passengers when the gentleman who had eyed me previously protested at my presence, and so because of his rank I was made to climb up and travel along with the luggage once more.

The night was pitch dark with a wind driving from the west and I sheltered as best I could behind the coachman's back while those more privileged below passed around a flask refreshed at the inn, and thinking of those warming drops I felt regret, for I hadn't dared order anything in the taproom on account of the noise there, as after the quiet of my cell the roar of people's voices seemed to crash about me like a breaking wave.

But I had little time to reflect on this for when we reached the town of Dumfries, where I would break my journey before catching the Portpatrick mail for Ireland and then afterwards who knows, a crowd soon gathered at the King's Arms, where we were to rest. My identity had been divulged by the gentleman inside the coach, who by a stroke of ill luck turned out to be a Mr E. Douglas Sandford connected with the court, and who had seen me there, and as word spread, more and more people of the town and beyond poured into the street, then through the inn doors to catch a glimpse of the notorious murderer.

As the crush grew, forcing me to take refuge in a back room, mere curiosity other than a desire for retribution seemed to be prompting those crowding in on me. Indeed, I was offered a dram and an invitation to speak freely, but my tongue clove to the roof of my mouth, and so the mood quickly changed to one of shouts and anger, and if it had not been for the police breaking through and taking me under their protection I might well have suffered the same fate as Willie, only with a lot less finesse in the execution of it.

How I got clear of Scotland and those thirsting for my blood there, word having by now travelled near and far, is down to the efforts of the constabulary, who seemed as determined as myself for me to vanish from the public eye for good, and to put the mob off the scent a chaise was brought to the inn yard, prepared, then driven at high speed with the townsfolk in hot pursuit. Then another, but with me inside it this time, was commandeered and raced towards the safety of the jail.

However, discovering the trickery, the crowd besieged the building, rioting until the late evening, breaking windows and the gas lamps in the town, and listening to the noise behind the bars of a cell I firmly believed my time had finally come.

But at one in the morning under cover of darkness I was escorted out of Dumfries without my bundle or my cloak and left on the roadside, the officer in charge advising me not to travel to Portpatrick as the mob was active there, even as far as the coast itself.

And so, heading south in the dark, I entered on the next stage of this journey of mine towards heaven or hell, although given my history I doubt if the former had much likelihood of being a final destination for Mr Black, as I had now decided to rename myself, Mr White not even in the running as any sort of alternative.

My Lord Beckford

Despite the keen interest from other collectors, notably the great Sir Walter himself, I am pleased to inform you my efforts in securing the item you requested have borne fruit, and even though copies already are in circulation be assured the article in question which will be shipped shortly to your house in Bath is the original Signor Fontanello cast.

As I write this the object itself is sitting in front of me in my lodgings in this place a little way from the capital where the person whose dead likeness it is plied his dreadful trade, and even though a lively or overheated imagination is not something I would associate myself with, ever since the thing has been in my keeping there have been occasions when I have felt a chill as though in the presence of something diabolical, despite it being merely a replica in plaster of Paris.

Yet the head itself seems perfectly natural, that of a normal individual, cheeks clean-shaven, eyes closed as though in sleep, lips pursed, and even though the cast was taken shortly after he was cut down, there is no sign of a grimace or similar expression, given the final agonies, for in my experience rarely does the 'drop' end cleanly, no matter how skilled the hangman is about his work.

Perhaps the wretch made his peace with his Maker before the rope snapped tight, as some have intimated to the Press. Yet others insist he shrieked like a demon as though feeling the fires of hell scorching the soles of his feet through his Irish brogues.

However, while I remain here as a private investigator in your Lordship's service I will persevere in sifting the truth from the dross that continues to boil and bubble, as everywhere one goes the talk is of little else. At times it seems as if Arthur's Seat, once an active volcano, so I understand, had erupted for a second time, pouring its lava on to the crowded rookeries at its foot, the mob crammed in there would still cry and clamour for retribution.

Only the other night a crowd gathered outside the now infamous Dr Knox's house, breaking his windows and hoisting a straw effigy on a pole before burning it, for your man in the street considers him as culpable as our two murderers on account of his dealings with them. Indeed, many are convinced he actively encouraged them in their foul trade.

In this present climate the wildest of rumours and counter-rumours continue to circulate in the streets and alehouses, some of which Mr Slack and I have visited in pursuit of our enquiries, gathering information even from the lips of scarcely the most reliable of witnesses.

Here in this city the English are not much liked, as seems to be the case throughout the rest of the nation, so I have kept a still tongue in my head, listening and observing from a corner seat, a habit acquired in my Bow Street days. Merging with the masses often can furnish one with more information than extracting it privately with a length of African hardwood, although I continue carrying my 'persuader' in the same inner pocket as notebook and pencil.

Thus far I have not found it necessary to employ my trusty ebony friend, but the presence of a six-foot former prizefighter with a shaved poll, albeit dressed in a fine satin frock coat and the best linen your Lordship's pocket can provide, makes even the most aggressive of Scots or Irish think twice about tangling with him.

We make an odd pairing, Mr Slack and I, he with his splendid gladiatorial aspect, and me the nondescript enquiry agent, short, stout, dowdy, and when your Lordship insisted on his accompanying me I confess I doubted the wisdom of such an alliance, accustomed as I am to proceeding alone and at my own measured pace.

However, I am pleased to report we have adjusted well to one another's company. His taciturn ways and private demeanour suit me fine, likewise my preferred way of moving towards a resolution. Even the Bible reading, which I admit surprised me in someone whose previous profession entailed reducing others to a bloody pulp, I now consider to be merely the eccentric mark of an otherwise fine and thoughtful individual.

As reported, the Burke death mask will be with you by the next posting, but I will not rest in my continuing endeavours to procure further items of interest, one of which I trust will come into my possession through a fortunate encounter in Dowie's Tavern, as it's known, near the Surgeons' College, for I made it my purpose to acquaint myself with an area associated with our two assassins and their fiendish trade.

Sometimes a stroke of blind luck can play a crucial part in an investigation, and I use the latter word from habit, even if not actually engaged in bringing a person or persons to justice, as the law in this case has already run its course, the proof of which, as regards one of the perpetrators, at least, will soon be in your private cabinet of curiosities in Beckford House. However, the occasion referred to was such a curious one, I intend setting down the circumstances in full, knowing your wish to be kept informed of every twist and turn in this present enquiry.

On the night of the first, a Saturday, when the alehouses are at their busiest, for much of the population go sober on the Sabbath, Mr Slack and I were in Dowie's establishment, as already mentioned, he with his nose in his little leather-bound testament, and me discreetly eavesdropping. We were seated in a side alcove with our backs to the wall so as not to draw attention to ourselves, when a party of the young College fraternity poured into the premises, all rowdy and merry.

Among them were those I recognised as Dr Knox's assistants, having been awaiting an opportunity to make myself acquainted in a casual manner before gaining their confidence, for these were the same three individuals who had direct dealings with our pair of 'sack-'em-up men', which was common knowledge, so now they had an even worse name for themselves, having already a reputation for drunkenness and dissolute behaviour despite their education.

Stories of skirmishes among their opposing factions were legion, for there was bitter rivalry between the followers of the two senior surgeons, Drs Knox and Monro. Gruesome tales of what took place in the dissection rooms, and their students' callous disregard for the specimens laid out for their experiments there, are perhaps too shocking to put down here, but I have heard accounts of human limbs being used as bludgeons, and even unspeakable acts of depravity carried out on some of the younger female cadavers.

Strong drink has much to answer for in all of this, and seeing these apprentice anatomists carousing into the small hours, I sincerely trust none are ever allowed near a living patient, at least not until they have learned their craft on the unresisting dead.

On this particular evening the trio I had managed to identify as Knox's youthful go-betweens were in a huddle at the bar counter, and as they talked together I observed them from my corner seat. Already I knew them by name, Messers Fergusson, Miller and Wharton-Jones, easily the most fanatical of all the Doctor's pupils, as I was to discover on this occasion when events took an ugly turn.

Somewhere a man began to sing, for the Irish with their taste for giving voice when tipsy evoke a ready response among their fellow Celts, unlike our own countrymen, who rarely if ever break into song on such occasions. In this instance, instead of the customary ballad of ancient massacre and bloody revenge, the singer chose something as fresh-minted as a new penny piece, and as the verse rang out the place gradually stilled, for the words were intended to taunt and to sting, expressly directed at the three leaning on the bar.

It was a street rhyme already enshrined in the popular repertoire. 'Down the close and up the stair, But and ben wi' Burke and Hare, Burke's the butcher, Hare's the thief, Knox the boy who buys the beef.' And although mention of the murderers caused no affront, that of the Doctor did, and one of his young defenders hurled a glass at the singer's head and a fine old ruckus ensued.

Safely distanced from the commotion, I observed the melee develop, the air ringing with curses and insults, followed by the first blows, our three young heroes fighting back manfully with boot and fist as their attackers swarmed about them.

Strongly outnumbered, as they were, they stood little chance against a mob who intended chastising them for their arrogance, and normally I would be reluctant to become involved as I quite enjoy a good rough and tumble so long as I'm not a participant, but this seemed a situation where my future concerns might suffer, like the very individuals I intended becoming acquainted with.

All this time Mr Slack was immersed in his gospel studies, but a nod of the head was sufficient to alert him to my wishes, and rising he made his way to the forefront of the scrimmage, stationing himself there like some great human bulwark against the tide of drinkers besieging our young heroes, who seemed almost as surprised at his intervention as their attackers. Foolishly, however, one of these same angry citizens threw himself at his manly form. As though taking hold of an unruly infant, Mr Slack hoisted him clear off the floor, setting him to one side as though weighing less than a feather.

But before any of the brawlers' friends could avenge him, I moved rapidly to join my burly associate, murmuring my apologies as I threaded my way through the throng, and I do believe it was the shock of hearing a cockney accent delivered in such a place and in such polite fashion that cleared a path for me.

'Gentlemen, it would appear we're no longer welcome here,' I said to the three young students, and one of them laughed, while another demanded, 'Who in God's name might you be, sir?'

'Merely an interested party,' I told him, and so after a moment of hesitation we all of us trooped out the way we came, with Mr Slack holding the door until we were safely in the street.

My new acquaintances were in celebratory mood, craving more drink to seal the victory, as they saw it, so they led Mr Slack and myself to another alehouse, but quieter, more private, this time. Pressed to join them, I accepted a glass of beer, while Mr Slack refrained as was his custom, but in a mannerly way, and soon the questions were flying across the table towards us as to our precise business in the city.

Deciding to be frank and open, I said we were on a quest to procure certain objects of interest pertaining to the Burke and Hare affair on behalf of our patron, who had been mightily intrigued by the case, yet not in a crude or sensational way, being a gentleman of refined and scientific bent. I mentioned the death mask, which they said they were aware of, but with some levity Mr Wharton-Jones declared his own professional interest lay more with those other parts as there were more of them to 'play around with'.

I could see Mr Slack was displeased by such crude humour, but not wishing to appear prudish myself I ordered up more drink, and soon any suspicions the three might have held regarding our motives melted like snow off a ditch, as the saying has it, in particular Mr Fergusson, who appeared most agreeable and might yet be even more forthcoming, and my intuition proved correct, for at a certain point in the evening he produced something from an inner pocket, laying it on the table in front of Mr Slack and myself for our consideration.

All three young men observed us intently to gauge our reaction, but the object itself seemed nothing more than a leather purse or wallet of the sort I carry myself.

'What's inside?' I asked, and Wharton-Jones replied, 'More to the point, what's it made of? Go on, take a hold of it, it won't bite.'

He laughed.

'Not now it's owner's molars are safely in a jar along with the rest of him.'

Tiring of the jest, Fergusson explained that after Burke had been cut down and, as the custom with felons, offered up for dissection, certain of the younger assistants privately appropriated portions of the flesh of the corpse and had them tanned and made into mementoes, bookmarks, wallets and the like, one of which lay now before us.

'And are there others similar to this?' I enquired, knowing your Lordship would be interested in obtaining such items.

To which Mr Miller, who shared Mr Wharton-Jones's same coarse sense of humour, remarked, 'If all the tales of such remnants were gospel, our friend must have had a hide on him the size of an elephant's.'

'Or the Redeemer Himself. Enough relics behind glass to reconstruct half a dozen such, which may come as a shock to some of our papish friends on Judgement Day.'

Noting Mr Slack's displeasure at such blasphemous talk, I concentrated my attention on Mr Fergusson, who appeared the more sensible of the three, and seeming to recognise our own seriousness, he enquired, 'Would you be interested in acquiring this?', pushing the purse across the table, and a silence fell, as in my experience any reference to hard cash usually brings people to their senses and the matter in hand.

'Possibly,' I told him, handling the object, 'if you can vouch for its authenticity.'

'You have my word on it, as I was present when the actual dissection took place and the specimen of epidermis removed. However, I don't condone such practices, as neither does our dominie,' by which I took it he meant Surgeon Knox.

At this point, heeding a call of Nature, he excused himself, and after he'd left, Mr Wharton-Jones remarked, 'Poor Willie, a mite over-serious for his own good. Theology might have proved a better calling, looking into people's souls instead of their insides. Still, he's the best apprentice anatomist the College ever produced. At least that's what the good Doctor says.'

'As well as treating him like his own flesh and blood,' his friend concurred.

Before I could glean any fresh insights the subject himself returned and, more drink being called for, Mr Slack dutifully crossed to the serving hatch returning with four pint pots clasped in his fists as though they were no bigger than eggcups, and Mr Miller, who was pretty far gone by this stage, expressed a professional interest in his physique, fulsomely admiring his biceps while he sat there tolerating the fondling even though I felt convinced he must be holding back a desire to chastise this young pup.

And sometimes, despite it being ruinous to my own discreet interests, I have felt an urge to witness some of that mighty power unleashed, the way one might long to see a slumbering volcano erupt, for truly he is a magnificent specimen, like one of those same Roman statues that grace the grounds of your own great house, and I can well imagine when first you saw him in the ring – unbeaten in thirty-five bouts, so I hear tell – you must have been struck by the resemblance, except here was living, breathing flesh and not Italian marble.

But, forgive me, I digress in a fanciful manner which is uncharacteristic and unprofessional of me.

Mr Fergusson, who wasn't nearly as boisterously drunk as his friends now engaged in chaff with the landlady, enquired if I would be interested in acquiring any further relics.

'You mean there are other parts preserved as well?'

'Not of Burke. Hare.'

'But surely he's alive still.'

'True enough, but I might be able to help you lay hands on a life mask made when he was in jail awaiting sentencing, only to evade it by his own low cunning and treachery. I sincerely wish we had a piece of him in front of us right at this moment, instead of that of his dead partner.'

Such vehemence came as something of a surprise, as up to then he had seemed as calm and even-tempered an individual as one could wish to meet. Why he harboured such intense resentment towards this Hare creature intrigued me, for not so long hence had he not himself acted as an agent for his superior, putting silver in his palm on receipt of his morbid cargo? Often it's said, the truth hurts, some much more than others, but my trained nose detected a deeper, more personal reason for his animosity.

But then, instead of being the interrogator, it seemed I was the one being quizzed, about your Lordship, no less, and what it was which had attracted someone such as yourself to two brutish labourers and their murderous personalities, and so I informed him I was merely a go-between and it was not my business to enquire or ask such questions of an employer.

'Well, Mr Speed, if you are telling me you are here merely to titillate the jaded appetites of some wealthy collector of the lurid and sensational, keep your master's English bawbees. Better still, give them to my two colleagues here, who will be happy to supply you with all the keepsakes your employer desires.'

I could see he was in deadly earnest, so I said, 'Mr Fergusson, I assure you my patron is not the sort of person excited by the penny-dreadfuls and their tales of murder and mayhem. On the contrary, he is a cultured individual who happens to be fascinated by the criminal mind. And may I say, I, too, in my own humble fashion, share some of those same interests. Before I became a private investigator, for a considerable time I was a London detective and once a policeman, as they say, always one.'

It was quite a speech for someone such as myself, and only when it had finished did I realise just how involved I had become with this case and its malefactors. Strangest of all, I felt this burgeoning desire to get close to them, as close as possible, even though one had gone to his just reward, and the other had vanished, leaving nothing but a whiff of sulphur in his wake and the loathing of the person now sitting across from me.

After I had stopped speaking he stared into his glass for what seemed a long time before lifting his gaze.

'Certain things regarding this business only I have knowledge of. So if you are as genuine and sincere about uncovering the truth as you say you are, perhaps we two should meet again, but this time more privately.'

'May my colleague be permitted to accompany me?'

'I have no objection. At least there will be little risk of him interrupting us.'

On hearing this, Mr Slack permitted himself a fleeting smile, something of a rarity, and shortly after my new informant and I shook hands, arranging a time and place for the morrow, and Mr Slack and I adjourned to our lodgings.

But here I must also take my leave, on paper this time, concluding this first report of mine. In my next letter I hope to bring your Lordship news of further twists and turns in this strange drama and its cast of characters.

One final note. Regarding my expenses thus far, I have managed to remain within the budget of your Lordship's generous bounty. However, if additional funds are required to extend my brief in pursuit of information, or seek out and acquire other items of interest, naturally I will keep you informed.

Yours
Percival Speed

My Lord Beckford

I am in receipt of your letter of the 15th and am relieved to learn the second mask arrived safely in good condition considering the state of the roads south to Somerset.

Concerning its acquisition, the price required for its purchase was not near as high as that of its companion piece. The elusive Mr Hare, it would appear, has not stirred the popular imagination to the same extent as his dead accomplice. Perhaps a public hanging increases the value of such commodities, as with that other most curious item which I have also forwarded to you.

Although I don't consider myself overly squeamish, I have to confess I am glad to be shot of it. The notion of handling an object fashioned from flayed human flesh is not something I feel at ease with, even if contact with others deceased was part of my career for many years. I am glad the object is now behind glass in one of your Lordship's cabinets where you will be able to gaze on it while reflecting on its history to your heart's content.

As mentioned in my last report, I have become friendly with this young Fergusson person, who appears more than keen to unburden himself regarding his involvement in the case. Unlike most of his fellow students, as rough a band of young ruffians as one would wish to avoid, he seems to have a genuine conscience regarding the victims, and yearns to make amends for turning a blind eye to the manner of their deaths.

As I understand it the bodies were brought to Knox's private quarters and there purchased on the spot by his assistants before being inspected by the great anatomist himself, no questions asked as to the nature of their demise, even if in most cases the subjects had barely time to grow cold.

To dispose of a fellow human in such a fashion, then have it haggled over like so much butcher's meat, is something hard to comprehend in a Christian society. However, with the help of this forthcoming young witness, I trust I will find a way into these individuals' minds despite an abhorrence of their foul deeds.

From what I've been able to glean from my meetings with young Fergusson, his own early involvement in the acquisition and subsequent purchase of the subjects from our two Irish assassins occasioned him barely a tremor of unease until he recognised a corpse belonging to someone he himself had spent the night with before she was murdered. Without being mealy-mouthed about it, this was a young prostitute well known in the Grassmarket area, by the name of Mary Paterson, who despite her addiction to drink was still strikingly beautiful. So much so, Fergusson had become infatuated with her, and talking about her even now, it is clear he is still greatly affected by her death, especially as at the time he would have been the one expected to mutilate that peerless form to prepare it for Knox's dissection class.

But before any of that took place Knox was himself smitten by such perfection lying lifeless on his marble slab. On the orders of one of the other assistants, Burke, or it may have been Hare, had cut off her hair in readiness for the knife, but despite such an outrage she still had the appearance of some young, auburn-haired Caledonian Venus.

Recalling all of this, our young friend wept bitterly, and despite having been drinking, his sincerity appeared heartfelt and Mr Slack and I listened in respectful silence while he unburdened himself.

'When we laid her out she still had twopence ha'penny clasped in her hand, and I was unable to unclench it, so I left it as it was, the last paltry possession she was to take to her grave, and the Doctor and I were alone with her, and he said to me, "John Oliphant should see her like this," and when I enquired who might that be, he said he was an artist friend and he should make a sketch of her for posterity before we went about our business, and then he said, "I wonder what her name was, and how she ended up like this," and so I told him, Mary Paterson, and from the drink, having been found in an alleyway.'

'"When we come to destroy something as perfect as this, William," says he, "we still must shut our minds to everything save the blade in our hand, for if you have learned anything under my guidance it is that under the skin we are all of us nothing but a rotting parcel of tripes and guts. Our curse is to see another being as simply a subject on which to practise our profession. I fear I myself have lost much of my humanity following my grisly trade."

'Never had I heard the great man speak in this fashion before, for I still consider him to be such, despite the lies his enemies have put out about him, for you must understand my master has been brought low, not on account of anything he himself has done, but because of two devils from hell, one of whom is now surely burning up like a taper there, while the other is as free as a bird God knows where.'

And once again there was that same rancour in his voice matched by the expression on his face.

'This Hare, did you yourself ever come face to face with him?'

For a brief moment I feared I might have touched a raw spot, but after a time, lifting his gaze, he replied, 'He came with Burke, who did the talking, while he stayed like a wraith in the shadows.'

'Can you recall his appearance?' I enquired, so far having only seen a cast of his features which made him look like a frozen waxwork exhibit, even though it had been taken while he was still breathing.

'Tall, gangly, ill-looking, as the newspapers have reported.'

'And you consider they got the essence of the man?'

'Essence?'

'His personality. From my reading of the case a much more detailed picture seems to have emerged of his more famous accomplice.'

Here he gave me a penetrating long look, before enquiring, 'Tell me, Mr Speed, does this noble employer of yours share a similar fascination with Hare?'

'Perhaps all three of us do, but for different reasons.'

'And what might they be?'

'I can only speak for myself and the person who sent me here. *His* interest lies in the background to the case and the mentality of those involved because of his studies into the criminal mind, while I am here merely to provide him with those articles for his collection which you so generously helped procure for me.'

'Nothing more than that?'

'Well, a career as a police detective leaves its mark, so I still can't help delving into the minds of murderers, and this particular pair under review are far removed from the normal run of homicides I have encountered in my time.'

'And myself, Mr Speed? What do you think is *my* interest?'

'Judging by your reaction to the very mention of his name, I would say he may have wronged you in some fashion. Perhaps in regard to the young woman he may have choked to death?'

On hearing this, he went deathly pale and, rising, cried, 'Damn you, sir! Don't dare sully her memory!' and events may well have turned ugly if Mr Slack hadn't intervened, lowering him gently but firmly into his chair, where bowing his head he wept once more.

Hardened as I am, I must confess I was touched by this loyalty to someone who in life had been no more than a common streetwalker, and after a time he said, 'If you could have seen her lying there while Mr Oliphant drew her, and afterwards Mr Knox himself couldn't bear for her to be opened up, placing her in a barrel of whiskey for near on three months before the first incision was made. As God is my witness, none of us knew at the time she had been done to death, or even the manner of it, for suffocation leaves no marks, as those two devils were aware of full well. Still, if we had cared a little more she might be alive still.'

'And do you believe Hare was the one who carried out the foul deed? Did it emerge at his trial?'

'No, but he's still the one who escaped punishment for all of the others he did away with, and as God is my judge, I won't rest until he has been made pay for his crimes.'

'And pray how do you intend doing that? The law, after all, has run its course.'

'There is another law, Mr Speed. The law of terrible and bloody retribution.'

And raising his head from his little testament, Mr Slack murmured, 'Thou shalt not kill, sayeth the Lord. Deuteronomy, five, seventeen.'

So unexpected was this interjection, we gazed at him for an instant, before Fergusson replied, 'To me belongeth revenge and recompense. Sir, I, too, have been grounded in the Scriptures.'

Not wishing to be trapped on the sidelines of some verbal theological tennis match, I said my farewells, promising to meet the following day, and so Mr Slack and I left the young man to his hopeless dreams of reprisal.

On the route back to our lodgings, lurching from the shadows a woman attempted to proposition us, and for an instant I wondered if she might have known this young Mary Paterson who had so captivated our grieving young friend. But the urge to question her passed, and we made our way onward with her curses ringing in our ears.

'Twa English jessies! One big, one sma',' she shrilled,

although how she knew our nationality was a mystery, an unsettling one, for anonymity is something I prize above everything else when embarked on a case, which in this instance seemed to be moving slowly and steadily like a stone downhill.

Yet the crime, or crimes, had already been solved, admittedly more by chance than any true detective work, and the offenders brought to book, one ending up dead as mutton at the end of a rope, the other walking free, having turned King's evidence and peaching on his partner. And so more and more topsy-turvy this present investigation would seem to appear, as normally I begin at the start of one rather than the finish.

My Lord, on reading this I trust you will forgive me setting down my personal thoughts in this fashion, but when I accepted the commission you insisted I should spare no details of its progress. However, if you feel I have fulfilled my obligations in procuring the replicas and that other most curious item for your collection, I will, of course, bring my enquiries to a conclusion, and Mr Slack and I will return south.

Accordingly, I await your instructions on this matter.

Your humble servant
Percival Speed

Footsore and with an empty stomach save for a turnip pulled from a field and dipped in a burn, I made my way south towards England, having understood that country to be more prosperous than the one I'd left. But when I crossed over I was sorely disappointed, for everything appeared much the same, mile upon mile of desolate moorland, and any houses to be seen not so different from the one I'd been brought up in, sharing quarters with the cows and with a dung heap in the yard halfway to the thatch.

I smelt turf smoke on the wind, too, and whenever there was a village at a crossroads or strung out along the roadside I hurried past keeping my head low, dogs barking and stones flying as the children pelted me on my way for being a Gypsy or a beggar, which was possibly my lot for the little money the authorities had given me must soon be gone.

For two nights I slept in barns, emerging at first light like a scarecrow before the farmer rose himself. There was no rain but the cold seemed to congeal the very marrow in my bones until the blood flowed once more and the thoughts swarmed and buzzed in my head like a hive of bees.

Perched on a drystone wall with a flock of black-faced ewes regarding me, I held my head in my hands, but the voices within would not be denied and for near an hour out there on the moors I endured their clamour, now roaring, now singing, for Burke had been the great one for the ballads and come-all-ye's whether drunk or sober.

'Damn you, Hare,' I'd hear him cry, 'give us a tune, will

you! Am I the only Irishman in this stinking house with an air in his head?' and then as was our wont we would set about one another before falling back on the bed together where the old Inishowen woman was stretched out drunk. So then Burke lay on the top of her, holding a hand under her nose, the other beneath her chin in the manner he had perfected, keeping it there for a good ten minutes until the deed was done, sending off yet another client to eternity without a sound or struggle, for we always took care to employ the services of Mr Whiskey on such occasions.

But then that turned out the one time that proved to be our undoing, Burke with more drink taken getting careless and putting the body under the bed and Ann Gray the neighbour seeing it before we carried it off in a tea chest to Surgeon's Square and Dr Knox's hired man there.

Sitting on my granite throne out in the middle of those Cumberland moors, a flock of mountain sheep my only company, I felt about as forsaken as they were. But they had grass and heather to sustain them, woolly coats, too, and so I bade them farewell, tramping on my way hopefully towards a night's shelter and something more filling than a raw root plucked from the soil and washed in a brook.

At a place where the road climbed straight to the sky I saw a figure coming towards me, first human I'd seen that entire day, and the closer he got the more anxious I became, not from fear of being recognised, which would have been unlikely being already so far from Scotland, but because I doubted the very usage of my own tongue so long had it remained silent. While the words roared inside my head, to exchange the simplest of them with another person felt far beyond me, so I kept my head low, hoping to get past without the need for any sort of civility.

Under my brows I shot him a glance as he approached, someone in his later years, but sturdy and with a strong step, a pack on his back, face dark and weatherbeaten, unlike my own, pale as tallow after being denied sun and light in a dark and penitential hole for so long.

About a stone's throw off the stranger came to a halt in the middle of the road, turning his gaze directly upon me, and as we came nearer the more fixed his stare became.

Unslinging his pack and laying it on the ground, he stood blocking my path, and while never one to shrink from a fight, which judging by the look and age of my opponent I would surely win, I had no stomach for it. Indeed the hunger I felt in that part of me, for no food had come my way for near on a day and a half, only served to make the feeling worse.

Taking care not to trade looks with him, on I came. But when we were about a dozen paces apart I heard him call out, 'Good day, friend,' with a sort of a foreign lilt to it. So then I stopped myself.

'Come far, have we?'

And with that he sank down on the ditch as if inviting me to do the same, and nodding to his query I joined him, as it would have seemed strange proceeding on my way without any form of acknowledgement or reply.

'Looking for employment?'

Again I gave a jerk of the head.

Unbuckling the straps on his pack, the stranger said, 'These are my wares. See?' displaying a variety of scarves and kerchiefs along with beads and buttons and other suchlike feminine fancies.

'When Farmer John is off in the fields about his work his good wife opens up her purse. Oftentimes that privy other little pouch of hers, as well. So, what do you say, why not throw in your lot with me? These lonely agricultural wenches would surely welcome a strong, strapping travelling man like yourself into their homes. The hay loft, too, I'll wager.'

Although far from a prude or puritan, hearing such talk out here instead of in a tavern turned me against this swarthy little jackanapes with his greasy ringlets and earring, added to which no one had tried puffing me up as some sort of fancy man before, not with this horse face and present pallor.

'Anyway, mightn't a change of occupation suit you? And if I may be so bold in enquiring, what exactly was your former employment?'

For an instant, foolish as it may seem, I had this urge to reply, 'I do away with people, or did. But the rewards in the end proved not worth the risk or bother,' just to see that Gypsy face of his change colour.

Instead I told him I had once been a boatman and after that a navvy on the Canal.

'The Union, eh? And then what?' meaning when the digging had finished and Burke and I were out of work and lodging in the same house with our womenfolk and entered into the business of suppliers of fresh cadavers to the scientific community.

But he didn't need to know any of that. No one did.

Yet he kept on and on until I grew weary of hearing his voice, wary, too, for he seemed over-keen to learn more about my history than I cared to divulge.

So I fell silent, and after a while, glancing at me, he said, 'When a man's on the road he's either walking away from something or making his way towards it. Which is it with you, friend? Still, no matter, come, share a bite with me. This oaten bannock is all I can offer until the next good wife takes pity on poor Rudolf, although everyone calls me Rudy,' reaching out a hand dark as tar, and in spite of my reluctance I offered him my own.

'And yours?'

By this time I had a lump of dry bread in my mouth, giving me time to conjure up a reply.

'Black,' I told him. 'Bernard Black.'

Which indeed became my name from that day forward until there were times when I came near to forgetting the one

I'd been baptised with, and all the better for it if I was to put the reputation I had earned behind me.

'And a fine ring it has to it, although I wouldn't recognise it as Irish, for that is the place I take it you hail from,' and again it seemed to me he was going beyond the remit of a mere passing roadside acquaintance.

'So now it's bonny Scotland again. Like a fair number of your fellow countrymen. To the big cities. Edinburgh, in your case.'

The dry bread I had been given was proving hard to swallow and as a burn ran nearby I scooped up a handful of water to help it down. Had I let slip any mention of a connection between myself and the capital? I convinced myself I had not, and staring at my wet hands wondered how they might look tightening around a certain brown throat, and for an instant the urge to revisit old habits took hold of me, telling myself here in this desolate spot with only the curlews mewing above the deed could be accomplished without fear of discovery.

While such diabolical notions were going through my head, this Rudy fellow lay stretched on his back taking the sun, the very image of contentment. Close by rested his open pack and the thought of what it held made the proposition of his despatch even more tempting, for after the deed was accomplished, why not take over the trade of hawker myself? After all, I had sold fish from a cart, although female gewgaws and trinkets would demand a softer line of patter. So then I thought of Burke and how he would have found it no bother with that personable manner of his, especially prior to plying some wretch with strong drink and sending her off to sleep one last time.

But the man taking his ease on the ditch wasn't drunk, so the notion left me, and looking down at him lying there, I said, 'I must be on the road, for I've a long way ahead of me,' pointing south, even though the truth was I had no proper destination in mind.

'Sure and certain you won't join me? We could have a merry time of it travelling together sharing the burden of the pack as well as the profits. It gets lonely on the road, as soon you'll discover, for it's clear you're a newcomer to the life.'

But I thanked him for his offer, leaving him enjoying the sun with his eyes shut, not realising how near he'd come to having them closed for good.

Some time later that day, thinking over what the packman had said about the farms in the area and their womenfolk, I determined to throw myself on their mercy. Tired and hungry, my remaining senses must have also been affected even considering such a step, this walking ghost appearing out of nowhere bearing nothing in the way of goods or cheeky banter, either.

However, in that place steadings appeared scarce. Barren hillsides and stretches of burnt moorland bore no signs of life other than the sheep I had come across earlier. Not even a solitary shepherd with his dog could be seen or heard in the distance, and the road was more like a track bare of signposts, so my only way of determining the route forward was by the sun, which by now had started its slow descent towards the coast, which I still was anxious to avoid.

I had this notion the further south I travelled the better the chances would be for an easier life in a land of rich pastures and, consequently, gullible citizenry, but where the idea had sprung from I had no recollection. Burke may have put it there, for he was greatly given to such opinions with the drink on him, and even though I knew he was spinning another of his webs some of that must have stayed with me. And as I tramped on I thought I heard his voice and saw his face along with other apparitions from the past reproaching me for my actions.

'Why, Willie, did you turn against me so? Sure, didn't we have the great times of it while the work lasted and the money rolled in, ten pounds a shot, remember, which we shared half and half, for I never cheated on you, never the once. I hope you're satisfied taking the King's sovereign like one of them turncoats back home. If it hadn't been for your black treachery, I wouldn't be lying on this slab now naked as the day I came into the world with half the population of this city sniggering over my poor manhood. And Maggie, tell me, do you ever give a thought to her, your own wife? Or did you abandon her as well?'

It was like being back in the dock again, having accusations flung at me, but refusing to respond, as I did then, I walked on until the faces faded and the voices ceased.

So intent was I on the buzzing of it in my head, I hadn't taken much heed the countryside was changing to a softer, more pleasing aspect. Foliage had started to appear, and the stone walls separating the fields, which now looked neat and green, seemed better cared for, and soon, too, I saw smoke rising from a clump of trees giving cover to a farmhouse, for I had seen the like in Ireland where the English had settled bringing their custom with them.

As I drew nearer I heard dogs barking, regretting not having cut a stick from the hedge, for I knew the sight of one made them wary and less liable to attack, but I was so low from lack of food and shelter I had only my boots for protection.

At the mouth of the lane leading to the farmhouse I drank from a spring, catching sight of my face in its still depths. Not having had the luxury of a shave for near on a month this bearded ruffian stared back at me, razors not permitted in the prison for fear of putting them to more deadly use, not that I had any intention of harming myself as I wanted to see how events might unfold even if it led to the final jig at the end of a rope.

Yet, strange to relate, all along I convinced myself I would manage to evade such a fate, unlike Willie, who seemed reconciled to his end, condemning himself out of his own mouth when it came his turn to stand in the dock, and so it seems to me there are two sorts of people in this world, those like Willie who enjoy holding forth, and those content to watch from the wings while people like him perform. Often my colleague and former business partner would chide me for being this dull dog sunk in his own thoughts while he charmed all and sundry. But then that was of little benefit when Mr Hangman slipped a hempen cravat about his neck, for not too many jokes are uttered on the scaffold, or so I've heard tell.

Sure enough, when I reached the yard of the place, a double-storeyed, slated dwelling in sore need of upkeep, the windows dark with dirt, its smoking chimney listing at an angle, a pair of collie dogs were waiting for me. Yet all of this cheered me up, for in that first moment I was able to single out at least a dozen tasks needing doing, and those only pertaining to the outside of the house. The outbuildings appeared almost as neglected, with a great steaming midden leaking its load on to the cobbles.

The two curs, mother and offspring, I decided, lay on their bellies eyeing me as I stood judging my approach towards the front door, and keeping my eye trained on it I waited to catch some sign of movement within. Snake-like, red tongues lolling, yellow eyes glaring, the dogs had started to crawl towards me making low growling noises. I knew they were poised to spring at any moment, as sneaky a pair of black and white brutes as one might wish to turn your back on, that's if one were foolish enough to do so.

Catching a glimpse of what I took to be a face peering out at me from the back of the door, I must have ignored my better judgement, for I heard a tearing sound and felt the nip of teeth through the leg of my trousers. The younger animal had gone for me first, hanging on to the cloth as I tried to swing it up and off the ground. Then the second cur made a dart for the other leg. But before it could get a grip, I caught it with the toe of my boot, sending it off yelping.

Still battling with the first animal, I got it by the hindquarters, squeezing its ballocks, and as I did so I felt the entire bottom half of my corduroys, from the knee down, come away in the brute's jaws, and enraged at being reduced to such a state I was fully intent on dashing the beast's brains out against a wall, when a voice called from the doorway, 'I'd take it as a favour not to harm my two dogs any further. They're only being playful.'

But still inflamed at what they had done to my apparel, rough as it was, I cried out, 'Playful, is it? Left me like a bare-legged savage, so they have. The only pair of breeks to my name.'

'Aye, so I can see by the light manner in which you travel.'

Standing there with her arms folded across her bosom was this great brute of a woman near filling the doorway with the size and the girth of her.

'They're not used to company. Not the masculine sort anyway,' meaning the dogs, who still watched me hungrily as though hoping for a final try at my other leg making a match of it, which might have been more fitting, for there was something shaming and pitiful having to stand there, one leg bare, the other not, like a living scarecrow, or the makings of one.

'What's your business here anyway? By the look of things you've nothing to sell or barter.'

But thinking quickly, I replied, 'Sure, didn't my partner send me on ahead of him. Left him, I did, with his wares, on the roadside sunning himself.'

For the first time something like a smile crossed her lips.

'And what might he look like, this partner of yours? Maybe I know him.'

'Small, swarthy, a wee gold ring in one ear.'

'His name wouldn't be Rudy, would it?'

'The very man,' I told her, feeling my spirits rise, for I felt she was beginning to thaw with full-blown cordiality not so far off as long as I kept up the pretence. Strangely enough, I was also starting to enjoy fencing with this great ginger-haired lump of a country woman. Burke would have been proud of me, I was thinking, when she said, 'I trust you're not a thief, for if you are, you're out of luck. There's no rich pickings here.'

Feeling about as naked now as my left leg, I said, 'I'll have you know I'm no robber, and never have been,' although, to be truthful, on occasions me and Willie had helped ourselves to the odd trinket, and once a watch belonging to that old man Joseph whose remains we sold, but then he was dying of the fever and had no need of such an article anyway.

'Where are you from?' she asked.

'Scotland,' I told her, for I felt it prudent not to mention the other place, knowing those of us from that side of the water had a bad reputation on this, something that had swung public opinion against Willie and me nearly as much as the charges brought before us.

'So if you're not a robber, and you have nothing to sell, for Rudy was here himself not two hours hence, just what *is* your business here?'

My expression must have given me away, for she gave vent to a guffaw, leaning her mighty backside against the jamb of the door, and another time, another place, woman or no woman, I might have wiped the grin off that face, for I have a temper not always easy to keep in check. But my time in jail had chastened me.

Still, I couldn't help wondering how she might feel to discover who it really was before her right now, albeit with only one good trouser leg left to his person. A trifle more fear and respect might well have been the outcome. But that was mere wishful conjecture, so I walked away, leaving any dignity lying there in the shape of a remnant of cloth wet and chewed on the cobbles.

However, hearing the words, 'Acquainted with agricultural work, are you?' turning, I told her, yes, for digging on the Union Canal must come mighty close to such labour.

And so that is how I came to find employment with Mrs Howland of Troutbeck Farm in the far north country. Far older than herself, her crippled husband spent his days and nights in an armchair while she ran the place. A servant girl fed him gruel from a spoon, wiping his dribble with a rag. A tongue-tied, simple creature from a Home, she tended to him like he was her own babby, while his wife left him solely in her care.

All this I observed on the few occasions I was allowed into the house, for I slept in the barn, burrowing out a hollow in the hay, half-bitten alive by ticks and other creeping things.

No wage was ever mentioned, but I was content to work for mere sustenance and a covering over my head, even if it did show the starry firmament through a hole in the roof.

The first task I was set was to reduce the dung heap in the yard by spreading it on the fields. But the more its size diminished the sooner I feared would arrive my walking papers, with me tramping the moors in the dead of winter once more. Hard labour never bothered me, for I was used to it in those times before Burke and me took up the easier trade of providing human joints for the learned butchers of Surgeon's Square.

At the start of my time there I ate my meals outside, brought to me by the servant girl, barely staying a moment at first, but gradually lingering more and more, watching me eat, as if observing some strange foreign creature and its feeding habits, and I bore her presence, for my sole interest was the food. After the diet I had endured in jail a pot of potatoes in their skins with the rare addition of a lump of boiled bacon or mutton seemed fine fare indeed. She brought me buttermilk, too, enjoying my relish for the stuff, for it was what I used to drink in my mother's kitchen after a day roaming the fields wreaking mischief with my young companions.

After I had scoured the plate clean to Hannah's satisfaction, for that was her name, hearing her mistress yelling it like she was on an equal footing with the dogs, all I longed for was a pipe and a dram. Both commodities I knew were in the house, for I had smelt the one on Mrs Howland's person, and the other on her breath, for while possessing most of the physical attributes of a man she enjoyed those other masculine vices as well.

As the days passed I started getting the notion the girl, in her own simple fashion, was taking a fancy to me, so I played along in the hope of her bringing me what I craved, for every time I smelt a waft of plug tobacco coming from the kitchen the harder it was to keep my mind off what I enjoyed most, for Willie and me were never short of either items when carousing the night away. Truth to tell, I also missed the heat and fury of a good set-to with some Highlander who had insulted my accent and race, and sometimes, just for the sport of it, with Willie himself, who always gave as good as he got, although both of us knew who was the better battler.

Because of her infirmity, Hannah, the servant girl, didn't speak, and so neither did I. But she seemed to know what was on my mind, for one day along with the midday dinner didn't she bring me what I longed for. I must have been chewing on a straw in lieu of the real thing for her to act as she did, slipping me from under her apron a clay pipe, its bowl crammed with sweet-smelling shag, yet without a solitary syllable passing between us. But her simple-mindedness had led her to forget the necessity of a light, so I had to perform a dumb show of striking a match, until a cry from the house had her scurrying away.

Buxom, but not near as heavy-set or broad in the beam as the one indoors, she reminded me of that quean Mary Paterson, who, still warm, had her own reddish locks sheared off by Burke on the instructions of the students in the dissecting rooms.

That same night Hannah came to me in her shift, a lighted candle in her hand, and after we shared a puff of her mistress's best tobacco, I tumbled her in the hay without much protest or disinclination on her part. In the middle of it she moaned a little, and fearing she might be heard I stopped her mouth with my hand, but not in the manner Willie and me employed with those other women, for even though the urge to stifle returned, it quickly faded, best buried like all those we had hastened to their final destination.

The second night the girl came to me, she brought a small jug of liquor, and I pressed her to join me, for it seemed a shame to drink alone even if it was in a barn with the moon shining through a hole in the rafters. But she seemed content to watch. As it was the first time I had felt merry in a long while I started humming an air, and this time it was she who put a hand over my mouth. The feeling was a strange one, yet not unpleasant, making me wonder if it might have been like that with those others, most of whom rarely put up any sort of a struggle.

But the notion passed, and I took her a second time, and afterwards, needing my sleep, I made her return whence she'd come, taking her candle with her as I had no wish to risk it setting fire to the hay.

Over the next nights her visits became a habit, and I performed to the best of my ability, having no wish to forfeit the offerings she brought me bundled in her apron, not just drink and tobacco, but now foodstuffs as well.

After we had lain together we shared a pipe, and she became affectionate like we were sweethearts, something I had no wish to encourage, never having much taste for the like, not even with my own wife, who, truth to tell, was as lacking in ardour as myself, the closest we came to passion the blows we dealt each other, the same she-devil able to hold her own with any man.

John Fisher, the jailer who had befriended me, informed me she, too, had escaped justice, as the law said a wife could not testify against her husband, but as to her present where-abouts he had no knowledge. I imagined he thought I must be pining for her, but the truth was I was glad to see the back of her, as my ardent wish was to begin life afresh with no encumbrances, and so though the girl's cooings and caresses were irksome to me I bore them for the sake of what she pilfered from her mistress's larder.

That night, after she had gone creeping back to the house, I fell into a deep sleep, but awoke as first light was beginning to appear. Still in the throes of the dream I'd been having, I lay there reliving its horrors for a second time, for I was back in my house in Tanner's Close, the door barred, and Burke feeding the boy they called Daft Jamie with drink and me alongside them on the bed waiting for the right moment to finish off our business with him. Yet the more Burke plied him with whiskey the more he refused it, crying for his mother. But things having gone too far for us to turn back, I lay on top of him while Burke took him by the nose and under the chin. Yet instead of giving in like the others, he struggled like someone twice his age, all three of us landing up on the floor together, which is where the dream took another and contrary turn, for instead of the one being despatched he was now the one subduing us two, all our strength and energies ebbing away, and before we knew it we were bundled into the tea chest we had ready to carry the body off. Crammed into that dark, foreign-smelling space, limbs intertwined, we hammered on the lid, and a little later felt the chest being lifted and borne out into the street, for we could hear people's voices and the noise and bustle of traffic.

Fortunately the dream ended there, before we finished up on Dr Knox's cutting table still alive, for that was where I convinced myself it was taking us, and lying on the straw soaked in sweat I tried to comprehend what it meant, never having suffered the pangs of conscience or remorse before as Willie had done near his end, and next day about my labouring duties I could think of little else, and at nightfall dreaded taking my rest in case the nightmare returned.

Staying awake as long as I could was no easy matter, for

forking dung by the barrow-load, then wheeling it to a far pasture, stretched limbs and sinews to the utmost, but that night the girl stayed in her own bed for once, for if she had visited me and I had performed as was expected I would have become even more drowsy, for men like to sleep after the act in my experience, while women remain awake desiring more.

But the hours passed without any repeat of the previous night's horrors, and in the morning I went to the pump in the yard to take my ablutions, and while drying myself on my shirt I heard a disturbance coming from the house, Mrs Howland crying out and swearing, followed by a banging of furniture. Minutes later she emerged trailing Hannah the servant girl by the hair, bawling at her for one rascally, thieving, ungrateful young bitch after she had taken her in and given her the benefits and comfort of a good home, which normally would have given me cause for mirth if the girl's looks weren't so pitiful, unable as she was to make a noise save a pathetic mewing sound. However, judging it prudent not to interfere, I filled my barrow and took the first load of the day off to the fields.

By the end of the week I reckoned my task was near done, for there was little left of the dung heap save some scrapings on the yard, and I wondered if my stay might be prolonged with further work, as I had no desire to face the snow I could see covering the distant fells.

At midday I waited for the girl to bring me my dinner, but she didn't appear. The door of the potato house had a bar across it, and when I drew near I heard moaning coming from within, so it came to me she had been locked in with the rats in the dark as a penance, but as it was still no business of mine I went to the house, my belly empty as a drum.

Rapping on the door, I heard the mistress call out for me to enter, and when I did so I saw her sitting at the table all disarrayed in her dress, still in her stays, a bottle of spirits in front of her along with a mess of cups and glasses.

It was clear she was drunk, near half the day gone already,

but more important to me there was no sign of a pot on the fire. She stared at me with red eyes, as ugly an example of womanhood as ever I did witness, although to call her female was an insult to the sex.

'Come to plunder some more of my liquor, is it? You and that young bitch have near drained me dry of my supply for my medical ailments, watering it, too, thinking I wouldn't notice the difference,' shaking the bottle at me, even though it was clear she was the one doing most of the draining.

'I suppose you've been prodding her with that papish prick of yours as well. God help us, but she must have been afire down below to let someone like yourself sprinkle her with holy water. Still, you know what they say, the older the fiddle, the sweeter the air,' and getting to her feet she made a grab for my private parts.

Up close she smelt rank like the slops she fed her swine, but she had a hold on me like the grip from a pair of nippers.

'What's the matter, Master Charley not fit to raise his head this time o' day? A real woman is what you need, instead of some young thing just lost her ha'penny. In a proper bed, too, instead of hay stubble pricking your bare arse.'

For the first time the absence of her own man drew my attention, and she must have noticed me glancing in the direction of his empty chair, for, brazen as brass, she said, 'Play your cards right and *you* could be sitting there. Judging by the coughs and whistles of him, that dotin' old fool in the bed back there won't have use for it much longer and a woman has her needs and must satisfy them where she will.'

'Thank you kindly for the offer,' I informed her, 'but if it's all the same, I'll take the wages owing me and be on my way.'

Dropping back in her chair, she burst out laughing.

'Wages, is it? Grub in your belly and a shelter over your head was our bargain. If you want to earn yourself a bonus you'll need to exert yourself a bit more. Anyway, you won't be doing your duty by two women. We wouldn't want you to be taxing your strength while you remain at Troutbeck Farm.'

Never had I longed to squeeze the living breath from another human creature as I did right then, taking pleasure in it, too, not having experienced the like before in spite of what was said about Willie and me, for all those desperate souls we had hastened to their Maker had been nothing more than ciphers to us. Willie kept a tally, names and sums paid out for each one, and I recalled him burying it in a canister at the back of the house when the hue and cry was at its height and the constables came sniffing around. For all I know it's in the soil there still, the only written evidence of our crimes. Not that any such material was sought when we stood in the dock, for we already knew the verdict, except, as it turned out, I was to be the lucky one.

So, confronting that great she-whale of a creature, I resolved to employ some of that same cunning which had stood me in good stead then, and by the look on my face she must have seen I was willing to surrender to her wishes, for going to the larder didn't she take out a platter of cold meat, setting it in front of me along with a jug of buttermilk to wash the victuals down.

Luckily she didn't demand satisfaction then and there. But I knew that when the day's work was over I would be called upon to fulfil my part of our bargain. And so to my shame I started servicing her on a regular, often nightly basis, until my prick was red raw, on occasions getting ridden like she was the man and not the natural and proper way of it, the great weight of her pressing me deep into her feather bed, and I bore it thinking only of the lucre I was earning to pay my return passage to the land of my birth.

My Lord

In pursuance of your most recent letter, as requested, I have broadened my investigations into the history and background of our subject.

Despite the universal condemnation of both his character and intelligence as someone barely on the level of a brute beast, he has succeeded in evading not only the full might of the law, but those who still thirst after his blood, for it seems young Fergusson is far from being alone in this regard. The family of the murdered lad Daft Jamie, for instance, took out a private prosecution against him, but failed, as his immunity stands. It would appear that, fearing further rioting, those in authority made certain the object of their fury should disappear like a ghost and Knox and his assistants would themselves become the target of the mob's wrath.

As to the present whereabouts of the elusive Mr Hare, there have been several reported sightings of him each one more absurd and fantastical than the previous. It was said, for instance, he was spotted in the village of Buckminster in the county of Surrey, then, even more farcical, New York, and, finally, cornered and hung by an angry mob in Londonderry in the north of Ireland, where he hails from. Naturally I have decided not to waste my time and your money in pursuing these so-called 'leads', concentrating instead on interviewing those who had a more direct involvement with him before he was spirited away, for it is not too fanciful to deduce that was what took place.

Surgeon Knox is someone I felt I should approach because of his business dealings with our purveyor of fresh corpses, but when I made clear my desire to young Fergusson he was not in favour of it.

'A day barely goes by that the muckrakers don't knock on his front door. He has had to barricade himself in his own home. If people are not pushing filth through his letter box, they are stoning his windows. Forgive me, Mr Speed, but the good Doctor has been badgered enough.'

Accordingly, I decided to act without his help, and so Mr Slack and myself kept watch on our target's house in Newington, and an uncomfortable time we had of it, on account of the chill mists that enshroud the city at this time of the year.

Not a solitary soul came or went from the place, its windows heavily barred and shuttered against further onslaughts by the stone-throwers. In an upper storey a light showed dimly, so we knew he was present, taking refuge like a beleaguered lion in his den. But having begun to form a notion of the man and his temperament from young Fergusson, I felt convinced he would emerge to face whatever the fates held in store for him. Opinionated, arrogant, outspoken, fearless, all of these adjectives seemed attributable to such an individual.

During the daylight hours relays of his students posted guard on the residence, but Mr Slack and I still withdrew to a discreet distance so as not to draw attention to our presence. An ability to merge with one's surroundings, brought about by long, often wearisome periods of surveillance, becomes almost second nature until a suspect emerges, or a voice is raised, or in this case a figure muffled in a cloak with a hat pulled down over his face, letting himself out with barely the whisper of a key being turned in the lock.

Cautioning Mr Slack to withdraw even further, fearing the sight of him might frighten off our quarry, I waited until he was close before showing myself and greeting him with a polite, 'Good evening, Dr Knox.'

A gas street lamp was nearby, and taking advantage of its light he peered at me.

'Do I know you, sir?'

'No, but my employer does, and sends his most cordial greetings and good wishes.'

It was pure fabrication, of course, but I hoped out of curiosity it might detain him long enough for me to make myself better acquainted.

'And who might that be?'

'Lord Beckford of Bath, a scientific gentleman like yourself.'

'A surgeon?'

'More a serious student of the workings of the criminal mind.'

At this he stared even more fiercely at me.

'Sir, my specific field is the dissection and study of the human body. The brain and its inner workings, fascinating though they may be, I leave to others.'

Tipping his hat, he walked on.

But, calling after him, I cried, 'Not even that of William Hare?'

It was a last despairing throw of the dice, but it brought him to a standstill, and turning, he said, 'So you are a reporter, as I suspected, after all, rooting in the gutter for carrion like the rest of your damnable tribe.'

'No, sir, what I have spoken is the truth. All I beg of you is a little of your time, no more than that.'

'And to what purpose? To have me indulge in idle speculation about a person I never once met?'

'But you had dealings with him. Not directly, perhaps, but via his deputy.'

'Have a care, sir, whatever your name is, or whoever your employer happens to be. I have no truck with the sentimental mewings of the mob, and as regards my personal opinion of Mr Burke and Mr Hare and their activities they are well known. Not to put too fine a point on it, sir, I am of the conviction they were doing society a service in ridding it of the dregs of our city while helping to advance the cause of scientific endeavour. That may sound shocking to you and your soft southern mentality, but the greatest evolutionary threat we face to our Anglo-Saxon nation on this island of ours is the Celt, and of its three branches the Irish are the most dangerous on account of their ingrained criminality and indiscriminate breeding. If we are to survive as a race they must be cleared from our land by fair means or foul. At any rate my conscience is clear, condemn me at your peril. How I practise my calling is between myself and a Higher Power.'

From the expression on his face I felt sure he was about to strike me with his blackthorn, and Mr Slack must have had a similar inkling, for suddenly he materialised from the shadows.

'Ah, so you intend forcing a false confession out of me, you and your pugilistic friend?'

'You recognise him from the ring?'

'No, but sustained damage to the occipital lobes and auricular area tells me all I need to know. Sir, don't waste any more of your time, or my own. As far as I'm concerned, the person you both appear so interested in might never have existed. Nothing remains of him and his ignoble history save the fiction you have created in your own head. Take my advice, there is nothing here for you, or your bruiser friend. Good night.'

After he had disappeared into the darkness, muffled up like some denizen of the night, heading God knows where, Mr Slack and I proceeded to our own address. As usual he was as silent as a stone, but I sensed an uneasiness and disapproval regarding my interest in this person Hare and his motives, that's if they even existed beyond the lure of easy pickings. But then I have always held the belief that every evildoer, no matter how horrendous his crimes, is worthy of study and analysis.

Admittedly this encounter with Dr Knox produced little to go on. Yet, out of stubbornness, I suppose, it made me even more determined to search out someone who had actually known our murderer and conversed with him in the confines of his prison cell.

But at this late juncture I must end here as it is now two in the morning and my eyes are weary and my pen refuses to follow the promptings of my brain.

Yours
Percival Speed

My Lord

The individual referred to in my previous letter, the last person to have contact with our man before he vanished like some human will-o'-the-wisp, I managed to locate from the newspaper reports of the time. As head turnkey in the Calton Jail he was responsible for the safe-keeping of Hare throughout the days following his trial, and by all accounts he took those duties seriously.

Your letter of introduction proved invaluable in gaining access to the prison itself, and even if I was forced to resort to lying, as in the case with the Surgeon, a combination of both opened the door, not only to the place but to the individual I was anxious to interview.

As before, I was made aware of Mr Slack's disapproval, even though I trust in time he will come to understand some manipulation of the truth can be a legitimate tool in obtaining results. As detectives, after all, we are not in the same business as men of the cloth, yet, odd to relate, both Slack and this particular gentleman appeared to share religious views bordering on the proselytising.

Armed with your recommendation, I arranged to speak with this John Fisher, as he's known, a man of middle years serious to the point of melancholy, Mr Slack and I meeting with him in his office, a room sparse of any form of decoration save for a small wooden crucifix attached to the wall, although he is not a papist.

To my bogus account of an interest in penal conditions in our nation's prisons and their population, he listened intently. Luckily I had been inside enough of them to appear reasonably well informed, but after pretending to take notes on the layout and state of the cells, the inmates' food and drink, punishment regimes, et cetera, I eased the subject around to their spiritual welfare. Instantly my interviewee's face shone, his voice becoming low and passionate.

'Sir, in addition to my statutory duties, my aim is to open closed minds to the glory that lies within each and every one of my charges no matter how heinous their crimes. Even if they are locked away within these four stone walls, the Lord can find a way to set them free through His bountiful message contained in this simple but beautiful Book,' and here he produced a Bible from a drawer, placing it in front of him.

'Are you familiar with the Good Book yourself, Mr Speed? Have you given yourself over to its powerful message in your own life?'

Not being any sort of religious individual, either privately or publicly, as well as sceptical about the transforming power of the gospel among the criminal classes, I hesitated about lying. But, fortunately for me, Mr Slack produced his own little leather-bound testament, laying it before him as a match for Fisher's own and proof of our good faith. And I readily confess I was grateful for my colleague's intervention, as from that point onward the way was made clear to pursue the true objective of my visit.

'As I understand it, this institution of yours is the most secure in the entire city.'

'The largest, too.'

'So the most notorious and dangerous offenders would end up here?'

'Sadly this is where most of them finish off the mortal span of their days.'

Here I pretended to scribble something in my notebook.

Then, without raising my head, as casually as I could, I enquired, 'These recent awful murders that have everyone talking, did those responsible come under your supervision by any chance?'

'Everyone detained here is equal under the law. As God's creatures all receive the same treatment. No one is excluded from His bountiful understanding, for if there exists even the tiniest jot of remorse in their hearts He will surely seek it out.'

This was proving uphill work, yet I felt I must persevere.

'Still, it must be a bitter disappointment when so many hardened criminals depart this life much as they entered it.'

Noting some confusion on his face, I elaborated.

'Without the peace and understanding you have described, I mean.'

'If only one is saved, then my heart rejoices, Mr Speed.'

And from Mr Slack there issued an almost inaudible 'Amen'.

Yet it didn't escape the notice of the man facing us, and so, realising this was the moment to strike, I put it to him, 'What a prize it would surely have been if your two most infamous charges had only opened up their hearts in the way you describe.'

For an instant I felt I had overreached myself. But, instead, it turned out to be one of those occasions when, forgive the angling analogy, one realises the fish has been well and truly hooked.

'On the contrary, Mr Burke sought solace from the teachings of his own Church, and I believe suffered genuine remorse right up to his final breath.'

'Unlike his accomplice, according to the newspapers.'

'Beware all the printed lies you read, Mr Speed, God knows there have been enough of them. The truth is he and I reached a private understanding after I presented him with a testament like your friend's here.'

'It also has been reported you were the last person to see him before he vanished.'

'There would have been others as well.'

'After you had seen him off on the coach from the city, you mean?'

'For someone who has recently arrived here you appear remarkably well informed regarding this dreadful case of ours.'

So then I reassured him my interest was purely professional, which seemed to satisfy him, and I asked him where he thought Hare might have taken himself off to.

'Unlike Mr Burke, he was not a person one could describe as forthcoming. But he did once confide in me a wish to see his homeland one last time.'

'And you believe that is where he might be?'

'After I put him on a coach to Dumfries I neither saw nor heard tell of him again, and so may the Good Lord take pity on him, for he has the rest of his life to repent no matter where he finishes up.'

'But you still suspect he could be in Ireland?'

'Well, here on this side of the water he runs the risk of being recognised.'

'The sketch artists portray him as a villainous-looking fiend from hell.'

'Which is how the newspaper writers and public perceived him, and still do.'

'But not yourself?'

'Mr Speed, if I were to suspend my belief in the inherent humanity in each and every one of us, no matter how dreadful their crimes, I would seek some other calling. But, then, it strikes me you, too, are just as wedded to your own profession, if you'll permit me saying.'

And at this point, having extracted as much information as I usefully could from Deputy Governor Fisher, I took my farewell, and Mr Slack and I left him to return to his duties.

Thus I have gone back to the newspaper reports yet again, hoping for some fresh nugget to leap out at me, and while I trawled through the *Edinburgh Observer* and the *Caledonian Mercury* Mr Slack sat patiently by, for truly he is a person of infinite forbearance, and although I have been granted some glimpses of his personality he still remains an enigma.

Alas, nothing useful in the newspaper columns emerged to capture my interest. So much ground has already been trodden over, any remaining clues have been muddied by crude speculation and a desire to satisfy the public's still-ravenous appetite for sensationalism.

Therefore, with your permission, I have decided to take passage on the coach our subject boarded himself on the fifth of February last in the hope the journey and its final stopping place may furnish some fresh information on his present whereabouts, and so when I have further news I shall report back to you.

As always, I remain, your faithful servant,
Percival Speed

And so the seasons changed and along with the rising of the sap I felt the urge to be on my way once more, for by my calculation I must be owed enough to get me to the coast and beyond with some left over. Further than that I had nothing in my head, having decided to allow events proceed at their own pace. All I yearned for was to turn my back on this country, even though I had first arrived here because of a lack of livelihood in the one I had left.

So the day arrived to confront Mrs Howland, still not knowing her first name, any intimacy between us confined to her own yelps and cries when I had pleasured her to completion, after which she would roll over and commence snoring, leaving me to return to the barn, for I had no wish to spend what was left of the night alongside some great lump of human lard.

Sitting across from her this midday dinner-time watching her chew on a mouthful of mutton, finally I spoke out.

'I think it's time for me to move on now that I've done all that's required of me here,' to which she made no reply.

Still getting no response, I said, 'Do you hear what I'm saying?'

Listening to the sound of my own voice seemed odd, having barely uttered a word since I'd been in this place, but my anger was growing at the sight of this half-drunk creature gorging herself in front of me.

'I said I'll take whatever monies owing me and be on my way, for I've a fair bit to journey.'

Finally she pushed back her plate.

'Journey, is it? That's a mighty grand word for a bogtrotter like yourself. Is it London you're bound for? Maybe King George himself has sent you an invite. A fine figure you'd cut among the toffs of Pall Mall in your present attire.'

There was a gulley knife lying on the table and my hand trembled at the prospect of drawing it across her throat, then watching the blood spurt the way the first cut is made in the killing of a pig hung and squealing on its hook.

'You'll get no brass here, Paddy Irishman, for there's none to spare. As a poor widow woman I need all the bawbees I can lay my hands on. Funerals must be paid for. Maybe it's different in *your* country, but I'd never be able to hold up my head if I sent my poor dead husband to a pauper's grave.'

Then she said, 'And it's no use you looking about you, for there's nothing worth robbing here, so take your bundle and good riddance. You're not the first stray to turn up on the doorstep and get his keep out of the goodness of my heart, and far better in the bed department, too, I'll have you to know.'

These were harsh words to hear, and harder to swallow, and the temptation to have her pay, and pay dearly, for them was difficult to resist, but adding another murder to my already rich tally might be something I would regret, and even though it was a poor substitute for retribution I made sure to give each of her curs a hearty farewell kick when they came rushing at me, jaws agape, to see me off.

During my sojourn there I had acquired several odd items, mainly cast-offs of the old man's, a fustian coat, a pair of boots, a waistcoat, as well as what the girl had smuggled from the kitchen, a ham hock, cheese, oatcake, along with some of the mistress's grog in a pickle jar. All of this I put in a meal bag tied with string and took my leave.

Young Hannah must have been at her milking in the byre, so luckily for me there were no tearful farewells, which would have been a bother, having no desire for someone clinging to my neck. In her own simple-minded fashion she had been good to me, and I had grown fond of her the way you might put up with the nuzzling affections of a pet, telling myself she would only get herself into further trouble if her mistress caught sight of her holding on to me.

The day was overcast, but mild enough, and so after a time I sat down on a ditch and took off the coat old man Howland had donated the one and only time he had appeared compos mentis. I wondered if he was still lying stricken in a back room, or stiffening with a sheet pulled over his face, something I wouldn't put past his wife, for a more heartless bitch I had rarely encountered. Nothing was too low for such a creature, although I scarcely imagined she'd try her hand at what Willie Burke and me had made our living at. Still, I doubted whether there would be much call for a carcass to experiment on in these parts, especially an ancient rickle of bones hardly worth the bother of harvesting.

With such thoughts diverting me I continued on my journey towards the coast, where surely there would be packet boats and with any luck the chance of boarding one, even if it meant going on my hands and knees and begging for a passage.

Just before I topped the crest of the road rising before me I took a last look at the place I had laboured in for so little reward. Smoke was rising back there, but not from the chimney, but the barn where I had spent the night, and minutes later flames leapt from its roof, spreading in a sheet of bright red fire. Then I saw a figure rush out from the rear of the house, making across the fields in the direction of the road, and I realised it was Hannah the servant girl bearing a bundle of some sort. Which was when the full horror of it struck me, not because of the plight of the girl, who must have carried out the deed, or the pair still inside the farmhouse, but for myself, who would surely be the one blamed for setting light to the hay.

Cursing the girl, I increased my pace, determined to get as

far from Troutbeck Farm as my legs could carry me, and I must have covered some two good leagues or more before dropping behind a stone wall to rest, asking myself just how fast might information travel in these parts anyway. Shanks's pony seemed the only reasonable mode of conveying bad news, but someone on a proper beast could move with greater urgency once the alarm was raised, which now it must be unless the woman of the house was lying inside insensible with drink.

At the next crossroads there stood a fingerpost, its wooden arms pointing four ways, but even if I was able to read their message the area's geography was a far greater mystery, so I took heed of the one bearing west. The Irish Sea lay there, that I knew, and there also was what I believed to be my best hope of embarkation, wondering whether I would be able to reach it before nightfall. In a sort of dream of longing already I thought I smelt a tang of salt in the air, and my head felt light even though I had eaten, and eaten well at the farm, which might well be a smouldering ruin by this time, and even though I was a long way off, once more I took a backward look.

Smoke no longer could be seen rising above those far-off, desolate hills, but something else caught my eye, a small figure trudging towards me. Suddenly, as if our gaze had met, crouching down, she dropped from sight, for it was a woman by her dress, and in that instant I felt sure who she was even at such a remove, the last person in the world I needed to be following me, the reek of her crime still about her person.

My only hope of evading her was to outpace her – she was a mere woman, after all – so I set off at an even faster rate, until I came to the first signs of human habitation I'd seen that day, a cluster of thatched cottages looking as if they had been dropped down all higgledy-piggledy in the same godfor-saken spot. There was no route around them, for the road ran straight as an arrow past their doors, so I pushed on, head bent, as though intent on some far-off destination, which, in truth, was the way of it.

Ahead was a tavern of sorts, and a poor enough establishment by the look of it, and as I drew near the door was flung open and two men came tumbling out, eager as I saw it to share their good humour with the world, and catching sight of me, the taller of the pair, a big ruddy-faced farmer by the cut of him, called out, 'Whither bound, brother? Come share a glass with us. This is no day for a fellow Christian to be out on the open road,' and his companion, who had a leaner, more cunning look about him, grinned, nodding assent.

Although fully determined to head on, for an instant my throat felt dry as dust, and I was sorely tempted, for I had sufficient in my pocket for a glass of ale, and seeing me hesitate the speaker held forth a great brown hand in a gesture I could not dismiss for fear of giving offence.

'My friend here and I have sold our winter ewes this day and are pruning our profits to mark the occasion, so come share a drop with us,' and giving in, I followed on after the pair as it seemed a refusal might cause affront.

Save for an elderly woman serving drink, the place was empty, but there was a fire in the hearth and I sat down with my back to it, savouring its heat and my first pint of ale in a long time.

'What's your name, friend, and where are you bound? Or are you one of those dedicated to a life on the road?'

Seeing no way out of it, I told him, Bernard Black, making up a destination in the Scottish Highlands, for I thought it unwise to say Ireland despite my brogue. However, they seemed to accept both, even addressing me as Jock after the second round, which I had no way of repaying, but they appeared content to continue treating me out of their own pockets.

The beer was working its way through me, and so I began to forget the trouble I had left behind, no longer taking thought of reaching the coast that day, but this was to be my undoing, for some little while later a man came into the inn saying that a young woman had taken a turn outside, falling down in a dead faint and the children were poking her with sticks.

'Shame on you, leaving the poor thing in such a state,' the landlady rebuked him, hurrying herself out the door, leaving the rest of us staring foolishly at one another over our tankards.

'Is she from these parts at all?' the big farmer enquired, and the newcomer told him, no, not to his knowledge, and hearing his words I began to have an uneasy feeling, cursing myself for being distracted from my original course, which was to put as much distance between myself and the locality as I could, and so draining my glass, I told them, 'It's time I was going, for I have a fair bit to travel before nightfall, and so I'll be thanking both you gentlemen for your kind fellowship and generosity this day.'

But the smaller one spoke up.

'Scotland's surely a long way off, but it's still uncivil to depart the company after having enjoyed our hospitality this long.'

'Aye, come, content yourself and take a last drop for the road,' said the big man, more reasonable in his cups than his companion, who like so many short-statured individuals was wont to conjure up insult where none was intended, and many's the time I've taken relish in chastising such individuals on account of their bad manners. But now was not the time to draw attention to myself or past habits.

'A parting glass, friend, for it's not often we have travellers passing this way. Even some young damsel dropping down in our street.'

And as he spoke didn't the landlady return half-holding, half-carrying the one person I had been endeavouring to distance myself from most of that day and now here she was in my very presence, eyes closed, face as white as a bedsheet.

'Sit the lass down and pour her some brandy,' ordered the landlady, and taking a bottle from the shelf the big farmer filled a tumbler, and the woman put it to the girl's lips, and after a moment she gave a cough, then a splutter, staring about her as if she had emerged from a bad dream, landing up in some equally fearful place with all these strangers gaping at her.

'Poor creature, she's near scared out of her senses. You men get back and let her gather herself,' and I was the first to withdraw to a dark corner, although I felt certain I had already been recognised.

Moving her nearer the fire, the landlady started into questioning her.

'What do they call you? Where are you from? Where are your people?'

But the girl hung her head, twisting her hands in her lap.

Then the small farmer said, 'Speak up, folk in these parts don't take kindly to foreign vagrants,' and she looked up at him, the tears blinding her, and without thinking, I said, 'She can't speak,' and all turned to stare at me, and I knew I had done a foolish thing, and rushing to repair the damage I said, 'Sure, look at the state of her, anyone can see she's beside herself.'

But Mister Midge, as now I preferred to call him, would not let things go.

'You know her, then, do you? Are you on the road together?' and avoiding the girl's eye, I told him, 'Not at all, she's nothing to me,' and after I'd said it I still felt the right Judas despite my stony nature.

But that scurvy little runt of an English cur continued tormenting her.

'Well, if you won't, or can't talk, how about a dance then? I'll gladly pay for the privilege of seeing you hoist up your petticoats,' throwing some silver on the counter, and rebuking him, the landlady said, 'Leave the poor lass alone, Rob Brown. Have you no pity in you for a lost soul far from home?'

'Gypsy folk have no home, or the wish for one, for they travel from place to place stealing as they go. Or cadging drink from them that have to toil for their living.'

From his words it was clear who he meant, and having put up with his foul tongue and rotten manners long enough, in a rush of blood I took him by his scrawny throat, ramming him against the wall, which of all the foolish actions I had carried out that day, starting with entering the establishment in the first place, this was the worst, being outnumbered two to one and with his larger friend the breadth of a barn door.

With the shock of it still hanging in the air, no one spoke for some time, until the landlady announced, 'If you need to resolve your disputes take them out to the street, for I want no trouble here,' and releasing my adversary, I stepped back, expecting him to retaliate.

But rubbing his neck, he dropped into a chair instead, reaching for his glass, his friend telling him, 'Lucky you are this gentleman here didn't lay you out cold as mutton, for you were well out of order as often you are with the drink in you.'

And so the storm passed, even though I had made an enemy, last thing I needed on my flight from all the rest dogging me. But crouching by the fire was someone who was still an encumbrance, a millstone about my neck, so I made my way to the door, for if I stayed I might not be so fortunate a second time if Hannah tried to follow. But luckily the landlady was pressing some nourishment on her, and as I left she was supping soup from a bowl.

Outside the day was fading fast, and unused to taking drink for so long I stood in the street to get my bearings. A group of urchins were watching me, and presently a stone flew, then another, so I took a race at them with bared teeth and they scattered until a curtain twitched and faces appeared at windows, so I took my leave, making off up the road to where the late sun was making its final descent.

But it wasn't until I had travelled a good distance that I realised I had left my bundle behind, and so I thought of it lying there by the feet of the one who had helped fill it with her own thievery. Yet that was of little consequence to me or my stomach, and when darkness fell I took refuge in the lea of a haystack with gnawing hunger as a bed companion, and waking at first light I managed to forage a handful of mushrooms, then some potatoes from a clamp in a nearby field. Both tasted of the soil in which they grew, but I gulped them down having no other choice.

Later that morning, from a laneway came a cart with a young lad dangling his legs over the shafts. It was laden with sacks, but there was room for a passenger on top, and as it drew near I waited by the side of the road, hoping to rest my own two legs a spell. But as it drew alongside I found myself unable to shape a sentence, or utter a syllable to the young driver, who looked at me oddly as he passed by, and gazing after him, I wondered where he was going, envying him his youth and his existence, hard as it might be, for never had I felt so low, and falling into some kind of a daydream, I was back in Ireland once more the same age as the boy on the cart, roaming the countryside in search of divilment, robbing orchards and gardens, dropping sods down people's chimneys.

But wakes and weddings were where I got a first taste for the drink, wakes my favourite, for when the poteen was flowing and the fiddles screeching himself would be brought up from the corpse room and propped against the wall in his open coffin so as not to miss the crack as well as the remarks being made about him. The priest, of course, was not too pleased and lectured us of a Sunday, but as it was one of the few diversions we enjoyed no one paid much attention to him raining down thunderbolts of censure on our bared heads.

Still, looking back, I sometimes fancy such nights might have been when I formed a careless indifference to the look and notion of dead people, nothing more than a parcel of rotting flesh and crumbling bone, soon to be mixed with graveyard soil, leading me to what rankles still, Burke and me getting called resurrectionists. For why go to the bother of digging people up when they're in your kitchen enjoying your whiskey until they're insensible and at your mercy? As Burke would always say, 'Me and you, William, are merely filling a gap in the market before anyone else thinks of it.'

And so with all this coursing through my brain my pace began to falter, then slow, until it seemed I would never reach my destination. More and more I would drop down by the roadside, studying the clouds drifting overhead, travelling from the place I was trying to get to before this tiredness took a hold of me. Rising up from the grass became harder and harder until I thought this might be where I might end my days, here on a lonely byroad in a country still very far from my own.

Wigton
Cumberland

My Lord Beckford

In regard to the matter of expenses and continuing outlay, I am pleased to inform you that the monies have now arrived safely. The enclosed premium was also greatly appreciated, and I trust I will shortly be in a position to repay your generosity by running our man to earth and hopefully bringing him to Bath in accordance with your latest set of instructions.

As you may gather from the heading on this letter, our travels have now taken us southwards, although the dreary landscape and its inhabitants on either side of the Border are little different save for the sound of the bagpipes and the wearing of the tartan, as following our own monarch's recent royal visit to his Caledonian subjects there has been a tremendous fuss about all things Scottish. Naturally this fervour has further inflamed the public ire towards Messers B. and H., if additional fuel were needed, given their nationality and their bringing disrepute to the host nation.

In my previous correspondence I reported my intention to retrace our subject's tracks while seeking statements from those who claimed to have seen him, or someone very like him. But yet again I have been forced to discount all of these so-called witnesses as their accounts were conflicting, clearly fabricated, or both. So, instead, I have been poring over a map of the entire region in the hope of tracing a likely route for our quarry, and surprisingly Mr Slack has proved himself a most valuable ally, albeit a mute one, while I allow my conjecture free rein and he listens.

'After Dumfries and the trouble there we know he was secretly conveyed out of that town and left on the roadside to Carlisle, where he is forced inland away from the Scottish coast as every port and seaside village its entire length is aflame with rumours of him attempting to cross by ferry. The authorities almost certainly would have warned him about this, so he travels away from the danger, seeking some place where he can escape public suspicion and possible recognition, desperately needing to go to ground, you might say, like his very own furtive animal namesake.'

However, seemingly unimpressed by such imagery, taking the map from me, Mr Slack began tracing a line away from the busier routes leading south, yet not too far distant from the sea, as our runaway might still be aiming to reach his native land and find refuge among his own people there, an instinct I might very well turn to my advantage, as often the smallest glimmer of human sentiment can lead one closer to one's quarry, even the most cunning and resourceful. And I say this despite having never clapped eyes on him, with nothing tangible to go on save a cast of his features now residing in your cabinet of curiosities in Bath, along with several ill-drawn courtroom caricatures from the Scottish broadsides.

Even so he appears to have taken shape in my head as a construct of flesh and blood, more importantly, a mind and personality which I might yet be able to infiltrate, and as we studied the map on the table in front of us I felt I could almost see this lonely figure trudging the remote and muddy Cumbrian byways, biding his time until the coast was clear, literally.

But what if he never was to be found? What if he had already met his end, even dispatched by his own hand? However, I quickly discounted the theory as all my professional instincts told me he would never countenance such a thing, not from any religious considerations, which appear to trouble him little, or not at all, but because his true talents, if they can be described as such, lay in harming others.

For a long time my companion and I pored over the ordnance sheet spread before us as though it might yield up an answer to our conundrum, and addressing Mr Slack directly, something I had rarely done before, not from any feelings of social superiority, I may add, but in consideration of his silent, reclusive ways, I enquired, 'Tell me, where would you yourself suggest we travel next in our search for this person?'

He kept his gaze lowered to the map before making a reply.

'Unlike yourself, I have no experience in detective work, but from what I have heard from your own lips and those of your informants, I suspect he might have it in mind to make a sea-crossing somewhere around here,' indicating an expanse of water to the west of the town of Whitehaven.

And so in preparation for our journey to this port we have remained here another day and a half, studying the map along with a gazetteer so as to be thoroughly familiar with the locality, and throughout my companion and I conversed freely as if a portal had been opened between us for the first time.

Mr Slack possesses a soft and pleasing accent, and gently quizzing him I learned he was Bristol-born and bred, apprenticed early to a bell foundry manufactory, where his great strength was nurtured and developed, in his leisure time achieving prowess in the grass ring. Joining the ranks of 'the fancy', as it is known, soon he was performing regularly for the noble gambling fraternity, where, I understand, he first caught your Lordship's eye before becoming British bare-knuckle champion, beating the great Tom Cribb for the title and holding the belt for two years before retiring undefeated.

However, when I attempted to question him about this departure from the ring by someone in his prime, I formed the impression I might be trespassing on private, possibly sensitive, territory. Yet I continued to be intrigued by my companion's history, and at times it seemed as if two men of mystery had taken a hold of me, not just the one we were seeking. But then I have always relished a puzzle, in human form or otherwise.

Early on the morning of the twenty-third we set off from our inn and, Mr Slack having hired a small chaise, soon we were trotting through the sodden countryside as a damp westerly was beating in from the Irish Sea.

As the day wore on into early afternoon, for we had a good forty miles or so to cover, I turned over in my head the prospect of coming across even the barest trace of our quarry, for even if he had travelled this same route and on foot he must be far distant by now, and so could be anywhere in the country off to the left of us.

Yet, as someone used to the city and its busy streets, the prospect of scouring those same misty fells and muddy upland tracks was an unappealing one, probably fruitless, as well. Accordingly, taking heed of Mr Slack's counsel, I have decided to go in the direction he himself suggested in the hope of some sighting of our Mr Hare there.

But at this point here I must end my report, hopefully promising some more rewarding news in my next letter.

I remain
Your obedient servant
Percival Speed

Two long days and longer nights it took to get within sight and sound of the sea, eating what I could find in the fields, and sleeping under hedges, for luckily the weather was fine except for the dew which soaked my clothes until they dried with my walking in the air. Before reaching the first houses of the port I washed my face in a brook, combing hair and beard as best I could, brushing my outer garments with twigs from a bush. But when I met the first townspeople they seemed as rough as myself, the screeching of gulls only adding to the noise, something I was unused to after being so long away from other humans and their daily concerns.

At the harbour I could see no sign of a packet steamer, just a row of fishing boats with their catch being unloaded on the quay. An old man sitting on a bench was watching the work, so I asked him if there was a ship crossing to Ireland.

'Not from the likes of here there isn't. You'll need to travel on to Heysham for one sailing to the Isle of Man first.'

'And whereabouts might this Heysham be?' I enquired, even though I had no intention of landing on some rock halfway in the middle of the Irish Sea despite it being a stepping stone to the place I was aiming for.

'Fifty miles or so along the coast from here. But there's a coach bound for there at noon. You can catch it at the Turk's Head if there's still a place to be had.'

'But I want the direct passage.'

'Then, Fleetwood's the port for you, which is even further away. Is it a bereavement or a death in the family, for you have the tone of a man anxious to get across in a hurry? Still, I'd beware of the stench, if I was you.'

'Stench, you say?'

'Aye, from the incoming boats. Aren't their holds packed with the dead like herrings in a barrel? Even travellers coming off have the look of a corpse about them on account of the smell.'

I saw he was expecting me to enquire about such traffic when there were burial plots a-plenty in the country the people had perished in. But I knew how ravenous the men in white coats were for subjects, no matter where they hailed from, even those not near as fresh as the ones me and Willie had once provided.

'I know of a man who might take you straight across if you have the wherewithal, for he sails there for the fishing.'

'Would he be willing for me to work my passage, do you think?'

The old man paused before looking me in the eye.

'Have you experience of labour on the boats, for only the fittest can withstand such work?'

But it was clear I had none, this whey-faced pauper, the few coins in his pocket barely sufficient to buy him the heel of a loaf, and so then I thought of my missing bundle and what it contained, enough to last me for a week if I rationed myself. Even my prison fare seemed like the scraps from some rich man's table, tormenting myself, as I walked along, with the smell and the taste of it, even the gruel and oaten bannocks as dry and lacking in nourishment as the flaking, scribbled plaster on the cell walls.

There were beggars in the streets, some with stumps for legs, or missing an arm, or blinded, those who had come back from the foreign wars. But even if I were to join them they had more hope of charity than myself, and with nothing better in view I took myself across to the inn the old man had pointed out to me.

Sure enough, in the courtyard a coach was being readied

with the luggage brought out while the owners watched from the taproom, one in particular more anxious than the rest, for he came out to supervise the loading of a large brass-bound chest. An elderly waiter and a young boy were making heavy weather of it, and the traveller kept ordering them to be careful as it contained valuable merchandise, a full dinner service from Paris for a Lady Denbigh, so he said.

At one point the old servant stumbled and almost fell, and the traveller cried out in alarm, telling the two to set their burden down. He kept looking back towards the inn, but the coachman who was responsible for the stowing of the luggage was nowhere to be seen. Yet the traveller seemed reluctant to allow his property out of his sight even if such an object could ever be carried off by thieves. Red in the face and sweating, he pulled out a spotted handkerchief, fluttering it in the air like a flag of distress. But still no one came to his aid.

Seizing my chance, I came forward, offering to help, and for a moment he scanned me up and down, for I knew I presented the appearance of someone pared to the bone by poor diet. But to his surprise, almost as much as my own, I hoisted the chest up on my back, heaving it on to the roof of the carriage alongside the other pieces of luggage, and he handed me a sixpence before returning to the taproom, and for the blink of an eye I was tempted to follow, but having learned my lesson I walked away with the coin intact in my pocket, permitting myself a smile, for the man's chest was near enough the same size and weight of those I had carried through the streets of Edinburgh on my trips to Surgeon's Square, but with a very different cargo inside.

At a stall in the marketplace I bought a ha'penny bun, washing it down with a draught from a public fountain. Sitting on its stone steps, with the buzz of commerce all around, I watched the farmers' wives selling their eggs and butter and pullets, while the spin of the wheel and dice merchants gulled their menfolk.

I also observed those who slithered through the crowd on the lookout for a purse to snatch, or a drunkard to waylay, as when a farmer came reeling out of a public house one of the Gypsy women would thrust a bunch of lucky heather in his face, while others offered more personal favours, taking the man back inside with them to an upstairs room.

Yet the more I studied these various forms of criminality the less I realised my own chances were of taking advantage of them. The risks seemed too great for someone only a few months away from public denunciation, even if it was in Scotland. But news also travelled south, and my likeness was still on a broadsheet, and moving through the streets I came across similar posted facsimiles of others wanted for their crimes, and found myself looking to see if my own face was among them.

But as the day lengthened, from my perch by that fountain among the crowds I caught sight of someone familiar, someone I had not expected, or ever wished to see again. First the red hair, then the shoulders and waist, then, as the head turned, the face. She was by the entrance of the Cumberland Arms, where the drabs of the town congregated to cajole, then fleece their next victim, chattering like painted cockatoos, bare bosoms rising up out of their gowns, although not all were bedecked in silks, for many were like those I had sometimes prodded in the Canongate myself with the risk of a dose of the pox at the end of it.

Curiosity at how Hannah came to be here, and what she was doing in this place, made me study her discreetly from the shelter of an entry across from the inn. Had she become so desperate she was reduced to selling herself? Or attempting the like, for amidst that band of red-lipped professionals she was not making much of a fist of it, holding back from the rest, looking like a plain, simple girl fresh from the country, which in truth she was.

In my head ran the notion she might have followed me

here. But how could she have done, unless there was a touch of the witch about her? Such theories were whimsical, I knew, yet still I couldn't shake off the notion she and I were bound together in some strange fashion, even if I was determined never to be in her company again. But then anger took a hold, for she might yet spoil my chances on account of our past association, fleeting as it was, two strangers rutting in a hay barn in the dark with never a word exchanged on account of her disability and my own disinclination for any sort of conversation.

As I was about to move away from the danger of discovery, a man came out of the inn, yet unlike the rest, with no hint of a stagger in his gait, not a farmer, not a businessman, either, closer to one of the travelling tricksters in the market square, a rakish air about him, a smile playing on his lips. Instantly attracting a rush from the females besieging the place, but holding them at bay with good humour, he made his way to the edges of the throng, where he stood for a moment, his eye moving from one face and figure to the next as if intent on choosing a woman for himself.

Noting this, three of the bawds returned to the chase, penning him in, but he refused all of them. Instead, he made his way towards the least promising of those gathered there, and I watched as he approached Hannah, murmuring something to her while she stood with lowered head staring at the ground. Angered by this, two of the rejected whores attempted to pull her by the hair, and rake her face with their nails, but the man raised his walking stick and they withdrew, yelling abuse at the pair of them.

All the while smiling and whispering in her ear, the stranger drew Hannah away, and she accompanied him like someone with no power over herself, borne along like a twig in the water, and even though it was not in my interest to do so, I began following them, drawn by something beyond sense or reason.

The route the man was taking seemed to lead towards the harbour, and staying hidden in his wake, I vowed I would turn on my heel once I had seen the place he had in mind for his victim, and for me that would be the end of it, and a little while later with my quarry's boots sounding on the quayside, and not wishing to make the same kind of noise myself, I hid behind a fisherman's hut until the ring of steel on stone ceased.

The foppish-looking gentleman, for his attire was of a superior cut to anything I had seen in that place, looked to have his eye fixed on a vessel apart from the others moored there, Hannah standing meekly by his side as if held by an invisible tether to her captor, for it seemed to me that was what he had become by this stage of the game, and one which still remained a mystery to me.

Keeping up my surveillance, I saw him signal to someone on board the ship, and a man in a seaman's jersey appeared on deck, bearded and swarthy, the two of them exchanging some words, but in a language unknown to me, and moments later a gangplank descended to the quay with Hannah being urged to set foot on it.

She held back, so taking her roughly by the arm the man began pushing her towards it, and as they struggled on the quayside I heard her give vent to one of those odd muted cries of hers, and raising his stick the man began beating her while the seaman above watched. But then, as though alarmed by the spectacle, he called out, which only made the man below become more vicious, yelling at his victim with a torrent of foul abuse no so-called gent should allow pass his lips, and in a moment of the purest folly I emerged from my hiding place, showing myself, and forcing Mr Fancy Britches to take a step backward.

'Have a care, my good fellow, this is no concern of yours. Merely a private matter conveying a young lady the worse for wear on board this ship.'

But, advancing, I made him, coward that he was, retreat

until he was close to the water's edge with the girl still in his grasp, staring with surprise and joy at the sight of her champion arriving to save her. At least it seemed that way to me, until there came a moment of doubt her struggle had been mere play-acting and I had misconstrued her true motives.

And as though reading my expression, the man said, 'Why quarrel over some slip of a girl when there's a score or more arriving fresh from the provinces every day? Come, what will you pay for her? If you're willing to match what my friends are prepared to offer, you and I, Irishman, will shake hands on it.'

And it was the word 'Irishman', as well as his tone, that incensed me, for as yet I hadn't opened my mouth.

'My friends have been at sea a long time and are in want of some recreation,' adding, with a fresh look of contempt, 'Still, if your funds won't stretch to it we might be able to share the profit. I'm a reasonable man, after all.'

But feeling far from reasonable myself, I moved closer, and raising his stick, he warned, 'Take heed, for I have some influence in these parts, unlike you and your sort, who have a poor reputation here.'

'Hers, as well?'

'So you know her?'

And so furthering the lie, I said, 'Why wouldn't I, when she's my own flesh and blood,' and the instant the words left my mouth Hannah gave a cry, pulling herself clear of her captor's clutches.

'So, robbery's your game, Irishman? A family concern?'

Prior to laying him flat on his back, I felt like calling him Englishman in return, but before I could give in to the urge Hannah made a rush at him, and backing before her didn't he go over the side of the quay while the foreigner on board started drawing up the gangplank as fast as he could, leaving his former partner flailing in the water below, hat and stick floating alongside him in the swell.

Which is when I fled the scene with his cries ringing out

behind me, but whether the yells of a drowning man or not was of scant concern to me. What was, however, was the girl racing at my heels, swift as a young colt, holding up her skirts as she sped, and staying in my wake, just as I now suspected she had done all along since fleeing Troutbeck Farm, and the memory of that establishment going up in smoke and now this latest outrage of hers made me even more determined to see the back of her.

Yet she hung on until, reaching an alleyway, I ran ahead, and waiting for her, pulled her into a dark corner, taking her by the throat. Casting her eyes up without a sound or struggle, she sank in my arms, and so enraged was I by her persistence in my affairs I was fully intent on throttling her.

But she gave vent to a moan like she would sometimes utter when we were bare-backed in the hay together, and didn't I feel a quickening below, and so confused was I by it, I loosened my grip, and she dropped to the ground, and seeing her lying there I felt doubly adrift, for never had I drawn back from protecting my personal interests when it came to a matter of murder before. But there could be no gain or profit in this case, so then I cursed myself for not heeding the man in the water and taking his money when he offered it.

'Damn and hell roast you, go back where you came from and leave me alone, for I'm off across the water tomorrow on the first sailing. Well, do you not hear what I say? Are you deaf, as well as dumb?'

But if she had little usage in the way of speech, her understanding of it was far from deficient, and her expression changed to one of eagerness and she began tugging at my sleeve, so I let her lead me, for I had become weary of battling towards a goal which in my heart I now realised was beyond me, for despite my talk of catching a crossing the likelihood of such a thing happening in my present circumstances seemed as distant as ever.

Our journey took us to what appeared to be the poorest

part of the town itself, as low and dirty a neighbourhood as any I'd seen in the Scottish city I had left, the houses little better than sod-thatched hovels, and stopping outside one of these my guide looked to her left, then her right, before pushing on its door, which hung half off its hinges. From the state of the dwelling it was clear no one lived here, or had done for a long time, and when I followed her inside a smell of damp and decay hung heavy on the air. In the far wall was a ruined fireplace, and Hannah was on her knees before it, her hand deep in its sooty maw.

Drawing something down from the back of the flue, she laid it on the hearth, a look of triumph on her face near as unexpected as the object itself, for there was the bundle I had left behind in my haste to escape that upland country inn. Taking it up in her hands, she held it out to me like a pet expecting to be rewarded for a task well done.

But I was only intent on what it contained, and lo and behold wasn't everything still inside, old Howland's donated coat and waistcoat, his boots, but best of all the provisions she had taken from the farm's larder, and in a moment I was sinking my teeth in the bread, stale and all as it was.

And as I ate she watched me with that same dog-like expression of hers as if waiting for scraps to fall her way. But none were forthcoming, and when I had my fill I shouldered my pack, a good deal lighter now, and she held on to me, so I told her, 'Here is where we go our separate ways. One burden on my back is more than enough to see me where I'm bound. You must take your chances in your own country.'

However, she began crying out in an unexpectedly loud manner, and fearing she would draw attention with her noise I put a hand over her mouth and might have carried on if the tears wetting my hand hadn't made me desist, for they felt like they would burn my very skin, so I told her, 'Get up and make no more noise if you value your health.'

Putting a hand under her skirts she drew out a small

leather purse, and still warm from the heat of her body it felt heavy in my hand, and when I loosened the string about its neck I saw there were coins inside, silver at that.

'Where did you get this?' I put it to her, and again just as fruitlessly, 'Where did this come from?'

She only stared at me, so then I wondered if she had earned it on the flat of her back. Yet even if she had, despite her rawness at the game a sum like this could only come from many such transactions. So only one explanation made sense, hard as it was to swallow, for bad enough to be blamed for the firing of Troutbeck Farm, but now to have a robbery on my head as well meant a double hanging matter, for I knew no one would listen to a plea of innocence from someone with a record such as my own. Still, what I held in my hand meant the answer to my prayers and a passage across the sea.

As though gauging my intentions, didn't she snatch back the purse, burying it under her petticoats once more with a look that told me if I tried wresting it from her she would let out a hullabaloo despite her limited means of protest.

'What is it you want from me? Surely you know full well we are nothing to each other.'

Yet even as I spoke the words, something about them rang false, and so wearying of our battle, I told her, 'Very well, come with me, and we'll share the money,' and she rose up, and watching her brush the soot from her dress, comb fingers through her hair, then pat and pinch her cheeks like one of the whores at the Cumberland Arms, it made no sense to me when there was ample money to spare tucked away in her drawers. But never having been an object of amour before, it was even harder to accept she had kept it, not for herself, but for me, like the bundle back in my keeping once more.

Outside the day was beginning to dip towards evening, yet I had hopes the old man might still be on his bench by the quay, and indeed there he was smoking his pipe, and when I came up to him, without a word he made a place by his side, not for myself, but for the girl, who blushed becomingly before accepting the offer.

'Found yourself a young companion, I see,' said he, and without thinking, I replied, 'No, she's my daughter,' thus adding substance to the lie fed earlier to the man landing up in the water.

'Travelling home together, is it?'

Ignoring the assumption, I pushed on with my enquiries regarding a place on the fishing boat, and the old man said, 'The man I referred to is taking her out before dawn to catch the early tide. I can bring you to his house if you wish, but if you have the money you'd be better off on the coach to Heysham and catching the packet from there.'

But, no, I told him, I was determined on getting across without delay.

'Very well, I'll show you where he lives. He and his son handle the boat on their own, for it's only a small craft. I'm not certain if it can accommodate more than two on board.'

And so off we set, the old man hobbling ahead, for he said he should speak to the fisherman first as he had a surly manner when faced with strangers.

While he entered the house, which had a figurehead in the form of a mermaid in the garden, the girl and I waited outside. In the town behind us lights were coming on, and the sky was darkening over the sea, which we could hear breathing softly where it washed against the harbour wall. The sound spelled freedom for me away from a place where I would be forever on the watch for those who sought revenge for what I'd done to their kith and kin, or, to be more truthful, those they themselves had abandoned on the street, for our case had stirred up an ants' nest of hypocrisy from mealy-mouthed protesters eager to join in the cries of outrage.

Burke had sated some of that appetite for retribution after they had seen him dangle from a gibbet, but it had given them a taste for it, as I had experienced for myself with the mob breaking windows and people's heads after a hanging, and the more I pondered the more determined I was to put as wide a stretch of salt water between myself and my pursuers as was possible.

To which end I told Hannah to hand me the money before the old man returned, for it seemed sensible I should be the one to make the transaction, and at first she hesitated, before reaching under her skirts. But when I told her to remain outside, she shook her head, so I bade her follow when the door opened and the old man beckoned us to approach.

'This is the gentleman desiring passage to Ireland,' he announced by way of introduction when we entered the dwelling, a rough-enough-looking place, clearly lacking the attentions of a woman. On either side of its fireplace sat the skipper and his son, a youth of similar age to my companion, who having heeded my advice hung back in the shadows by the door.

'He has money to pay for a crossing if you're willing to accommodate him.'

But neither of them deigned reply, the father spitting in the embers, the son following suit, and eager to push my proposition forward I produced the purse, and finally the older one spoke up.

'Has the man himself not got a tongue in his head?'

And it was on the tip of my own to respond with, 'Well, one of us has,' for I felt my chances of persuading these two unmannerly brutes were slipping away before our business was even established, my own appearance no great help. However, what was in the purse was, so I spilled some of its contents on the table as a taste of what might be forthcoming.

'How much have you got?'

'Enough,' I told him, even though I had no true notion of the amount.

'A sovereign,' says he, then adding, 'For the pair of you,' and I heard Hannah sigh as though relieved.

But setting all thought of that aside, I emptied the purse

on the table, a rapid calculation telling me there was at least twenty, maybe more, in gold coin there, robbed, it now seemed clear to me, from a woman and a farm I knew only too well.

'Agreed,' I said, scooping the money back in the purse, before enquiring, 'How much for one to travel on their own?'

'The same, for there's little difference in the stowage.'

So, giving in, I told him, 'One sovereign it is.'

'With another as a gesture of good faith.'

But being too fly to be taken in by such a hoary old trick, I informed him he would receive half the sum when we went on board and the rest setting foot on Irish soil.

And so, with the money safe in her possession once more, my travelling companion, now to be, led the way back to the ruined dwelling, and once inside, by gestures, intimated we should shelter there until dawn, and spreading a covering of coats on the earthen floor she prepared to lie down, and I joined her, staring up at the bare rafters, brain busy with how to regain the initiative by fair means or foul, as for all her guile she hadn't considered the person lying next to her might, instead of lovemaking, squeeze the life from her, for she was already fast asleep as if all her cares had drifted away, one hand bare, the other under her clothing holding tight to what I desired most, yet not the thing another man might lust after in a similar situation, and so in the remaining hours until the sky turned a shade paler through the holes in the roof, I lay torn between the urge to throttle and rob and a more ardent alternative.

Yet I must have slept as well myself, for I was stirred by a pulling on my shoulder, and rubbing my eyes found her looking down on me, and when she saw I was awake her hands began a kind of dance, summoning me to make haste, and again it seemed odd she could be so insistent about something that by right should be of no concern to her. But even if we were fated to continue on our way together, I vowed the instant I felt my native turf under my feet that link would be broken for good.

Despite what he had promised about setting sail without

us if we were late, our fisherman was waiting for us when we arrived at the harbour, or, rather, for the first instalment of his money, which I had ready to hand and which he took without the barest pretence of gratitude or civility, and so we went on board, where the son led us to a rank cubbyhole below, stinking of fish. Above our heads we could hear the preparations for sailing, and a short time later felt the play of the waves on the sides of the boat.

I had neglected to enquire how long our passage would take, so I raised my head above deck where the father was steering while the son busied himself with the nets. But both ignored me even when I called out to them, so I gazed up instead at the patched sail bellying in the wind beating in from the south-east.

Soon it brought rain, so I went below, where, no longer controller of events, Hannah was being sick with her head over a bucket, receiving no pity from me. Laid low in this fashion was what she deserved, I told myself, enjoying her suffering even more on seeing me finishing off the last of the bread and a mouldy rind of cheese in my knapsack, an old army relic of Burke's, for he liked to talk about his time 'fighting Boney', as he referred to it. Of course, I knew full well he never got within a musket ball's flight of any Frenchie as they never set a boot on Irish soil.

Still his stories were worth the hearing, even if the half of them were made up. He had been a fifer in the Donegal militia under Lord Leitrim, which I do believe to be true for he played the flute with some distinction, regaling us with marches as well as jigs and reels in our kitchen, as having had a surplus of drink often we would end up there after the alehouse. And my own wife herself would birl and spin with the rest until she dropped down light-headed, then rising up and reproaching me for being a blight on the festivities with my long face and watchful ways.

After her first husband Logue died, she and I wed, more

as a business arrangement than any love match, as she wanted me to help her run the house and keep the tenants in order. Not that she was ever backward about raising her own two fists, and I was happy to oblige for I was sick of hawking fish around the town with an ass and cart. And when I married her I knew what I was letting myself in for, as my opinion of her was of a she-devil with a temperament to match, and able as any man, she also fought like one, often sporting a black eye.

But I was content to accept all that in exchange for a cushy billet, and now that everything has been aired like dirty linen, I admit we shared a bed together while I was still a lodger and before old Logue passed away of a fever, although some of our enemies have suggested his widow herself hastened his demise.

Everyone who came within range of her was fearful of her disposition, but in court, I've heard tell, she put on a great show of injured innocence, which may have softened the judge, for, like myself, she too escaped justice despite knowing full well what me and Willie Burke got up to, as well as sharing in the proceeds.

In his testimony Willie said she stripped Mary Paterson, taking the clothes off her back for her own use, then helped fit the corpse in a tea chest for transportation, all of this relayed to me by one of the turnkeys, who swore he was there when he said it in the dock. But then towards the end Willie would have implicated his own mother to cheat the rope, and, to be fair, me and Margaret were the same, and as events turned out, he himself ended up the scapegoat for all our crimes.

So it looked like Lady Luck continued to smile on me, a brisk wind at my back, and a vessel carrying me to a place where those who once knew me there had no inkling of my subsequent career as a 'burker', my former ally and accomplice having given his name to a new word in the dictionary. But then, better to be a live nobody than a dead somebody, says I.

Even though our boat still battled with the waves, the girl seemed to have recovered from her bout of seasickness, and so as we squatted in that dark miserable hold, two people bound together by chance with nary a word between them, once more I wondered what was in the head of this woman clinging on to me.

My own actions, too, were a puzzle to me, one minute ready to choke her, the next giving in to her, yet not entirely for the sake of the money, either, and even though I had been grateful for her silence thus far, getting her history from her own lips was something I still felt an urge to hear for myself. But, given her infirmity, I knew that to be impossible.

Caught up in my own thoughts, I wondered if she had been born that way, or smitten later, as it was not unusual, so I heard tell, for people to lose their power of speech because of some event or great shock to the system. But if such a thing had occurred, only she had the knowledge of it, locked away within in much the same manner as my own secrets remained hidden.

Once when her mistress had wrung her satisfaction from me, and I was lying in that great bed of hers with its rotten canopy and carved posts, an itch for conversation took hold of her, a rarity, as normally she would roll over and commence snoring like one of her own fat sows, and she began taunting me about the girl and our trysts in the barn, having guessed at what we had been up to when I wasn't servicing herself.

'No more ploughing Miss Mousie's furrow for you, Mr Irishman, while she rots in that shed out there and repents of her pilfering. But then thieving comes natural to someone who was locked away before with others like her. Bad blood always will out, I should have told myself, instead of showing pity to a young trollop and taking her in. Took you in, too, with her silent ways, so best spend no more of your seed where you might regret sowing it. Better a barren field than one that might sprout a squalling keepsake before another three seasons come round.'

And recalling those words, it occurred to me a certain queasy turn earlier might have less to do with the rise and fall of the keel under us than the time me and her spent in the hay together, might explain, too, her desire to cleave on to me, and the more I turned it over in my head the greater my impatience grew to reach dry land and put paid to such intentions.

The wind had dropped when I got on deck, for we were becalmed with the sail falling straight as a sheet hung to dry and the boat's owner gone from his place at the tiller, now tied with a rope, and the son, also, nowhere to be seen.

Piled up in the stern was the tangle of fishing nets I had seen the younger one working on earlier, and coming closer I spied a pair of waders such as fishermen wear sticking out from under it. Nearer still, legs, then a body, recognisable on account of the jersey, for it belonged to the skipper, fast asleep, and judging by the bottle close at hand, dead drunk.

The whiskey looked tempting, at least half a naggin untouched, but rage taking precedence over thirst, I dealt the brute a hearty kick, provoking nothing more than a low moan. Another kick, but he was beyond pain, and the more I thought about it the less I felt like trusting this pair of blackguards, not only with our money, but our safety as well. Clearly the older one was now incapable, but the son, wherever he was, had a brooding, treacherous look that didn't bode well, and when I returned to our quarters below there he was stretched out, proprietorial as a young lord, while the girl crouched facing her unwelcome visitor, who must have slid down the companion ladder when my back was turned, silent and slippery as a rat.

'Why are we making no headway?' I demanded, and he grinned up at me, and by the look and smell of him I could tell he had been at the whiskey bottle as well.

'Why don't you whistle up a wind for us, Irishman, if you're so eager to be on your way? Anyway, what's the great hurry? Sit yourself down so we can all get better acquainted,' and he winked across at the girl, and there was lechery in his tone.

'I've been trying to get a civil word out of the lass here, but she's like a stone. You should teach her to be more sociable when a person's being agreeable to her.'

When first I'd come across this youth, sitting across from his dour relative spitting in the fire, I'd dismissed him as a mere stripling with no more wit or cunning than a block of wood, yet here he was treating me like some feeble fool with a ward as powerless as himself. But despite the same young whelp being misguided on both counts, I reined in my temper, knowing, for the moment at least, he held the advantage.

'So when do you reckon the wind will lift and take us on our way again?'

'Why don't you climb up and consult the weather while me and the young lassie here pass the time together? No harm will come to her, cross my heart,' and as he made the gesture the girl shot me a look of distress, mouthing something, and the boy laughed.

Already my foot was on the bottom rung of the ladder, for why jeopardise the chances of landfall over two people both young and lusty engaging in the beast with two backs, even if one wasn't as agreeable as the other? Besides, why keep up the pretence of caring if another put their prick where mine had once been?

But then didn't this young pig carry his behaviour a shade too far, laying a hand on her breast, while crudely remarking, 'Sure isn't the same young damsel hot and eager as a bitch in heat.'

And so I went for him stretched out there defenceless, with a grin still on his face. But before I could squeeze the breath from him, up sprang Hannah like a young tigress, a knife in her hand, and in the blink of an eye pressing it to her tormentor's throat as if bent on despatching him herself, and pulling her back I could feel the rage burning up inside her like a fire.

Meanwhile our would-be Galahad was whimpering for his

life, more fearful of the girl's intentions than my own, it would seem, so I let her torment him some more, crouched in the corner as he was by now, close to pissing himself.

However, knowing we were still dependent on him and his drunken parent, I said, 'How far are we still from shore?' and to speed a reply I cuffed him a few times until he cried out he couldn't be certain, so then I gave the girl licence to prick him some more with the knife, which I now saw was of the kitchen variety, yet another plundered memento from Troutbeck Farm, I suspected.

'A league, maybe two,' eventually was forced out of him, even if there was still no breeze to carry us that distance.

'And how long before we can be on our way?' and wary of the knife, he said, 'All we need is some wind to fill the sail.'

'For your own sake that better be soon, for our patience is fast running out,' says I, beginning to relish the feeling of power, having so long been denied the sensation, and the girl seemed of a similar mind, giving him another jab of the blade until he bawled out, 'Take your damned money, and I'll get you there for free if only you keep this she-devil away from me!' and hearing the words Hannah gave a smile of satisfaction.

'What about the one up above drunk as a monkey?'

'Forget him, I can sail her by myself.'

Then, cocking his head, he cried out, 'Listen! Listen! The wind's up!' and sure enough the lapping on the sides of the boat had grown stronger, and following him up on to the deck I could see the sheet creak and tighten, and as I watched he untied the tiller and the craft began slowly to turn.

But the girl who had come up with us took hold of my arm, with concern on her face pointing towards the stern and a low dark line on the horizon, for instead of making for the land, we were sailing away from it, and seizing this young English dog by the scruff of the neck I shook him like the treacherous cur he was.

'Do you think we're blind, or what? Turn about this instant

if you don't want to join the fishes along with your pig of a father!' for I was quite prepared to tip the pair of them over the side, just as I now was convinced they themselves had planned on doing with us all along.

'No, no, we have to tack to take advantage of the wind!' giving the steering a tug, and the boat started to zigzag, each flap of the sail edging us closer to that promised rim of coastline, and going aft I strained ahead for a column of turf smoke, a flash of window glass, and the girl joined me, and I felt her hand take mine, and again came that curious wordless murmur in my ear, and for an instant I felt I could understand what she was trying to communicate, that no matter what the next stage of our journey might bring, I still had need of her.

Returning to our steersman, I demanded, 'Where do you intend setting us down?' to which he replied, 'A port by the name of Dundrum with a decent harbour.'

However, having no desire to land where people might gape and gossip, I told him, 'The nearest stretch of shoreline will suit us just fine.'

'Better a place, surely, where the young lady can step ashore dry-shod?'

And so once more I ordered him to watch his tongue, and to reinforce the command the same 'young lady' pressed the blade of her knife to his neck, making him tremble afresh, with my warning, 'Just do as you're told and no harm will come to you.'

Yet my companion, it seemed, had a harsher fate in mind, for drawing my attention to the drunkard sleeping it off on deck, she made a cutting motion across her own throat, a face on her like an angel itself, and hardened as I am by the life I've led and sins committed, I felt shocked as well as apprehensive, recalling, as I did, my own darling spouse, who would also stick a knife in one as soon as look at them, and now here I was with another vixen with similar tendencies.

When we were near enough a cable's length from the

shore, which was low-lying with a sheltering ring of sand dunes, I bade our steersman take us into the shallows where the water was clear and the bottom pale shingle. And so the girl and I prepared to lower ourselves over the side while he watched with a hand steadying the rudder.

Once our soles touched the water I knew we would lose our power over him, so, lying, I warned, 'We have friends in these parts, and it will be the worse for you if you try to return. So count yourselves lucky and go back where you came.'

And the words seemed to have their desired effect, for, lifeless as the wooden tiller he held in his hand, he stood there watching as I went over the side followed by the girl hoisting up her skirts, and then we were wading for the shore, and the water was cold, and she clung to me, shivering. But I hardened myself, knowing the parting of our ways must come once we made landfall, and so reaching the shore and taking her by the wrists, but not in a rough or unmannerly way, I told her, 'All you've done on my behalf, I'm truly grateful for, but this is where we must take our farewells. You have enough still in your purse to get you to wherever you care to go, but for now I must travel on alone for I have business to attend to and folk to meet.'

While the last part was pure invention, it had a plausible ring to it, something I'd borrowed from Willie when he was embroidering yet another tale to soften up some client before despatching them.

Nevertheless this was not some street doxy lulled into submission with strong drink and soft words, for sinking to her knees, she clasped me by the ankles, and instead of pity a sort of rage came over me at her making a show of herself in this way when up to now she had been like a wildcat ready to strike without fear or conscience, and so I told her, 'Rise up and give over your grovelling, for I no longer have need of you, or the money you stole in your own country,' and closing my ears I left her crying there, already starting to feel like the old William Hare again, dependent on no one for his livelihood or future salvation.

Where the beach rose up to meet the dunes, foolishly I turned to look back, later wondering if my life might have taken a different course if, instead of being curious like Lot's wife and the pillar of salt, I had marched straight on. But then the here and now, not the hereafter, has always been the main consideration for someone such as myself, and just then what the present threw in my face was the sight of the girl running pell-mell into the water already waist-deep with her skirts billowing and filling up.

The boat was lying some little way off, our young steersman having turned it about ready to sail away, and I could see him looking shore-wards, both of us intent on what would happen to the girl. But then I saw the sail start to fill and the craft put out to sea. Yet the girl kept on wading further and further until I could only see her head bobbing, then no more of her, so dropping my bundle I ran down the beach and into the water, striking out to where she had gone under, for floating there was her petticoat like a bright marker, and I followed it down until my hand grabbed the rest of her clothes, then finally their drowning owner, for I knew if I lost hold of her that must surely be her fate.

Struggling with her to the shore was like hauling a double burden as her sodden garments seemed to weigh as much as herself, and when I laid her out on the sand I lay down alongside her to get my strength back, and after a time she coughed up some seawater and began weeping, and so I lifted my hand to her for I was angry at having to take to the water a second time when in all good sense what I should have done was leave her there, and all the time I was beating her she lay mute, and it was if I, too, had lost the power to speak when inside there raged the question, why, why had she done such a thing? Was it her intention to reach the boat and take her chances with those on board? Or, worse, do away with herself? Yet even if I continued battering her to within an inch of her life I still knew I never would discover the truth of the matter. But what was more pending was what was to be done with her. I had, I suppose, saved her life. But for what? To leave her lying here like a drownded rat?

Down along the water's edge lay the bundle she had abandoned before rushing into the sea like a lunatic, so I went to retrieve it before the tide did, for by this stage my mind had been made up by what it might contain, namely any money remaining from what those two reptiles at sea had extracted from us.

The bundle, in actual fact, it was nothing more than an old pillowcase, the neck tied with hay rope, and when I delved into it all it appeared to contain was clothing along with some articles of a more personal nature, hair ribbons, a comb, a little cake of soap, a scrap of mirror. But at the bottom lay the knife and, of more import, the purse, and with both items safe in my own pocket I went back up the beach to where she lay as I'd left her.

Soaked to the skin, we both were, so I told her to take off her wet garments. But she only stared at me like someone who had left her wits in the water. So, once more, I commanded, 'Do as I say if you don't want to catch your death a second time.'

Getting no satisfaction, I decided to take care of the matter myself, but it was like dealing with something inanimate, stiff as a block of wood. So then I began stripping off my own wet clothes, and after a moment didn't she start doing likewise until there we stood on that lonely strand as naked and bare as Adam and Eve themselves save for a hand covering her modesty and myself long past caring.

Still, never having seen her in that manner before, as in the hay we had always done the deed in the dark, it came as a surprise, for she had as fine a figure as ever graced some artist's work, flesh pale as milk, with a dusting of freckles across shoulders and arms, and, God help me, but didn't I near allow lust take advantage of the moment, until withdrawing a short distance away I spread my shirt and breeches on the sand to dry.

Judging by the elevation of the sun, it was near enough noon, and out on the ocean our former transport could be seen sailing off towards the east, and watching its progress, I told myself those on board had got off lightly, regretting not chastising them more for their villainy, as well as recovering the passage money they had got from us. But some little consolation, small as it was, was they would be returning without a haul of herring in their nets.

Having covered herself by now with what she'd plundered from her former place of employment, for I thought I recognised an outer garment once belonging to her old mistress, Hannah came and sat by my side, her borrowed apparel big and loose-fitting, unlike my own, for old man Howland was of a meagre build, and even though my recent diet had left me lean as a lath we must have looked like the pair of us had escaped from some kind of pantomime show. And even though our present situation could scarcely be described as comical, I uttered a sort of a laugh, something she must never have heard from my lips before, for, leaping up in fear, she looked as if she might plunge into the sea a second time.

But keeping a tight grip on her, I managed to reassure her I was not some sort of madman after all, and sitting down she started going through her belongings, and I could tell she was looking for the purse, and to prove it was safe and in my keeping I showed it to her, and first she looked at it, then at me, and from her expression I could tell I was the person in authority once more, with her ready to follow and do my bidding.

Rising together, we looked back across the water towards a country we no longer could see, yet was in our blood and bones like an affliction still not cured. And in that at least we were as one, and so with her by my side it was time for me to return to the place I had fled near half a lifetime ago. But how it would receive me, and how I would fare there, were something only fate would decide.

The Turk's Head, Whitehaven, Cumberland ✖ 27 April

WHITEHAVEN IS A bustling fishing port, its boats harvesting the waters of the Irish Sea, and having found rooms at the above I set up quarters there and Mr Slack and a young local lad were despatched to post up a quantity of notices bearing a likeness of the person we were seeking, although I took the precaution of removing his name in case his notoriety should attract the wrong kind of attention.

A reward of two guineas was offered for information on the same gentleman, quickly producing several hopefuls from the town, all claiming to have seen him. Most of these were quickly dismissed as sham-merchants, but a travelling huckster captured my attention with his account of meeting our man on the road some weeks earlier and engaging in conversation with him.

Lounging at his ease, a pint of porter before him, he recounted the following.

'Half-starved, he looked, the cheeks on him pale as that sheet of paper in front of your Honour, and so I shared a morsel of bread with him for which he was grateful even if he didn't speak much.'

'And when he did, could you tell his nationality?'

'Scottish, I'd say. Or, Irish maybe. Aye, Irish, for the entire region is rife with his sort seeking employment.'

'Employment?'

'Aye, he intimated as much.'

'And did he volunteer any further information?'

'None. He seemed mortal anxious to be on his way.'

'In which direction, may I ask?'

'Keswick, I reckon. Aye, somewhere towards them parts.'

Here he paused, with a sly look, enquiring, 'But what would two fine gentlemen such as yourselves want with someone like him anyway?'

'A private matter concerning a debt to be paid.'

'Well, I wish you good fortune, for he looked like he had nothing but the clothes on his back, and even they looked as if they didn't belong to him.'

'Not all debts concern money.'

'In my line of business, they do.'

'And you are still of the belief this is the man whose likeness is in front of you?'

Once more he studied the drawing, before nodding his head.

'Aye, I'd swear it on the Holy Book itself, even if he looked a deal rougher as if fallen on hard times. But then times are hard for all of us on the road, unlike gentlemen such as yourselves.'

I knew he was angling for the reward money, but even though he appeared to know things about our quarry we ourselves were only privy to, I held back for I still had hopes other witnesses might yet come forward, so thanking him politely for his time and generosity I bade him good day.

But holding forth a filthy palm, he refused to budge.

'There's still the matter of the brass referred to in your handbill.'

So once more I informed him I was more than grateful for his information, but no money could be forthcoming as I had other claimants to interview, and at this he became irate, using foul language, and Mr Slack was obliged to expel him from our presence.

After he had left, still cursing in a fury, Mr Slack sent one of his disapproving glances my way, and relenting I handed him a shilling, telling him to give it to the packman when he found him, which wasn't difficult as he was with some of his cronies in the taproom below.

Unfortunately, his tongue having been loosened by drink, a stream of other would-be witnesses came knocking on our door, and even though it was hard not to blame Mr Slack for having such a generous Christian nature, I told myself thereafter I would pay more heed to my own less trusting instincts.

Over the following days I ventured into the streets alone, as already my companion was attracting too much attention for my liking. Children had started following him in the street, men, women, too, of the lowest kind, jostling for a closer glimpse of his imposing presence and exquisite turnout, being most scrupulous regarding his appearance, as your Lordship will attest.

Having enjoyed an entrée to your mansion in Somerset, I can well imagine him silently moving up its long corridors graced by your collection of classical antiquity, all of those marble heroes in athletic poses, recalling you also telling me of his expertise in the art of massage in the Ottoman style, when ministering to your needs in your splendid bathhouse.

Hearing of those powerful hands kneading a naked torso, yet with the delicate touch you intimated, strikes one as something of a contradiction. But then Mr Slack's outer appearance belies a personality of the most sensitive and private nature. In the rough world of detection, however, I fear he may be too guileless for his own good, so I have decided to leave him to his religious studies in his room rather than have him by my side in the streets, where I can pursue my enquiries anonymously and apart.

In my pocketbook I have taken to carrying a drawing of our runaway in the hope someone might recognise his features, bearded or not, but no such happy outcome has so far taken place, and here I must confess to losing faith in the success of our venture for, as though receding in a mist, that same countenance seems to have faded and lost shape until nothing is left save a sheet of blank paper.

Yet as sometimes transpires when all appears lost, a fortunate accident may occur, and whether brought about by the power of concentration, or some such divine interference of the kind Mr Slack himself believes in, I am always glad to take advantage of it.

How it came about is as follows.

One afternoon, while strolling by the harbour, I found myself staring westward towards that invisible shoreline where the person on my mind might himself be walking free as air at this very same moment. Then, again, he might be skulking somewhere deep in the landscape behind me. Both possibilities kept see-sawing in my head until, so low became my state of mind, I contemplated writing to your Lordship offering to abandon the entire project, for even if I did manage to track down this Hare person, what then? I, personally, harbour no fierce animosity towards him, save a loathing of his crimes, while you have made it clear your own interests are of a purely scientific and clinical nature.

As I say, I felt the quest might well be a hopeless one, and it might be better if no more time and expense were squandered on someone leaving no living trace since stepping out on the Carlisle road some months previously. But even that seemed doubtful, for he might have been at large a much greater length of time given the conflicting reports surrounding his disappearance.

With all these thoughts tumbling through my head, I sat down on a bench facing the sea, studying the likeness of the wanted man, as I had done a hundred times since receiving it from the printer in Princes Street, at which point an old man came hobbling up and sat down alongside me for no other reason, I presume, than this was his favourite seat.

In no proper frame of mind for conversation, I made to rise, but detaining me, he said, 'Don't hasten away on my account,' and so out of politeness I resumed my place by his side.

'At my time of life I like talking to folk and hearing their stories, and even if they don't care to humour an old man these old eyes can often tell me more about them than they wish to divulge.'

Mercifully he made no attempt to offer a reading of my own personality and history, not that there was much likelihood of him coming even near, priding myself, as I do, on keeping both well hidden.

After a time, filling a pipe, he puffed away, before remarking, 'So you're the London gentleman who's seeking the one on the handbill.'

'How do you know that?' I asked, alert and interested for the first time.

'This is a small place, as I'm sure you've realised, so scarcely anything escapes my notice.'

Producing the sheet in question, I showed it to him, and taking it in his hand he studied it, before observing, 'By the look of the same gentleman, he might well be someone you wouldn't care to cross.'

Feeling constrained about supplying too much information, I told him I wished to contact him on behalf of a gentleman who desired to remain anonymous.

'And you think he might be in these parts?'

Suddenly all this seemed tedious, having no wish to waste any more of my time on some old salt with a penchant for other people's private business, and so consulting my timepiece, I told him I must be on my way.

'Bustle, bustle, like all you southern folk. Still, you might regret not having more patience with an old man and what he might have to say.'

The tide had started on the turn, its wash rocking the fishing boats moored to the harbour wall, while on the horizon the late sun was bathing the sea in a rosy glow. Suddenly all about seemed peaceful, unlike the turmoil in my head concerning someone as fleeting as a ghost, and I must have been still staring at the repeater in my hand, for the old man said, 'Perhaps it requires winding.'

But the hands continued to move relentlessly and silently, just as they had done every hour and every minute since the piece had been presented to me on leaving Bow Street, Speed by name, speedy by nature, my reputation in the force. But that was another time, when I had spies in every den and rookery from Clerkenwell to the Seven Dials.

My face must have showed my mood, for the old man said, 'You might be a lot closer to your quarry than you think. Let me take another look at the gentleman.'

Peering at the portrait, he enquired, 'How long since this likeness was taken?'

'Two, three months. More, maybe.'

'Aye, so I can see. For in this, his cheeks have had the benefit of a razor.'

'You recognise him?'

'Indeed I do, and was able to be of some service, although it was the young woman I felt sorry for.'

'Young woman?'

'Aye, the daughter. But with fiery red hair, unlike her papa.'

Up until that point my hopes had been raised. But with the appearance of a strange female on the scene, they sank again, for it appeared I was the victim of yet another fraudster despite his years and outward semblance of sincerity.

'I suppose you're aware a reward is offered in connection with this matter?'

'Aye, but I have no interest in a penny piece of it, for it would be on my conscience to be a Judas Iscariot.'

'Still, what if I were to inform you the individual concerned happens to be a murderer?'

'Murderer? Murderer, you say?'

'Aye, and several times over.'

'God forgive me, and here was me helping him on his way,' said he, gesturing seawards.

'But there is no ferry from here.'

'True enough, but he arranged his own sailing.'

'And you saw him leave?'

'No, I only put him in the way of someone who might accommodate him.'

'Is it possible to speak with this person?'

'You may, but I doubt if he'll care to talk to you, for his manners are not near as refined as your own.'

Arranging to meet the following day, the old man and I shook hands, and despite his protests I pressed some money on him, and returning to our inn my mood was a buoyant one as, finally, Mr Slack and I might be about to reap some reward for all our hard work.

That evening we pored over a chart of the coastline searching for possible landing places on the other side and next morning after breakfast armed with the information we set out together, for I had decided to bring my colleague along in case events should take an ugly turn.

As promised, our guide was waiting for us in his usual place, and although a mite disconcerted at seeing Mr Slack for the first time, he soon was at his ease, for despite his forbidding exterior, Mr Slack, as you and I both know well, has a calming effect on most people after they have been in his presence for a time, and so the three of us sat looking out across the water as though in no particular hurry to carry out the business in hand, for I have learned it is better to allow the person supplying the information to believe he is the one in the driver's seat, in a manner of speaking, and so I waited for the man seated alongside to make the first overture, and after a time he enquired, 'This person you seek, is he sought by the authorities?'

But I told him on account of the extreme delicacy of the case my colleague and I were not at liberty to divulge any of its details, and this seemed to satisfy him, and so, finally, I broached the subject of the boatman who had arranged passage for our pair of fugitives, even though I still had my doubts about Hare having company, an additional puzzle being the money needed to hire the craft, unless, of course, he had resorted to old habits.

'That's her over there, *The Western Maid*,' replied the old man, indicating one of the vessels bobbing in the water. 'But as you can tell she's seen better days. Still, I imagine our two travellers weren't greatly particular, being in such a hurry,' and here he glanced at me.

'Is the owner normally on board?'

'Aye, but he don't take kindly to being confronted with strangers, especially after indulging too freely the night before,' and leaving him to observe the forthcoming encounter from his bench, Mr Slack and I made our way towards *The Western Maid*, where I hailed its skipper.

At first nothing stirred above or below its decks, so again I cried out, 'You on board there!' trusting an official tone might produce a response. Yet still there was no movement.

Between craft and quayside was a space of a foot or so, making it an easy matter to step across, and weighing up the risk, even possibly a breach of maritime law, I looked towards Mr Slack, but he gave sign of neither support nor opposition. But I had come too far to be foiled by some drunkard of a fisherman, so in a trice I was on board, leaving my companion standing on the dock.

From one of the masts hung a brass bell, so I tugged on it, and ringing out across the still waters, its sudden din stirred the seagulls from their resting places, their shrill cries enough to wake the dead, or in this instance someone from a sodden sleep, and there came a yell from below, and moments later a half-dressed, crazy-eyed figure thrust his head through an open hatch, crying, 'Pirates! Pirates!' like someone in the horrors of drink.

He had an upraised axe in his hand and appeared intent on using it, so Mr Slack leapt on board, and at the sight of this giant of an individual, dropping his weapon, the man cowered back against the side of the vessel.

'We mean you no harm,' I called out to him. 'I merely wish to speak with you regarding some people you conveyed to Ireland.'

Instead of placating him my words seemed to rekindle all his previous terrors and he began yelling, 'Ned! Ned!' who I took to be the son the old man had mentioned, and now this youth also appeared from below, but unlike his parent, showing no fear, and taking hold of the axe he made a rush at Mr Slack, who, sidestepping neatly, pinioned both his arms, forcing him to relinquish his weapon.

But the lad, a coarse, loutish-looking creature, continued to struggle, and so Mr Slack struck him with his fist, felling him to the deck, where he lay moaning. Certainly the blow might have been delivered with much greater force, coming as it did from a former professional in the art, yet I was still shocked by this uncharacteristic display of violence on my colleague's part.

However, his action had the desired effect of calming our two assailants, and so once more I informed them I simply sought information for which I was prepared to pay, and at the mention of imbursement the son became almost affable in a sly, cringing sort of way.

'Are you two gentleman seeking passage for yourselves?'

No, I told him, I was only interested in another couple he and his father had taken across some time before, a man and a young woman.

'What do you want with them?'

'That's neither here nor there. All I wish to know is whether you transported them or not.'

'First let's see the colour of your money.'

All this time the father had been lying stretched out on

the deck, half-soused, still, by the look of him, and now he was heard to mutter, 'That Irish pig and his female spawn still owes us money. Tell 'em, Ned.'

But the son became angry.

'Don't listen to him, he's drunk. Put 'em overboard, we did, him and that whore of a daughter of his makin' eyes at me while me and her were below. I could have had my way with her if I'd wanted, but she weren't to my liking.'

'Never mind that, just tell me where they went ashore. At which landing place?'

'Haven't I said they got their feet wet? Over the side in too much of a rush to care about a soakin'.'

Producing the map Mr Slack and I had been studying the night before, I spread it on a raised hatch, instructing him to point out the spot where our two travellers had disembarked, and that if he did so to our satisfaction he would be paid for the information, but not until I was convinced he was telling the truth, for I had a way of knowing when someone was fabricating, and being the gullible young knave that he was he swallowed it, and after peering at the chart he indicated a stretch of what looked like barren coastline near a place by the name of Dundrum.

'There, that's where we left 'em to their fate. Not that I care much what happened to them. Good riddance to the pair of them.'

'I trust for your sake you're not spinning us a yarn, for if you are, my friend will be back to pay you a return visit, depend on it.'

'On my life that's the place, I swear,' says he, all the while keeping his eye on Mr Slack standing nearby with folded arms.

Tossing him a shilling, over-generous for such a rank specimen, but satisfied I had got from him what I wanted, I left him there, and as Mr Slack and I walked away I saw him biting on the coin, part of me wishing it had indeed been counterfeit.

Passing the old man on his bench, I saluted him with a wave of the hand, which he returned in the same spirit as though he and I had pulled off a fine coup together, and truly I did feel as though a way ahead might finally have opened up for us in our quest, and back at our lodgings my mood continued to be jovial.

Yet Mr Slack seemed unable to share it, a cloud having settled over him for some reason, and when I enquired what it was that ailed him, he declined to answer, pacing up and down, his great fists clenching and unclenching by his side.

'If I have said or done anything to upset or offend you, I am truly sorry,' I told him, 'for you must know I hold you in the highest regard, as does the man who first brought us together.'

Dropping into a chair, he bowed his massive shaved poll bearing the scars of his many past encounters, and, lo, it transpired it was that very history that was the cause of his upset, for after a time, holding up his right hand, he confessed, 'I swore an oath never again to raise this to another living soul,' and so I realised he was referring to the youth on the boat.

'But you only did it as a last resort.'

'Even so, I broke a promise, and a man is only as good as his word, even if it is only to himself.'

'Jack,' I said, addressing him by his Christian name, for to adhere to polite usage at this precise instant would have seemed graceless, 'Jack, no one knows better than yourself what the Good Book says about forgiveness, no matter how awful the act involved.'

And so having put two and two together, I went on to enquire, 'When and where did this occasion of sin, as the saying has it, take place?'

He looked up, and there were tears in his eyes.

'Ten years ago in Bristol's Clifton Fields with people present I knew well, but where vanity took me beyond the bounds of sporting decency even when the one facing me was a newcomer to the ranks. Still only a lad, yet already a fine prospect, he was hungry for my crown, and God forgive me, but when I heard those fine gentlemen of the fancy yelling for him, and not for me, the champion, I became no better than a brute bent on taking the contest to the very limit, even death itself.'

'His own, I take it?'

'Aye, and since that day I have never trod the grass circle again, or raised a hand to another living soul.'

I could see he was greatly overcome, so I said, 'But don't you see, those were the risks attendant on such a contest. You were unlucky, that's all, just as, in the end, sadly, he was, too, but in more tragic circumstances.'

But despite my words nothing it seemed could heal the hurt he had lived with for so long, and so I told him the time had come for us to pursue our quarry across the water, and at first light take a coach to Heysham and there board the first packet steamer to Ireland, where, back among his own people, and thinking he would be safely out of reach, we would have the advantage of him.

A man who once knew the pair of us, or was of the opinion he had our measure, used often to remark we reminded him of the knave of spades and the king of hearts, Burke being the merry one of the pack, and me the dark, gloomy-visaged one. But even if we were not playing a hand of cards at the time, I never took offence, taking it as a kind of a compliment, just as Willie did being likened to the old red monarch.

Holding my tongue with an expression to match came easy to me, just as being Master Joviality was second nature to him, except when drink was taken and he and I fell out, so tramping the roads of Down with a silent companion was far from irksome. In truth, I much preferred it, as most of the women I had previously known would deafen one with their dinning, especially my wife, having a tongue on her that would etch glass.

The first few days the climate was agreeable enough, so at night we made our bed in the lea of some haystack, or in a barn one time, well away from human habitation. But when the rain set in, as it does at that time of the year, I told the girl we must seek some proper shelter and decent covering, for the clothes on our backs were near destroyed by seawater and the weather.

'And sure isn't there more than enough in that purse of yours to provide us with sustenance and a place to lay our heads until I find employment,' I told her, even if a far quicker and easier solution would be to end the association there and then with no witnesses.

But she was young and fit, as well as sober, unlike those others we had despatched, so instead of encircling that milky young neck of hers, rising up, I said we should be on our way once more before darkness set in.

In a place called Comber, with one Catholic chapel, but half a dozen churches and meeting-houses of the other sort, I realised my accent might give rise to suspicion, then enmity, so I hit on a ploy to play dumb like my companion, as though a double weakness ran in the family, but thinking I was making mock of her and her disability, she became enraged with a flurry of hands and a silent mouthing of what I took to be swearing. But when I explained the reason for my plan, she became calm and indeed appeared willing to be a party to it herself.

Accordingly, I decided to give it a try in the first lodging house we came to, a rough and ready sort of a place, but then my life up to then could hardly be described as spent in the lap of luxury, and the bed at least was raised off the floor and the tick was horse hair instead of straw.

The woman who owned the house, and judging by the holy pictures on the walls, was of my own persuasion, was a harmless old biddy who never seemed to budge from an armchair, for she suffered from the dropsy, and cradling my head in a parody of the need for rest, and holding up two fingers denoting the number of nights I wished to stay, I succeeded in getting my intentions across without uttering a solitary syllable, which came as much of a surprise to the other mute member of my 'family' as myself.

When the bedroom door was closed behind us, I wedged a chair under the latch so no one could enter while we took our rest, for each of us was dead tired as well as footsore with the walking.

A good half a day I must have slept, because when I opened my eyes the sun was streaming through the casement, while alongside me lay a young woman fast asleep, for I was still in a dream, thinking she must be a stranger and some stroke of luck had brought us together, most of her clothes being absent, both bare arms flung out enticingly, and just as I was about to press home my good fortune, I heard her murmur something, and so the spell and the dream were broken, and even though I was still standing to attention in the nether parts, I drew back, so then she woke herself, turning her face towards me with an expression nearly as surprised as my own had been moments earlier.

Next thing she was out of the bed pulling up the sheet to cover herself, while laying bare my own readiness to take advantage of the situation. Clutching the sheet to her bosom, there she stood like we were strangers who hadn't done the same thing many's the time in the hay at Troutbeck Farm.

'It's me,' I told her, 'do you not remember?' and was on the point of telling her my name, until, using the one John Fisher had hung on me at Dumfries, 'Bernard Black. Barney,' I said, and mouthing it back at me some little while later she got into the bed again.

But the urge had left me, so like a couple of shy newlyweds on their honeymoon night, even though it was now the middle of the day, we lay apart, and not really enquiring of her, I said, 'I wonder what o'clock it is,' and she began rummaging about under the bed for her precious bundle which she had placed there so as to be close to it, and finding what she was searching for, she laid the object in my hand, and to my great surprise it was a hunter watch, still working, for when I put it to my ear I could hear its steady tick, and we passed it back and forth between us, admiring the sound and solid feel of it.

The case itself had all the heft and appearance of gold, yet I doubted if it really was, as it seemed unlikely such a valuable piece would have found its way to Troutbeck Farm, for that was where I suspected it had been pilfered, or was the property of some rich mark she had robbed, as the closer my acquaintance with the person alongside me in her shift grew the more

I was coming to realise she might prove a match in villainy for myself.

After a time, lying there, I put it to her it might fetch a decent sum which would keep us off the street until I could find employment, and I could see she was pleased at hearing the word.

'But first we must find ourselves something to put on our backs.'

And next thing wasn't I translating the words back to her in some form of mummery all my own just as if the pair of us were dummies, and a little while later we set out together, still conversing in sign language in the street for the benefit of anyone seeing us there.

In a poor part of the town we found a shop where they sold other people's cast-offs, and laying down her money, Hannah made it clear to the woman who owned the place what we were in need of, a skirt and a frock for herself, and a pair of trousers and some class of jacket for her parent, for that was the role I had now decided to take for myself.

On the back of the door was a mirror, and after we had gone behind a curtain to change, coming out we looked at one another in the glass, she in a wool coat with a rabbit fur collar, and me in a serge topcoat and moleskin trousers, and I caught her smiling to herself as if I was now the comical-looking one of the two, while she had turned into a fashion plate. But her opinion was of little consequence to me. The watch and what it would fetch were of much greater import, so we went off in search of a Iew who might give us a decent price for it.

In the staunch Presbyterian city I had previously lived in, the sign of the three golden balls was a rare enough sight, but in the Grassmarket was a pawnshop I would sometimes visit with whatever trifle Willie and me had taken from those we had hastened to a place where they no longer had need of such things. Not that we ever received much for our pickings as our clients were as poor as ourselves.

Yet one time, I remember, there had been a fine ring on the finger of that jade Mary Paterson, which young Master Fergusson must have given her on account of being enamoured of her, and Willie and me did everything short of sawing it off, but thinking the absence of a finger might lower the price we left it for her lover to retrieve when his colleagues came to get their hands on the rest of her.

Still, even in a stiff-necked Protestant hole such as the one we now were in there must be someone who dealt in usury. Yet coming on such a person was like seeking a needle in a hayrick, especially for a pair of mutes, for I was still determined on playing the part even if it became a hindrance to our prospects.

In the town's Irish quarter where the gutters ran with whatever filth was thrown into the street from the cabins there, I settled on the roughest-looking shebeen I could find, signalling to the girl to remain outside, as only the lowest class of whore or trollop ventured into such places.

Inside, a drunk man was singing some sort of rebel song, while the room itself, scarcely bigger than somebody's kitchen, was dark like a cavern on account of the turf fire and the usual fog of tobacco smoke. Having spent a fair bit of my days in dens of a similar nature, it was like coming home, and after the first glass of porter my vow of silence left me, and easing myself into conversation with one of the customers I enquired if there happened to be such an individual as a shylock in the locality. In true Irish fashion he, in turn, enquired of the company at large, and so my query was passed from one end of the place to the other, until a frail-looking man approached, doffing his cap as though in the presence of someone higher in status than himself, for the first time in my life a reasonable suit of clothes elevating a ruffian like myself in another person's eyes.

Treating him to a glass in the manner expected, I told him I wished to pawn an article an elderly aunt had left me.

'Well, as it so happens there is a person of that class even if the priest wants to drive him out. But poor folk have need of his services even if he is a Hebrew who would drain the last drop from you as his forebears did to our own good Lord Himself.'

But having no time for such hoary old pulpit beliefs, I enquired where I might find this man, and he told me of the shop where the Jew bought rags, while in the back people put their belongings in pawn never to see them again, and so pleased was I with the information I ordered up more drink, for after being denied good Irish stout for so long it tasted like the very nectar of heaven itself.

Enjoying the taste so much, didn't I forget the person waiting without, and when I got into the street neither hide nor hair of her could be seen, and cursing myself for a fool I ran all the way back to the lodging house, expecting to find her gone and leaving me to my fate.

However, she was still inside the room with the door barred, and after I began hammering on it, fearing the noise would alarm the old woman below, she unlocked it, standing inside with a knife in her hand and looking ready to use it, so I told her it took longer to complete my business than I thought, but sure now that I had, couldn't the pair of us seek out the old Israelite at our leisure?

Coming closer, and sniffing my breath for evidence, she made a fierce lunge at me with the knife, and taking it off her, I flung her on the bed, pressing her beneath me, and it felt strange lying on the top of her like that with her looking up at me as if reading what was on my mind, and God help me, but I believe if she had fought back I may well have carried on with what I'd started until there was not a drop of breath remaining in her. But pulling up her skirts, I entered her, and after a time she responded, matching my heat with her own, and at the moment of discharge, instead of withdrawing, I spent myself in her.

Afterwards we took our repose, and it was like lying with

a dead person, me thinking I might have despatched her after all, for she made no sound, unlike most of the other women I'd had who after the act and on account of the drink taken had snored like very thunder itself.

At five o'clock by the watch hanging on the bedpost, rising from our slumbers, we dressed in our new attire and set out through the streets together, and after travelling less than a mile in the direction the alehouse man had indicated, we came across the old Solomon's rag shop, its window piled so high with his merchandise you could scarce see inside, and within it smelt of all the dead people whose clothes were destined for the shoddy factories, and holding her nose the girl looked as if she would be happier if I handled the transaction by myself. But keeping a tight hold on the watch, she made it clear she wasn't to be left outside a second time, and so we pushed our way through the aisles of stinking bales towards the back of the place.

Observing us as we approached was this old greybeard with a skullcap on his head, sitting at a desk with a pair of scales on it, and when the girl handed him the watch, without uttering a word he took it from her and springing open the case held it to his ear. Then, with a glass pressed to one eye, he studied the inner workings before scratching its metal with a tiny instrument, finally saying, 'pinchbeck', or a word sounding something like it.

'Do you wish to sell, or redeem the item?'

Undecided whether to reply or not, I looked at the girl before mouthing the word 'sell', and she nodded, and taking her to be deaf as well as dumb, the man took a piece of paper, writing something on it then reaching it across, and she passed it to me, having no knowledge of figures unlike myself on account of my past dealings with the butcher boys of Surgeon's Square.

The sum the old Jew offered was two florins, which told me the watch was more valuable than he let on, so passing the scrap of paper back to him, I shook my head, and rubbing his beard and sighing he took some silver from a leather pouch, spreading it on the table.

'That is my final offer, for the piece is below average quality.'

I knew he was lying, so I continued to shake my head, but he refused to budge, so we took our leave with his money, and the last I saw he was holding the watch to his ear, so I hurried the girl into the street before he could change his mind as a pair of florins with some left over was better than expected for something that had dropped into our lap like a ripe fruit falling from a bough.

And so a small celebration seemed to be the order of the day for myself and my doxy, for what else was I to call her? Daughter may have been all very well in front of others, but unnatural in private when astride her on the bed.

However, when I brought up my hand to my mouth in a drinking gesture, I could tell from her expression she was agreeable enough, so the pair of us adjourned to an alehouse where women were served, but apart from the men, a custom common in the place I had just left. But though this was my own country, this northern corner of it seemed much like Scotland, not only in the accents, but in the dour nature of the people themselves.

Thus with old Isaac's cash jingling in our pockets she and I proceeded to make merry in our own private snug, and each time I put my head through the hatch the woman of the house afforded me a great smile as though honoured by the presence of two such well-behaved customers even if unable to manage a word between them. But all of this miming rigmarole was already starting to feel natural to me, never having been over-fond of gabbling anyway, so I was content to let my companion have her way, for if her tongue was tied, her hands and face made up for it, as the ale, then the whiskey, took a hold on her.

Even so, after a time her antics became irksome, as beyond the hatch I could see those present laughing as if at an entertainment, and unwilling to shift she became even more boisterous in her behaviour, bubbling and grimacing, and so I fetched her a blow that closed her mouth for her, turning her to tears.

At the rear of the premises another way led out through a yard where the customers relieved themselves, and dragging her there I got her into the air, where she clung to me still mewling like an infant, except instead she was this grown woman I needed conveying through the streets without drawing attention in such a small-minded, inquisitive place.

Keeping to the back lanes where only the pigs in the gutter took note of our passing, I got her to our lodgings and up the stairs, where I barred the door, and taking off my belt prepared to chastise her. But clinging to my legs, she looked up at me with the face of someone pleading for forgiveness, and so keeping my tones low so as not to be heard beyond the four walls of the room, I vowed if she didn't mend her ways I would leave her in this foreign hole, and, full of repentance, delving into her bosom she brought out a warm handful of coins which I then transferred to my own keeping.

For the rest of that evening she was as biddable and quiet as could be, and even though the kitchen knife was safe in my coat pocket I made certain it remained there, recalling how that hell-cat of a spouse of my own had often vowed to cut off my manhood while I slept, and even if there had not been much demand for its services at the time, I still had a fond attachment to it, intending to keep it that way.

What with all the drink she'd taken, my companion soon lay down in the bed, but unable to sleep myself I sat in a chair reviewing episodes from my past like they were on a penny picture machine I had seen at the Edinburgh Fair one time through an opening no bigger than a postage stamp.

And rolling back a score of years, there I was labouring on

the Union with as rough a crowd of spalpeens as one could ever have the misfortune to work alongside, a shilling a day our wage for digging out the cold, wet Pentland clay, then wheelbarrowing it away, and on the banks of the Canal we lived in huts like Hottentots, drinking and fighting on our day of rest. But if we were given to faction fighting among ourselves, according to the counties, even townlands, we hailed from, the common foe was still those great ginger-haired, shaggy brutes, the Highlanders.

One battle, I remember, was arranged near a place by the name of Broxburn in the county of Lothian, where about a hundred of us lined up against their own men on the far side of the water, and even though it was the Sabbath the well-to-do from the city flocked to watch us tear into one another, even the ladies with their fine dresses hiked up above the clabber, along with farmers keen to see carnage, detesting us as they did for tramping through their oats and barley fields on our way to and from our day's toil.

With the drink flowing in our veins, our blood was also well and truly up, and on the higher slopes already folk were taking bets on the outcome, even the ones singing psalms and hymns earlier, and though I was young and ignorant I thought, instead of trying to maim one another, we might have turned our spades and billhooks on those looking down on us, as hearing them squeal, scampering for their lives, would have been surely something to savour.

But their hopes of witnessing a bloody massacre from a safe distance that summer's day came to naught, as an alarm had gone up in the town, and the militia arrived to place the leaders of our faction under arrest.

Looking back on it, Burke might well have been there himself that day, for even if barely five and a half feet in stature, and light in the frame, with enough whiskey in him he would take on any mortal being. Many's the time when wrestling and I had him in a Chinaman's grip he would never give in, so I let him think he had the beating of me and he would prance about crowing he was descended from the mighty Finn McCool himself.

And so then I was remembering how it was we first met up, not in the muddy swamps of the Canal, but some few years later in the city itself.

At the time the pair of us were married, he to Nellie MacDougal, and me to Logue's widow, for I had risen from being her lodger in Tanner's Close to sharing her bed, although amour, as it's known, had little to do with it, having been singled out to keep the other tenants in order when her husband died.

But the life suited me well enough, despite having to put up with her tongue and the weight of her fist, for the same blade, may she dance a hornpipe in hell, could out-box, out-drink, out-curse the majority of men.

The first time I saw her she was running up a plank with a barrow-load of stones, the arms and bare legs of her a match for any one of the Kerrymen themselves, being the very divils for work. But then it was hard to see any great difference between the men and the women in the camps, as, foul-tongued, unwashed, or ready for a drink, fight, or an argument, they marched alongside us with no quarter given or received.

After the Canal was finished our services were no longer required, and we were on the move again, picking up work wherever we could. Myself, I hawked fish about the streets for a time with an ass and cart I stabled in the cellar in Tanner's Close, and according to his own history Willie took to the cobbling, being as neat and nimble with his fingers as he was on his feet, for he liked to dance as well as sing when the drink and the notion took him. He also loved to talk about his time in the militia and his adventures there, though I reckon he might have been handier with a fife than a musket, when not employing that other flute inside his breeches.

'Begod, don't all the fine ladies dote on a man in a uniform, and sure didn't I cut the grand figure in my corporal's green and gold facings and army shako on my head.'

And listening to him blow air in this fashion, I gained an inkling into the person who was soon to be my partner in the cadaver procurement business.

But then all that was to come later through chance when the old pensioner Donald died under our roof of the dropsy while still owing us rent, which by another stroke of luck I recouped for near enough the amount outstanding, and thus a small profit was turned for myself, with a bigger one for my partner, splitting the proceeds, as we continued to do in most of our other dealings with our buyers in Surgeon's Square.

Sitting there in that darkened room, a long way from where the events took place, I fell to wondering how the person in the bed across from me would take it if she were to uncover that history for herself. But then who would be the one to tell her? Supposing I did, however, would she turn a hair or not? I thought not, somehow, and so once more made certain I had possession of the knife, for if murder would be no great bother to her, she might as easily turn a hand to it herself if I crossed her.

Leaning close, I studied the rise and fall of her bosom, listening to her soft breathing, the face on her the very picture of childish innocence. Yet I still couldn't banish my doubts, and for a long time I sat on in the chair unable to give in to sleep.

It must have overtaken me at some point, for when I awoke the pair of us were in the bed together, and the dream I had been having was still with me.

More of a nightmare, it had left me sweating and shaking, for it concerned the poor half-witted lad Willie and I had despatched between us and transported in a tea box. But in the dream he kept knocking from the inside, calling for his mother, just as he'd done when we were plying him with whiskey, and so people in the street were looking at us, then at the chest, and the further we ran with it on our backs the louder came the knocking and the pitiful cries from within, and so then we were at the porter's lodge, where we delivered up the bodies. But one of the young students there refused to take it, saying, 'What have you brought us this time? Is it a dog, or a cat, you're trying to fob off on us?' and sure enough didn't there come a scratching on the wood like that of claws, and Burke told him we'd run out of bodies and had to make do with whatever was available, even if it had four legs and a tail.

'Sure, the Doctor won't know the difference if you skin it first. Tell him it's a babby,' for there was always some infant or other crawling about the house nobody would miss anyway.

But there was no changing of the young man's mind on the matter, so we had to carry the thing, whatever it was, back to Tanner's Close, and when we got there, handing me a chisel, 'Open it up,' says Burke, and so I started in on it, and the lid started coming up, and the instant it did, I let this tremendous cry out of me and woke up, trembling like a leaf, running with cold sweat, and my yell of fright must have stirred and wakened the one lying next to me, for next minute I felt her reaching under the bedclothes for my thing, trying to coax it into life, and when she persisted with her handling of my prick, and it as limp as an old stalk of rhubarb, finally taking it in her mouth, sickened by such a filthy French whore's trick, I leapt up, wondering where she had learned such a thing, certainly not from observing the livestock in the yard at Troutbeck Farm.

Rebuffed, she began blubbering, burying her head beneath the bedclothes. But an urgent need for the hair of the dog coming over me, I proceeded to shake her out of her humour, and some little time later that same day we took to the streets again.

Alas, as things turned out, after a week of carousing for the pair of us, my companion having now acquired a taste for the drink about as fierce as my own, nearly all our money had run out, and unable to pay the bill for our board, we did a midnight flit, and sorry as I was at playing such a low trick on the old woman stuck fast in her chair, for she had treated us fairly, it was time to move on and either seek employment or starve.

With just about enough left to sustain us for another wee while, our days were spent tramping in the open, and our nights under the stars, and a great melancholy took hold of me, for in the place I grew up in there had been folk like ourselves travelling the roads, and if you asked them where they were bound, none could give an answer save a wave of the hand beyond the next hill, and the one after that, and it seemed to me a terrible sort of a life entirely, roving on and on until you dropped down dead in a ditch, for I recall such sights, men like living skeletons, discharged from the war, still in their uniforms, quartering the country with barely a sole to their boots, and unable to bear the silence between us a minute longer, trudging along, didn't I begin talking, her listening as if storing it up inside for later, and hearing my own voice out there in the wilds like that was more than strange, even if there were plenty others the same holding conversations with themselves to keep the black dog at bay.

I started telling of my younger days in places like the ones we were now passing through, and the tricks my companions and I would get up to roaming the woods and fields in the dead of night in search of divilment and folk to annoy, and later terrorise, for I joined the Whiteboys, so named on account of the bedsheets we put on, burning and destroying the landlords' property, as well as maiming their animals, for it was a war against high rents and rank prejudice, no quarter given or received, for if the Volunteers hunted you down it was the lash followed by the gallows in short order.

One time, I recall, we took captive one of Lord Dufferin's prized Friesian bulls, putting it on trial like we were judge, jury and executioner, finding it guilty, then butchering it with all due ceremony, and after hearing the story my listener betrayed not a hint of surprise.

Spurred on, I was on the brink of confessing what Willie and I had turned our hand to, but the words curdled in my mouth, for after giving evidence in court I vowed never to disclose that side of my history to another living soul, and so all of it went back inside to fester and provoke bad dreams like the one I'd had with her in the bed that time, making me wonder if more were to follow as in Willie's case, him crying out in his sleep from the horror of them.

More pressing, however, was the emptiness of our bellies, and coming upon a trim and tidy farmhouse, for we were in a rich part of South Antrim, I instructed Hannah to approach the place and ask for food. But returning with a face black as thunder, she made it clear they had chased her off, so that day we dined on turnips and potatoes dug from a pit in the nearest field.

Still, thieving on this modest scale would scarce keep the hunger pangs away, so I decided to beg for work myself at the next farm we came to, although I doubted if any such contract would include the services of my prick in such a God-fearing community.

Arriving at the door, I was confronted by a large, red-faced man with a dish in his hand as if in the middle of his dinner, but before I could open my mouth he yelled for me to be gone as he wanted no 'Fenian trespassers' on his land, while at the back of the door a gun was primed and ready for such riff-raff, and looking as if he meant it, too, so I took my leave without further ado.

Yet what exercised me more than the likelihood of getting a backside peppered with pellets was how he could tell my religion, politics, as well, even though I had adhered to neither since roaming the countryside in night attire, simply by looking me in the face, people being the same here as always they had been, and now I was plunged back into it all over again as if I had never been a day away.

Seeing an old man cutting reeds in a nearby meadow, I enquired if he knew of anyone looking for a labourer in the locality, and for an instant we eyed one another, weighing up each other's pedigree and allegiances, as getting them wrong, as I knew to my cost, could land one in bother.

Resting on his scythe, finally he said, 'Sure, amn't I fortunate in getting half a day's work myself. But you could try the hiring fair, as it's that time of year again, except they have a preference for the young and lusty that can work and slave all the hours between dawn and dusk.'

Seeing as I could give him near a score or more years himself, I took it ill. But being in no position to show my displeasure, I asked him where the fair was held.

'The town of Ballyclare, about twenty miles hence, the people there as tight-pursed and miserly a crowd as ever you'd chance to meet, the farmers around about near as bad, so I wish you good luck in your endeavours. By your tongue, you're not from these parts, I take it? Travelled a fair wee distance, have you?'

'Far enough,' I told him.

'By your present attire, you don't look like someone accustomed to labouring the land.'

I could tell he'd be content to keep the pot boiling in this manner for as long as I let him, but wearying of his enquiries, I bade him farewell, and he stood watching until I disappeared from view, and when I returned to the girl sitting on a bank by the side of the road I had no need to utter a word, my face telling the full story.

After a good day's walking we reached the town the man had told me about, its noise and hubbub greeting us before we even set foot in the place, the streets thronged with buyers and sellers of horses, calves, pigs, poultry, with other wares as well set out on stalls in the market square ankle-deep already in straw and dung. Yet, despite the clabber, stepping high in their buttoned boots and Sunday best, the women there were flitting hither and thither like mayflies atop a flowery carpet.

Present, also, were hurdy-gurdy men, trick o' the loop merchants, a foreign person with a monkey on a chain, Gypsy women telling fortunes, others selling taffy, liquorice and similar sweetmeats, making one near faint with the smell, while every public house had its doors flung open, waves of whiskey fumes and tobacco smoke pouring forth.

Making our way through the crowds, the girl and I pushed forward, until by the market-house steps a line of mainly young people caught my eye, each holding a meagre bundle of possessions sufficient for a twelve-month, a spit in the palm and a handful of coin sealing the contract, and so bringing Hannah along with me, I fell in at the tail end of the group myself.

As our future employers seemed in no great a hurry to make their choice, most still drinking in the public houses nearby, we stood a long time waiting for them to appear. But then they did, sauntering up and down, feeling a forearm here, squeezing a calf there, even peering into some of our mouths as though judging one of their own beasts, and it was hard to bear their patting and pummelling. Yet the girl endured it better than most, for some of the farmers seemed to take pleasure in fondling the women, one brute in particular lingering, then returning again and again, until I felt close to putting him to the test himself, but in far rougher fashion.

As the line thinned out, and those chosen went off with their new masters, it seemed my own chances of getting hired were as dust. But the man who had hung fire over Hannah came back, and, lifting up her chin, asked what they called her. Unable to answer, she hung her head, so he said, 'Where are you from? Do you not have the English?' thinking she might be an Irish speaker.

About my own age, he was, but heavier, especially around

the girth, someone not given to stinting himself in the way of provisions, liquor, neither, for I could smell it on his breath. Finally, spitting on his palm, he took hold of her by the wrist and, pressing some money in her hand, announced, 'The deal's done,' and before I could intervene, even if I wanted to, he started dragging her towards a cart close by with a horse yoked in the shafts, and all the while she made no protest, so then it came to me maybe she was content to go with the man, preferring the taste of proper victuals to what the pair of us had been foraging for in the open these past number of days.

Manhandling her up and into the bed of the cart, the farmer climbed in himself. But, standing up, she flung his money in his face before leaping down and running back to where I stood, whereupon there arose this great cry of derision from all those watching. So then the farmer, he, too, jumped down, yelling, 'Come back, you foreign bitch, we made a contract, you and me!'

Clasping me close and gesturing with all the silent means in her power, she signalled that she and I were not to be parted, and coming up to the pair of us, he started shouting, 'Take him, too, is it? I might as well hire a cripple. Two tongue-tied foreigners instead of one.'

And even though I favoured the notion of sheltering under another nationality, I kept my gaze lowered to the ground.

'You're not in your own country now. Here, when a handshake and money's exchanged, a deal stands and can't be broken, so you'll work out your time with me until the year's out,' and taking hold of her by the hair of her head, he looked set to have his way by brute force.

But still she held on to me, and the crowd started to titter, then laugh at the farmer doing his utmost to pull her away, and tempted as I was to let her go, for surely it was better for one of us to find employment, the man's manners deserved a rebuke and, temper getting the better of me, I dealt him a blow with my fist, sending him reeling backwards.

Although he had the advantage in both strength and weight, he was slow and cumbersome, and lowering his head he came at me like a bull at a gate, but, sidestepping, I got in another and better dig before he came charging a second time, but slipping in the dung he provoked another great cheer, enraging him even further.

Still, how long I could keep him at bay was a worry, as I was not as fit as I once was due to the lack of proper nourishment and all the walking to get here, but before I could gather my remaining strength didn't the girl grab up a handful of mud and clabber, hurling it at my attacker, blinding him, and so tripping him up with a trick I had often employed against Willie back in our wrestling days, he fell again, rolling in the mire, clawing at his eyes, and seeing him in that state the girl and I looked about for a safe passage through the crowd, fearing some of the man's friends might yet thwart us.

Yet our luck continued to hold, as it seemed we had vanquished a bully nobody much cared for, and a path was cleared for us, with more cheers, even back-slapping, sending us on our way.

Certainly it was a sweet moment, made even sweeter when my companion opened her fist, disclosing a guinea, of all things, which she had somehow held on to after throwing the bulk of the farmer's other money back in his face, and so pleased was I by her cleverness didn't I kiss her full on the lips, leaving her nearly as surprised as myself, being unused to such displays of affection, either given or received.

In an eating-house, sufficiently removed from the market square, we ordered up a fine feed of bacon and cabbage, currant bread and black tea, gorging ourselves until our bellies were tight as two drums, and lying back at my ease I sucked on a clay pipe the woman of the establishment filled for me, and all the while Hannah wore a smile on her face as if revelling in her recent victory. So then I began thinking maybe I had been hasty in my judgement after all, and should trust her more, something which had not been a habit of mine with other women in the past. But now the present was upon us, and here we were like two turtle doves, for, reaching across, she placed a titbit in my mouth, then another, until I made her stop, having no wish to draw more attention to ourselves than we had already done that day.

When the reckoning came, money was left over, maybe a month's wages, going by the farmer's calculations, which I reckoned was compensation for his unmannerly behaviour. Yet because of the business with the same gentleman any chance of finding farm work hereabouts seemed more remote than ever, so I decided it was time to move on to a different neighbourhood before our funds ran out like water through a sieve.

Carrying our bundles, the girl and I made our way along a side street as deserted as any thoroughfare should be in the middle of the day, for it appeared everyone had left their houses to attend the Fair, and it was like walking through a graveyard, nary a sound to break the silence save a low, distant hum where the townsfolk were enjoying themselves, and so the temptation to turn it to our advantage entered my head, before telling myself any pickings from such a poor collection of dwellings would be limited to sundry sticks of furniture and cheap pictures of a religious nature, none of which we could carry off with us anyway.

So then the notion crossed my mind we should have robbed the old Jew when we had the chance, returning to his shop at dead of night, getting clear before he was found with a rag in his mouth. But what if he were not? What if he were choked by a scrap of his own merchandise? Getting off scot-free for the same crime a second time was about as unlikely as being offered a day's work in this place.

However, as events transpired, all sense was turned on its head in a manner of speaking, for on our route away from the town and into the green of the countryside a most curious sight met our eyes, causing us to slow our pace, for we were both keen to put the locality and its inhabitants behind us as swift as our feet could carry us.

Appearing over a high hedge, there rose the ridge of a great tent with flags fluttering from its pointed end poles. Cooking fires sent smoke into the air, and voices could be heard, women and children, mostly. But then a man began shouting in what sounded like a foreign tongue, answered by another in the same Gypsy lingo. Yet even though I had seen tinker people camping by the side of the road before, never under canvas like this, the tremendous bellying breadth of it the colour of sailcloth, bright triangular pennants fluttering from each corner.

The girl appeared near as surprised as myself, but with more of a childlike amazement, as though coming upon something dropped from the heavens as in a storybook, the strange voices making it even more of a wonder, and so, curious to discover what manner of encampment this could be, we came close to the hedge to peer through a gap, drawing back when a face thrust itself forward, grinning and girning, seemingly that of a child, but the features far too old, too wizened for that, the girl uttering a cry of alarm, at which the creature, in a high-pitched voice, told her, 'Don't be frightened, little lady, I'm as much a man as your tall friend there, and if you care to come closer I'd be more than happy to prove it to you. Come inside and meet the rest of my merry companions.'

He must have been standing on a box, or something similar, to meet our gaze as he did, for now I realised he was a midget, and part of a travelling show along with other oddities, having been to the like in Edinburgh during my time there.

In spite of her earlier fear the girl seemed willing to take up the dwarf's invitation, having, I reckoned, never seen such a person, even a show before, so both were a great cause of wonder to her.

However, anxious to press on, I commanded her, 'Come,

we mustn't delay. There's nothing for us here.'

Stubborn as always, instead she went on ahead of me to an opening in the hedge wide enough to let a cart pass through, intent on viewing what lay beyond, and so nothing for it I followed her, coming on her gazing at the sight before her, for, there on the grass in front of the tent, a troupe of tiny people no higher than my belt buckle were somersaulting and leapfrogging with great skill while an older dwarf in a cut-down military coat but normal-sized helmet, for his head was the same size as my own, was putting them through their paces, shouting instructions in a deep voice more fitting for a human twice his size.

It was hard to take one's eyes away from such a spectacle, but there were other sights as well, a scattering of brightly painted wagons of the Romany variety, plus a score of smaller tents pitched about the field with some older women attending to the cooking fires we had smelt outside. Children, too, along with a few hungry-looking mongrels and creatures in cages.

But just then the acrobatics came to a finish, and one of the midgets, whose ancient face I recognised from looking at us through the hedge, came skipping towards us, and stretching up on his tiptoes he took hold of the girl's hand in his.

'Welcome to our little band of players, pretty lady. Permit me to show you where we perform. Nightly at seven. See?' pointing to a banner above the entrance to the tent, words painted on it in red and gold. But having no mastery of the reading, or writing, for that matter, they were foreign to me, and even if the girl had some learning herself, it was still beyond her powers to translate, even if she wished.

As dainty as some little lordling, across the grass the dwarf led her, the pair of them entering the tent together, and though it was no concern of mine what she did, I followed, having heard stories of these manikins and their hot appetites, for if the rest of them was in miniature, their private parts, so I had been told, were not.

Standing in the mouth of the tent I looked inside where there was a sawdust ring of the circus sort with penny seats all about made ready for the night's entertainment, while balancing on its rim our little midget friend was putting on a show of his own for the girl, performing a trio of somersaults like those he had been practising outside. Then, on his hands, legs high in the air, he scampered around the circle, and Hannah clapped her hands in childish glee, and never having seen her like this before, and after all the bother I had endured on her behalf, here she was blossoming for this upside-down Tom Thumb of a creature she had only just met, and carrying on in the same fashion the midget continued, becoming more energetic with each new trick and variation.

To be truthful, for myself, I had never seen the like before, and might once have paid good money to see such a thing. But the girl's clapping must have carried beyond the canvas walls, for through a flap at the back suddenly a face appeared, angry and threatening.

'How many times have I told you, Tito, no punters until the doors are opened.'

Tall, broad of build, the man had a full reddish beard, and wore a military frock coat with a row of medals across the front. He also carried a whip in his hand, and eyeing it, Tito, as he was called, dropped from his perch, and kneeling in front of the other's boots, begged, 'Forgive me, master, they strayed in before I could stop them. They're only country folk. You know how simple they can be.'

'Unlike yourself, you mean? Back to your wagon, and don't be drunk like last night or your arse will smart from a touch of braided leather,' and a chastened Tito ran from the place, disappearing beneath the skirt of the tent, leaving Hannah gazing after him.

'Well, you heard what I said, young lady. No public entrance until curtain-time and the playing of the overture.'

But as though tethered to the spot, she stood there, and

angry at the man's rudeness I came forward, and taking her by the arm made to lead her away.

'So, there's two of you?'

Then, peering closely at me, he said, 'Here, hold on, aren't you that pugilistic fellow from the Fair? Damn it, sir, I like a man who defends a lady's honour. May I ask your name?'

But I had no intention of replying, and shaking my head, and pointing to my lips, I backed away with the girl alongside.

'Can't speak as well, eh? The pair of you, is it?'

Then, 'Tell me, are you still looking for employment?' and so I turned to face him.

'I can't give you a wage, just your bed and board. But it will be better than tramping the roads in the wind and the rain.'

Our work, as he explained it, would be to sweep the tent before and after each performance, as well as helping with the general upkeep of the company, and at first we were to sleep in the great marquee itself, and it was strange waking up to the smell of canvas and sawdust and the leavings of the people who had filled the seats the night before.

The company was a modest enough one, comprising the dwarfs and their dancing and leaping act, and a collection of human oddities, Polly O'Grady, the Fat Irish Child, John Chambers, the Armless Carpenter, Eliza Jenkins, the Human Skeleton, the Yorkshire Giant, Leonine, the Lion-Faced Lady, Hairy Mary from Borneo, who was really a monkey.

In the midst of all these human wonders, the girl and I stood out, yet kept to ourselves. However, strange to relate, several of Tito's friends were themselves devoid of speech, and having their own sign language they would try to converse with us, and one tiny creature in particular, Anita, the Living Doll, took a great fancy to Hannah, and one day I caught the pair of them waving their hands and girning away as though deep in girlish discourse, and it was a worry seeing them sharing secrets, as I saw it, for I was still wary of our past history being broadcast even if it was to a dummy barely the height of my navel.

If the day was fine we all would eat together on the grass, although the Colonel, as he was known, dined in his own caravan with his wife, Madame Juno, who had been a high-wire balancer, and although I never once set eyes on her while I was there, I understood she was a rare beauty with raven-black hair to her waist. All of which I learned listening to the chatter around me as I went about my duties, refreshing and raking the sawdust in the ring and tending to the seats and tent generally.

Meanwhile, Hannah, who could wash clothes, patch and sew with the best, was also picking up gossip from her little friend, and going by certain nods and gestures it seemed I had made an enemy, and that was Tito, having set his sights on Hannah. But despite all his efforts in that direction she spurned him, and so he blamed me for spoiling his chances, having the vanity and conceit of a dozen normal-sized men.

That first night, curious to see the full performance for myself, I crouched down near the back of the tent, fearing that the farmer I had upended might be one of those present, ready to be dazzled by 'The World's Greatest Collection of Human Marvels and Oddities!', while the music played, for there was a band of midgets in toy soldiers' uniforms with children's instruments. As fine a military band as ever I heard, they kept the audience entertained while Tito and his brothers and sisters vaulted and danced and spun at the end of ropes, followed by the rest of the 'human marvels' and their acts.

Two more nights we spent in the field, and to my great relief I saw no sign of the farmer among the evening crowd of townsfolk. Then, again, he might have been one of those with no time for such devil's amusements, being too tight-fisted to spend money on the like. And so the more I pondered on it, the luckier I considered Hannah was to have escaped his filthy paws, knowing how such brutes treated their maidservants, bedding them as part of their contract, there being little difference between themselves and their Scottish kind, and all my life I hated their sort, taking great satisfaction in burning their stacks and crippling their livestock when I ran with the Whiteboys.

But all of that was behind me and I could barely remember the half of it in this new life the girl and I had fallen into by chance as well as good fortune. The food was nourishing and plentiful, the work far from back-breaking, and all the while the pair of us were treated with consideration, save for Tito with his evil little roaming eye, and so I made certain we kept out of his path as much as possible.

To our face he nicknamed us the Two Bumpkins, as though we were some kind of a double act ourselves, and even though the word was foreign to me, clearly it was an insult, and so I determined to bring him low when the time was ripe, for a taste for revenge still smouldered even if its fire had been banked down for preservation's sake.

But his taunting continued, and it was hard to absent ourselves from his company at mealtimes. Casting an eye around the table and raising his glass, as he always liked to drink wine at such times, he crowed, 'A toast, brothers and sisters, to all gathered here, even if we do have the misfortune of playing to a crowd of Irish bogtrotters each night. Am I not correct, my tongue-tied bumpkin friends?'

Signalling neither yea nor nay, I kept on eating, but from what he'd said, I felt sure he had guessed my nationality, that little bloodshot eye of his piercing part of my armour. Yet playing dumb seemed still the best option, even if he had suspicions about that as well.

However, as events turned out I wasn't as clever as I should have been at staying in character, which was proved one night when it was late and the girl and I were in the tent and we were weary after having swept the ring and cleaned beneath the benches, for the people who sat there threw down all manner of filth and rubbish.

Our beds, or what served as such, a heap of old patched stage curtains, were apart a dozen feet or so, but after a while, feeling amorous and starved of affection, didn't Hannah come creeping across to get under the covers with me.

Taking hold of her, but not in any cuddlesome fashion, I ordered her back to her own couch in case someone might discover us, but she persisted, for the heat was on her, not having had the benefit of servicing since we landed up here, whereas my own desire had near shrivelled away like Mr Maggot himself. Yet still she kept blowing in my lughole, while seeking me out beneath the bedding, and so rising up from my nest I stood over her in my pelt, which only seemed to inflame her the more.

'Do you want us to get found out and so ruin everything? Go back to eating turnips in the raw? You and me must be as silent as the grass grows. These canvas walls are thin as paper.'

And as I whispered the words, a loud laugh was heard outside and someone fell against the side of the tent, the girl rushing back to her own bed, while I dropped into my own, the pair of us feigning sleep.

After a time came another burst of merriment, for it was Tito, no one else, prowling about outside, and the worse for wear by the sound of it.

Hoping he would tire of his antics, leaving us in peace, I lay listening for his retreat. But he continued stumbling about, until finally his head appeared under the tent flap, and one eye open I watched him swaying there, still in his boy-soldier's scarlet tunic and striped breeches.

'My, my, my, what have we here? A couple of sleeping beauties pure as the lilies of the field. More like rank stinkweed, I'd say.'

Stumbling over to the girl, he stared down at her lying there with eyes shut.

'Little Miss Muppet, hand on her ha'penny, eh?'

Bending low, he whispered, 'Still play-acting like your fancy man over there? Not up for it, was he? Never fear, Tito's here.'

And drawing back the covers, didn't the dirty little tyke try to climb in alongside her.

Unable to keep up the pretence, drawing clear a bare arm, she dealt him a blow with her fist, sending him back on his haunches. But changing his tune, he threw himself on top of her, trying to throttle her with those tiny hands of his, yet with all the strength of someone thrice his size on account of his acrobatic skills in the ring.

Reluctant as I was to come to her aid, the same lady more than capable of holding her corner herself, I could hear her choke for lack of breath, so rising up and wrestling him off her I flung him backward on to the ground.

Startled as he was, he rallied quickly, capering on his toes like some fairy-weight prizefighter, and if it had been some other occasion I might have been amused by the sight of this human flea challenging me to fisticuffs. But, darting forward, he delivered a jab to my privates, and recovering from the low blow, advancing and belabouring him right and left, I sent him scurrying around the ring moaning and crying, fully intent on his despatch.

But his guile saved him, and he seized the end of a rope still hanging from the night's performance, and speeling up to the roof of the tent, he hung there.

'Come, take a hold and haul yourself up, Mr Irishman. Or maybe your young bed-partner would care to try. I bet it's not the first length of tackle she's handled in her time.'

And didn't the filthy dog unbutton himself, directing his flow on us below, as sure of his grip as Hairy Mary the chimpanzee, and knowing it full well, continued crowing.

'On the run, are we? Never mind, half this lot 'ere have left a rotten smell behind 'em, even the Colonel himself.

Even so, he won't take lightly to bein' deceived. Most likely he'll get the hump when I tell 'im about your dirty little double game.'

Content as a canary on its perch, he was enjoying himself, his tone growing more cockneyfied by the minute, all those dandy airs of his as much a pretence as our own.

'Still, being a reasonable sort of a bloke, I might just keep my trap shut if her Ladyship cared to take her chances with a proper man instead of one with a worm between his legs,' holding out a crooked little finger as he said it.

In vain I cast about for something to bring him down, but after my careful sweeping of the tent there lingered not a bottle, not a cup, not even a child's plaything, and despite my pledge to myself to hold my tongue, I called up, 'If it takes till first light I'll wait for you to come down, and then see if I don't settle your hash for good!'

But, laughing, he cried, 'Hark, he speaks! A miracle, no less!'

Then, 'Roll up, roll up, and behold Tito the Great, Tito the Magnificent, lord and master of his aerial universe! See how he floats, soars like a bird!' and arms outspread, he did appear in truth to hover above our heads.

However, running forward, the girl took hold of the rope, and with all her strength began hauling on it back and forth, and laughing at her efforts to dislodge him, he called down, 'Bell-ringer or no, you'll never shift this human clapper!'

But being drunk, as well as overly confident, following yet another tug on his life-line, losing his grip, he tumbled to the ground, falling like a stone on to the rim of the ring, the crack of his skull striking the wood drawing the breath from us.

Sinking to her knees, the girl began to moan in that strange keening way of hers, and no sound or movement coming from her victim, I went to where he lay, praying he was a goner, for our fate surely was sealed if he recovered to tell the tale. But his body was bent and broken, while his head oozed blood, and not needing to touch him it was clear he would trouble us no more.

Lamenting still, the girl was carrying on as before, and fearing she might be heard, I took hold of her to shake some sense into her.

'Forget him, the world's well shot of him. But if we leave him where he is you and I will get the blame.'

But she only stared at me as if now deaf as well as dumb.

'Do you not understand? We must carry him off and place him somewhere else so they'll find him there.'

Hoisting him up, he felt as light as a child, and when I got to the opening of the tent I laid him on the grass before peering outside. The night was dark and silent, and with the girl watching I carried the body across to his home on wheels, a richly painted wagon with Rosie his mare tethered at the rear, the intention being to lay her master at the foot of its steps as though he had fallen and split his crown trying to climb inside, for I had often heard him attempt the same with many starts and stops because of the drink in him, singing, also, for he had a fine voice, drunk or sober. But I felt not a jot of pity, for he had been a thorn in our flesh, and now it had been plucked clear and we were free of his biting tongue and spiteful ways for ever.

By the time I got my burden to its destination, I was sweating, not on account of the weight, but from fear of being discovered with a corpse on my back, as in those earlier times. But then a dog began to bark, and another took up the call, and crouching low, instead of dropping the body where intended, I went around to the back of the wagon in case the dogs got a sight of me.

Tito's old horse was there in the dark, his head in a nosebag of hay, the last it would ever receive from its master's hands, and scenting my load, it shied and snorted, horses being alarmed by a dead body, like the one I had in Tanner's Close that balked at carrying the old Donegal woman that time. But then didn't it occur to me, why not leave the body here so the horse would be blamed for stoving in its master's skull, for everyone knew of his ill-treatment of the animal.

The rest of that night little sleep came our way, the girl and I lying in our separate beds waiting for the first cry of discovery, and when it arrived we pretended to slumber on, until in great distress Anita the Living Doll came into the tent.

'Oh, my dears, my dears, I hardly know how to tell you, but a most dreadful occurrence has taken place. Poor Tito is no more. He must have fallen under his horse, and it has kicked him to kingdom come. Oh, the blood, the blood!'

And hearing that word 'blood' was a blow, for I had forgotten to sweep up where our enemy had fallen and the sawdust was still dyed with his gore, and so after Anita had gone I quickly remedied the situation until nothing remained to show where Tito the Magnificent had flown for the last time.

After a deal of lamentation from the rest of the company, but not for long, for he had never been popular, the show continued without him, and the townsfolk came as usual, the passing of a midget less than nothing to them. As for myself, I felt no remorse for the death of such a treacherous little swine, and once or twice caught myself wondering how much such an interesting specimen might have fetched in Edinburgh if only I had been able to transport him in a barrel marked Fine Salted Herring.

Still, I kept a close eye on the one who had hastened his end, but she seemed to have recovered well enough from the business, and so the pair of us carried on for our three good meals a day, as well as a canvas roof over our heads.

One day when washing down the Colonel's caravan, I heard him remark to the Yorkshire Giant, 'I reckon, George, we have milked this particular Irish udder as long as we're able. The takings are getting poorer with each performance, so it's time to move on to another pitch and fresh pastures. Bonny Scotland looks ripe for another tour, so we'll start off in the Borders, then Glasgow, then Edinburgh.'

And just as earlier the word 'blood' had given me cause for alarm, 'Scotland' and 'Edinburgh' were doubly concerning, and so that evening lying in my bed, the smell of canvas all around, I determined we must move on, too, but not back across the water where enemies with long memories still were waiting.

Belfast ✖ *24 May*

HAVING HAD NO RECENT correspondence with Lord B. these past weeks I have taken to keeping a journal, for no other eyes save my own, putting pen to paper each evening and setting down a record of yet another fruitless day trawling this city's drinking establishments, of which there are many, in the hope of getting a whiff of our quarry, for it has been my feeling he might land up in this city where work is so plentiful for someone like himself, for never have I heard such a din, and witnessed such a bustle of industry as goes on here, the great brick chimneys of the factories where linen is manufactured belching out smoke and steam, hanging in a perpetual pall over the streets and poor dwellings of the workers clustered at their foot.

I doubt if there exists another part of this island kingdom of ours that can aspire to the progress made here since it first sprang from a mere cluster of huts at the mouth of what was little more than a muddy fording place. And the folk who have made their fortunes on the back of this transformation seem mighty pleased with their own elevation, proudly proclaiming their city to be a veritable Athens of the North, although I have not seen much sign of refinement in the arts, or pursuits of a similar nature, mingling with those not so different from certain individuals I once spent my days and nights with in the stews of Whitechapel and Smithfield. There, at least, I could understand what they were saying most of the time, unlike here, where the accent is even more rapid and brutal on the ear than in Edinburgh.

As for their general temperament, the people are more forthcoming than their Scottish cousins, as on that side of the water Mr Slack and I were able to watch and listen without being pressed to participate in the evening's entertainment, whereas the custom here is for all present to contribute, usually with a song as more and more drink is consumed, black porter for the most part, along with tumblers of whiskey and water.

One can quickly gauge the political and religious complexion of those present by the choice of such ballads, and in one of our haunts close to the city's heart by his quick thinking Mr Slack saved the day, possibly our skins as well, when I myself got called upon to regale the company with a stave or two.

The person making the request, a surly-looking, red-headed fellow, had been sending bleary-eyed looks our way for some considerable time, so much so I thought it might be advisable to take our leave. But then his invitation arrived, not in the customary polite usage of that word, but bawled in a hoarse, carrying voice across the room.

'You in the corner with your big man there, make a name for yourself and give us a song! Or are youse far too high and mighty for the company?'

After he'd spoken, a hush descended, all eyes settling on us where we sat with our backs to the wall, a worrying moment for the pair of us, already aware of the excitable and violent temper of the times, rioting in the streets as rival factions clashed, breaking each other's heads, in addition to their windows. Having a close and personal regard for my own cranium, I was not about to run the risk of an assault upon it here. Yet there might be no way of avoiding it given the volatile nature of those present.

Racking my brain for a ditty, not a solitary line could I muster, none at least that would satisfy my listeners, for going by the flavour of the songs rendered so far only the most bloodthirsty of Orange ballads would satisfy such a gathering.

'Well, are you true blue or not? Or is it another colour you favour?' a murmur running through the room as if our fiery-headed friend had indeed detected a whiff of popery about our persons.

At my side I could sense Mr Slack steeling himself. Yet this present pickle was far more perilous than the time in Edinburgh when he had forced a retreat into the street, so thwarting young Mr Fergusson's assailants. But these Northern Irish patriots, blood inflamed by drink and various toasts to 'King William, of pious and immortal memory', accompanied by vows of hellfire and damnation on his enemies past and present, were another matter, ready at the first sign of what they took to be perfidy to rend us limb from limb.

Nor could I talk my way out of it, for my accent would further inflame a suspicion they had an English papist spy in their midst, even if I had been baptised in a church similar to their own. Ruing the day I had ever even come to this barbarous country on a doomed mission, never had I felt so much under present threat.

But to my tremendous relief, as well as astonishment, didn't my companion himself rise up and break into song, bringing his listeners to a universal pitch of open-mouthed awe and wonder at his choice of offering, the words ringing out clear and true in a fine, full-blooded baritone.

All people that on earth do dwell,
Sing to the Lord with tuneful voice,
Him serve with mirth, his praise forth tell,
Come ye before Him, and rejoice!

Halfway through the second verse, yet another seeming miracle, some of those present started roaring back the words, so that anyone passing at the time might have assumed they were by a church or gospel hall and not a public house, and not the most reputable one of its kind either.

After he sat down Mr Slack received an almighty cheer, accompanied by cries of 'No surrender!' and 'To hell with the Pope!' as well as similar expressions of an ardent Loyalist nature, and soon glasses of porter and whiskey were filling the table in front of us. But not being an imbiber, Mr Slack lifted none to his lips, so I was forced into doing the honours instead, as it would have been a grave insult to refuse such hospitality, the upshot being that by midnight I was well on the way to being more stocious than I had ever been, not even at my leaving celebrations in Bow Street ten years earlier. Yet despite my incapable state I was still aware it would be grossly disrespectful, if not dangerous, to leave after so much generosity coming our way.

To my great shame, though the occasion and the company were more the culprit than myself, I have little recollection of returning to our lodgings in Waring Street in the small hours, and waking in the morning with a head like a pounding Orange drum, at breakfast, being the person of discretion that he is, Mr Slack forbore from reminding me.

For once he was in a communicative mood, informing me he had managed to make some enquiries of his own regarding our venture. From what he had gleaned from the landlord of the Morning Star, as it was called, we were in the wrong public house and wrong part of town if looking for someone seeking a labouring job. According to the man, the city was flooded with Catholics pouring in from the western parts of the province in search of such work. His own customers, he said, were of a higher standing, decent tradesmen, a cut above your country 'teague', as he described them, with nothing but a spade and a strong back to recommend them.

Congregating in their own rough neighbourhoods, they boarded six, even more to a room, as no decent landlady would accommodate them on account of their religion and filthy habits, a reason why we should never entertain the notion of entering any area with a chapel close by.

Even though my brain was not functioning as clearly as it should, I still managed to congratulate Mr Slack on his good work, despite feeling a mite peeved he had somehow stolen some of my thunder, leading me to consider that perhaps the servant was taking over the master's role. But I knew it was the drink making me reflect in this manner, so I pushed such an uncharitable notion away from me.

Still, it would appear we had been frustrated yet again, for even if we were able to disguise ourselves in some fashion, though well-nigh impossible in Mr Slack's own case, we would never be able venture into these places where the low Irish had their domain, and even if we had some way of distributing handbills there no one would cooperate in betraying, as they saw it, one of their own, or now, more properly, two, in my obsession with her companion having forgotten the young woman.

And so it came to me I should have given her more of my attention, even if any knowledge I had been able to glean was scanty. Young, with reddish hair and sturdy of build, and passed off as Hare's daughter, was all I had to go on, the latter a clear falsehood, as he had no offspring. So how and where had they met, and why?

In previous cases my custom has been to allow an image of the one I was pursuing take shape in my head, and helped by the broadside sketches and, indeed, the mask, already he had become almost established there as if we were in the same room together and reaching out I could take a hold of him.

But the more I closed my eyes no picture of the girl emerged, nothing but a featureless daub. Was she Irish like Hare? Yet no hint of an accent had been mentioned, first, by the old man at the seashore, then the young ruffian on the boat maligning her for his own low purposes. Still, what if he were not so far out in calling her a whore after all? She and her 'father' might well have come to this place where there would be more call for her services than in the rural parts they had been travelling through.

The only advantage coming out of this was that now we knew there were two of them, and such a pairing might jog people's memories of seeing them as a couple, and not someone travelling on his own.

Belfast ✖ *Tuesday*

THIS MORNING finally a letter arrived from England bearing fresh instructions, Lord Beckford requesting me to visit an acquaintance of his at a place not far from where we are at this time, as this friend, it transpires, is himself a keen devotee of criminal matters and those engaged in such pursuits.

'While at Oxford University, Viscount Massereene and I in our own juvenile fashion experimented on some local felons made available to us, achieving some interesting results with, first, nitrous oxide, or laughing gas, as it's crudely known, and later, electrical shocks applied to those parts of the brain which govern behaviour.

'Therefore I feel convinced my friend might prove a valuable addition to our little team of "detectives" in bringing a fresh eye to the case, not to mention an intimate knowledge of the territory Mr Slack and your good self now happen to find yourselves in.'

On reading the foregoing my appetite for breakfast was quite spoiled, my gorge rising at what I took to be a slight to my professional reputation, despite it being delivered in the silkiest of terms. Ordered to go traipsing off to some lordly seat in the middle of the countryside put me in an even blacker mood, and when I told Mr Slack the news from his employer he appeared uneasy, and so I asked him, 'Have you heard of this gentleman? Has your master ever referred to him?'

After a moment, he replied, 'He visited Bath on several occasions and was entertained at his Lordship's residence.'

'And what manner of man might he be?'

There followed yet another uncomfortable silence, accompanied by a lowering of the head.

'I cannot say. I merely served him at table.'

And there I left it, for there was something in his manner that advised me not to proceed, allied to a feeling some sort of mystery existed there, and so I made preparations for our trip later in the morning.

As it appears there is no direct coaching service to the locality we are bound for, I have hired a driver, or 'jarvey', to get us to the village of Randalstown, where Viscount M. has his country seat, for like all these landed folk, despite their Irish titles, he spends near half the year at a conspicuously grand address in Mayfair.

This information was forthcoming from our driver Dermot, although I hadn't the heart to tell him I was fully aware of the custom, having a thorough working knowledge of such swells and their London habits, even though my dealings were usually with those in the business of robbing their houses in their absence.

Determined, at least, to see something of those parts of the city we were warned against, and where Hare might have gone to earth among his own kind, I instructed him to drive us in that direction.

'And why would you be wanting to go up over Divis mountain when there's a far more convenient and picturesque route via the coast road?'

But I insisted, and taking his displeasure out on his horse, he whipped it through the narrow, cobbled streets climbing up from the heart of the city, our car followed by half-naked children yelling abuse while their mothers watched from doorways, heads covered in shawls like Arab women, and soon stones were rattling off the roof of our conveyance as a cursing Dermot used his whip to clear the way.

'Didn't I tell youse not to come this way? If we halted for a minute, sure, they'd have the very coat off your back. You'd need to be armed, or soft in the head, to venture among this tribe of savages.'

Which I thought curious, him being so hard on his own kind, for by his name I could tell he was a 'left-footer', a term, so I'm given to understand, derived from a type of spade used in the digging of turf, which judging by the prevailing reek in the air is the only fuel burned here, whereas in the better-off areas Scottish coal seems to be the choice.

But soon the urchins fell back, the patter of missiles dying away, the countryside asserting itself, gorse- and heather-covered and desolate at this height above the capital cupped on its northern and eastern flanks by high blue hills.

When we reached the summit I told our driver to rest his horse, and let us stretch our legs, and while he sat smoking Mr Slack and I looked down on the city below, and it was like studying a busy hive with no hope of singling out a solitary human insect from all the rest.

After a time Dermot came up to us, and removing his pipe and spitting out over the steep decline, he enquired, 'If it's not too bold to enquire, is it business or pleasure you two fine gentlemen are engaged on?'

I felt like telling him it was scarcely diversion which had brought us here despite the scenery, so I told him we were taking some documents to be signed by Viscount Massereene's own hand, to which he replied, 'Well, they must be pretty important to bring you all this way, from London, by your accent. I can't judge your friend's here, as he's been quiet as a mouse this far. An almighty big one at that.'

Yet his familiarity didn't strike me as offensive, for I had learned Belfast folk spoke their minds freely, having little or no respect for ceremony or refinement of manners, and

I found it refreshing, if confusing at times, to be in a place where a man felt himself to be as good as the next, even if he was seen by the other as an underling.

'I can imagine in your occupation you must be pretty knowledgeable with all that goes on down below us there.'

'Don't I know every cobblestone as well as them that have often used the same as ammunition? Ask me any question concerning its history, past, present or future, and I'm your man. Amn't I near enough what you might call a walkin' encyclopedia on the subject.'

However, it was not a lecture I wished to hear, but the possible whereabouts of one of its present inhabitants, for despite my recent setbacks I still hoped for some sort of an outcome in the matter.

'Mr Slack, would you be good enough to fetch me my portmanteau?' and, going to the carriage, he retrieved it, and unstrapping it I produced one of the monotype renderings I had procured of our quarry at the time of his trial.

'By any chance might you have come across this particular individual in the city?' and taking it from me as if it was some rare and precious relic, our driver studied it up and down, back and forth for some considerable time.

'He may well have been in the company of a young woman.'

At this he seemed even more respectful of the drawing in his hand.

'Well, is the face at all familiar in any way?'

Sighing, as though reluctant to return it to my keeping, he held out the sheet.

'It all depends what your interest might be.'

'How do you mean?'

'Well, is he respectable or is he not? If he is, then he'd more likely be residing in some of the plusher parts such as Malone or Bloomfield.'

'I would scarcely think so.'

Grinning, as though a light had come on in his understanding, he said, 'Ah, so that's the way of it, is it?'

I could sense Mr Slack growing as impatient as myself at
this tedious cat and mouse game so, putting the sketch back
in its case, I said, 'I think we should be going on with our
journey. His Lordship will be expecting us.'

However, he had no intention of letting the matter drop,
and after we had been on the road for a time, over his shoulder
he remarked, 'I might be able to be of some assistance with a
little more information on your man, the one you're looking
for, I mean. Goin' by the cut of him, I'm reluctant to think he
would be mixing in the same circles as yourself.'

'You can tell that, can you?'

'Aye, there's something about the face, as well as the
clothes, what one can see of them, anyway, that says they're
not his normal attire, but put on specially for the taking of the
likeness. I mean, would he have had some class of a run-in
with the authorities at all?'

Despite my irritation at his persistence, some other part
of me couldn't help but be impressed by his amateur sleuth
work with only a pen and ink sketch to go by, so I said, 'He's
a countryman of yours, and could be looking for work of the
labouring variety.'

'And has he a name at all?'

But deciding I had disclosed more than enough, I told him
that was all the information we had at this time, which seemed
to satisfy him, and so we proceeded on our way, Mr Slack and
I leaning back and surveying the changing countryside as it
slid past.

At the village owned by the Massereene estate our driver
stopped to ask the way, and was directed towards a high stone
wall with a splendid archway opening on to a long gravelled
sweep leading to the house itself, more like a turreted castle, in
truth, with its many fine windows reflecting the now dying sun.

Almost as though expecting our arrival, the moment we

drew up a liveried footman came trotting down the steps and with an unexpected show of deference Dermot doffed his cap, for despite all his proud protestations of being under obligation to no man, he still was greatly impressed by 'oul' dacency', something I had often remarked in my dealings with the Irish generally, even the most rebellious of them.

After our luggage had been carried off by this same footman I paid Dermot what we owed him and we shook hands.

'May I enquire, will you be returning to the city when your business is concluded here?'

I told him, yes, almost certainly, and he said, 'If you like, I could look into into that little private matter of yours and report back to you at your lodgings. In my line of work I come across all sorts and classes, so a couple of runaways would scarcely be a bother.'

Taken aback, I asked, 'Why do you say that?'

'Well, reading between the lines, it seems to me they might not be all that overjoyed at being discovered.'

In my previous occupation I made a habit of recruiting a select little band of informants who were invaluable in many of the cases I handled at Bow Street during my time there. But all my 'grasses' then had gone through a rigorous testing of their trustworthiness and reliability before receiving a sou for their work on the streets and in the public houses and brothels of my beat. So why then should I put any faith in this Dermot character after being merely half a day in his company? Yet, on the other hand, supposing he did manage to find my two 'runaways', what could *they* offer him in exchange for his silence?

And so handing him half a crown, I told him, 'Take this, and if you bring me news of the people in question there'll be more of the same. But only if you're discreet, do you hear?'

'Indeed I do, and if they're anywhere to be found, with or without a name, I'll seek them out, for I never forget a face even if it only is on white paper.'

Mr Slack and I watched him drive away, raising his whip in a light-hearted gesture of adieu as he did so, and standing there I felt I could sense what was going through my companion's head, so I said, 'Seeing as there's no other option open to us, all we can do is trust him and hope he has better luck than we have had, for I am well-nigh ready to call it quits and admit defeat,' to which he said nothing, having, I suspected, more pressing and private concerns on his mind, which, as events were to turn out, I would soon be involved in myself.

Some little while after, yet another footman, of which there appeared to be a small platoon, led us to our sleeping quarters, in my case a fine clean room near the top of the house, and standing at the window gazing out over the grounds, I spied someone by a grove of trees engaged in what looked like some form of open-air callisthenics. Even more unusual, a Negro, black as tar, and even at that distance, of a fine physique, exercising with a set of Indian clubs, his bare glistening torso rippling with muscle, my first real indication of the exotic nature of the place, its owner, and those under his roof.

After resting an hour or so, at seven by the clock I was aroused by the sound of a gong being struck below, and shortly after Mr Slack and I descended the splendid staircase to meet the Viscount, as he is known, with a couple of dogs in tow, a breed of runny-eyed, yapping little spaniel more commonly seen in the arms of some London lady than a country gentleman.

'Mr Speed, Mr Slack, I have heard so much about you I can scarcely wait to hear of your thrilling adventures. Come, meet my other guests, who are equally a-tremble with anticipation.'

Having no wish to perform for a party of jaded nobs there to be titillated, this was not what I relished hearing, but there was no turning back, so we followed our host, a pale, slim, slightly precious individual into the dining room. Luckily there were only three others at the long table, an older man and woman, and a curious-looking gent with a large domed forehead and wispy hair, with the air of the scholar about him.

'Friends, permit me to introduce Mr Percival Speed, our famous London sleuth, and his trusty auxiliary Mr Slack, come to regale us with their experiences in the fascinating under-world of crime and those who frequent its shadowy purlieus. Mr Speed, I trust you will forgive us, for we simple rural folk are starved of such heady excitements.'

Thereupon the one in the snuff-stained frock coat and with the bookish appearance coughed and took a sip from a glass in front of him filled with some dark heavy stuff, but not wine like that in the decanter in the centre of the table.

'Pray forgive me, my dear De Quincey. No one could possibly accuse someone such as yourself as being any sort of country bumpkin, for I know Mr Speed and you have much in common when it comes to delving into the darker recesses of the mind of *Homo sapiens*.'

Already I had taken a dislike to this popinjay, whereas the De Quincey character seemed far more agreeable, and he and I exchanged glances as Massereene prattled on about his own modest studies into mayhem and murder and the motives of those practising the like.

'Mr Speed, it would give me the greatest of pleasure to introduce you to my own little collection of curios despite it being not nearly half so extensive or fascinating as Lord Beckford's.'

At this the wife of the man across the table, putting a hand to her mouth, murmured, 'The very thought of such awful objects is enough to give one nightmares. Really, Perry, I've never been able to fathom how you came to be so absorbed in such an interest, which is neither normal nor natural.'

'Quite the contrary, dear lady,' interjected the other guest, 'for the art of murder is as old as time itself, and has been indulged in by its practitioners since Cain had a serious falling-out with his own brother right up to the present when Mr Speed's assassin, along with his fellow countryman, enlarged the tally, so to speak, as well as refining the technique.'

Clearly his female listener had no earthly notion what this De Quincey person was talking about. Neither did her husband, who seemed more interested in refilling his glass. As for myself, detecting a twinkle in his eye, I was uncertain of the seriousness of the little man with the greying, wispy locks and bulging forehead, and a moment later my suspicions were confirmed when he pronounced, 'Once a man indulges himself in murder, very soon he comes to think little of robbing, and from robbing he comes to drinking and Sabbath-breaking, and from that to incivility and procrastination. Once begun upon this downward path, you never know where to stop. Many a man has dated his ruin from some murder or other that perhaps he thought little of at the time.'

I saw Mr Slack look down at his plate, a darkening expression on his face. But moments later something else occurred which appeared even more of an affront to him, but in a far more personal manner.

On the table was a little silver handbell, and our host rang it, and after a brief interval the door opened and in came the Negro I had seen exercising in the grounds previously. But now he was dressed in a fine uniform of almost military cut showing off his mighty frame, near on a par with Mr Slack's own. Indeed it was hard not to see similarities, not merely in physique, but in a certain scarring of both their features.

'Gentlemen, this is Ptolemy, whose talents are many, not just in muscularity, as you can see, but for someone of his race, intellect, as well.'

This was aimed at Mr Slack and myself, but I noticed a look passing between the Viscount's black body-servant and Mr Slack that made me realise no introduction was necessary between the two, the Negro smiling in a sardonic, knowing fashion, while my companion's face remained stiff with disapproval.

'While you are my guests Ptolemy will be at your service day and night. No one knows better than he how to satisfy every request or demand made upon him. Isn't that so, Ptolemy?'

With the same slightly mocking expression on his handsome features, the black bowed, and the lady said, 'Does he speak English? I confess I have never heard him utter a single syllable since he's been here.'

'My dear cousin, Ptolemy adheres to that age-old adage about actions invariably speaking much louder than words. But for your information, he is fluent in several languages, including our own.'

'Really? How fascinating. Don't you think so, Tom?'

But her husband merely grunted, helping himself to more claret.

After Ptolemy had been dismissed the conversation swung back to what I had understood was the reason for our visit, something I was still unhappy about, even more so now on account of the company.

'So, what news of this Hare person, Mr Speed? My good friend in Bath has me nearly as intrigued as himself regarding our mysterious will-o'-the-wisp. I understand you are of the opinion he is now in our own country. May I ask how you arrived at such a conclusion?'

But here De Quincey answered his question for him.

'Without attempting to trespass on Mr Speed's territory, knowing what we already know regarding the background and history of the same gentleman, surely it must be pretty obvious?'

'What do you mean?' asked the woman.

'Well, here he would have a much better chance of sanctuary, if such a term is appropriate, rather than in his adopted country on the other side of the water.'

'So he could be at large anywhere, even close to where we are as we speak. Merciful heavens!'

'No need for alarm, dear lady. A peaceful retirement from his old trade would be far more to his liking. True, Mr Speed?'

'Peaceful and retirement are scarcely the words I would associate with the person we happen to be talking about.'

He laughed.

'Bravo. Well said. Forgive an amateur with an amateurish interest in the subject, although I must confess to possessing an advantage over your good self in that I happen to have actually seen the one we're discussing, having been as near to him as to that wall there.'

At this those around the table went silent, while Mr Slack and I did our best to appear impassive, for this was not what we had expected to hear, especially coming from someone like the person opposite.

'Having lived in the city of Edinburgh these past number of years, naturally I followed the case, attending the court as often as I was able to, as did most of my friends who also were avid with curiosity regarding the proceedings, unlike your good self who came to the business much later, so I'm given to understand.'

'Correct,' I told him. 'I am merely here at the request and on the instructions of my employer. As far as I'm concerned, the case is closed, unlike most of the others I have worked on.'

'But in tracking down a suspect, you might still be inclined to employ similar methods of detection?'

'Forgive me, but the use of the term "suspect" in this particular instance is neither relevant nor accurate.'

'Bravo yet again, Mr Speed, I'm put in my place, and rightly so. Here's to your modesty, for your reputation and well-earned success as a thief-taker precede you.'

Raising his glass, he took a sip of the contents, which by this time I reckoned to be more medicinal than the fine claret the rest of us were drinking, save Mr Slack, of course. Tincture of laudanum was my guess, and indeed later I was to discover this De Quincey character was none other than the acclaimed author of *Confessions of an English Opium-Eater*, despite taking it in liquid form, being the preferred usage for those also sharing his particular addiction.

But none of that was of any real or abiding interest to me just then. Such topics I was happy to leave to those with a more intellectual bent like those at the table, with the exception of the couple, the wife, in particular, who still persisted with her own lurid fancies.

'It's said such terrible people bear the stamp of their crimes on their features. Like an indelible mark.'

'I think Mr Speed must be the one to answer that, although in Hare's case, despite what the newspapers wrote of him at the time as some decadent freak of nature, I have to say I merely saw someone you might easily pass by in the street without another glance, the very reason, I suspect, he may have evaded public scrutiny thus far.'

'Would you care to hear what *I* think?' interjected our host. 'I firmly believe if you two were to join forces you could flush out this specimen of human vermin from whatever den he happens to be holed up in pretty damn quick, you with your sharp intellect, De Quincey, and Mr Speed here with his workmanlike, forensic skills.'

Sitting there, I wondered just how much longer I could bear being patronised in this manner, but Mr De Quincey took away some of the sting of the insult by countering, 'I scarce think Mr Speed is so bereft of imagination as to ally himself with a poor desk-bound scribbler such as myself. However, if at any time he would deign to discuss his investigations with me, I would be greatly honoured.'

Thankfully, the meal ended soon after, and the couple, having some distance to travel, rose to go, and so I, too, made my excuses, saying the journey had finally caught up with me.

Before turning in, however, I decided to take a stroll

outside to clear my head, for my brain was still buzzing with everything I had heard earlier.

A slight dampness was in the air, cooling on the brow, and the smell of some night-scented flower came wafting up from an arbour at the far end of the terrace. After the hubbub of the city the peace of the countryside was hard to get used to, and I wondered how long it would be before my senses slowed to a crawl and I lost the sharpness I had always relied upon to get me to the heart and guts of a case.

Next day I again took myself off with my thoughts, but this time further from the house. In the distance lay a broad expanse of calm water which I understood to be the famous Lough Neagh, and as I made my way towards it I saw a jetty and a person poised there. It was the one called Ptolemy, naked as the day he was born, and causing barely a splash, in he dived, but not wishing to be seen I made my way some distance off to where there was a stand of young trees, and there I sheltered in the shade, for the sun was already climbing high in the sky.

For a servant our swimmer appeared to enjoy an unusual degree of freedom, privilege, also, some might say, sharing a certain familiarity with his master, and moments later I was to discover just how close that particular relationship happened to be.

Alerted by the cries of approaching dogs, I withdrew deeper into my hiding place, and soon Massereene himself strolled into view, making his way along the length of the jetty. His three spaniels were now barking like the very dickens, so he hurled a stick out for them. But reluctant to get their pampered little pelts wet, they ran up and down in a great state of excitement, and next moment I heard their master shout something to the swimmer, his dark head bobbing like a cork out in the lough.

I took it he was being ordered to return ashore, and sure enough his strokes accelerated, that powerful upper body forging effortlessly through the brown water. However, what occurred next transformed something entirely innocent, for to my disquiet I saw him take hold of the floating stick in his mouth and swim with it like a dog to its owner.

Hauling himself up on to the jetty, still in retriever mode, he knelt at the Viscount's feet, and after laying down his burden was dutifully patted on the head.

Sickened by the sight, I withdrew even further into my hiding place. But before I could make a retreat, a worse scene of shame and degradation met my gaze, for, raising the Negro to his feet, his master embraced him in all his nakedness, nuzzling, then kissing him on the neck, and not wishing to witness any further indecency I made my way back to the house.

The shock of what I'd just seen lingered with me, and in my room I wondered why, being no stranger to such practices, in my time having brought a fair number of sodomites and their catamites to prosecution. Yet the more I pondered, the closer I came to thinking I might have become tainted myself in becoming involved with such deviants even in a purely professional capacity. Even more disturbing was the notion my present employer might himself share such tendencies, recalling, as I did, that curious look passing between Mr Slack and his black counterpart at the dinner table.

Some time later he, himself, came to my room, enquiring how long I intended remaining under his master's friend's roof. I could tell he was thinking of the business that had brought us here, and somewhat snappishly informed him there was no immediate urgency as the trail had gone cold by now and must be dry as dust anyway.

I could see he was put out by my manner. But I still was beset by doubts whether he was the person I thought he was. Perhaps I had grown a little too close to the man with the battered brow standing now before me, for normally I would have invited him to sit himself down on the window seat with his back to the beautifully tended, romantic landscape beyond the glass, but blighted now for me by what I had witnessed out there earlier.

'Mr Slack,' I addressed him, and again it was clear this formal approach was puzzling to him, 'I would like to think you and I have been frank and open with one another since first we joined forces in this undertaking, and so while we are in the company of these people I would appreciate it if you would be equally forthcoming and tell me what you know of them and their private habits.'

Bowing his head, which I knew to be an indication of his unease, he murmured, 'I merely served the Viscount at table when he was visiting Lord Beckford, as I have already informed you.'

'And his servant, was he present at Bath as well?'

'He was.'

'Both appear pretty free and easy for master and man, wouldn't you say?'

I saw I had touched a nerve, but, pressing on, I said, 'Am I correct in thinking this Ptolemy and yourself have had your differences in the past? Is it a matter of his colour and race?'

He stared at me, and for the first time there was anger in his eyes.

'I would never judge a man in regard to either of those two things.'

'But something else, perhaps?'

'Mr Speed, I have been more than happy to assist you in whatever course of action my master desires, but I think it scarcely fitting for you and I to go beyond the boundaries of such a professional arrangement. So, if there is no further call for my services at this time, I should prefer to spend some time in my own room reading,' and rising he crossed to the door.

'Well, to hell with you, Master Jack Slack, and your precious Bible studies,' was my reaction after he had gone. 'And I trust you will take heed of a place by the name of Sodom, and the practices of the inhabitants of that same city.'

But here I wavered, disappointed at being concerned with something having no proper bearing on the case in hand, telling myself the sooner I left this house the better, for I was beginning to feel a cloying sensation already even in contact with the very furnishings of the room I was in, with its heavy brocaded curtains and Oriental furniture. And, later, going down the staircase, the array of ancestral faces lining my descent seemed also to hint at past depravities.

Happily, below, no sound of yapping dogs was there to greet me, the house silent as the grave, and pushing on a door, I saw it led to the library, also like a tomb, albeit lined with more volumes than I had ever seen in a single room, not even in Lord Beckford's own study when he received me there.

Standing there, awed by the sheer weight of knowledge surrounding me, I heard a cough, followed by a voice enquiring, 'Is that you, Mr Speed?' and De Quincey poked his head from an alcove.

'Are you, too, a lover of literature?'

He was sitting hidden away in a corner with a book on his lap and a slew of papers about his feet.

'To my shame, not at all,' I told him, and gesturing to a chair, he said, 'No need for shame, Mr Speed. I would give more than you might imagine to live in the real world, even an unruly one such as you yourself inhabit, instead of spending my time merely dreaming about it at a safe remove.'

I noticed he had another of his vials of reddish-brown stuff by his chair, and intercepting my glance, he said, 'I see you have discovered my little secret, not that it would take tremendous powers of detection to recognise such a habit. Have you yourself ever indulged in the chemical delights of *Papaver orientalis?*'

'No, but often in my career I have witnessed the effects on others close to hand.'

'And like those poor wretches you refer to, in time you

believe I, also, may join their ranks. Yet each one of us began our fall from grace for differing reasons all our own, whether weakness of will or some other cause. In my own case a debilitating illness led me to enlist the services of my liquid friend quite early on. And so now I still need my purple draught much as some suckling babe craves the maternal teat.'

As though to prove the point he raised the glass to his lips and, after the draught had gone down, closed his eyes.

I felt sure he had fallen asleep, for he looked as though he needed his rest, his face drawn and parchment pale. But after a moment the colour crept back into his cheeks once more and I heard him sigh, 'There, I am renewed, and so we are ready to converse like two people without prejudice or preconception, for unlike your mighty companion, you yourself are no Puritan.'

'All of that after one brief meeting? Bow Street surely has lost a recruit of exceptional promise.'

He laughed.

'Perhaps our host was not so far off the mark when he suggested we join forces after all. But, no, I was referring more to your man Slack and his reputation.'

'Reputation? How do you mean?'

Leaning forward, he stretched out a hand scarcely bigger than a child's, the skin white as milk, as though never having seen the light of day.

'I am merely relaying what has come from our host. He and Lord Beckford are close friends, and closer correspondents, both sharing a high opinion of Jack Slack, and indeed your own good self.'

But despite having a keen nose for flim-flam and flattery, I still felt uneasy, and was relieved when the conversation moved on to something much more pressing and pertinent, which was the person who had brought me here.

'Unlike most of my Scottish friends, who fastened their attention on the character and personality of Burke when he was in the dock, perversely, perhaps, I felt myself concentrating instead on his accomplice. As I say, I was practically alone in this, and the more the public vented their fury on him, again, perhaps perversely, the more I formed the opinion he might not be quite the beetle-browed, mindless brute they determined he should be, as better the devil you know than the one you cannot fit inside a box with a neat label attached. But then, Mr Speed, as we both know, this same Irish hobbledehoy succeeded in confounding all those who had sought to place him there, so perhaps the label was incorrect in the first place.'

I felt I should offer some reply, but what? Agree with him for articulating what did, indeed, appear to prove a degree of low cunning in our quarry? Yet at the same time I resented yet another amateur sleuth putting his own gloss on someone who in some strange way I had come to regard as my own personal property.

'Nevertheless, I still prefer to concentrate on a person's movements rather than their cast of mind.'

'But surely the latter must influence much of his subsequent actions?'

'No one, no matter how gifted, can foretell what a criminal will do next. One must wait and watch until he makes a mistake, as in my experience invariably they do.'

I could see he was far from being convinced, but I was determined not to give him the satisfaction of victory, even though he was correct about getting inside an offender's head. Indeed, it was a cardinal rule which had guided me through a score or more of years in my chosen profession.

'Fascinating as the subject of Mr William Hare might be, I trust you will forgive me if I resume my reading, for I must prepare an article for *Blackwood's Magazine*. Indeed, it was what brought me to this part of the world in the first place. Regarding which, I have a proposition I wish to put to you. But not just yet. Perhaps in a day or so?'

'Well, I hope to return to Belfast much sooner than that.'

'Have you informed our host of your intention? I under-stand he has a proposal of his own which may delay your departure.'

And so some short while later, when Massereene met up with Mr Slack and myself to inform us of his 'proposal', we looked at one another dismayed by the man's gall.

'I have taken the liberty of arranging a little outdoor diversion tomorrow for some sporting friends who are partial to a wager like myself. Are you a betting man yourself, Mr Speed?'

No, the urge had never taken a hold on me, I told him.

'This particular contest might well change your mind.'

'What kind of contest?'

'Why, the most manly of all. An exhibition match between my man and yours, or should I say Lord Beckford's.'

Which was when Mr Slack and I exchanged those glances of disquiet, although in his case the reaction appeared more muted, even though beneath that calm exterior a fury must surely be near bubbling to the boil.

'I take it you have consulted Lord Beckford regarding this "contest".'

'A gentleman's wager involving our servants is of no concern but our own, and anyone prepared to lay money on the outcome. So, are you tempted to back your fancy, or are you afraid our large friend here may not come up to snuff?'

A sneer was on his lips, as he said it, and tempted as I was to take him up on his challenge I was keenly aware of the person by my side listening to all of this as if he were a mere piece of furniture, or, in this present case, a human chopping block.

'With your permission, Mr Slack and I would like to discuss the matter.'

'By all means. Make ready your man while I see to it my own is himself up to the mark.'

And there we left it, with his Highness going off to tell

his 'man' the news, although I felt pretty certain the bout had been planned in advance, even convincing myself it might well have been the real reason we had actually been summoned here, and nothing to do with what I had been commissioned to carry out in the first place.

It was now close to noon and time to take our midday meal, so Mr Slack and I went below stairs to the kitchens on the instructions of the head footman, a rather grand individual who had disapproved of Mr Slack being invited to eat with his master at his table the night we arrived.

Soup, a boiled fowl, cheese and bread, with ale for myself and water for my companion, had been laid out for us on the great scrubbed table, and having the place to ourselves we sat eating in silence, until after a time I spoke out.

'Jack, I am far from happy concerning this thing Massereene has foisted on us. He has no right to demand it of you, and at the risk of incurring his displeasure, I will stand by you no matter what your decision turns out to be.'

I could see he was distressed and unwilling to speak. But I pressed ahead.

'This Ptolemy person. Have you and he clashed in the past?'

'No, but he has longed to prove himself against me for some considerable time.'

'And you have never accepted his challenge? Until now, that is?'

Looking me in the eye, he said, 'The Good Lord alone will guide me in this matter.'

'And Lord Beckford?'

But I could tell our conversation was at an end, and we finished our meal, leaving the table and going our separate ways soon after.

That evening Mr De Quincey and I dined alone. Our host had business elsewhere, which was a relief as I was in no mood to put up with his crowing about his champion, who I had spotted in the grounds earlier exercising with a skipping rope while Mr Slack was grinding away in his room at his Bible studies, which if he were preparing himself for a contest in the grass ring seemed a singularly odd regime to follow. But I had still no inkling what his intentions were, and had no wish to press him on the subject.

To take my mind off the matter, I allowed the little writer free rein to talk while I listened and he sipped his purple potion. His topic, as before, was murder, and those engaging in it, but on this occasion it was the Williams case, popularly known as the Ratcliffe Highway Murders, a score of years earlier. When he enquired if I myself had been involved in the investigation, I told him it fell outside the remit of Bow Street and was handled by the London Marine Police Force, who had jurisdiction over the river and dockland areas of the city.

'But you must still have been acquainted with the case.'

Certainly, I told him, for everyone was gripped and horrified by the unusual ferocity of the attacks, half a dozen people butchered in their own homes. De Quincey, it transpired, was himself familiar with the gruesome details, referring to the implements used, a ship's carpenter's mallet and chisel in the first murders of the Marrs, the linen draper's family, and a knife to cut the throats of the publican John Williamson, his wife and their old female servant a dozen days later.

'In point of fact I was of the strong opinion those particular killings may have been carried out by someone other than Williams, or Murphy, as he was sometimes known, as he had no proper motive for the second murders. However, for convenience sake, I suppose, the police and the public felt happier about one killer taking the blame for both, rather than another being still at large among the population.'

'You seem to have a low opinion of the police.'

'Not at all, but they are human like the rest of us, and pressure of popular opinion often forces them into arresting the wrong person, usually on the basis of his or her character, instead of employing the kind of calm, reasoned detective work such as Mr Percival Speed is well known for.'

Recognising when I am being soft-soaped, I said nothing, and after another sip of his elixir De Quincey leaned back in his chair.

'On another and very different topic, but perhaps one much more pertinent to present circumstances, how confident are you your man will win tomorrow?'

'Why? Do you intend betting on the outcome?'

'My dear chap, I've never wagered a penny piece on anything in my life. But if ever tempted, it would not be on the kind of barbaric spectacle planned for tomorrow.'

'And is the Viscount aware of this aversion of yours?'

Laughing, he replied, 'You have a disconcerting knack, Mr Speed, of cutting to the quick, so I will return the favour. Are *you* comfortable with Mr Slack taking a beating to gratify the bloodlust of a clique of wealthy gambling men?'

'It may well be the Negro whose pride will be dented, not Jack Slack. But the decision is solely his, no one else's. He is his own man.'

'Twere only so. Alas, in this society of ours we must all bow the knee to those with power and privilege. I myself take no particular pride in accepting the crumbs of patronage that fall from rich men's tables, for I have a wife and children to feed as well as clothe. A married man yourself, Mr Speed, are you?'

'Once, but the demands of my occupation put paid to it.'

'I, too, have been close to sacrificing the joys of domesticity for this addiction of mine. But I love my children, and my Margaret is a good mother, tolerating, as she does, this rival for her affections,' indicating his glass, which by this time was pretty near drained to the dregs.

'These past fifteen years or so I have been in thrall to this chemical mistress of mine, so I trust you will now excuse me, for already I hear her siren call reminding me of my other obligation of a thousand words a day.'

But instead of rising he remained sitting where he was, staring into the lees in his glass, as if, indeed, he might have been listening to some private voice murmuring in his head, for nothing would surprise me about this curious little man in his worn frock coat and ink-stained linen, fulfilling, as he did, all the popular perceptions of the eccentric, other-worldly scholar.

Later that evening a nightingale sang outside my bedroom window, for I had the casement open as the weather was heavy and sultry, and between the bird in the tree and the turmoil in my brain it took me a long time to get to sleep. I kept thinking of Slack on the floor above, pacing, testament in hand, for how could he lay his head on the pillow with such a weight hanging over him?

Perhaps he would find consolation in the Good Book, for even a hardened unbeliever like myself was familiar with all those biblical references to other lone men in the desert wrestling with their consciences.

Morning came, with my songbird no longer serenading its mate. Instead another much less mellifluous sound drifted up, the crunch of carriage wheels ploughing up the raked gravel below. At least a dozen broughams, gigs and outside cars were disgorging their male occupants, who stamped about restoring the circulation in their limbs. Their voices rang out, and a relay of Massereene's footmen came trotting down the steps bearing stiffeners of punch and whiskey on silver trays.

Making a hurried toilet, then dressing as swiftly as I could, I made my way up to Mr Slack's bedroom. Already garbed in his best black, he was sitting on the bed staring at the floor, and even when I entered, he neither raised his head nor spoke.

Needing no excuse to announce what was on both our minds, I simply said, 'Jack.'

But still he made no reply.

'The people who have come for this bout are down below, but if it is your wish to withdraw I will inform them myself, for I feel responsible for this business. We never should have come to this godless place.'

Raising his head, he stared at me, before murmuring, 'Godless, aye, godless indeed,' as if shaken by the word. 'For their abominations they shall be smitten and brought low. Their faces shall be ground in the dust, their pride humbled.'

But far from being in the mood for a sermon at this hour, any time of day, for that matter, I continued to press him.

'These people are waiting and will not be pleased to be denied their sport.'

At which point he rose.

'Very well, go down to them, and I will follow presently. Never fret, Percy, what needs to be done shall and will be attended to.'

It was the first time he had ever addressed me by my first name, and the surprise of it made me turn away in some emotion, for we were both individuals who rarely, if ever, openly displayed our feelings.

'What will I tell Massereene?'

'I will look to the matter myself.'

And so in some confusion still, I left him sitting there as though dressed for a funeral, which in the present circumstances might well turn out to be the case, for I had seen enough of these bloody contests at Marylebone and Paddington fields to be fearful of the result.

By the time I made my way downstairs and out through the entrance doors, the crowd had moved on to the lawn at the front of the house. A roped-off square had already been marked out on the freshly mown turf, and around its perimeter the sporting types I had heard earlier were milling about in what appeared to be a high pitch of anticipation. Massereene himself was holding court under a striped umbrella, while lounging by his side was the Negro, already stripped to a pair of pale-coloured breeches setting off his tawny hide to its best advantage.

As I crossed the gravel, one of the uniformed lackeys pressed a glass of something on me, but I refused, even though I could well have done with it just then, for I was still in turmoil regarding Mr Slack's fate, uncertain if he would even enter the ring. But whether he did or did not, I knew he would be made to suffer the consequences of his actions either way.

As I came on to the sward, raising a pale, womanly hand, Massereene summoned me to join him and his champion under the umbrella, and when I came up he greeted me with a smile, while the Negro showed his white teeth as though at some private jest of his own.

'Well, as you may observe, my dear Speed, we have a fine turnout today. Some of these gentlemen have come from as far away as Dublin itself, for it's not every day they are afforded the opportunity of seeing two such splendid heavyweights matched against one another. And speaking of combatants, where is your own man? I trust he has not conceded the contest before the first blow has even landed.'

'Mr Slack is on his way and will be here presently.'

Having still no clear notion of 'my man's' intentions, it was pure invention on my part. Torn between wanting him to trounce this black devil, which was how I now saw his opponent, or seeing him turn and walk away, I could only wait while observing the crowd. From their bearing and dress most were of a similar station to their host, but present, too, were those not so well connected, men of the professional class, even a clergyman or two, red-faced farmers, gambling types, and a group of large men bulging out of their attire obviously gathered there to size up the competition when the time arrived.

As expected, of De Quincey there was no sign, and so I thought of both men in their rooms, apart, yet united in their abhorrence of the blood-spattered spectacle about to take place in this beautiful setting, and I wished I was with them instead of standing in the shade of a parasol alongside a decadent aristocrat and his catamite, for after what I had witnessed by the lake nothing now could convince me otherwise.

The crowd was growing impatient, several of those present taking out their pocket watches and glancing at them before turning their heads in the direction of their host, and as time ticked by a short, round-bellied man, who I took to be the umpire, for he had his own timepiece hanging about his neck, came towards us and whispered something to the Viscount, who instantly smote his knee with a slap of bad temper.

'Damn you, Speed, fetch your man this instant. I will not be treated in this fashion in front of my friends by a mere servant.'

'Mr Slack may well be as you say, but I, sir, am not,' I replied, for I'd had my fill of this noble nelly and his arrogance.

'Mister? Mister, you say? Rest assured your employer in England will hear of this.'

'So be it, but when reporting back to him myself I will make sure to acquaint him with what is taking place here this day.'

After I had spoken the wrath on the other's face was a sight to behold, with Ptolemy looking poised to dole out some form of chastisement if called upon.

But, for my sins, just then I was saved by a combination of factors, one, his master being reluctant to sanction such a thing in front of his guests, and, second, Jack Slack coming down the steps of the great house, and at the sight a tremendous huzza arose, for he, too, was bare-chested, clothed only in his long white under-drawers and gartered stockings, and having only ever seen him fully clothed up to then, I could share in the admiration of all those present, for here was someone awesome indeed in his breadth of shoulder and great, heavily muscled arms, while the shock on his opponent's face was a match for his master's, and it was a sweet moment made even sweeter when a fresh flurry of betting broke out which

I could hear swinging in favour of the man making his way towards us.

Staring straight ahead, he moved directly to the ring, the crowd parting before him with some slapping his bare back and calling out his name as he passed, it being clear his reputation had travelled before him.

Climbing through the ropes, he took up position in a corner, arms folded, waiting for the Negro to join him, and now the little umpire clambered into the ring like some pygmy preparing to hold the line between a pair of giants, one with flesh pale as milk, the other's dark as mahogany.

Summoning both men to the centre, he could be heard announcing that the bout would be conducted strictly to Broughton's Rules, which each of the contestants knew well.

Massereene had seen to it his man was attended by two of his own footmen bearing towels, water and rubbing oils, whereas Slack had no one, so I made my way through the crowd to take my place where he leaned against the ropes.

We exchanged looks, but said nothing. Then, to everyone's consternation, including my own, he sank to his knees with closed eyes, murmuring something, and, near as I was to him, I strained in vain to hear the words, until it came to me he was praying, and looking over at Massereene under his umbrella, I realised he, too, had caught the drift of what our muscular Christian was about, for he was laughing with one of his toady friends, the Negro Ptolemy, also, revelling in the sight while having his shoulders rubbed by one of his seconds.

Motioning the combatants to come to scratch, Mr Umpire withdrew, and the fight was on, the challenger circling Slack still with his arms by his side as though waiting for his opponent to make the first attacking move, which he did, quickly darting forward. Backing out of range, Slack slid away, and now the most remarkable bout of prizefighting those present that summer's day had ever witnessed ensued, for ducking and weaving in the most wonderfully light-footed and adroit manner for someone his weight and size, the former champion continued evading every punch and lunge the other sent his way.

Not even on a stage had there been a performance the like, the crowd standing dumbstruck, the only sound to be heard the grunts of the black man and the whistle of his fists meeting empty air.

Finally came the inevitable impact, however. Yet, as before, Slack avoided any real hurt, parrying the blow with his forearm and sending his opponent reeling off balance, the crowd erupting as if finally scenting some full-blooded sport. But the cry also contained an element of derision at the black's inability to score a single point, and, enraged and forsaking all his vaunted fighting skills, he came at his opponent swinging his fists windmill fashion, which surely was the moment when Slack should have put him down, and caught up in the excitement of it and with the cries of 'Drop him! Drop him!' ringing in my ears, I, too, called out, 'Jack! Jack!' and for an instant he looked directly at me, and whether it was the sound of my voice, or something much deeper, compelling him to act as he did, he dropped to one knee and the crowd howled in unison like a pack of wild dogs denied their prey.

Yet even in their rage they were aware of the rules which said he was entitled to a half-minute count to recover, although why he should need such a respite when he was as fresh and untouched as the moment he first stepped into the ring was a mystery.

Above the noise of the crowd could be heard Massereene's cries of *'Foul! Foul!'* despite there being no grounds for it. But his voice went unheeded, for all eyes were on the umpire counting off the seconds as though his very existence depended upon it, which might well be the case, ending up a target himself if the man at his feet remained kneeling after the small hand on his watch moved past the point of no return, thus marking the finish of the bout.

Halfway into the count the crowd fell silent, nothing to be heard but the trickle of water from one of the great stone fountains behind us. Even the mighty Ptolemy hung fire, mouth open, panting, yet every sinew of his black torso taut and straining in readiness, and the instant the umpire raised his hand to signal his victory, instead of being overjoyed, he sprang forward and struck his kneeling opponent a savage blow to the temple, the onlookers boiling up in a storm of disgust and outrage at such a blatant and cowardly act.

Yet a fair proportion of that same anger was directed at the one who had cheated them, not only of their day of sport but, for some, their winnings, also, and it seemed only moments before the ring would be stormed by angry, waving punters, and so once more I called out to him, 'Jack, Jack, you must get away or you will be undone!' and slowly he rose to his feet, a tempest of abuse breaking about his head.

As he stepped clear of the ring a man rushed forward and spat in his face, and in spite of all my earlier caution I dealt him a blow, knocking him to the ground. Luckily he was scarcely my match, although his friends looked more than capable of taking up his cause. But before Slack could intervene, which seemed doubtful, for he appeared still to be in a world of his own, shouldering their way through the mob came a handful of men of the sort I had noticed earlier, who by their bulk and deportment I took to be pugilists themselves, and flanking the pair of us they proceeded to force a passage through the baying crowd.

Without uttering a word, with faces as though carved in stone, they conducted Slack and myself across the grassy lawn towards Massereene, who had fallen back in his chair as though drained of all his previous spite and fury. Looking neither at us nor at our silent escort, he sat there, and although it appeared a moment of moral victory for the man by my side, I feared he was not yet done with Jack Slack and, possibly, Percy Speed as well.

At the foot of the steps leading to the house, our little praetorian guard came to a halt. Their leader, a squat, powerful, older man, yet bearing the signs of countless bruising encounters on his face, took Slack by the hand with still not a word uttered by either, and this mark of silent respect for a past champion and fellow battler impressed me deeply, while reinforcing my regard for the person receiving it.

One by one our remaining protectors shook his hand before walking off to where the crowd appeared to be already breaking up and dispersing, several calling for their carriages, and Slack and I watched them go, and it felt like a signal for us to leave the place as well, although I doubted if any of those so-called patrons of the noble art would be willing to share their conveyance with the man who had cheated them of their day of sport.

'Jack,' I said, 'let us leave this place, godless or otherwise. You have had a notable victory this day, even if others might not see it that way. But I still believe it will go down in the annals of boxing, despite you not delivering a blow, but because of it.'

Overly fanciful though it sounded, it was what was in my heart. Yet still I couldn't help enquiring, 'If it had gone the other way, do you think you could have beaten him?'

After I'd said it I could have bitten my tongue for spoiling the moment, but in a soft tone he replied, 'Thankfully, conscience was my guide and protector. But if the Lord had ordained otherwise I would surely have smote him as Asa in Deuteronomy smote the Ethiopian.'

Up in our rooms we packed our few belongings as we were no longer welcome in that great house, by now strangely silent, as if the events earlier had plunged the entire household into some kind of mourning. Before that mood wore off, however, and retribution took its place, it seemed sensible to depart as quietly as we could, and there being no likelihood of transport being provided, it was a case of going on foot, and so carrying our traps Mr Slack and I left by the servants' quarters along their underground, stone-flagged passages and out through the kitchen gardens at the rear.

To our surprise the same air of despondency seemed to hang over the entire village itself, no sign of life or anyone stirring we could ask regarding a car and driver. Yet even if we managed to find someone, he would be unwilling to assist us, Massereene holding his entire estate and its workers in the palm of his hand, and so our situation looked bleak indeed, two foreigners set down in strange countryside like this, made even more alien by their appearance.

After a time Slack relieved me of my portmanteau, being better equipped to bear the burden than myself, and we tramped on in silence past the empty gaze of cows in fields which were lush and green, for this was land very different from the boggy upland wastes surrounding the city we had set out from some days earlier.

Even though it was far from being an occasion for humour, I couldn't help think it ironic that here I was on the same footing as the person I had travelled all this way to confront, and Mr Hare and myself might well be within a reasonable distance of one another under the same sky with the same breeze blowing on our cheeks, although he had the advantage of knowing the terrain, whereas I did not.

After about a good hour of walking a kind of despair set in. Dependent on some form of miracle, as I saw it, I envied the man alongside me and his fortitude, and when we came to a bridge, I said, 'Let us rest,' even though he was as unpuffed and fit as ever, and while I sat down he leaned on the parapet staring into the stream below. But I had long given up enquiring what was on his mind lest I be treated to yet another parable, this time on the waters of life, or some similarly appropriate text.

Ever since we had set out on this winding country road we had not seen sight of another human soul, neither on foot nor in a vehicle of any kind, not even a farmer's cart, yet the fields around us looked well tended and fertile.

Then, as if all my previous cynicism was overturned, and my companion's silent communing with his Maker finally had been answered, in the distance there appeared what looked like a modest four-wheeler.

As it came closer, I feared the driver would bowl right past us as though we were of no more consequence than a pair of stones standing by the wayside, but to my great joy, pulling back on the reins, he brought the conveyance to a halt, and in even greater wonderment I heard a familiar voice announce, 'Well met, gentlemen, for I deeply regret not making our farewells in a more decent and civilised manner,' and it was De Quincey riding inside, and whether he had come upon us by chance or set out to overtake us out of regard for our plight, he still was a saviour in human form.

'Come, gentlemen, step up.'

And the driver, who might well have been one of Massereeene's own men, for he looked straight ahead with that same severe, unquestioning expression on his face they all favoured, clicked his tongue and the horse moved on.

'I trust you have no strong objection to saving your feet, as like myself, I take it, you are both accustomed to a more civilised mode of transport.'

I told him we were indeed indebted to him for his generosity, and replying, he said, 'It's the least I could do after the shabby treatment you received.'

Realising he must be referring to Slack and not myself, I enquired, 'So then you heard about the match?'

'I had no need. I observed the entire shameful episode from an upper window, almost as good as the proverbial ringside seat.'

Then, turning to my companion, he said, 'Seldom, sir, have I witnessed a nobler example of man's innate moral superiority over those of a brutish and bestial nature. I am privileged to have made your acquaintance,' and extending his pale little hand he watched it taken captive by Slack's immense, scarred one, even though none of those marks had been incurred that day.

'May I ask if you are both bound for Belfast city?'

'Someone is presently making enquiries on our behalf there, but I imagine he will need some time to carry them out.'

'In that case allow me to put a proposition to yourself and our mighty Achilles here. At this moment I am currently engaged on an assignment for the good readers of *Blackwood's Magazine*, and am bound for a place not all that far distant from here, and as a student of the odd and strange yourself, you, too, might find what I hope to see there equally intriguing. And by the time my researches have been completed, your man in the city may have some news for you.'

Turning to Mr Slack, I said, 'Are you agreeable?' and after a moment's reflection, he replied, 'Well, if you are so minded, Lord Beckford, I'm sure, will have no objection when informed of our movements.'

Leaning forward, the little man seated across from us cried, 'Bravo!' and putting his head out of the carriage window, he called up to the coachman to make haste as he and his two friends were anxious to reach their destination before nightfall.

The night before the Colonel was planning on taking his people on the road, I told the girl, having grown attached to her tiny friends, and they to her, she should go with them, and as was our habit we were lying apart in the tent, even though our tormentor Tito had since been laid in the ground, where he rightly belonged.

Yet the news didn't make her go all tearful on me as on those other occasions when I suggested the like, and expecting far more of a fuss, if truth be told, I was a mite put out, for it seemed she had somehow managed to work her charms on me, if charms is the proper word for one so middling in looks, some of the female midgets, if one set aside their smallness, being far finer specimens of pulchritude, especially Anita the Living Doll, who had all the men, dwarfs and otherwise, panting after her.

But she, it seemed, preferred Hannah's company, laughing and caressing, the pair of them, until I began to think they might be heading down the Sapphic highway, for in Edinburgh there was a bawdy house called the Happy Land where both sorts followed their inclinations, and often Burke would talk of waylaying some of the more prosperous when they fell out into the street of an evening the worse for wear. But for a matter of a purse or a watch and chain it seemed too much bother when we had a far easier way of making money with our medical friends in Surgeon's Square.

Nature and desire being such contrary creatures, I half-expected the person across from me might yet wish to bid farewell to Nebuchadnezzar, as he's known, it being the last time she might get to call upon his services. But, turning her back, she went to sleep instead, and so reining in my own urges, to hell with her, I told myself, if she prefers nuzzling up to her own kind, for there would be plenty not so particular walking the streets of Belfast the price of a bob or two.

Next day barely had we time to rouse ourselves before a great bustle and commotion got under way as preparations were made to depart with the tent near taken down over our heads. The girl and I lent ourselves to the work, and it was odd seeing all those little folk scurrying and swarming about, each with a task to perform, as though born to it, so that before the morning was advanced the field had been cleared, with only a bleached square remaining on the grass where we had been sleeping the night before.

Bundle in hand, I stood waiting for the convoy of carts and caravans to move off, with Hannah alongside, ready, as I thought, to climb up beside Anita. But before she could join her, whip in hand, the Colonel came walking along inspecting the line.

Coming to where we waited, he shook my hand.

'My friend, you may well be mute like your relative here, but I know you are no dummy within. So if you care to travel with us, I could introduce you to some of the tricks of our calling.'

But pointing to the bundle at my feet and shaking my head, I signalled my intention to remain, and taking out his purse he put some money in my hand like the true gentleman he was.

'And you, young lady, are you set on taking your leave of us as well?'

To my surprise, however, she, too, signalled her desire to stay, and cracking his whip the Colonel sent the first caravan trundling on its way.

Immediately Hannah broke into blubbering and bawling, and running to her, Anita clasped her about the knees, and it was a truly pitiful sight to see, like they were mother and child parting from one another. Yet I knew if I tried forcing Hannah into changing her mind, an even worse scene of wailing and lamentation might take place, bringing unwelcome interest to bear on us, yoked together as we were, nothing tying the knot but our crimes, for she had been the one to despatch our old enemy now in the local graveyard, where the company had buried him in a child's coffin.

After the last conveyance had gone from the field, leaving nothing save a patch of bruised pasture and horse droppings, we stood there alone with our thoughts, and she seemed in a similar frame of mind, expression downcast, hands at rest, for in her time with these people she had mastered a kind of dumb lingo of her own, taking tuition from those with the same failing. And sometimes I, too, would enter into the conversation, putting fingers to my lips, as they did, and found myself enjoying this new game, for words could be treacherous things, even lead to one's downfall as in Willie's case, when, in his cups, he allowed his tongue to get the better of him while I stayed dumb in a corner.

Yet little was I to know that same pretence of mine would change my fortunes. But before all of that came about we must make our way to the city, regretting, as I did, not taking up the Colonel's offer to travel with the company, at least as far as the port of Belfast.

The rest of that day she and I tramped along with nothing passing between us in the way of an exchange, even a glance. Her tears had long since dried, but she was sullen and locked up in herself, and as there is nothing worse than being in the company of a sulky woman, after a time I could bear it no longer.

'In God's good name, why didn't you stay with your little playmate back there when you had the chance, for I'd rather be on my own than along with some surly bitch poisoning the air?'

Halting on the instant, she turned on me. But before I could raise my hands, spitting like a wild cat, she came at me, her nails raking my face, so I dealt her a blow, knocking her back on her heels. But her rage being so hot, she retaliated, and throwing her down on the bank, I wrestled with her there, having forgotten she was as fierce as an animal when it came to taking affront.

Still, my appetite for the fray was not near as keen as her own, having no stomach for throttling her as I once would have done without thought or conscience, so I cried out, 'Bad cess to you, will you desist? It was your wish for us to stay together, not mine.'

But if I hoped this might pacify her, I was mistaken, for resorting to her teeth, didn't she bite me, and seeing the blood on my hand I took her around the throat, squeezing, fully determined on despatching her there and then, having put up with her craziness long enough, telling her, 'Be sure you won't be the first poxy jade I've hurried on her way to hell.'

Before I could carry out my intentions, however, wasn't she reprieved by the sound of wheels on the road, and I pulled her into the ditch, and as if the dread of being discovered was on her as well, she, too, crouched down, waiting for the carriage to draw near, a neat four-wheeler with a driver on its box, and a single horse between the shafts.

As it came closer I could see three men inside, two older than their companion, who, though seated, towered above them, dressed in black, and broad as a door, for I got a good look at him, and it was he, with the air of a preacher despite the great shaved head on him, I felt certain I would remember and not the others, a thin, pale, skinny individual, and a red-faced person about the same age in a billycock hat.

After they had gone, disentangling ourselves, we rose from the ditch without a word, for it seemed our recent tussle had taken all the fire and fury out of her, telling myself never in this wide world would I understand the workings of a woman, any woman, putting me in mind of my own wife, who had vanished after our trial as if she and I had never spent a day together, rumours reaching me she might even have fled the country to the one whose roads I now walked myself. But even if she chanced to turn up around the next bend, there would be no falling on one another's necks, affection of the sort common to other couples sharing a bed as well as a roof over their heads having no place between us, for like Burke and his woman it was more an exchange of blows and insults than any billing and cooing, and so now it looked as if I might have ended up with another younger version of the same, even if this one had only her teeth and fists to fight her corner with, unlike the other, who had a tongue that could flay the skin off one.

At the first crossroads, a choice of three routes lay before us. As neither of us could read what was on the fingerposts there I heeded the one pointing east as smoke was rising over the hills in that direction, and when the sun was low in the sky we reached the city's outskirts, and a more unwelcoming introduction to a place was ever likely to be seen, cabins, as far as the eye could travel, thrown up as if from the day before, with barefoot, bare-arsed weans tumbling about in the dirt, while from those same hovels their mothers stared out, heads covered with shawls like Romanys, recalling as it did the Scottish canal encampments when I laboured there, more like shelters for Hottentots than white people, even if our own faces were near as black with all the dust and stour of the digging.

Pushing on, we came to the dwellings of those more fortunate, yet not a great deal given the filth in the streets and the rows of ugly kitchen houses packed with noisy humanity, the voices of the people grating on the ear like a thousand corncrakes. And then, roaring away full pelt, great mills started rising up, and the girl and I walked in their shadow, gazing up at the chimneys, the names of their proprietors painted on them even though the letters were beyond our comprehension, at least my own, never having seen her with a book or a newspaper in her hand. But then she was still a riddle to me, the lack of a voice making her even more of one, for who could tell what other secrets lay in her past history.

In a street called Frederick Street, for we heard someone make mention of the name, we found lodgings, but only after I had shown the woman who owned the house the money the Colonel had placed in my hand that morning.

The small upstairs back room was not the worst I'd ever stayed in, but then I only craved a bed to lie down on, so weary were we after our journey, falling asleep the instant our heads touched the pillow, even though it felt stuffed with Belfast brick instead of straw, feathers and down being something I had only ever heard Burke speak of, like the time he was in the Donegal militia and a sergeant major's widow had taken him to her bed. But like so many of his tales, especially those concerning past love affairs, they were only fit for to go in one ear and out the other.

How long I slept was a mystery, shocked awake by a tremendous din going on outside the window, which I had left open on account of the noxious air due to the low-lying nature of the place. The roaring of the factories and the cries of the women who worked in them was enough to waken the dead, yet not the one lying alongside me, who appeared to have joined the deceased herself until I felt the damp heat of her, and so I decided to leave her as she was, for like those of her years she never could get enough of her bed. However, when I ventured into the streets, it looked as if most of the population up and about were the same age as herself.

Pouring into their places of work, these young hussies filled the air with their hoarse cries. Bold as brass, with linked arms, they pushed aside anyone or anything before them, and as a shouting wave came towards me I stood in a doorway to let them pass, and spotting me, one of them called out, 'Lookin' for a sweetheart? A kiss'll cost you tuppence, a coort a tanner,' and her friends screamed at her effrontery, and having heard tales of these young she-devils and how they would turn on a body as soon as look at you, I ducked down an entry with their cat-calls following me, away from where they ruled the streets at this early hour.

Prior to arriving here, the word was work was plentiful in the factories where linen was manufactured. But after seeing the hordes of young ladies from hell employed there I decided it would be safer to search out some other manner of earning a living, putting me in mind of breaking my fast, for I had eaten nothing for near a day and night, and the smell of new bread coming from the bakeries drew me to an eating-house where people were standing being served all manner of good things, rashers and eggs and chops and kidneys, while all I could afford was a saucer of tea and a Paris bun.

As was my habit by now, I pointed to the teapot, then the cakes, without having to explain myself, even though a tremendous hubbub was in the place, with all classes of people calling out their orders to the great sweating woman behind the counter exchanging quips and insults with her customers, for the people here are known to have a quick and ready tongue in their heads, and so it wasn't long before a man engaged me in conversation.

'I haven't seen *your* face in here before,' says he. Then, grinning, 'Whiskers, notwithstanding.'

'Sure there's no better barber than Archibald Brand in Fountain Lane,' another man joined in. 'Go on, feel for yourself. Smooth as a babby's backside.'

But, declining his invitation, I put a hand to my own face, then my lips, followed by a shake of the head, and the first man said, 'Forgive me, friend, I didn't know you suffered from an infirmity,' and the second man said, 'Aren't we all God's creatures, whether fully manned or not? Tell me, have you been to the Deaf and Dumb Institute on Peter's Hill? Even if you're passing through they'll attend to your wants whether great or small. Never let it be said the business folk of Belfast turned their back on those less fortunate than themselves.'

Having seen the state of some of those same 'unfortunates', I felt disinclined to agree. Yet keeping a still tongue in one's head had a lot to be said for it, and as all around me others' tongues were busily clacking away I wondered what it would be like pretending to have my ears stopped up as well.

But I supped my tea, and finally my two fellow diners left me in peace, departing for their places of work.

Out in the streets the early morning din and bustle had lessened considerably, and so I could wander freely without having to fight my way through the throngs of mill-women in their factory uniforms, coarse shifts of linen that left the arms bare to work the machines that thundered away as noisily as ever, prompting me to realise it was that that made them screech like parakeets, half-deafened as they were by the looms they served, and as I walked past the great mills on either side of me it seemed everyone was employed save myself in this city where work was God.

Yet, as I was to discover, the Almighty Himself was first and foremost in certain others' concerns, and soon a set of circumstances, as well as a stroke of luck, was to bring me into His Fold myself.

Still at a leisurely pace, for there was much to see, I moved on, marvelling at some of the fine buildings, for it would appear money was plentiful for those who controlled the city's commerce.

As for the girl, when she awoke she was smart enough to realise I would be back, for my bundle was where I'd left it. Yet it felt good not to have her dogging my heels at every step, and as the time went by I began to regret having to return for my belongings, meagre as they were.

Recalling what the man in the eating house had said about me needing a shave, I looked in a shop window, and seeing myself stare back from the glass like some bearded stranger, I stood half-transfixed until the proprietor came out, giving me a fierce glare, for his wares were women's dresses and bonnets when what I urgently required was to be found in a grocer's, not a haberdasher's, my insides hollow as a drum, and so a second time I was drawn towards the scent of food even though my pockets were near as empty as my stomach.

The smell of soup was what my nostrils detected, and the closer I came to where it simmered away the more my mouth watered. A ham bone to give it flavour, barley, marrow-fat peas, passed through my brain in a list, for my nose had become as keen as any hound's, and led by it I made my way on until I arrived at what looked like a meeting-house, doors thrown wide the better to let the heavenly aroma escape into the air.

However, like all such gifts from above, a price must always be paid, not in cash, of which I had none, but taking the Redeemer's shilling, as the army saying has it, and plucking hold of me by the arm, this person dressed like an undertaker invited me inside.

'Friend, you have the look of someone who could do with some nourishment. Never fear, everyone is welcome here no matter their faith or religion. Are you a papist by chance?'

Without thinking, in reply, I crossed myself, cursing my stupidity in ruining my chances of a bowl of decent broth. But in no way did it appear to discourage him, for growing even warmer he led me into the hall, where a row of men in greater need of a razor than myself were lined up at a long trestle table with a great black pot on a trivet sending out the smell that had drawn me to the place.

'Just as our Heavenly Lord and Master once fed the multitudes, we, too, in our own modest fashion endeavour to follow His example. Feel free to join your brothers in Christ and be served at His table, and afterwards, if you are of a mind, stay and give thanks to the One who embraces all, whether believer, heretic or heathen.'

As my own new-found religion was now to worship at the Great Stock-pot on Earth, I took my place, shuffling forward along with the others until I reached the front and was given a bowl, and after I had drained it to the last drop I had it filled for a second time.

In this hall were rows of wooden benches, and after we had been fed some of those present took their places there and I joined them, being curious about the people doling out the food and what lay behind their charity, for it has always been my belief nothing is ever free in this world, and maybe in the next as well, that's if there happens to be such a place. Certainly the one in the claw-hammer coat who had invited me in from the street believed so, for after the empty pot had been carried away by the woman serving us he rose to address us, Bible in his hand.

Yet what he had to say was nothing I hadn't heard in the Grassmarket, the same religious rigmarole urging us to change our wayward habits and accept the Saviour's love, just as earlier we had partaken of His bounty like it was manna from on high instead of plain kitchen broth.

For a good half-hour he sermonised us until I grew tired of hearing how we were all bound for the hot place, despite some of those around me half-asleep already. Yet it didn't seem to bother our host, a minister by the name of Dunwoody as I was to discover. Like all such reverend gents, he greatly enjoyed the sound of his own voice, every so often coming out with a prayer, and following the example of the others I bowed my head too, having decided to go along with this show as long as there was free food for the price of my presence. Finally a hymn was sung, and while most of the rest joined in I remained silent and afterwards as I was leaving Dunwoody approached me.

'Even if one is unfamiliar with the melody, it is still good to raise one's voice in some semblance of praise. Or do the words offend you, coming as you do from the other side?'

And so I performed my dumbshow for him, which was as easy as breathing by now.

'Are you a foreigner? A stranger to these shores?'

Once more I worked both hands, even waggling my tongue for good measure, until finally he said, 'Ah, so you are dumb. From birth, is it?'

This being something I hadn't considered, taking a gamble, I shook my head, and he said, 'Aye, indeed, a sudden shock in one's early years can sometimes result in such a disability. Yet the Good Lord Himself cured those whose voices had been taken from them. Believe me, miracles can still happen, if one's belief is strong enough. Here,' says he, pressing a piece of paper into my hand, 'take this and present it on your next visit. It will gain you admittance and more sustenance, not only for your body but your soul as well.'

So, with a full belly and a promise of more where that came from, I took to the streets again.

All around the din of industry carried on, and the people walking past seemed in as great a hurry as ever, while I dawdled with my thoughts, for if there was a place where soup and charity were doled out to people like myself there might be others as well, and if all you had to do was put on a poor mouth and swallow their message like their broth, money might also be forthcoming, enough to keep a person out of the gutter until finding his feet.

It put me in mind of John Fisher, my jailer in Calton lock-up, and how eager he was to draw me into the fold while slipping sops my way. This Dunwoody, too, seemed equally hungry for fresh souls, and never the one to let religion stand in my way, with spirits uplifted and a spring in my step, I decided to share my good fortune with the one I'd left sleeping in her bed, as together the pair of us might gather in an even richer harvest.

Back in the lodging house, she had the door barred, so I called out, 'It's me, let me in,' and she opened up, and wary of what to expect, for I still bore the marks of her teeth on me, I found her back in the bed with her face turned to the wall, which was worse than if she'd come at me like a banshee, preferring that to someone tearful and moping in the worst sort of womanly fashion.

'Our luck is in, for I have found a place where we can be fed free of charge and get money, too, if we play dumb as we have been doing.'

The part about the money was a shot in the dark, yet it was enough to bring her upright.

'All we need is show this bit of paper, and these people will dispense their bounty. Here, see.'

But whether she could read what was on it was another matter, and even if she did possess such skill, how could she inform me of its message anyway?

Unable to help myself didn't I start into the laughing, for it seemed a great joke the pickle we were in with our double shortcomings in the matter, but drawing back in the bed she looked at me as if I had lost my reason. So then I told her not to be alarmed as I was only celebrating our good fortune, and after a time she began smiling herself, and taking advantage of her good humour, like the dirty dog didn't I climb in alongside her, the bed being warm while the room was not, and it was like old times all over again when we enjoyed each other in Mistress Howland's barn, only it wasn't dry straw jagging our bare backsides but Ulster linen caressing them for a change.

The rest of the day we stayed lapped up together as the room was paid for and I was determined to get my money's worth. Or my bed companion's, I should say. But I was easy with the arrangement, herself holding the purse strings, even if they were well loosened by now, while being pleasured to her heart's content, so that by the time it was getting dark and the factory whistles were blowing for knocking-off time I was as hungry as a hunter all over again, as so must she be, having had nothing save the food of love since the day before.

'Come, make yourself look decent, for we don't want to appear more desperate than we can help.'

Turning the tables on me, she rubbed a palm across my cheek as if to say, what about yourself? And she was right, for my beard was as rough as a whin bush, and to my surprise didn't she produce a razor, and so I said, 'Did you rob that as well?'

Not a whit abashed, she started combing her hair with yet another toilet article she had in her possession, that bundle of hers more like a bottomless bag than some old rag of a thing tied at the neck with hay rope, and tempted as I was to have her spill the rest of its contents on the bed, I was in no real mind for an inventory just then, so I went to the basin the landlady had provided and shaved in cold water with a scrap of soap while she watched as if she'd never seen a man do such a thing before, and maybe she hadn't, given her innocence, and I scraped off as much growth as I was able, the cut-throat being dull as could be, yet something of a blessing if it crossed her mind to draw it across my thrapple while I slept, for I was still wary of her temper, having suffered the brunt of it previously.

And so, primed and primped for our venture, we set off for the gospel hall, and passing by several of the city's many public houses, open-doored and in full cry, some change here, thinks I to myself, bound for a place of religion instead of one of those same hostelries with the chance of a good brawl at the night's end of it.

A little way short of our destination, I said to the girl, 'Certain are you now you can carry off this business?' for I had explained to her what we must do, two sinners dumb as Balaam's ass, yet eager to repent.

Nodding, she put her hands to her mouth.

So then I told her, 'Very well. Just keep your eyes and your ears open and do like I do.'

However, as we got closer to the mission, it was the sound

of hymn-singing, not a smell of soup that greeted us, and when we arrived at the place and I presented my paper to a different person at the door this time, the hall inside was filled with worshippers very different from the desperate and destitute of the morning, Dunwoody beaming down from his pulpit on a new congregation, men in Sunday go-to-meeting suits, their wives in feathered hats, a smell of money and good living rising off all of them, while at the back, apart, stood a row of souls like ourselves, and we joined them, and knowing what was going through the girl's head, I gave her a look urging patience, and when the singing finished we sat down alongside the rest.

'Brothers and sisters, as the Scriptures tell us, the wages of sin are death. But before that fate awaits certain of those amongst us, I say to you, you can still be saved from the scorching fires of hell if you repent and beg forgiveness for every iniquity either contemplated or committed ...'

And so it went on, all those hypocrites sucking on Dunwoody's message like it was mother's milk, until it came to me he wasn't preaching to the converted, but to us on the sinners' bench, which was why we were there, not to take his soup, but sit with bowed heads while the rest took pity on us for being what they were not.

Alongside me was a man about my own age in what looked like a hand-me-down off the back of one of those same do-gooders, and suddenly, rising to his feet, he started shouting, 'Hallelujah! Hallelujah!'

Yet, instead of showing him the door as he deserved, for I could smell drink on him, Dunwoody cried out, 'Come, brother, testify, and let us hear once more the wondrous story of your deliverance from the Great Serpent himself. For as the snake led our first forebears down the path of sin in the Garden, so he still strives to coat us with his slime. Indeed, he might well be in very this room this instant waiting to wrap the unwary and weak in his coils and tentacles.'

Some of the ladies present shrieked at this, while their husbands put on their bravest faces, and surveying the lot of them, thinks I to myself, these gulls are ripe for the plucking, and when the one alongside me commenced spewing out a catalogue of every bad thing he had ever turned his hand to before seeing the Blessed Light, with barely a morsel of truth in the entirety of it, in my estimation, what a tale I could tell myself, I thought, and one that would make the same gent on his feet sound like a teller of bedtime stories for little children.

Still, that was where he had the advantage of me, cursed by not being able to open my mouth, and didn't his friends follow after him until the place rang out with their own confessions, those in the good seats at the front becoming more agitated with each fresh history, Dunwoody waving his Bible about like he was smiting Old Nick himself, and when it was all over the girl and me were left to the side while the ones giving their testimony, as they called it, were doled out their reward, not just soup, but all manner of fine victuals, even sweetmeats, served by the well-off ladies with their own dainty gloved hands.

The smell of the food was making the girl and me feel faint, so the pair of us went up to the big long table, near cleared by now by the flock of human gannets there before us.

Dunwoody was standing alongside it, and when we came forward he gave me a look very different from the one he had met me with earlier that day.

'In our nets this night we have gathered in a mighty haul of sinners willing to give themselves over to the Redeemer's love. By confessing their shortcomings they have reaped their own bountiful harvest of redemption. Are you yourself prepared to join them?'

Nodding my head as eagerly as I could, I signalled, oh, I was, truly I was. But still he fixed me with the same quizzical look.

'And is this young woman with you also ready to testify?'

I wanted to say, give her a morsel of grub and she'll dance a jig for you, as will I. But all I could do was point to her mouth, then my own.

'Is she similarly afflicted? If so, may the Lord have pity on you. Never fear, return tomorrow and there will be nourishing soup for both of you.'

Close as I was to taking him by the collared throat, I swallowed my rage and left the place with the girl at my heels, and out in the street I saw the man who had been rewarded for his story with a fine feed of ham and sausages, eggs and oaten bread, for I had taken a keen note of what had been denied us.

Tipping me a wink, he gestured for us to follow him around the corner, and setting himself down on a low wall there invited us to do likewise, and if there was ever proof a full stomach could make a great change in a person, here it was, for he was as merry as a cricket when half an hour previously he was crying out about his past career of sin with a croak in his voice and tears in his eyes.

'Why didn't you give them the fine song and dance like me? Haven't I been livin' high on the hog these past two months? Sure, they can't get enough of debauchery and backsliding, especially the women. Wring their heartstrings, as well as their loins, and you'll be fed like a fightin' cock. Here,' and taking a paper parcel from under his coat, 'have this for your supper, for I'm already full as a badger,' and the girl and me fell on the meat pie he offered us.

Watching us devour it, he grinned.

'No need for thanks. Sure, wouldn't you do the same for me any time?'

Bringing my dumbshow into play once more I nodded back, and he said, 'Ah, well, it looks like it's only the broth and gruel for you two. A pity, for I'd dearly love to hear the young lady's secrets. I'm sure she has a good few tucked away under that chemise of hers,' laying a hand on her knee.

Yet even though I was an instant away from knocking him from his perch, I wanted no trouble, and as we got up to leave, he said, 'Only a miracle will get the pair of you a decent diet in this place, barring the lassie puttin' her talents to some other use on the street.'

Making our way back to Frederick Street and our room there, I began to notice other places of worship, some great, some like the one we'd left, and it came to me people here had only two things of import in life, making money and going to church, and as we walked along I began to turn over in my head some way I might employ the two to benefit us, and by the time I climbed the stairs to our room the first glimmerings of a scheme was taking shape in my head, the man on the wall having said only a miracle would save the pair of us from starvation, and even though he was making a joke of it, he had planted the word in my head.

'Tomorrow night you and me will go back to that hall, and this time I promise you we will fill both our bellies. Are you listening?'

And turning to me in the bed, she put her hand on me under the sheet, which was I suppose as a good a way of saying yes as any.

Ballymena ✖ *County Antrim*

THESE PAST SEVERAL DAYS Jack Slack and I have accompanied Mr De Quincey on his quest for material for his article on the curious goings-on in these parts, and for someone so puny and light of frame he seems tireless, eyes bright as stars, recording every anecdote he draws from these people with their taste for 'hard blow', as it's referred to hereabouts. Attracted to the subject on account of his own addiction no doubt, so far he hasn't attempted drinking any himself, for it is highly dangerous and damaging to those who indulge in the practice. He calls them 'etheromaniacs' after their choice of 'poison', far cheaper than alcohol and readily available from grocers, druggists and doctors short of patients.

Before arriving in this backwater he enlisted the services of a local subscriber to *Blackwood's*, an admirer of his work, a priest by the name of Mulcahy, not only offering himself as guide and interpreter, for to an English ear the local accent is as hard to follow as Bengali or Burmese, but allowing the three of us the run of his parochial house, bed and board supplied by his housekeeper, a Miss Nora McCartney, who has taken a great shine to Mr Slack, waylaying him at every opportunity with tasty titbits and offerings of one kind or the other.

'Sure a fine strong man such as yourself requires feedin' on a grand scale entirely. By the time you leave here, if I have the way of it, you'll be as well padded out as the Prince Regent himself,' as if our mighty friend needed even a superfluous ounce on that tremendous frame of his, already the wonder of every cabin we peered into led by our noses, the fumes of the ether being impossible to disguise. Not that the drinkers appear concerned in the least to conceal their habit, for it is as widespread as any other vice, as our priest acquaintance terms it, fully determined, as he is, to stamp it out.

'This deadly craving for a few short-lived moments of oblivion is destroying our entire community. Families are going without food or clothing while the breadwinner lies helpless on his back clutching a glass of the vile stuff. Men in this parish, not yet forty, already beaten wizened wrecks, are only fit for the asylum or the workhouse. I pray to God, Mr De Quincey, your article will move the authorities to ban this foul substance, making it only available to the medical profession and those using it for its proper purpose.'

To his credit De Quincey looked a trifle shamefaced, torn as he was between his own attachment to an equally notorious relaxant and reassuring his host.

'My dear sir, I am here merely as an observer wishing to throw light on the phenomenon, which I feel certain will provoke great discussion and debate once the piece is published.'

The Reverend Father appeared satisfied by this, although whether his guest was being totally sincere with him was another matter, and later when the priest had gone off to deliver yet another of his fierce sermons on the subject, De Quincey unburdened himself.

'Our clerical friend is, of course, rightly passionate in his crusade and has scientific reason on his side, but the irony remains he and his fellow agitators are the ones responsible for the very thing they wish to put down, as the present temperance movement is to blame for the public houses being forced to close their doors while the illegal distillers in the hills have been harried to near extinction. Human nature being what it is, so an alternative was sought, and one which has been in use long before the ether drinkers of these parts came to my attention. But, then, you, my dear Speed, must have had some first-hand experience yourself in your forays into the opium dens of Wapping and Shoreditch. Tell me, have you heard of a substance called Hoffman's Drops?'

I confessed I had not.

'They were first prescribed as a tonic for women suffering from depression, and so while their menfolk did their drinking, they themselves indulged privately in their own genteel form of intoxication, three parts alcohol, one part our old friend ether. So even your fine ladies of Mayfair and Kensington enjoyed the pleasures of inebriation, although not quite in the uncouth manner of our farm labourer in County Antrim, thus proving my contention most mortals, even the most exemplary, can quite easily fall under the spell of some form of addiction, otherwise existence would be as flat and stale as water in a ditch.'

It was clear he was intent on getting an argument out of us, his eyes brimming with mischief, already having taken three draughts of his own particular tincture. At such times his entire body seems to shake and shudder with the demands of his intellect, whereas Mr Slack and I are as two clods with barely a word to throw back at him, being tired tramping from one bothy to another hearing those within testify to their debilitating habit even if Father Mulcahy had to translate most of what they had to say on the subject.

'Come, Speed, what is it that makes your own blood race, your cranium buzz?'

'We can't all be at full pitch most of the time.'

He laughed.

'Like myself, you mean? No, I wouldn't wish to prescribe my narcotic friend here for everyone, least of all someone requiring steely control and a clear head in pursuit of his line of work.'

'Those days are over.'

'Yet they were heady and exhilarating ones. Perhaps that is *your* addiction, Percival Speed, the chase, the running to ground, that final confrontation.'

Mr Slack rose to go.

'If you gentlemen will excuse me, I'll seek my rest and leave you to your conversation.'

After he had gone De Quincey remarked, 'Even the great Jack Slack himself has an indulgence of his own, reliving the bloody battles of the prophets as opposed to those in the grass ring.'

'You appear to know a great deal about the pair of us, even after such a brief acquaintanceship.'

Rising and going to a cabinet, he proceeded to take out a whiskey bottle.

'As I cannot persuade you to join me in a glass of the ruby nectar, at least will you take a glass of our host's finest Bushmills? Come, indulge a poor insomniac and keep him company.'

More mellow than its Scottish counterpart, the malt was surprisingly easy on the palate, and so I prepared to listen and be entertained, although it seemed he was more intent on getting *me* to talk, and whether it was the whiskey or the heat of the fire, or a combination of both, I began to relax, recounting some of the cases I had solved in the past, even voicing theories of my own on the detection process, such as people being the sum of their parts with certain aspects of their inner life being imprinted on their features.

'And did the life mask of our friend betray *his* inner life?'

'Possibly. Yet I still must confront him, watch him breathe, see him move.'

'Hear him speak, too?'

'Well, I know his accent is Irish, coming from these parts as he does.'

He looked at me over the rim of his glass, refreshed yet again from his own little bottle alongside my own much larger amber-coloured one.

'And if and when this fateful encounter takes place, what then?'

Noting the look on my face, he laughed.

'Aye, there's the rub, for with the law on his side, you're still powerless to lay a hand on him, so that moment of triumph, of gratification, is denied you.'

'Those are *your* words, not mine.'

'So why proceed, then?'

'Because it is what I am paid to do. Isn't that what you, yourself, are here for?'

Suddenly he looked drawn, as though exhausted, the laudanum no longer supplying the energy required to confound as well as dazzle, and so I told him, 'I think I, too, will make my way to my bed. It's been a long day.'

But before I could set down my glass, reaching forth, he clasped my wrist, a pitiful look on his pale face.

'Please, I beg of you, indulge a poor scribbler with a modicum more of your company.'

There was something strangely pathetic about the man slumped in his chair, so I took pity on him, and he continued, 'My work here is almost complete. All the material I require is in this notebook,' pointing to a small, leather-bound journal on the table by his side which never left him and in which he jotted down his observations wherever he went. In its pages, I suspected, there might well be even some concerning Mr Slack and myself, possibly this very conversation, transcribed at a later date and reworked for his own journalistic ends.

'So I take it, then, you will be travelling on to Edinburgh and not rejoining Lord Massereene?'

'My dear Speed, life among the leisured classes and their like quickly begins to pall. Also I have been far too long absent from family and friends, which I suspect also applies to yourself.'

'You forget I am a widower.'

'Indeed I do not. I was referring more to the society of those like your employer in Bath.'

'Lord Beckford and I met only the once, and that was on a professional and purely business footing.'

'But you have since been in correspondence with him?'

'Not recently. The distance separating us may have something to do with it.'

'You are convinced of that, are you?'

Annoyed at what I felt was presumption, I rose to go, but in the instant he was all fulsome apologies.

'My dear Speed, please don't be offended, I merely wish to be of service, being privy to certain information connected with this commission of yours. Your employer back in England may not have relayed his most recent instructions to your good self, but he *has* corresponded with his friend the Viscount on the subject.'

Detecting a whiff of treachery, I dropped back in my chair determined to hear more.

'According to the contents of this particular communication, Beckford, it now would appear, has lost all further interest in Hare, and intends to abandon the pursuit along with your own involvement in the matter. This change of heart may have been influenced by his noble friend's antipathy towards Mr Slack and yourself after his champion's humiliation, and knowing these people and their kind I can well imagine that to be the case.'

My initial shock at hearing this had now become cold anger compounded with disgust that something like this could happen to someone who had always prided himself on being nobody's fool, and as though guessing what was going through my head, De Quincey said, 'Take some comfort from the fact that I too have been used and on occasions abused by these same people. As a class, on account of their power and influence, they are fickle in their pursuit of diversion, toying with people as well as their livelihoods.'

A brief pause followed while he observed me intently.

'And so now the cat is out of the bag, as it were, I take it you will be calling a halt to your enquiries?'

'Not until I receive my final quittance in writing,' I told him, and before I could raise a hand to deter him he had poured me out another good inch of whiskey.

'But what if there is to be no letter, no correspondence? How far would you persevere in this thankless quest? Until your expenses run out?'

'Those are well-nigh exhausted already.'

'And what of Mr Slack? Do you propose telling him of your intentions?'

Truth be told, I was beginning to feel a trifle drunk, while still unable to fathom just why this person opposite should be so concerned about something that by reason or logic shouldn't involve him.

But then, leaning forward, face ablaze, he pleaded, 'Allow me to help you in your efforts, for can't you see you have planted a murderer in this head of mine. Faceless, he may be, a wraith, yet he has taken up residence there, and so you and I, we must flesh him, flush him out if we are to have any peace.'

Growing more and more agitated, he was now on his feet, pacing about, clutching his glass as though it might break.

'Look, I, too, have funds. Not as much as Beckford, certainly, but easily sufficient for our purposes.'

But I had heard enough, my head swimming, not merely with our host's whiskey but with all I had learned to my cost and confusion this evening, and seeing I was intent on going, finally he fell back in his chair.

'Forgive me, I have burdened you more than I should for one night. Take away what I have said and in the morning we will talk further, that's if you still wish it. But I give you my solemn word you will not be subjected to any further verbal battery.'

Next day I awoke to the sound of Miss McCartney preparing breakfast for Mr Slack and myself in the kitchen below. The clatter of pots and pans and the patter of her feet on the tiled floor set off a throbbing in my head, and I lay vainly trying to keep my thoughts at bay before they came crowding in like a pack of creditors demanding their dues. Both Mr Slack and the housekeeper were early risers, as was I, so fighting the demons inside my skull, and after a splash of cold water and the rub of a cloth, I went downstairs to join them.

'Eat up, gentlemen, for you'll need the benefit of it hunting down more of Father Mulcahy's and Mr De Quincey's hopeless cases. I only pray their combined efforts will save some of them before the gates of hell slam finally shut in their faces. A religious man yourself, sir, are you, like your friend here? You'll forgive me, Mr Slack, if accidentally I happened on some of your bedtime reading material attending to your room. It does you great credit, and you'll surely have your reward alongside the blessed saints, unlike them sad creatures pouring poison down their throats.'

There seemed no way of stopping her, for we were both captors in her domain, and could only listen while she heaped more food on our plates.

'Once the craving takes hold it grows like a canker until there's no curtailing it. As for the way they go about their foul habit, first they swallow a great mouthful of spring water, then a tablespoon of the stuff, which creates this almighty rift of wind in their insides, which if it doesn't get out will be the mortal end of them. Sure a man in this very parish went to light his pipe after a dose and if it wasn't for somebody with a jug of water to pour down his gullet and quench the fire he would have gone to his Maker a lot sooner than anticipated.'

Luckily there arrived a blessed lull in this lurid account, and taking advantage of it I informed her Mr De Quincey had completed his researches and was ready to depart.

'And yourself and Mr Slack along with him, is it?'

I told her, indeed so, as we had some business of our own to attend to in another place.

'More poor wretches beyond the reach of redemption, is it?'

I looked at Mr Slack, who by now had pushed back his plate, and told her, 'One only in this case, as it so happens.'

Sighing deeply, for she had grown more and more attached to Slack as the days progressed, she left to change our bedlinen, and he and I were alone, and after a time he enquired, 'So we are ready to move on from this place, our present dealings with Mr De Quincey concluded?'

'He may still be accompanying us.'

'Having business of his own in Belfast?'

'No, it seems he has become interested in our own venture himself.'

I could see he was displeased, and it was in his voice when he said, 'With the object of writing one of his articles, I take it.'

'Not necessarily.'

But he had voiced something I had managed to put out of my head in my desire to rescue our project, so plunging in, I said, 'I have something I must tell you which determines what you and I do next.'

After I had reported everything I had learned the previous evening while he was up in his room with his own concerns, we sat facing one another across the scrubbed kitchen table while the clock on the wall seemed to measure out the ever-widening gap between us.

Finally, I said, 'Jack, I have decided to continue with this undertaking of ours even without Lord Beckford's sanction or support, for I have expended too much time and effort to walk away now, when I believe we are within closing distance of a resolution.'

'And if that resolution should fail to appear?'

Having shot my bolt, I was unable to answer as I scarce knew myself.

'Very well,' said he, 'you must follow your conscience, as indeed must I. But, as ever, my first allegiance is to my employer.'

'But what if he has forfeited that trust by ending our contract? Hear it from the lips of the person above our heads right now.'

In my heart, however, I knew it was hopeless, despite De Quincey's attempts to smooth away even the tiniest fragment of the other's noble granite with liquid charm and a silver tongue, and so we both rose, shaking hands.

'Jack,' I said, and he replied, 'Percy,' as plain and simple a farewell as could be, yet two words never contained such a depth of respect and affection.

Later that afternoon we took a carriage, all three of us, for Slack would be travelling to the city to make the crossing to the mainland and then south from where he had come at the start of our venture, and as we set out the mood was a sombre one, the same dreary countryside streaming past, same clusters of cabins we had peered into, same ragged children and desperate-looking women around the doors with invariably, as we now knew, the man of the house within with a vial of his 'medicine' to hand.

Earlier in the day, when I informed De Quincey I would accept his offer, he seemed more concerned about Slack's future movements than our own.

'But will he be able to resume his duties as before, and, on a more delicate matter, has he the wherewithal to make his way back to Bath?'

'Jack Slack is his own man and is more than able to stand on his own feet.'

'But you will miss him.'

'More than you can imagine.'

When we were within viewing distance of those familiar pillars of factory smoke rising high above the city's circle of blue-green hills, De Quincey raised the subject yet again, but with the person concerned sitting directly opposite this time.

'Mr Slack, despite you and I only being acquainted a few short days, I have been mightily impressed by your commitment to this present mission of Mr Speed's, and even though it appears it must now proceed without your services I should like you to know I would much prefer it otherwise.'

A lengthy silence followed, and not until our driver was taking us past the first rows of thatched dwellings on the outskirts of Ligoniel, as it is known, did the big man facing us offer a reply.

'Sir, complimentary as your comments may be, yet I must still follow the promptings of "that still small voice within", as the Scriptures have it.'

Which appeared to be the end of it, and so when we arrived at our destination and our lodging house there, I told him, 'Our driver will convey you to the docks, where you will be able to arrange a sea crossing at your own convenience.'

But to De Quincey's and my own immense surprise, instead he got out, gesturing for his traps to be handed down to him.

'You intend walking? But the coachman has already been paid and is at your disposal along with the carriage.'

'There is no need, for I no longer require either.'

Even more perplexed, we stared at him, for where did he intend going, if not to the waterside and the next vessel leaving there?

'In the name of all that's sensible, Jack, what are you about?'

For a moment he regarded us with the same unflinching expression, before replying, 'Despite escaping justice in this world, a transgressor must still pay for his sins in the next. Even so, it remains our Christian duty to ensure those who commit murder are made to confront their crimes. So if you gentlemen are still of a mind for me to join you, I will continue to offer my services in the hunting down of this man.'

'Bravo!' applauded De Quincey. 'And if you will permit me to paraphrase something I feel certain you are also familiar with, "a threefold cord is not quickly broken", Ecclesiastes, four, twelve.'

As for myself, still bemused by this fresh turn of events, I said nothing, for welcome though it sounded, I still wondered how it might yet affect the unfolding of the next instalment in the tracking down of the devilish and elusive Mr William Hare.

Last night I had this bad dream, as instead of being in my bed in our Belfast woman's lodging house, I was in the pitch dark in what seemed to be a wooden cask of some kind, knees drawn up to my chin, as tightly wedged in as herring in a barrel, and when I called out in my sleep my bed companion put her hand over my mouth for fear I would be heard, and so I then awoke, and it came to me what the dream was about, as one time when call for our merchandise was at a near-unreasonable demand Willie proposed we should import fresh bodies from our own country, where there was a glut, and they could be kept in brine until Knox and his apprentices took possession of them.

Being drunk at the time he was mightily fired up with the idea, stamping his feet on the floor, and even though there was only the pair of us present I urged caution for he was raising his voice, not caring who might hear and, as was also the case when the whiskey was talking, he started upbraiding me for being a hindrance to him, yoked together the pair of us, and if it wasn't for him I would still be hawking the streets with an ass and cart instead of having money in my pocket and an idle life of it like one of the swells promenading in the Grassmarket.

Yet it still was my roof over his head, I reminded him, and he was my lodger, like his wife. But he laughed it off, insulting me further, and if I had been near as drunk as himself I might well have grappled with him on the bed, but instead that was the night Mary Paterson was sold for ten pounds to Doctor

Knox, who kept her for a good while in a barrel like the ones Burke proposed shipping over from Ireland.

And so lying there, I recalled Willie saying how the two of us were like chalk and cheese, himself the quick and venturesome one, and me slow and over-cautious like in that old fable of the tortoise and the hare, except on account of my name it should have been the other way around. But still in a sweat on account of the bad dream, I was in no mood for amusement.

Nevertheless, Willie was the one who had his neck stretched, and I was not, determined as I was instead to turn my fortunes about without any advice, mocking or otherwise, from that dead quarter, and the way forward as I saw it was through the front door of Dunwoody's gospel hall, where I must make my mark alongside that other collection of would-be penitents with their past transgressions, a favourite word of the pastor's, along with corruption and depravity, and given half a chance I would provide him with sufficient of all three as would keep him and his followers happy for a good twelvemonth.

However, two obstacles stood in the way of a full stomach and money in my pouch. One, I would need to confess my crimes, but two, I was supposed to be dumb like the one warming the bed right now beside me, and so the more I pondered on it the more despondent I became, trapped, it would appear, by a pretence of my own making.

Although it was still early I rose and made my way down the stairs, keeping as quiet as I could, being behind with the rent and the Protestant woman of the house starting to lose patience despite our joint afflictions. At this hour the street was like a grave, the factory horns not yet calling the workers to their looms, and it was as if I had the city to myself, the sky in the east barely changing colour from grey to a pale rosy tint. Ahead lay the port and with no real purpose in mind I bent my steps in that direction, the crying of the gulls guiding me through the narrow lanes leading to the sea and the ships lying there.

There was a smell of tar and fish and bilge water, but idling along the quays my nose caught another scent, that of cooking coming from one of the vessels moored at the quayside, the flag flying from its mast blue and white with a stripe, but the name on the side upside down for all I could tell.

It could have been the hunger affecting me, but I stood stock still, taking in the aroma of frying rashers wafting down like very manna itself, except this was more real and nourishing than the Reverend Dunwoody's heavenly variety, and after a time someone leaned over the rail and called down, 'Good morning and good day to you, Irishman. Tell me, have you a sister?'

The shock as well as rudeness of it knocked me back apace, and seeing my expression, the man laughed.

'Don't take offence, friend, but it's my habit to ask everyone that, for sometimes fortune smiles on a poor sailor hungry for female company. After all, if a man doesn't ask he will never receive. Am I not right?'

Small in stature, he had a face like a monkey. Indeed, all the appearance of one, like Bongo in the travelling show, for *he* also had a brass ring in his ear and smoked cigars. But this one had the advantage of reasonable English in spite of being foreign.

'What do they call you, Irishman?'

Already my hand was edging towards my mouth to explain my lack of a voice, a motion now as natural as breathing itself. But, instead, I heard myself reply, 'Bernard Black,' the sudden surprise of it causing me to near choke, and the little ship's cook, for that was what he was, said, 'Come aboard and take something for that dry throat of yours, Irishman.'

And truly it was my lucky day, for not only did he offer me a dram of some foreign firewater but a generous dish of fried ham, which he told me was for the crew as he was forbidden to eat of the pig on account of his religion, for although the ship was a Greek one he himself was Turkish and the Turks were a hospitable race the same as the Irish, he said.

While he continued with his cooking in his cubbyhole of a galley, barely bigger than a closet, I gorged myself not knowing where my next meal might be coming from, and he remarked, 'In my country we have a saying. A full stomach and a willing woman are riches indeed. Have you a woman yourself, Irishman?'

I shook my head, and he sighed.

'Ah, then we are indeed brothers, you and I. But, tell me, if a man has money can he find some agreeable female company in this place?'

'Where sailors are, such a thing is always possible.'

'Cooks, also?'

'Tin's the same no matter whose pocket it comes from.'

'Tin?'

'Gold, silver, copper.'

Without another word, going to a cupboard, he took out a wooden box and proceeded to empty it on the table, and there spread for my consideration was a hoard of notes and coins, none of which happened to be currency in the country we were in. But boodle is boodle no matter whose face is decorating the front of it.

'Some of these same agreeable ladies, might they be known to you, Irishman?'

The riches heaped now in front of me looked near as tempting as those dangled before the Redeemer Himself in the desert that time. But the one in the parable which Dunwoody had used as his text only the night before was the Lord, while I was this mere mortal without a sou to his name, and so I told him I might be acquainted with someone like that after all.

'And might she be young, well favoured, clean?'

'All of those,' I said, and taking my hand, he kissed it.

'Irishman, I have not been near a woman since leaving the port of Piraeus three long months ago, and no matter how sweet his mouth might be, a boy in a barrel can never take the place of the real thing. If you can accommodate me in this matter I will be happy to share my good fortune with my shipmates, for they have money as well, and so your lady friend will be richly rewarded for her favours. But now you must go, for I must prepare the captain's breakfast. Here, take this as a sign of my good intent,' presenting me with a parcel of more of the food I'd had earlier, along with a loaf of bread and some hard, bitter-tasting berries with stones in them which I later found were something called olives, but not to my liking, nor my companion's, either, for that matter.

Making my way back to her, I told myself what I had promised my little foreigner had all the prospects of a happy outcome, for even if she required some persuasion to accommodate him and his friends, the rewards for an hour or so of her time would be enough to keep the pair of us in victuals and shelter for a month, even longer. As for any reluctance on her part, I remembered her hawking her honeypot on the streets of Whitehaven, and walking on with my parcel under my arm I wondered whether a fresh line of business might not be opening up for me providing flesh to those requiring it, yet young and still alive this time with no bother from the law at the other end of it.

So in lively mood, and with a good round belly on me for a change, I returned to Frederick Street, and when she saw the prize I had brought with me she became all loving and tender, me telling her, 'Sure isn't there more where that came from, as well as money,' and when she gazed at me seeking further information, with a wink I told her, 'All good things come to them that wait,' and she laughed, not knowing what lay ahead of her, and so instead of going to Dunwoody's gospel meeting that evening the pair of us set out together in another direction.

But the nearer we got to the water and the craft berthed there the more I held fire about telling her what was in store for her on one of those same ships, and the more my mind ran on her giving herself over to the little Turk and his shipmates the slower my feet dawdled on the cobbles.

Already I could see the ship's striped ensign standing out from the rest of the flags, for this port of Belfast, as I'd discovered, was as busy in its overseas trade as those on the far side of water I'd come from. So then I thought of all the other seafarers in heat presently anchored there like the Turk, but kept on board, for that was their captain's orders, he'd said, thus needing the services of a pander like the fat Englishman in the beaver hat in Whitehaven, who for his impudence had ended up in the tide arse over tip with his hat bobbing alongside him.

And so unable to delay the business any longer it was on the tip of my tongue to tell her we were invited on board a ship for some entertainment and all she need do was be pleasant and accommodating in return. The words as I say were on my lips, but before I could come out with them, taking hold of her by the arm, instead didn't I move her further on along the quay away from temptation, for what had entered my head was Willie and me with Mary Paterson that time, her, also, not knowing what was in store for her, and the thought of the one by my side being ravaged and rummaged made me turn on my heel, even if good money was to be lost on account of it.

So I told her I must have taken a wrong turning after all, but we were still in good time for the evening gospel meeting where there would be food and something to help it down, and she seemed to swallow it like the notion of nourishment itself.

Travelling back, our route took us past a parcel of the city's whores parading for custom, and it came to me I might still be recompensed for my trouble if I could get one of them to return to the ship with me. But just as earlier I'd shied away from dealing in quim, I had still no interest in the trade, and in my head thought I heard my old colleague chiding me for going soft over some young thing near half my years, having neither means, nor a voice to her name, and letting it suck the very marrow and evil intent out of me.

However, that was the very night I was to prove him wrong, hitting on as cute a trick as ever he and I manufactured together, and, best of all, with no murder at the end of it.

By the time me and the girl arrived at the hall, Dunwoody's crusade, as it was called, was going at full blast, the place packed with seekers after salvation eager to enjoy other people's misfortune not having any of their own. A hymn was being sung, and under cover of the noise the pair of us slipped into seats near the back alongside as scabby a crowd of black-guards and scam merchants as ever you'd wish to avoid.

As a member of the same fraternity myself, but doing my best to hide it, I kept my head down, putting on the poor mouth, as the saying has it, for, unlike certain of my coun-trymen, tugging the forelock never bothered me, even though I would still derive pleasure from clapping a hand over the mouth and nose of those same whited sepulchres at the front and keeping it there, better them than some of the other poor divils I once despatched for profit.

Still, this was neither the time nor place for any of that, so instead I waited for the food to appear. But, as ever, a price had to be paid for forbearance, and shortly after the first confes-sions started ringing out like the cries from Hades itself, and getting hungrier by the minute, me and the girl sat there, for if this riff-raff were singing for their supper any crumbs falling to us would barely feed an ant, and praying the thing would soon be at an end I kept my eye on the one on the platform with the Good Book in his hand.

'Brothers, sisters, once again we have all heard yet another outpouring of remorse from those who have strayed from the proper path of righteousness, and we pray they receive the balm of forgiveness for the wounds they have inflicted on them-selves as well as others. Yet even if tonight's harvest has been a bountiful one, other sheaves still remain to be gathered in.'

And here he sent his gaze roving out over the heads of the faithful to where we sinners sat on the hard seats at the back, and it seemed to me he had his eye fixed on me and my companion when he announced, 'Let the halt, the lame, and those afflicted by the loss of their speech come forward unto me,' and so I felt like heading for the door, having no desire to be made a holy show of for this crowd of forked-tongued liars and hypocrites.

But it was the one by my side he had his sights set on, for, next minute, all heads turning in her direction, he cried out, 'You, yes, you, with the fiery red hair, stand up and come forward to His Table.'

For an instant I felt sure he intended feeding her before the rest of us, and so must she, for, rising from her place, didn't she make her way to the front, where he stood, arms outstretched, and taking her by the hand helped her up on to the platform, and there she remained gazing about her like she was dumbfounded, as in very truth she was.

'Sister, be not afraid, for your defect only makes you more precious in the eyes of the Saviour.'

Now, whether it was the heat of the moment or everyone looking at her, expecting her to perform in some fashion, didn't she start into humming and hawing, and the vermin sitting alongside me took to laughing, making mock of her, and losing my temper I rose to defend her, and pointing his finger, Dunwoody cried, 'Behold, yet another mute witness is himself called to the Mercy Seat!'

But the anger still had a hold on me and it erupted in a bellow of rage, and it was like the roof itself had come in, only down on my own head, as the chances of our eating in that place now seemed about as meagre as the flesh hanging off both our sets of ribs. Yet instead of being banished into eternal darkness for being the right pair of fakers, didn't Dunwoody cry out, 'Hallelujah! Rejoice and give thanks to the One who has made possible this two-fold heaven-sent intervention. Not only has our young sister here been miraculously granted the gift of speaking in tongues, but her relative has had his own larynx loosened as well.'

And next minute wasn't I up alongside him and the girl, mouthing along to some hymn tune the words of which were as double Dutch. But who was I to quibble when fortune had smiled so unexpectedly on me, and by the look of things might continue to do so as long as I supplied these Belfast holy fools with what they hungered after, even it was to give them nightmares.

The Commercial Hotel, Belfast ✖ 10 July

HAVING QUIZZED THE PEOPLE here as to whether anyone
has been enquiring after us, and receiving no joy in the matter,
the hunt for our quarry seems to be thrown back yet again,
and so we can do nothing but wait in the hope that Dermot
the coachman I enlisted to scout for us will still show his face.
As for the hotel, it's a decent enough place, the proprietress
a Mrs Abigail Bunting, who takes more than a keen interest
in her guests with accents different from her own, especially
Mr Slack.

As ever, he retains his customary dignified composure,
reading in his bedroom, or in the little downstairs parlour
apart from the taproom where the local business folk gather
and conspire, Mammon being worshipped assiduously here,
to which the many fine new manufactories rising from the
city's sloblands bear testimony. But churches, too, are in
the ascendant, De Quincey informing us that a veritable tide
of fervour and revival is currently flooding every home and
hamlet throughout the entire province.

'As a staunch Christian, Mr Slack, surely you yourself must
be tempted to observe what is taking place here in this corner
of our commonwealth, respectable men and women falling
down insensible in the street, hardened criminals crying out for
forgiveness, entire classes of little children beating their tiny
breasts, housewives rending and throwing off their garments
in public, for, unfortunately, there has been a deal of unbridled,
even lewd behaviour in some of the remote country parts ...'

The more he appeared to revel in it, the more I began to

doubt the wisdom of involving him in our present project, being first and foremost a scribbler forever casting about for fresh material for his pen. Yet he had given his word he was prepared to put his money where his all too ready mouth was, and so I enquired, 'Well, Jack, do you intend seeing some of these happenings for yourself?'

We were in the sitting-room at the time taking tea, which already had set us apart as oddities in this city, where only spinster ladies drink from china.

'Remember you are under no obligation to restrict yourself to what brings us here.'

'If you can spare me, and Mr De Quincey wishes me to accompany him, naturally I will be happy to place myself at his disposal.'

Delighted by this, De Quincey clapped his pale hands.

'Nothing would give me greater gratification than to have my own personal "muscular Christian" at my back on these occasions.'

As he said this I glanced at Slack and he sent me a look in return and it seemed to me we were in accord as to our opinion of this little patron of ours, and so I debated whether I might not have exchanged one fickle employer for another, even if this one was far less patrician in his manners.

After Slack had retired to his room to immerse himself in more of his reading material – by now surely he must have digested the entire Old Testament – De Quincey, too, took himself off, eager to seek out further instances of religious mania. As for myself, I had not the slightest interest in such goings-on, having a private demon of my own in human form to concern me, and so after staring out the window at the building opposite and finally tiring of seeing all those mournful-looking devils trotting up and down its stone steps, for it was some sort of police office, I decided to try my luck once more with Mrs Bunting behind her gleaming mahogany counter in the front part of the hotel.

For once she was absent, in her place this elderly individual in a brass-buttoned frock coat. Saluting jerkily like some war-weary veteran, which, in fact, he was, and missing a leg, he enquired if he might be of assistance, and so I repeated the question I had put previously to his employer without success.

For a minute or two he observed me warily before asking, 'Mr Speed, you say, from London?'

'No, that's *my* name,' I told him a touch tetchily. 'Not the gentleman's I'm enquiring after.'

But with a flash of irritation in those watery old eyes, he rejoined, 'Sure, don't I know that. But if you'll forgive me for further correcting you, the same gentleman you happen to be referring to is no gentleman.'

'So you *do* know him, then?'

'And why wouldn't I, as does Mrs Bunting, and everybody else, which is why he was sent away with a flea in his ear, a papish cur like that daring to show his face in a decent establishment like our own, and coming out with his lying stories.'

Hard as it was to rein in my rage, I still felt relieved, telling myself there yet might be some way of salvaging the situation.

'This "papish cur", as you refer to him, might he be found in some other place when not bothering respectable folk like Mrs Bunting and yourself?'

'There's a low class of stabling by St George's Market where he and his sort keep their mangy nags. But sure no decent Protestant would want to set foot in one of them oul' hackney carriages of his. Eaten alive with vermin, they'd be, as well as taking their life in their hands.'

Despite being annoyed at him and his mistress both for their interference in my private business, I still couldn't help but enjoy their presumption I must be as true blue as themselves, believing, as they seem to do, any person possessing even the slightest semblance of respectability must be such as themselves, similar sentiments, back on my old London beat, of course, being commonplace. But there a man's religion was never a consideration when hunting him down. However, I might have to adjust my opinions in a place where a person's appearance and, as I was to learn later, his accent, even turn of phrase, could mark him out as though he had a placard about his neck.

So, having waited long enough for this welcome ray of cheer, I interrupted Mr Slack's studies to tell him the news, and with the afternoon already in decline the two of us set out together.

The Markets, as it's known locally, is a very putrid pit of a place, a stench of rotting straw and dung infecting its yards and alleyways, and glad I was to have such a formidable ally by my side as we picked our way through its maze of dark and dangerous-looking courts and entries, like some forgotten rural outpost abandoned when the city closed in, encircling it. Ragged children stared at us, crones veiled their faces as we passed, while of menfolk there appeared to be none.

Finally attracting the attention of a young woman scrubbing clothes at a pump, I enquired if she happened to know a certain Dermot Mulholland, a coachman of about such a height, using one of Mr Slack's breast buttons as a gauge, and amused by this she withdrew her hands from the tub, patting her hair as if to draw attention to her looks, for despite the slovenly state of her dress and bare blackened feet she was comely enough for a washer wench.

'Well, good luck to you if he owes you money, for you'll never get a sniff of it, or of him, either.'

But, no, I told her, it was I seeking to repay *him*, meaning the other half-crown, if he had good news for us.

'Sure, why can't I give it to him myself and save you the bother?'

So then it was my turn to be amused, and becoming even more coquettish she winked at Slack, who came over all shy as any maiden.

'You, sir, would you care to spend some time with me?'

But shaking his great head, he declined, and taking no offence, she said, 'Never mind, sure won't I take you to him. But if you have any serious intentions towards myself, be warned, for he's my uncle.'

And so I gave her a shilling for her wit, and still bold as brass she repaid me with a kiss on the cheek.

'Come, he's seeing to a mare with a bad fetlock,' leading us along a cobbled back way until we came out on to a yard where half a dozen poor-looking nags were tethered.

Hands on hips, she gave a loud halloa and a runt of a fellow in a jockey's cap appeared in one of the doorways, a saddle clutched to his chest.

'Tell Dermot two gentlemen are here asking after him.'

'From the assizes, is it?'

'That's for him to find out, not for the likes of you.'

Still cradling the saddle, he returned to the darkness of his cave and the girl said, 'Are you gaming men by any chance? Eamonn there is riding in the Downpatrick races tomorrow.'

But I told her the sport held no interest for either one of us.

'Then you're surely not Irish.'

'Might that not already be obvious?'

'Maybe in *your* case. And your great friend as well, if he deigned to open his mouth.'

At that moment the individual I'd almost given up hope of ever setting eyes on again showed himself in the stable doorway, arms bared to the shoulders, a leather apron about his waist, greeting us with, 'Sure and the Lord be praised, but didn't I think you had decamped back to England and forgot all about me. Them ones at the hotel told me they'd never heard tell of you.'

'Well, as you can see for yourself, you were misled on both counts.'

'I'm glad to hear it, for I have some great news for you two gentlemen.'

'You've found our man?'

'As large as life and twice as ugly. And this very night, if it's convenient, I'll bring you to him.'

After we returned to the hotel I told Slack it might perhaps be wiser not to mention to Mr De Quincey any of what had taken place, at least not yet, and he nodded his head.

'And when we have upon this person?'

'Then we can tell him.'

'And afterwards?'

We were in the little snug with its brown leather armchairs and sporting prints on the walls, like any other inn parlour anywhere save for the smell of turf smoke drifting in from the hearths of the poorer homes outside. In our own grate burned a good fire of Scottish coal brought over from across the water, yet even with the recently installed gas lamps lighting the streets it still seemed a foreign place, making me doubt yet again what we were doing here and why, the very same question my companion himself had hinted at.

Yet I had still no satisfactory answer for him. All this time, all these long weeks, the pursuit had been the only thing in my head, leaving little room for anything else. But now when success appeared within touching distance, like the very collar of our quarry himself, what then? And when in response all I could come up with was, 'Let's wait and see,' I could tell from the expression on his face he was far from being reassured.

That evening, after De Quincey had returned looking wan, his energy only kept at a decent level with regular drops from his little amber medicine bottle, I told him he should take some rest, and he went to lie down in his room, so leaving the field clear for Slack and myself to meet up with our coachman friend, and at seven when the clock in the hotel struck the hour I heard a voice in the front office call my name. But before Mrs Bunting or her doorman could eject our man a second time, I went down to where he was standing in the hall, as if still afraid to cross the threshold despite our assurance we would be there to vouch for him, and when he saw us his face took on a positive beam of delight.

'Well, isn't it the great relief to be finally reacquainted, after that unfortunate misunderstanding earlier,' all of this announced in carrying tones for the proprietor's benefit, who, I felt certain, must be nearby with her ear cocked to our conversation.

'Tell me, do you find the hotel here to your satisfaction, for there's other establishments far more comfortable and not near as old-fashioned? Sure if I'd known I could have brought them to your attention when we met up at Viscount Massereene's great house in the country that time.'

Even Mr Slack appeared amused by his effrontery, as was I, thinking of it as tit for tat for his earlier treatment, and playing along, I replied, 'And it's good to see you, too, Mr Mulholland, after all this time. So, shall we resume our business where we left off?'

Out in the street he carried on as merry as could be, claiming, as he put it, to have near walked the soles of the feet off himself on the trail of our mysterious client, Mr Nobody, in a clear hint we had still not provided a name, merely a bit of paper with an artist's likeness on it.

'But sure didn't I still recognise him behind the whiskers, for the eyes in a man's head never change, like the devil's own carriage lamps.'

'May I ask where you intend taking us?'

'Sure, won't you find out soon enough. And nobody'll be as surprised as themselves when you light on the pair of them.'

'Pair? Pair, you say?'

'Aye, isn't that what you said? Your man and his doxy?'

After we had made our way deep into an area known as the Marrowbone, our guide came to a halt by the side of the street.

'This particular neighbourhood I'm taking you to harbours a very low class of people so I took the liberty of bringing this along,' producing a short wooden baton from his coat pocket.

'That's entirely up to you, but I promise you Mr Slack here is more than capable of looking after himself.'

'Aye, I can see that well enough, but he's not the one that concerns me.'

Thanking him for his consideration, nevertheless I assured him that in my previous occupation I had frequently found myself in tight corners and so was confident I, too, would be safe.

'And what class of occupation might that be now?'

But thinking he knew quite enough of my business as it was, I ordered him to keep going and, grinning, he pressed on.

The proceedings our guide introduced us to that night was scarcely what I expected, at least not in this particular city, familiar, as I was, with similar events in London, although infinitely tonier, including the clientele. Yet I had no proper inkling of any of this at first, being taken along a series of dank, dark alleyways where the city corporation's much vaunted new gas-lighting system hadn't penetrated, probably never would, going by the squalor of the locality.

'Stay close to my heels, for you'd never find your way back out again on your own. Only them that knows the geography venture here for their entertainment,' a word, it occurred to me, pretty improbable for such a setting.

Yet we would see what we would see, and so deeper and deeper I allowed myself be led into this maze for the unwary, thankful not only for Jack Slack's presence, but the comforting feel of my own police billy club as well, for our guide was not the only one with a persuader in his coat pocket.

Eventually we came to where there stood a great abandoned-looking shell of a building, its doors and window frames nothing but an ancient memory, our guide announcing, 'It might not look much from the outside, but inside is where you'll find our two beauties along with others of the sporting fraternity.'

'Sporting, did you say?'

'Aye, for even if our pair of lovebirds haven't a copper piece to rub between them there's no charge for spectators. Anyway, leave things to me when we get inside, and I'll point you in their direction.'

Despite my uncertainty, I followed him to a gaping opening where a fine door must have once hung, and beyond it lay near darkness and a strong smell of decay, and as in a game of blind man's buff, Slack and I edged our way along a dank passageway until a glimmer of lamplight pierced the gloom and a low hum of voices grew louder and louder until the hum became a roar and finally an almighty great hubbub as if a crowd were urging on two of their own like Slack himself had been in his prime.

But these were no human combatants, for now there came another sound, the barking of dogs and the animal squealing of their kill, and it came to me where I had heard the sound before, and here it was again filling a ruined chamber near the size of a ballroom, but in a Belfast rookery this time instead of a cellar in Clerkenwell.

As a contest was in full cry, the onlookers had their eyes fixed on the spectacle in front of them, so our arrival appeared to go unnoticed, even of our own Goliath himself and despite his fine tailoring, although the crowd was not universally rough, for quite a few of the local fancy were present, waving their arms and shouting the odds.

On account of the floor being raised on planks at the rear, we had a good view of the pit itself, about the size of a small boxing ring, but round instead of square, and inside it, already the jaws and front quarters of the black and white terrier despatching its quota of rats against the referee's clock were stained crimson like the walls of the enclosure itself, and the stink of blood and dead vermin piling up in the corners had the swells present holding handkerchiefs to their noses.

As we watched, for it was impossible not to be transfixed

by the carnage, the dog's owner plucked his animal from the pit, wiping its chaps with a cloth and letting it lap water from a bowl before lowering it to resume its deadly work, the record standing, as I recall, at fifty rats killed in four minutes, the tally of a Yorkshire terrier by the name of Jacko. Gruesome as it was, the spectacle had diverted me from the proper purpose of my visit, but as the dead rats were being swept up, and a squealing batch of live ones looked set to be released from their cage, I sent my gaze roving about the faces around me.

The rays from the half-dozen or so oil lamps suspended above the pit cast barely enough light, and I strained to single out just one set of features from all the rest. Yet not a solitary female form could be seen in the entire gathering, and just when I was about to give in to despair, I heard our guide whisper, 'There, by the pillar, do you see, talking to the gent in the beaver hat?'

'You are certain?'

'Don't I know him by the coat on his back, brown, with the collar ripped half off it, careless as can be.'

But it might have been black, even navy, because of the dim light where he stood in conversation with the other man, who now turned away, leaving him there.

'See? He's been touching up a mark, only coming up empty-handed.'

The next bout was about to begin, the assembled ratters in a barking frenzy, but my attention was on my target still, and determined to get a sight of his face, I ordered my two companions to stay where they were while I moved closer.

Slack appeared concerned, so I told him not to worry for I had something in mind and if all went according to plan I would signal to him.

However, putting in his penny-worth, Dermot cautioned, 'If he's cornered he might well turn nasty like one of them rats, for they've been known to bite back and take out an eye.'

'Never fret, this old dog still has his teeth, as well as a trick up his sleeve.' Or, as I might have said, a trusty wooden ally in an inside pocket.

Edging my way towards our man in the drab brown coat, I kept my eye fixed on his back, worried he might disappear before I could get near enough to engage with him. But it seemed he was casting about for another mark, as Dermot had intimated, and so I came up alongside and the trap seemed sprung, for finally here we were, the two of us within a hand's breadth of one another with me smelling the very reek of turf smoke and tobacco on his clothes.

Side by side, in our separate ways, we stood there pretending interest in the carnage before us, the dog biting the neck, then expertly snapping the back of its prey, and as the instant stretched I began to fear he would not make an approach after all, and so it would be up to me, thus alerting his suspicions, for as I knew only too well from his history he could sniff out peril if and where it existed as keenly as his animal namesake.

From what I could see of him, for the light was still poor here, there was indeed something of a resemblance in the set of the jaw and shape of the head, the hair grown longer and curlier than in the drawing the Scottish court artist had made of him, and so I waited for him to reveal some better form of identification.

With hindsight probably I was more nervous about letting this particular bird in the hand fly free than in all my previous years as a catcher of those like him. Yet even if he did decide to spread his wings and take flight, there was nothing in practice or in law I could do to restrain him, and so it looked as if Percival Speed, celebrated thief-taker and London detective, might have travelled all this way in pursuit of nothing more than a bundle of human feathers.

However, to coax our bird back in his cage, I made a play of rattling some change in my pocket as though considering a wager, and I saw him give a sideways glance from the corner of his eye, and so I waited for his move, and, finally, it arrived, but in a far more direct fashion than expected, even though the accent in which it was delivered was as I had imagined.

'Fine ratter he may well be, but he's still no match for the next one up, wee Welsh Bob.'

'You reckon he's a sure winner, then?'

For an instant I thought my London accent might have spoiled my chances. But then why should it? Some hint of a Caledonian cadence could well have done, but not a cockney one.

'I take it you're a stranger here,' he said in even more friendly tones, 'as well as to this particular class of sport.'

And so deciding to ratchet up this cat and mouse game a notch or two, I remarked, 'I've made my home in Scotland these past number of years, but there's no great appetite for such diversion there,' watching for a reaction, for even the craftiest criminal type it's been my experience will give something away if pricked in the right place.

But to my disappointment came there none. Not even the slightest flicker of disquiet.

And so I enquired, 'Ever ventured across the water yourself?'

He laughed.

'Born and bred here and never left it, except right at the minute I'm not as flush as I'd like.'

But to employ some of his own sporting parlance, cutting my losses, I moved away, as it had become crystal clear he was not our man, and never had been, despite a passing resemblance to the real thing, whatever that was.

When I returned to my two companions, our hackney driver had a broad grin on his face.

'Well, then, will we tail him when he goes back to his woman, for you're after the both of them, right?'

'I was,' I told him, and his expression changed.

'Tell me, his woman, as you refer to her, did you actually set eyes on her?'

'What do you mean?'

'Well, wasn't she meant to be also present here tonight?'

'Ach, sure mebbe she was indisposed, how should I know? Anyway, didn't I have occasion to exchange words with her on the street a couple of days ago, keeping it discreet, as you told me. But as rough-tongued a tinker as ever you had the misfortune to meet.'

'She spoke to you?'

'Why wouldn't she, seeing she was on the cadge same as his nibs back there?'

In the pit the ratter had finished his quota, and the referee, a stout man in a leather butcher's apron, for he, too, was spattered with gore, was sorting out the corpses, tapping their tails with a stick, so if any showed signs of life the still-eager terrier could finish them off.

Where I had left him, I saw the man in the brown coat waving to draw my attention to his 'sure thing'. But I had no further interest in either wee Welsh Bob or himself.

'Jack,' I said, 'we've drawn a blank. Our business is finished here.'

'Very well, whatever you say. I'm pretty sure I can find our own way back to the hotel easily enough.'

But our guide was not so sanguine, or quite so restrained.

'What about Mr Nobody over there? You're not letting the blackguard go after all my hard work, are you?'

'He's not the one, and neither is his woman.'

Downcast, as if he was the one whose hopes had been cruelly dashed, he shook his head.

'Ah, well, if that's the end of it, fair dues. Still, what about the rest of my money?'

'Come to the hotel in the morning and we'll settle up then.'

Leaving him there looking still despondent, Slack and I made our way back out into the air again without too much difficulty, just as he had predicted, and returning through the city streets alone together not a word was spoken, and never was I more thankful for my companion's customary reticence and forbearance.

Neither one of us had dined that evening, but I had no appetite, for it felt as if there was a stone in my insides, so I told him to eat on his own, knowing he required his full ration of four hearty meals a day, and leaving him, I said, 'You and I will talk more in the morning about this night's dreary business,' and we shook hands in curiously formal fashion, as though already we might have come to a parting of the ways, and it was in my own head as well, having reached about as low an ebb as a man can possibly find himself at.

And upstairs in my room, lamp trimmed and curtains drawn against any distraction from the street outside, I took up pen and paper to compose the following.

The Commercial Hotel, Belfast
10 July

My Lord Beckford

Further in regard to the hunt for the person known as William Hare, I must now inform you that, despite all my efforts in following his scent, barely detectable though it's been up to now, the search has proved in vain, our quarry nowhere to be found, either back on the mainland or in this, his country of origin.

To continue, therefore, with such a fruitless undertaking would, in my opinion, be a waste of both your own precious assets and my professional skills as a detective in your employ.

Needless to say, I will submit a more detailed report of the commission along with a record of all expenses incurred.

On a more personal note, may I add, that throughout this entire enterprise Mr Slack has proved himself to be a very bulwark of trust and unfaltering dedication, and so I feel confident you will be pleased to have him return to his previous duties as a valued member of your household.

Faithfully yours
Percival Speed

And so finally there it lay before me, a bare page of testimony to all the fret and turmoil pursuing nothing more than some aristocrat's whim, for I felt certain there would be no rekindling of that earlier enthusiasm of his, nor little hope of receiving the outstanding dues owed to me.

After I had sealed the letter in readiness for the first post in the morning, I went downstairs, for I was feeling parched, even if my stomach had still no hankering for food. As our old curmudgeon of a steward had retired to his bed, I helped myself to a glass of stout and sat down with it in the shadows, head still buzzing with recrimination and invective.

Yet it was Percy Speed himself, no one else, who must take the blame for this entire botched business, when he should have stayed at home in slippered retirement like the rest of his old metropolitan comrades, and not let vanity lead him into thinking he could recapture a time when he would have run this particular villain to earth with ease by following up the decent leads available instead of pursuing a clutch of worthless ones.

But then what were these so-called 'decent leads' anyway? A rumour here, a tall tale there, a ghost sighting like the one this very night?

I poured another glass, then another, until, 'Hell roast you, William Hare! And you, too, Beckford!' I let fly, and the list might well have continued if another voice hadn't broken in.

'Hear, hear, and amen to that.'

And it was De Quincey in his nightshirt, his puny little pale legs poking out like an infant's.

'Rest assured, friend, you are not alone. This poor hack has also had obstacles put in his path by those spurning his best endeavours. Pray excuse the attire, for I thought I might creep down undetected and retrieve something I left below earlier.'

As he spoke he kept glancing about in search of his property, until, darting forward, he snatched up a tiny bottle, not bothering to conceal it, for it was his constant companion, in the same way as another man might never be too far from his snuffbox or tobacco pouch.

'You are intent, so I see, on dissolving the frustrations of another long and tiring day. May I join you?'

Having had more to drink than I should, for he was right about drowning my sorrows, I nodded, and he sat down, smoothing out his night attire in almost maidenly fashion before setting his own personal elixir on the table in front of him.

'So, yet another fruitless exercise, eh?'

'Mr Slack, I take it, has been speaking with you.'

'Certainly he and I dined earlier together. Well, *he* did, for as you know I have barely the appetite of a mouse. But, despite my pumping, he still kept his counsel regarding your little excursion with our coachman friend this evening.'

'So how did you find out about *that*?'

He laughed.

'My dear Speed, seldom have I found myself in such a den of gossip-mongers as exists in this particular city. The entire place is addicted to knowing one another's business. Nevertheless, *you* are not the only detective here.'

'Perhaps then it should have been *you* conducting this investigation.'

Instantly his demeanour changed and, stretching forth

his hand, he implored, 'Believe me, I have not the slightest intention of rubbing salt in your wounds. But you mustn't berate yourself. It is not your fault this exercise in some noble-man's vanity has ended so disappointingly.'

'While only days ago you yourself pledged your support for it.'

Pouring out the barest thimble-full of brown liquor, then diluting it in a water glass, he studied the change in colour, before remarking, 'Throwing your reputation and my meagre resources after a doomed cause as cold as yesterday's mutton would be the purest folly. Your chances of catching our Irish renegade are as dead as the proverbial doornail, and those poor wretches he himself once put in the ground. Leave him be, leave him to a higher power, if, as Mr Slack so fervently believes, such an Entity exists.'

But despite his efforts to convince me, little did he know, having just written my letter of resignation, the battle already was won. However, I was not prepared to allow him the satis-faction of believing he had anything to do with that decision, for, in my book, he still was nothing but a literary scavenger drawn to the smell of carrion, in this case delivered in bulk to the knacker's yard by someone it now appeared he had lost all interest in like my patron.

'Come, your glass is empty. Allow me to refresh it.'

But I'd had more than sufficient for one night and rose to go, leaving him to his little apothecary's flask, as discreet as any lady's scent bottle, yet far less innocent in the contents.

'Percy, stay awhile and let you and I talk further about all this, for the truth is Slack and I have, indeed, had some private discussion on the matter.'

'Writing me off like his damned employer, is it? Behind my back? The pair of you?'

'No, no, nothing could be further from the truth. Forget this wild-goose chase of Beckford's and instead join us in an infinitely more rewarding venture.'

'Another murderer? Another fugitive?'

'Not one man, but other men and their salvation, or what passes for it in this present hotbed of religious hysteria. Help us investigate and expose it for what it is, gospel truth, as Jack Slack so passionately yearns for it to be, or something much less miraculous, as this old cynic here believes, not so much trusting in the Blood of the Lamb, but in something far more chemical and efficacious.'

And raising his glass and taking a sip, he closed his eyes.

But having indulged him long enough I bade him good night, leaving him with his tincture of laudanum. What the morning might bring seemed as unclear as the thoughts in my head, already beginning to throb. One thing remained certain, however, and that was what was lying on the desk in my room ready to be sent off by first post on the packet to England in the morning from this dark and damnable place.

They say it takes one faker to know another, and early on in our acquaintanceship hadn't I the Reverend Dunwoody pegged for as cute a hoor as ever put on a clerical collar and go-to-meeting coat to cover his trickery. But if he felt the same about me, he kept it to himself, treating me like this heaven-sent gift that had walked in from the street previously dumbfounded but now cured by prayer and redemption, and a terrible warning to every man, woman and small child present in his gospel hall off Clifton Street.

And to be honest, no one was more surprised than Bernard Black himself, the name being now as neat to the fit as a glove, sometimes even forgetting I once had another, only far more dangerous.

What I did need to recall for the benefit of the ignorant, however, was what I had turned my hand to before I took on that name. But being neither mad nor foolish, I had to shift the blame on to someone else, for eager as Dunwoody and his flock were to have their blood turned to ice water, hearing it from the lips of the very one who had done away with all them people himself would have been more than they could tolerate.

So after I'd served my apprenticeship, as it were, this was the way I would go about it when called up to give my testimony.

'Even if I never harmed another living soul myself, I once knew someone who did, and so maybe I deserve to end up in hell alongside him for not reporting it and he could be apprehended for his terrible deeds. Having travelled across the water in search of honest labouring work, I fell in with this person there, frequenting the same public houses, squandering our wages on whiskey and loose women, until one night didn't he tell me he knew of a way to make easy money without hardly having to lift a little finger, asking if I would be willing to join him in the venture. Well, brothers and sisters, the Good Lord must have been looking out for me, for, thanks be praised, I turned my face away from that person's offer, as what he told me that night was enough to make the blood in a person's veins run cold ...'

Which of course was my intention, and if Willie had been there he might have thought some of his gift of the gab had rubbed off on me, even if the blame for our misdeeds was being put squarely on himself, William Hare, as previously known, getting away with murder yet again, while being royally recompensed for it. And nobody was happier than Dunwoody as his congregation swelled and grew, none of the other breast-beaters on the back benches having a story to tell half as diabolical as my own.

'Thanks to your witness, Bernard, our harvest is growing more bountiful with each passing day. Even my own dear wife has been wrung to her very essence by your terrible narratives. Yet from this horror comes something truly inspiring and wonderful, persuading people to recognise the evil in their midst which can only be purged in the fire of true confession and heartfelt redemption. But I can see you are drained by your efforts, so I will leave you now to rest, for we must not allow that precious well of revelation to run dry.'

Not that I was near half as destroyed as I let on. Still, that was part of the act, me groaning and throwing my eyes up to heaven, then coming out with something you might run across in a penny-dreadful of the sort Burke's own wife used to read to us for our entertainment, while never knowing me and her husband were up to something as bad, if not worse. But, then, as long as I stuck to stories about resurrecting bodies from the ground, and not live ones, I persuaded myself my secret was safe.

Yet some might say I was getting too clever for my own good, so one evening when Dunwoody enquired, 'This fiend from hell who tried to snare you in his net, was he by any chance an Irishman like yourself?' no, I told him, as British as John Bull himself, and why I fell in with him something I would never know, having always associated with people from the same part of the world as myself.

'And so where might that be? From your accent, it's clear you're not from our own dear city.'

Hitting on a place off in the middle of the country, as far away from my birthplace as I could manage, again I lied. But still he continued with his prying.

'And this grave-robbing devil of an Englishman, did he receive his just, judicial deserts when his time came to face his punishment for his crimes?'

This was growing a mite close for comfort, so I told him I never did find out, didn't much care to, either, having nightmares still about some of the things I'd heard from his lips when he was alive and which now were being recounted for the spiritual benefit of the pastor's own congregation, and after I'd said it didn't he send me this knowing look as much as to say maybe his apprentice was learning his master's trade a touch too readily for his liking.

Still, he needed me as much as I did him, for as more and more newcomers poured in to have their blood curdled, didn't I see him getting puffed up with his own importance, the collection plate growing heavier with each night that passed, people sitting with white faces and hands covering their mouth and nose as if to ward off the smell of sulphur and damnation.

The money, he said, was for the glorification and propagation of the Lord's good work on earth, but I knew it was ending up in his own pocket. But sure wouldn't I have done the same myself, and as long as I was fed and funded along with my female partner, a fine new wool coat on my back, and a decent sprigged poplin dress on hers, I was content to play along. And, truth be told, I couldn't have set foot back home at a better time, for according to Dunwoody not just the city, but the entire North itself, was currently consumed with a dread of fire and brimstone raining down, our own tabernacle not the only one doing a roaring trade in sin and salvation.

Yet not too many testifying could claim close personal acquaintance with grave-robbing and them that carried on the trade, for if there was one thing that kept decent, law-abiding folk awake at night it was the fear of getting dug up and sold for butcher's meat, despite their posted guards and mortsafes placed on the top of them.

And as if things couldn't get any better, one evening, taking me aside, our benefactor said, 'It's not right and proper for you and your daughter to reside in that low-class lodging in Frederick Street where the city's jades ply their shameful profession. You must come and stay as my guest in my own house.'

Speaking for the two of us, herself still dumb as a post unlike myself after my miraculous cure, I told him we would be honoured to reside under his roof. But I knew he was only doing it so he could keep an eye on me in case I took my wares elsewhere, for the word had gone out one of Dunwoody's disciples had his flock near demented with his resurrectionist parables, as by this time I was stirring the pot of horrors for all I was worth.

'And when the coffin couldn't be brought up whole, wouldn't he take a pick and break a hole in the one end of it and pull the body out head first like you would prick an egg and suck out the marrow,' and the housewives at the front would be throwing up their hands and shrieking, while their husbands fumbled for their handkerchiefs, sick as dogs. But, sometimes, the very same ladies would be taken in other ways, loosening their neckbands and chokers, fanning themselves, and afterwards pressing in on me, begging for a meeting of a more private nature, and seeing this the girl would get heated herself, but in a jealous, wifely way, which was not something I cared for people to see.

Unlike Willie, now I've never had great fortune with women, a quick glance in a looking-glass explaining the reason why, yet here they were tumbling over one another to fondle me like I was the Great Panjandrum himself. But Hannah, as I say, did not take kindly to this, and when we were on our own together it was all I could do to keep her from going at me with both fists, being unable to employ a scalding tongue like other females.

To tell the truth, I was more concerned with getting marked about the face, and my fine new suit of clothes ripped, as this might prompt talk I had gone back to old ways. So I gave her a thump, grateful she couldn't cry out and alarm the house. But my heart wasn't in it, thinking this new evangelising life was making me soft as putty, as not long before I would have battered her senseless for daring to defy me, so maybe she was getting to be a burden now I needed no one but myself under Dunwoody's wing, for a day after his invitation we went with him to his country residence in a place called Lisburn a little way out of the city, and it seemed to me he must have been prospering rightly enough even before I came along, for the house was a fine, well-appointed villa with a garden and a lily pond and inside the very best that money could provide.

Keeping my eyes peeled and ears cocked, I soon ascertained Mrs D. was the one with the wherewithal, a pale mousy little creature given to taking to her bed with frights and upsets made all the more frequent hearing what I was filling her ears with of an evening. Yet as far as I could make out his wife's health was of scant consequence to the master of the house. Indeed, I got the impression he might not be all that greatly put out if her health got worse, thus giving him more freedom to enjoy her inheritance, myself thinking he and I made the right match in the villainy business, and as long as we played each other's game all would be fine and everyone happy.

But while his own woman was biddable and nice as ninepence, mine was not, clinging on to me like a spouse instead of the daughter she was supposed to be, even if we did have the looks of two strangers, her hair red as rust, and sturdy of frame, and me dark-featured and thin as a lath despite all the fine feeding I was currently enjoying.

However, if Dunwoody suspected as much, he never let on, even with her putting on the sour face when he led us to separate rooms, quick as a flash remarking, 'It surely does the heart good to see such a close, affectionate bond between family members. I only wish it were so in my own case, as my own dear Miriam and I have not been blessed with offspring due to her poor constitution.'

That night when we got back to the manse and, as was our custom, went down on our knees for a bedtime prayer on the fine Turkey rug on the parlour floor before retiring to our beds, I was hardly asleep more than ten minutes when didn't Hannah come climbing in alongside me in her night attire, and even though the chance of a ride was tempting, I rejected her, for the noise of her when she came off was fit to wake the dead.

'While we're lodging in this place, we must let on we're blood-related, as it's too cushy a billet to get found out. Remember when we had barely a crust, or a decent coat on our backs?'

Even in the dark I could see she was not well pleased, not merely for the want of a bit of the other, but because she was thinking I was getting ready to put her back on the street where I first found her.

'Just be patient till we milk this udder dry then find ourselves a fresh one.'

Putting it like that, it must have reminded her of being in

a byre at one time, so she gave me a dig with her fist before going back to her own bed further along the hall.

Dunwoody, however, was not the only one to watch out for, having a housekeeper with a big bunch of keys attached to her waist, and even though you could hear her coming because of it, I was wary of her on account of the sour way she looked at us when we were together, at mealtimes, usually, with her master making us go down on our knees, giving thanks for every mouthful she grudgingly put in front of us.

And one day about a week after we got there she raised this great commotion, accusing Hannah of helping herself to some trinkets, sundry rings and a mother of pearl brooch from the mistress's dressing-table while she herself was still in the bed, but scarcely able to know what day it was on account of all the stuff she was taking for her nerves.

Pouring oil on troubled waters, Dunwoody spoke up.

'On account of her sad condition Miss Black is unable to defend herself. Yet even so, I feel certain she would never venture into Miriam's bedchamber. Anyway, wasn't there a man sweeping the chimneys here only a few days ago?'

'Indeed there was, but that was Willie John Stevenson, as God-fearing and respectable an individual as ever set foot inside another Christian person's house.'

'And as Mr Black is, too, and those related to him. But these are mere gewgaws which will surely turn up in the fullness of time. And even if this sorry business was brought to poor Miriam's attention, I feel certain she would quote Matthew six, nineteen. "Lay not up for yourselves treasures upon earth which moth and dust doth corrupt."'

And there the matter was let lie, but not to my own satisfaction, for taking the same thieving young baggage by the throat when we were alone, I demanded, 'Where is it, for I know you took it?' and throwing up her eyes to high heaven, finally she gave in, handing the booty over, which at another time and place might well have fetched a tidy sum for the pair of us.

Still, that was then, and now was now, so once more I warned her not to provoke these folk, nor me neither, giving her a clout for good measure, and she fell to weeping. But when her tears dried I told myself she might try the same trick again, that being her nature and with me maybe teaching her far too well, and so I came nearer to getting shot of her, short of murder itself, a nicety which Willie would have found greatly entertaining.

But the pastor and me were by now like two business associates, and no longer addressing me as Mr Black, 'Bernard,' he would say, 'Bernard, I realise you were brought up in the false religion of Rome, but as you have now repented of your previous sinful ways there's no earthly reason why you shouldn't be welcomed into the bosom of the true and proper Church.'

Not having darkened a chapel door since I was a cub, I told him I was happy enough to 'turn' and 'take the soup', as the expression has it, and so he was pleased as could be, saying, 'Why don't we make it a doubly blessed occasion and lead your daughter to the fold as well,' not knowing she was a Protestant like himself. But then who was to find out, for she was not going to open her mouth even if she wanted to.

Now, as has been said, religion meant little or nothing to someone like myself, except now it was providing me with a fine living. But, as the Scriptures themselves have it, a price must be paid for blasphemy, for one day like a bolt from the blue there came a sudden change in our fortunes, due, according to Dunwoody, to some transgression on the girl's part, with me thinking she had been up to her pilfering tricks again.

But, no, said Dunwoody, something had been taken from *her*, her purity, innocence, her good name.

So then I thought he must have heard us talking that one time, me telling her to get back down the hall to her own bed in case we were discovered. But I was wrong again, with him saying some culprit unknown had violated her, as well as the sanctity of his home.

But if something bad had happened to her she had given no hint of it to me, I told him, and he bowed his head with what looked like a tear in his eye.

'Oh, Bernard, Bernard, no truer word was ever spoken, that a fond parent is often the last person to know the truth about his offspring, for Satan can take away that dewy bloom as a thief in the night, or in this case, someone having their ungodly way with them.'

Yet his words were still as slippery as soap, until, finally, he came out with it, that the housekeeper was the one who had brought the unwholesome news to him, telling him, 'Surely even you, Pastor, must have noticed how swollen she is of late, a belly on her getting bigger with every day that passes.'

Heaving this great sigh out of him, he went on, 'Sad as it grieves me to have to say this, the poor creature can no longer remain under the same roof as my own dear Miriam, for her health would not tolerate it, nor the shame of it getting carried back to the congregation either.'

Even though I felt like enquiring whether there might not be room for one more fallen sinner in his gospel hall, I held my tongue, being more concerned with my own situation, even if only two people knew who the culprit was who had been dipping his wick and getting the 'poor creature' in the family way.

Still, that was beside the point, for just as Dunwoody had been blind to what was in front of him, how had I managed to miss the bump in question myself? The housekeeper's womanly eye was the answer, along with her having it in for Hannah over the articles she'd taken.

However, things were going far too smoothly to have them ruined by bringing some wee by-blow into the world, and when I faced her with the truth of what she had been hiding under her shift, she denied it, saying it was the fault of all the rich provender she'd been enjoying since the two of us came off the road and ended up where we were.

Nevertheless, by not taking care of the matter as she should have done, she had spoiled a good thing for the pair of us, which was maybe the intention, wanting to put a burden on me, so I told her it might be best if she didn't come with me to the meetings any more, but stay in the house instead, and her eyes flashed as if about to defy me. But not having any of that, I lifted my fist to her and she put her two hands over her belly, so giving the lie to what she had sworn blind to a minute earlier.

Going into the city with Dunwoody that evening in his chaise, for he was able to afford to keep a mare as well as a man to look after one, says he to me, 'I am pleased to see you heeded my advice and left the young lady in her present delicate condition behind with my dear wife. You and I will be forgiven, I feel sure, for shielding our loved ones from some of the more awful accounts you are currently bringing to our meetings.'

Without any doubt here was someone who could teach Satan himself lessons in cant and hypocrisy. But even if he had the serpent's tongue on him, mine could do what his could not, and being aware of it, he went on, 'Have you perhaps something special for us tonight? Something more harrowing, netting us an even greater catch of penitents?' as if it was to our mutual benefit to cram in even more hungry gawks eager for a dose of hellfire and holy terror instead of his own heavy sermons.

But then they could avail themselves of that class of thing in any number of respectable churches throughout the city, whereas Barney Black, to call him by his rough street name, with no education save what he had picked up from the gutter, was the boyo to get the women fanning themselves and loosening their undergarments like they could feel the fires of Hades itself licking their private parts.

Well, this particular evening, taking heed of what

Dunwoody had said, and maybe I was getting far too comfortable in my work, to hell with it, thinks I, I'll give them a juicier morsel to whet their appetites, murder being the tastiest titbit of all.

Greedy as Dunwoody was, the hall was as full as it could muster, the faithful standing packed along the walls, men, mostly, although a crowd of mill women and girls, having just as much of an itch for a rub of the relic as their better-off sisters at the front, were also present in large numbers.

Now being the quick and dutiful pupil of the master himself up alongside me with the Good Book in his hand, I scanned the place as always, never lingering on any one face longer than necessary, spreading the pain, you might say, for tonight I was out to inflict as much of it as I could, not because of what Dunwoody had said in the carriage, but because I was still feeling vexed at what my companion had done in her sly, feminine fashion, only wishing she was here to learn what men turn their hands to when murder suits them better than soiling them in a graveyard at dead of night.

'Brothers and sisters, even if the heart has been sore scalded in you these past number of nights, believe me, you still haven't heard the half of it, or the worst by far. So if some among you are not sure you are able to bear any more hellish stories of what wicked men do when they have given themselves over to out and out iniquity, now is the time to take your leave and be spared the pain of meeting Satan face to face ...'

Up aloft there with them in the palm of my hand, I was near starting to believe some of the things I was coming out with myself, even though there was still sufficient truth in them to convict me. But it was like a wave sweeping over me, Dunwoody crying out his hallelujahs, and in my head I was seeing Burke and me suffocating them people all over again, only it was as if somebody else was doing it, maybe even the very one whose name I was taking in vain, Auld Clootie himself.

So there was me in full cry, my eye lighting on a woman weeping here, a man biting his lip there, telling them what it's like when you squeeze the breath from another living creature, then getting them to the surgeon before they turn stiff as a board, until at the back of the hall where the factory women were clinging on to one another for dear life, didn't my gaze fasten on two people, who by their expression hadn't given themselves over to the Message, one with a bird's nest of grey hair, a good couple of feet shorter than his companion, whereas he had his poll shaved clean as an egg, and seeing them together, as unlikely a pairing as you could ever come across, it came to me where I'd seen them before, riding in a carriage along a country road in the company of another and older man.

Yet so full of myself had I become, despite seeing the little scholarly one scribbling in a wee notebook, it never occured to me these same two people might cross my path again, and soon, and with dire consequences for myself and my future prospects.

The Commercial Hotel,
Belfast ✖ 18 August

SUCH WILD, UNSEASONAL storms have buffeted the port here these past few days, with no sailings in or out, there is nothing for it but to remain confined in the above with my two associates, even though they can no longer be termed such, having by now been informed of my intention to abandon my search for our Mr Hare and return to England as soon as the weather permits. But I have not attempted to encourage Slack to join me, as De Quincey has persuaded him to remain in pursuit of a separate venture of his own.

Having grown attached to the gentle ex-pugilist, I told him that in my letter of resignation to his former employer I had added a note of commendation regarding himself.

We were in the downstairs snug at the time, the gale outside rattling the windows in their frames, and the smoke in the grate skirling about every corner of the room.

'That was most generous of you, and I'm grateful.'

So then I said, 'But you still won't accompany me, even if Lord Beckford would be happy to retain you in his employ?'

'No, I must follow this other path that has opened up before me.'

'Mr De Quincey's, you mean?'

He looked at me before replying.

'Out on the street with him these past nights, what I have seen and heard has convinced me something truly wondrous is taking place here, even hardened sinners taken over by its power, cast down and smitten senseless.'

'Something Percy Speed has always done his level best to

avoid, for you know what they say, Jack, once a policeman, always one.'

'Yet there also comes a time to forsake old habits, as I myself once did.'

'Old dogs, Jack, new tricks.'

But as the days passed so the storms continued as fierce as ever, the slates falling from the roofs and the few people venturing abroad blown about like leaves in the wind.

Yet not even an Asiatic typhoon, as it was likened to, could deter my two fellow guests from setting out each evening, until I began to suspect Slack might have persuaded himself the End itself was nigh, with all the portents of flood and tempest his reading had prepared him for.

As for the one who had led him down that path, I still felt convinced he was seeking nothing more than fresh meat for his quill, and when he and I found ourselves alone together, and he had helped himself to a taste of his own private medicine from his little brown bottle, he said, 'Religion, you see, has become the opium of choice for these people, opening wide the casements of their souls, lightening the load of their repressed inner selves. But while all across this dreary northern city a new dawn is breaking, you, my dear Speed, cannot depart from it quick enough, not even allowing yourself to take note of it. But then I would hazard you have never allowed yourself to stray much beyond the boundaries of your professional calling anyway.'

There was a curl to his lip as he said it, making me tempted to take his little phial of slow poison away from him like you might withdraw the teat from a spoiled infant. However, history has a way of correcting such arrogance, the details of which I intend setting down in this journal before he writes it up himself, for if I wasn't totally convinced of his true motives before, the following day Jack Slack brought information which persuaded my instincts had been correct about the same gentleman all along.

As was our habit, he and I took our breakfast together, and the customary fine spread, it was, for despite her begrudging manner Mrs Bunting kept an excellent larder, ham, eggs, blood pudding, kidneys, along with the good oaten bread one finds here, setting us up for another day ahead even though no proper outdoor exercise was possible as the rain continued to fall from the heavens like stair-rods.

Mr Slack ate in silence, as did I, but he appeared more preoccupied than usual, though never much of a talker anyway, unlike his new patron above, not stirring from his bed until late in the afternoon, being a lamp-burning night-owl like all his tribe.

After a while, for want of something to lift the sombre mood, I remarked, 'You must have been well-nigh soaked to the skin out in all that deluge last evening. And Mr De Quincey, also. I trust he won't get a foundering, not being as robust as yourself. At times I swear he looks like he's knocking on death's door itself. But then, his medicine, I suppose, revives when it would lay others low.'

Rattling on in this fashion seemed ridiculous, as surely, by now, he and I must be easy enough in one another's company. But, finally, laying down his fork and knife, the big man opposite said, 'Percy, there is something I feel duty-bound to tell you which concerns you and the business that led us here.'

I could tell by his face whatever it was it troubled him greatly, so I waited.

'These past evenings Mr De Quincey and I have made our way to a particular place of worship in the city, as a man there has so captured and taken a hold on his listeners, folk of all sorts and classes have been flocking to give themselves over to the power of his testimony. Yet he is not a preacher like the clergyman whose church it is, but someone who appears to have come out of nowhere with an armoury of tales of the utmost dread and evil which you should hear for yourself on account of this person's intimate knowledge of a particular crime and those like it.'

'Of what specific sort?'

'Grave-robbing. But, of late, murder for the same financial ends.'

'Making you believe he may have some connection with the one who brought us here? Tell me, is Mr De Quincey also persuaded of this?'

A long pause followed, before he replied, 'I fear he intends to confront him himself.'

Lowering his great head, he stared down at his plate.

'Jack,' I said, 'I am truly grateful for this, as a friend and, I trust, colleague still, but would you be willing to accompany me, so we might meet with this man?'

As though considering this blatant play on his conscience, which in truth it was, he looked at me for a moment before reaching across and renewing our original contract with a handshake.

'And have you managed to discover where this person might be found when he is not about his evening's work?'

'Some way out of the city at his clergyman's residence, a Pastor Charles Dunwoody.'

'This pastor, as he's called, what sort of man might he be?'

'Without his Irish disciple he would be drawing a mere handful of converts. They only come on account of this Bernard Black person.'

'So we have a name for him.'

'If it's the one he was born with.'

But running this Mr Black to ground, when he was not putting the fear of God into others, might not be quite so easy on our own, so I said to Slack, 'Let's find the man we employed earlier, and trust he will be of better use this time,' hoping luck must shine on us for one day at least, and sure enough when we stepped outside, even if the sky was its usual slate-grey colour, the rain had ceased, and making our way on foot towards the Markets and our Belfast jarvey, we were dry for a change, and when we came upon him in the stable attending to one of his sorry-looking nags, he greeted us with a cheery, 'So what's it this time, then? Another will-o'-the-wisp, is it?'

No, I told him, this particular individual was as solid and real as himself, and well known in the city, yet possibly not so familiar to him given his profession and religious persuasion. But good-humouredly as ever he took up the challenge, and when he heard the name, he said, 'And why wouldn't I know the same gentleman, even if he happens to favour the orange lily over the green shamrock? A man's politics and denomination never meant a hair to Dermot Mulholland.'

'Still, might you know where he happens to reside?'

Scratching his head, he thought for a moment.

'Well, I can't promise to lead you to the precise dwelling itself, but I know the neighbourhood well enough to get you within spitting distance of its front door.'

So a short while later the three of us were in his chaise, with the same horse he had been grooming earlier briskly trotting in the direction of a pretty place people here call Lisburn, and despite the weather the drive was a pleasant one, the countryside all about fresh and verdant, the cottages neat with well-tended gardens, which Dermot informed us was because this was a Protestant locality and all who lived here were weavers to the linen trade.

When I suggested he ask for directions, grinning, he replied, 'I think it might be better coming from yourself, or your great friend here, for this lot would smell a papish a mile away.'

Leaning over the gate to his cottage was an old villager, so stepping down I made my way over to him, enquiring if he knew where the Reverend Charles Dunwoody's residence might be found, and he called out to a woman inside I took to be his wife, but without satisfying my query she in turn commandeered a neighbour, and before I knew it I was surrounded by a swarm of busybodies and gossip-mongers all eager to learn of my business with the clergyman, which was the last thing I desired as I wanted to approach my man as cannily as possible, and when finally I managed to escape, Dermot, even more amused by now, observed, 'Sure they'd have every last scrap of flesh and information off you if you let them.'

But I was still aggrieved at being trapped, and sharply ordered him to drive on past the white-painted villa which had finally been pointed out to me by my inquisitors, and when we were a short distance away and hidden by a high hedge, I told him, 'Stay in this one spot and don't stir from it,' and turning a shrewd eye on me, he enquired, 'Is it the same boyo we didn't run to ground the last time we were out together?'

'Never mind that, just do as I say, or no money will be forthcoming at the end of our arrangement,' for I'd had my fill of these people and their slippery ways, like trying to manage water in a sieve, and when Slack himself stepped down and made as though to accompany me, I told him it might be best for him to remain with the driver, and when he, too, looked at me in a questioning way, I explained, 'You may have been spotted at his meetings, whereas I have not,' and he replied, 'Very well. But this man is still a brute in spite of what he now professes,' and so I said, 'I think I'm sufficiently equipped to handle a mere man of the cloth,' even though we both knew he was referring to someone very different.

Set into one of the gateposts flanking the house up ahead was a nameplate which read Bethesda, an obvious enough choice for our so-called clerical friend, although from what my nose was telling me he was beginning to smell nearly as fishy as the one sheltering under his roof, the expression 'thick as thieves' coming to mind, yet something I was grateful for, as I always felt much more at ease dealing with land pirates no matter what flag they happened to be flying under.

Telling myself, first the master, then the man, I made my way up the trim gravelled path, reviewing, as I went, the proper procedure in such a situation, softly, softly, or bull at a gate. With Slack alongside, the latter might have its advantages, a shaven-headed Goliath appearing on one's doorstep driving home the message, and after I had rung the bell and waited and waited some more, an oldish woman drew back a downstairs curtain, peering out at me, and so I rang again, and finally she appeared on the step.

'Good day to you, madam, and would you be kind enough to inform the reverend gentleman within there is someone here who wishes to speak with him on a private matter.'

'Reverend Dunwoody is busy writing his sermon and can't be disturbed,' came the reply.

'I would be happy to wait.'

'I'm sure you would, but it's still inconvenient. Mrs Dunwoody is poorly herself and can't tolerate strangers in the house,' and she made to close the door.

'Is Mr Black at home?'

'Mr Who?'

I could see she had been well coached in repelling any form of unwelcome enquiry, so tipping my hat I stepped back, deciding to watch and wait until our two birds left the nest, as they must if they were to travel to the city for another evening of hocus-pocus, for that was how I was starting to see this couple and their knavery now, no different from any other pair of tricksters working the stews and taverns of Vauxhall or Shoreditch.

Knowing far too well how such slippery gents were apt to flee once their game was rumbled, I decided to reconnoitre the rear of the premises in case there was another exit.

It had been some considerable time since last I crept along an alleyway, or scrambled over a dividing wall, but that was forgotten as I crawled through a hedge and into a field where a herd of cows lifted their heads to stare at this curious creature appearing on their home turf. The grass was long and damp and spotted with their dung, and before I reached the far gate

Percival Speed was no longer this respectable caller, but an intruder mired to the knees, yet close enough to his objective to see its outbuildings and what did, indeed, look like some sort of tradesman's entrance.

Ahead, through the foliage of the intervening hedge, could be seen an orchard and someone sitting in its shade, a young woman, but with her back turned, so I couldn't see her face. Recalling what the old salt in Whitehaven had said about a female with red hair, my blood began to race, and moments later it seemed as though my hopes might be realised when over at the house a door opened and out stepped a person making his way towards the girl on the summer-seat.

Could it finally be true? Tallish, lean of build and wearing a decent-looking topcoat, this was not the skulking scarecrow figure I had long imagined. Straining to catch a glimpse of his face, I remembered Slack's description of someone who had come up in the world. But if his clothes were an improvement, looks were impossible to alter, so I would have no need to refer to a drawing, or even a life mask like the one I once held in my hand, to make the necessary comparison. All I required would be one clear look for corroboration.

At that moment, however, I became aware the cattle in the field behind me were growing restive and coming closer, and distracted, I turned around, and when I resumed my surveillance the scene in the garden had changed, for my mark had now the young woman by the arm and was dragging her towards the house. His back was still turned, yet it was obvious he was angry, his companion unresisting, both hands clasped protectively across her middle.

The door slammed, the pair vanished inside and, cheated yet again, I was left kneeling in a wet, muddy field surrounded by a herd of curious Irish livestock, who to a London townie like myself might be a lot more dangerous than they were normally given credit for.

First thing of a morning, lathered up, razor in hand, I'd look in the mirror in my room in the clergyman's house and say to myself, 'Keep your nose clean and your powder dry, Bernard Black, and everything in the garden will continue being lovely.' But, to employ another expression, there was still a fly in the ointment, and that was the oul' Protestant bitch of a housekeeper who had it in for me and the girl from the minute we first set foot in the place, and when her master wasn't present, wasn't a bit shy in showing her contempt.

Hannah, however, as I knew to my cost, had a temper on her as hot and fiery as the colour of her hair, and would have gone for her if I hadn't warned her to rein herself in.

'Just be patient and put up with it. Sure, won't we get our own back when the time is ripe.'

Still, all the while, Miss McBride, as she was known, was pouring poison in her master's ear, for listening in on the stairs one day I heard her at it when they were together in his study where he wrote his sermons.

'Take it from me, that pair, are not near as innocent as they let on. I mean, where did they suddenly spring from anyhow? And, while we're at it, no whiff, no hint, not even a bare mention of how the same young hussy got herself in the family way in the first place.'

'Now, Sarah,' I heard Dunwoody gently chide, 'should we not show charity and compassion towards all God's creatures, not least one who hasn't the capacity to answer back? And surely it's not her father's fault his own flesh and blood veered off the primrose path and now must pay the reckoning for her moment of weakness.'

Even if he did manage to put the slandering bitch in her place, I knew she wouldn't rest until she had pinned a label on us we might not be able to shift in a hurry, for I could hear her roaming about at night when we were in our beds, and might even have heard the girl scratching at my door that time, and so the thing preyed on me, until one night I decided to play her at her own game.

After the old grandfather clock in the hall had struck the chimes of three, down I crept to where I knew she slept, putting my ear to the door. Now, for someone so eager to remind others of her superior breeding despite being only a housekeeper, didn't the same lady snore like a trooper, and so listening to the snorts and whistles of her I knew I had her at my mercy.

From off the bed I had a sheet with me to put over my head like the Whiteboys, for many's the night my hooded companions and myself used to go on the prowl against people we had sworn vengeance on over religion and land, and so here was I at it again, except this time the enemy was not some landlord but this dried-up spinster with no property or cattle, yet Protestant, still, and just as bitter.

Soft on my two bare feet, I was in the room now, and there she was lying on her back, the snores of her rattling the very chamber pot under the bed, some sort of a nightcap covering her scalp, and standing there I studied her, knowing I could do as I liked with her for all the bad intent she had directed towards my young companion and myself, for what had we done to her to deserve such treatment? Nothing was the answer, save she was this out and out oul' rip who would not be missed if she never shook a room with her noise again, for hadn't I done the thing before, and even out of practice could again, lying on top of her gripping her mouth and nose, the weight of me and her shortness of breath putting an end to her malice.

But observing her in the bed, I had second thoughts, for she wasn't drunk like all them others, so maybe I should have brought the girl along to help in the task, hating the one in the bed as much as I did, maybe even more.

The longer I stood there the colder my feet grew, along with the resolve to carry out what I had come for, so, drawing the bedsheet over my head, I decided to leave with the satisfaction at least of throwing a scare into her without laying a hand on her.

So there was me ready to bawl '*Boo!*', or some similar expression, when didn't she let this almighty great fart out of her, loud enough to wake the dead, herself, as well, and starting up, saw this object all in white above her, a fierce yell emerging from her, and instead of gagging her for good, as intended, next thing I was out of the room and up the stairs before she roused the entire household with her outcry.

In the morning, Miss McBride, we were informed, had had a bad night and was still not herself, making a total of two women in the house now taking to their beds, Dunwoody calling me into his study with the big long face on him, and it was hard to keep my own straight when he said the housekeeper swore she had seen an apparition in the small hours in her room all clothed in ghastly white.

'You and I, Bernard, must pray for her and help convince her she was sorely mistaken.'

'Maybe she made it up,' says I.

'But why would she do such a terrible thing?'

'Sometimes women like drawing attention to themselves if they think they're not getting enough of it.'

'But she wants for nothing here.'

'Indeed and you're right. But instead of conjuring up ghosts out of her own head she might be better off with the holy variety, for she doesn't come to any of our meetings, so I've noticed.'

'You think you might be able to lead her over salvation's

threshold and through the gates of redemption?'

'Sure, haven't I helped the right few others in that direction?'

'Indeed you have, Brother Black, indeed you have, and long may it continue, for I see no end to this glorious mission of ours.'

And with all the right lingo at my command, wasn't I the lad revelling in it, and a minute later he led the way up the stairs to where I was able to view my handiwork from the night before.

Stretched on her back, a vinegar-soaked napkin covering her brow, there she lay, face as white as chalk.

'Oh, Mr Dunwoody, sir, do you think the house is haunted?'

'No such thing exists, Sarah. It's only in your head, and must be banished by prayer and turning away from worldly things.'

'But I have done nothing else.'

'And I believe you. But you still must have allowed some tiny shred of dark matter creep in and take hold unawares.'

'Aye, like a thief in the night,' says I, putting my oar in.

'Amen to that, Brother Black, amen to that.'

So down the pair of us go on either side of her, chasing out Satan with prayer, as Dunwoody would have it, yet never knowing the same boyo himself was kneeling across from him doing his utmost to keep from the laughing, and some time later when I told the girl what I had been up to, she gave in to merriment herself, so I put a hand over her mouth, but not in any bad way, as we were in her bed at the time, for with our old foe safely below raving about ghosts and demons, the urge had come over me to introduce Fagan, as the expression has it, even if she was carrying a keepsake from the last time he came calling, and wasn't she as tender and loving as if I was the papa already, the notion of it not nearly as bad as I thought, for why not turn over a new leaf as Dunwoody was always exhorting other people to do?

Lapped there in fine Irish linen, well fed with money put by, and the promise of more to come, who says a leopard can't change his spots, Jeremiah, thirteen, three, for even if I couldn't read the text, not everything I heard went in the one ear and out the other.

But life being like a see-saw, one minute up, then down, wasn't I bound to be set back as if all that stuff Dunwoody had been forcing down other people's throats about the wages of sin had stuck in my own as well. Yet never had I seen his eyes so bright or manner so eager, not even when the collection spilled over and a bigger plate had to be found.

'The wonder-working power of your witness, Bernard, has spread even further than we could ever have hoped or imagined, and so we can now go forward to a bigger, brighter, better church in a much more prosperous area. Not that we should withhold the gospel message from the poor among us, although your testimony of late would appear to have attracted a rowdier, rougher class of worshipper, and certainly we don't wish to be in competition with the music-hall and similar low places of entertainment.'

'Has something happened I don't know about?'

'Not some *thing*, Bernard. Some *one*.'

Lying back in his big leather chair, he closed his eyes as if about to come forth with a prayer or a text, peppering the air with titbits from the Good Book, for if most of the volumes I could see around me were only there for show, he did seem to know his Scriptures. At least to one who couldn't read a word, he did. But then for a fair part of my life I'd been bombarded by preachers, Bible-thumpers and the like anyway.

'It seems a most distinguished visitor has honoured us with a visit, and so impressed has he been with what he has seen and heard he has expressed a wish to meet with the person converting so many sinners with his reports and hellish testimony almost as if he had been present himself when they took place.'

Then, with a sly look, he said, 'Mind you, that is the mark of the true missioner. As for myself, I only wish I possessed even a ninth degree of such talent. But then that is why this famous writer wants to interview you and not Charles Dunwoody, even if it is his church.'

Rising, he went to a table where there was a pile of periodicals, and lifting one, set it in front of me.

'Here is the journal he contributes to, which despite being widely read all over, is published in the Scottish capital.'

'This same writer, might he be some sort of a small, sickly-looking individual with grey hair?' says I, recalling just such a person, but in the company of someone very different, being the breadth of a barn door, a great head on him naked as marble.

'So you have already met with him?' says he, looking disappointed.

'No, but I might have seen him in the hall one night along with another party,' making no mention of a third man, older, with the look of a bailiff or writ-server about him, and riding in a carriage with his two friends, while me and the girl kept our heads down in a ditch, and now I knew where all three were bound, and if Dunwoody had his way we would shortly be meeting face to face.

Having no intention of appearing in print again, despite it being in some gentleman's magazine, and not a broadside, I knew I no longer could afford to stay on here, and even though every night a miracle was promised, it looked as if I might have to perform one of my own without assistance from above.

That same afternoon up in my room I heard the front-door bell peal, then ring again and again, as if the caller, whoever he or she might be, was hell-bent on getting an answer. Thanks to my previous play-acting with the bedsheet, the housekeeper was still not fully recovered, but I heard her go downstairs anyway so as not to have her master disturbed at his devotions, as she referred to them.

Listening on the landing, for I was now as nervous as a cat regarding my situation, I became even more alarmed at hearing my name, for whoever it was on the doorstep seemed to be enquiring after a Mr Black, so I raced to an upstairs window. But by the time I got my eye to it, the door had been shut and my visitor gone, so I went below and out through the kitchen into the back garden in case he still was prowling about.

To my surprise, as well as aggravation, who should I see there but the girl Hannah taking her ease on a summer-seat, and having told her to stay indoors away from the prying gaze of the neighbours, even though the hedge was near as high as the house, I pulled her inside with me.

Up in her room, spreading herself out on the bed, didn't she come over all hot and amorous, quickly changing her tune on seeing me going through her effects in search of money, or anything else of value she might have laid her magpie hands on, and, taking hold of her, I hissed in her ear, 'Listen to me, there's people here who would make bother for us on account of what we done across the water, and to save ourselves we have to get away from here.'

Yet far from being put out by the information, rising up, she went to the chest I had been ransacking a minute earlier as if prepared to start packing herself.

'No,' I told her, 'you must stay here in the house so as not to raise suspicion, and after the evening meeting I'll come back for you.'

Dumb as she might be, she still could smell a lie better than most, and next instant she was on the top of me, but not in any affectionate manner, and so yet again I shivered on the brink of finishing the business with my two bare hands, for why be tied to a millstone who might yet drag me down along with her? However, changing my mind, for easy living had left me soft as a marshmallow, I surrendered, telling her, so be it, the two of us would go to the hall after all and under cover of the final hymn slip away together.

Yet never will I comprehend the crazy ways of women, for taking hold of my prick, which to my additional puzzlement had risen up stiff as a rod, the same jade directed it to a place it often had entered before, and it was like we were back in an English hayshed once more before a certain person present put a light to it and had us take to our heels and the open road, and now the same thing was happening all over again.

Lying there, I became restless, for the caller at the door was still a worry to me. An English voice, what little I'd heard of it, but would our famous writer person come out all this way only to be turned away? Why not wait until the evening and a more convenient time and place? The thing was a mystery that wouldn't let go of me, so leaving Hannah asleep on the bed, I went downstairs a second time and out into the orchard, where it was near dark by now with a mist creeping over the fields at the back of the house where there were cows, for I could hear the herdsman calling them home to be milked.

Off to the side of the house lay the stables where Dunwoody's horse was kept which would convey us to the city later. The boy who tended the mare and was to drive us there lived in the village, but I saw him with a bucket in his hand, so I asked him if he had seen anyone near the house that afternoon. Touching his cap, for he was a well-mannered young cub, he replied, no, he had not, for he had been home all day and had only just come to get the carriage ready for his reverence and myself, making me sound on a par with his master, something I now would have to turn my back on and would surely miss, for playing the big cheese had sat well with me, and far better than expected.

But whoever was on my tail was of much greater concern, and determined to scout further I bade good night to the stable lad, whose name was Albert and Protestant like everyone else here, myself being the oddity in the place, yet not for too much longer, I told myself, venturing down the back lane as though taking the air on an evening stroll.

My route led past this ancient graveyard full of near-toppled headstones all mossy with the names rubbed out through age and neglect, and entering I made my way to where an iron gate opened on to the main road that ran through the village. Above this same gate was an old lamp, as once upon a time it would be lit at night to keep intruders away, and so it was odd seeing such a thing in the light of all the stories of grave-robbing I had been recounting of late. Still I doubted if there were any pickings buried there to tempt someone with a bag and a crowbar, and had been that way for a very long time.

The gate was padlocked, and peering through its rusty bars I could see the road beyond, as dead and empty of life as what lay at my back, and about to give up on my search, suddenly I was rewarded by the sound of a horse approaching, then the glimmer of a carriage lamp, for it was near dusk by now, and into view came a chaise with its driver up on its seat, a rough-looking individual smoking a pipe, although if he had any passengers inside there was no way of knowing as the rig's curtains were drawn against the chill night air.

Some little distance on he brought his horse to a halt and, getting down, proceeded to make his water in the ditch until another person stepped out, and seeing him, shadowy and all as it was, I took in a breath, for it was the giant with the shaven head I had previously seen travelling in another coach, and then some nights later sitting alongside Dunwoody's writer friend, the pair of them close together at the back of the gospel hall.

From the sound of things, piss or no piss, the driver was receiving a right royal roasting, but being far too removed I was unable to catch the actual words. Yet I could tell the voice was not the same as the one I had heard on Dunwoody's doorstep asking after me, convinced it must have come from whoever was still in the coach.

From where I stood, it looked as if my visitors were settling in for a long wait. Even the driver had now some sort of horse blanket about his shoulders, while his passengers stayed snug inside. But my days and nights running through fields and sleeping in barns and under hedges were far behind me, and so I decided if I could reach the city and melt into its streets I might yet be able to slip the closing net like I'd done so many times before.

The young stable lad was still at his work when I returned to the house, and I stood watching while he combed and curried his master's mare like it was his private pride and joy, which fitted in well with what I had in mind.

'Tell me, how fast can she go, Albert? To outpace something on the road, say?'

'Another carriage, you mean?'

'Aye, about the same size and weight with a similar quota of passengers.'

'Nothing on four legs in these parts can touch her. But his reverence favours more a trot than a gallop.'

'Still, this evening he might think different, and so if I were to tip you the wink, would you give her her head?'

From his face it was clear he was up for it, so shaking hands with him I gave him a sixpence, and well pleased he was, touching his cap to me like earlier.

My next hurdle, however, was going to be harder to surmount, and over the light supper the housekeeper had laid out for Dunwoody and myself I approached it cannily at first. But he was in good form, which made my task easier, so I put it to him, 'This writer fellow you say who wants a story for his paper, surely he'd be far better off talking with somebody a lot cleverer than myself. After all, you're the one the people trust to lead them in the right direction after I've done my work with them.'

He smiled at this, and I could tell he was flattered, so growing bolder, I said, 'Still there's a deal of envy among your own kind looking down from their pulpits of a Sunday and seeing far too many empty pews for their liking. They might do you mischief if you let them.'

Despite my making most of it up, I could see he was worried.

'You've heard tell of such plots?'

'Only rumours and gossip. But you should take care, for there's those who would bring you down if they could.'

'Beware of men who will deliver you up and scourge you in their synagogues. Matthew, ten, seventeen,' quotes he, getting up and striding about.

'Well, you're the Bible scholar here, but not too far from where we are this minute there's people not so Christian-minded, and I fear they may mean you harm.'

'Here? Here, you say?'

I saw I had him nearly hooked, so I told him, knowing such dangerous types as I did, and him being only a man of the cloth, I had a plan to defeat them, and he said, 'Tell me what you wish me to do.'

'Allow me to handle these dogs before they get close enough to bite.'

He seemed content with this, and so when we had laid down our forks, I said, 'While these same curs are in the neighbourhood, I don't much care leaving my daughter here, so if she could come with us tonight I would greatly appreciate it, as would she, for she has a love for the gospel message and longs to be gathered in.'

After I'd spoken he gave me this sly look, and I thought sure I'd lost my fish and it was back in the water again ready to slide away as slippery as ever. But, instead, he said, 'So be it. If she pants after the Word, as the hart pants after the water brooks, then let her thirst no more. But for the sake of propriety, take care her condition remains as discreet as possible.'

'She'll be quiet as a mouse, you have my solemn word on it.'

But if there was a joke in that he was the last to see it, so bound up in his own importance was the same gentleman, and so I left him getting into his clericals ready for the night's performance, never knowing I had another and very different one in mind.

By the time I was above with Hannah in her room she was ready and dressed as if she couldn't wait to see the back of the place, even if it had been good to us. But our time here had run out, knowing, as I did, who was waiting on the road for us and she didn't, and seeing her standing there with her bundle all eager and willing to travel yet another part of the way with me, didn't a sort of a softness take hold, telling myself I might even be pleased I wasn't leaving her behind after all.

However, unwilling to go down such a namby-pamby road, I ordered her to hide her bundle under her skirts, padding out what was already there, and after she had arranged her clothes, she took hold of my hand and I thought sure she was going to go all lovey-dovey and tearful on me. But, instead, didn't she fill it with more of the plunder she'd filched from the minister's missus, and knowing it would fetch the right few bob when needed, I wasn't annoyed like the first time I'd caught her dipping her hand where it shouldn't have been.

'Well, and aren't you the right thieving young piece of goods and no mistake.'

Taking it as a compliment, she laughed, and I did as well, even though who knew what twist of fate lay before us, and when we got below and out into the yard our young driver was waiting for us, and seeing who was with me, being sappy and green, he got all flustered and taken aback, and I told him, 'We are in your hands, so I'm depending on you to see this young lady comes to no harm on the road tonight.'

Finally Dunwoody himself came down, decked out in his usual clericals with white collar band and Bible in hand, and with me and the girl already seated inside, he climbed in without a word or a look, taking his place on one side of our female passenger and me on the other.

A dense swirl of mist still hung about, for a river ran nearby, but I had told young Albert not to put the side candle-lights on so we could steal up on our enemies unawares, his master sitting all the while like a graven image with eyes closed as if whatever happened next was in the hands of the Almighty. But I knew it was myself, not He, who had the ordering of events, and when we were clear of the house and I could see the tail end of the other carriage sitting by the side of the road up ahead, leaning forward, I said to the boy, 'Drive on slow and easy till we get near, and then when I give the word go like the wind.'

And so, close, ever closer, we came, and still no sign we had been discovered, for the back curtain was pulled across, while it looked like the coachman was either asleep or drunk, or both, even better.

But when about a dozen yards separated us, someone in the carriage in front gave a shout, and the horse reared up, followed by another louder cry of, 'Damn and blast it!' and Dunwoody himself called out, 'Merciful Lord, save and deliver us from those who would undo us!' and without waiting for my command young Albert lashed the mare's rump and off she flew like a steam train, leaving our enemies, whoever they might be and whatever their intentions, surprised and confounded by the roadside.

Enfield, Middlesex ✖ 12 September

IN LIGHT OF THE RECENT piece in *Blackwood's Magazine* regarding the events of the evening of 20 August last, I should here like to record my own personal recollection of the occasion, as I happened to be present in the closing moments of the hunt for the former felon William Hare, and the author of the article was not, for while my colleague Jack Slack and I were pursuing that same slippery customer along certain Irish country roads, Mr De Quincey was already putting the final touches to what he would go on to write about his 'subject', as usual not greatly heeding others' views on the matter, as I recall at one of our after-dinner discussions back in Belfast's Commercial Hotel.

'Tell me, Speed, are you by any chance familiar with the term "antinomianism"?'

'No,' I informed him, reconciled to yet another lecture, his eyes growing brighter as his tongue tried keeping pace with the thoughts teeming behind that bulging brow of his.

'Well, for your information, it is associated with certain individuals who believe they are the Elect and can therefore absolve themselves of all of their past actions, no matter how heinous, by embracing the gospel.'

'Sounds to me a pretty convenient excuse for certain criminal types undeserving of either our sympathy, or understanding.'

'Which is precisely why you happen to be the policeman whereas I myself am not.'

'I doubt if there was ever much confusion on that particular score.'

He laughed.

'Nevertheless, not a great deal separates us, as we both seem to be striving after the same prize. Or have you perhaps lost some of your original zest and zeal for the enterprise?'

But if there was an answer to that, I wasn't prepared to give him the satisfaction of using it against me, one wily adversary being more than enough to be going on with without another treating me as his intellectual inferior, for although I had never heard tell of 'antinomianism', or 'justification', for that matter, neither expression was about to change my opinion of someone De Quincey seemed to believe had himself joined that same band of bogus believers, and so I was quite content to let our little writer friend scribble whatever he pleased, being faced some evenings later with something far more pressing in the Antrim countryside, yelling out to our dolt of a coachman to chase after our quarry presently disappearing into the gloom ahead of us.

Whip in hand, however, he continued sitting on his box as though stupefied, and growing near as agitated as myself, Jack Slack leapt to the ground as though prepared to take the reins himself.

But the man cried out, 'I want no bother with the law in these parts! Nor with them having it on their side, neither!'

'Here and now *I* am the law and you are obstructing a police officer in his duty.'

And only after I had thrown in some sort of sop of a reward, did he finally force his horse to go forward as I commanded.

But by now the vehicle in front had vanished from sight, its driver having no side-lights on, and so I said, 'Jack, I am afraid we have lost them.'

'Them?'

'Aye, two men and a young woman, for I caught a glimpse of all three as they raced by.'

'But one of them is the person we're seeking?'

'I'd wager my life on it, and even if he has just now slipped us, I know where he is yet to be found, and so this night I intend to finish what you and I both came here for.'

'I sincerely trust you may be right,' said he, before leaning forward and enquiring of the driver, 'You're certain you can convey us back safely to the city?' and with a flash of his old impudence the other rejoined, 'Sure, and if I succeeded in getting you two gentlemen out here in one piece, amn't I bound to return you to Mrs Bunting's establishment in the same condition?'

Even so, I wasn't convinced of the wisdom of heading directly to the hotel as he said, as our adversary might be making for the place he knew best, ready to rain down more bolts of wrath and damnation on the heads of his listeners.

And so after a good half-hour or so of brisk travelling, back in the city streets once more, I put it to Slack, 'Are you able to recall where this gospel preacher's hall is situated from here?' and peering out at the houses on either side of us, he replied, 'Aye, I feel reasonably certain of it.'

And unwilling to be excluded, the driver volunteered, 'Lavinia Street is where you're looking for, near the gasworks,' an area of the city I had never explored before, the dwellings close-packed and the lanes mired and narrow, with barely enough room for a conveyance to pass through. But our driver seemed more at ease with his present surroundings than those in the country and proceeded to take us through a warren of back streets and entries until we came out on to what looked like a square of sorts.

Head drooping, and blowing, the horse had come to a halt, and to be fair it had managed remarkably well, being almost as worn out as the conveyance it was drawing. Peering out to get his bearings, Slack was staring about him, but it was Dermot who provided the information we sought.

'Through that narrow opening up ahead of you is where it's at. So, will I wait for you or not?'

'No, I think we're sufficiently capable of making our own

way back on foot,' Slack told him, and handing over some silver I thanked our guide for his services, and after inspecting the cash, he said, 'Well, I trust you'll arrive at a satisfactory conclusion to your business, which I still never got to find out about, save a certain flighty gentleman seemed to be involved. But, as I always say, no names, no pack drill, so good luck to the pair of you,' and chirruping to his old plug of a mare he sent it wearily clip-clopping off into the darkness.

After the sound of hooves and the ring of iron-shod wheels on the cobbles had faded away, in the silence it seemed as though the very buildings themselves all around were listening intently, and if anyone dwelt there, they, too, seemed waiting to see what my companion and I were about next, into my head drifting the expression, so near yet still so far.

'Come, we must hurry, for the meeting should be well under way by now,' said Slack, a note of urgency in his voice, and indeed he appeared renewed, the great shoulders squared, prepared for whatever might ensue, and it was odd to think I had been the one to infect him with an eagerness for the chase, and now it was I who hesitated.

Leading the way, he plunged into the darkness, and not knowing what to expect, blindly I followed. Some sort of moon had risen by now, pale and watery after the storms of recent days, yet barely lighting the path ahead, until finally, hand in the air, my guide halted, but when I came alongside I could see a look of puzzlement on his features.

'Listen,' he said.

Yet nothing could be heard save the sound of some old shutter creaking in the wind.

'There should be hymn-singing, at least.'

'So we're near?'

'Look, there. See?'

And he was right, for there *was* a building, with a high arched doorway and matching side windows, yet all within as black as could be.

'You're certain this is the place?'

Not answering, he went forward to peer inside, then, taking hold of the door handle, he shook it until the metal rang.

'Jack, for pity's sake, come away. The place is as dead as the grave. Can't you see, he's given us the slip yet again.'

But, stubborn as an ox, strong as one, too, he continued pressing hard on the door, and next minute he had burst his way in, the legal terms 'trespass' and 'forced entry' coming to mind, and here in a place where the penalties for both might be considerably more severe than anywhere else.

Yet there seemed nothing for it but follow him, and so I, too, was inside, where what little light coming from a glass dome in the roof showed we were, indeed, in some sort of meeting-house after all, yet all its forms and benches empty as though a plague had scoured the place clean.

So yet again I queried whether we had come to the right place or not, but, clapping his hands and sending up a great echo, he called out, 'If anyone is here, in God's name, show yourself!'

'Desist, Jack, the place is as bare as the palm of your hand.'

Yet he would not be persuaded.

'I can still smell the stink of his abomination, hear his blasphemy. From these seats I watched and listened, yet not once did I raise my voice and cry out against his sacrilege.'

'And so now he has tricked us again. Can't you see the game is over, played out?'

Yet even as I spoke I knew it was too late for any kind of sense or reason, seeing him settle himself on one of the benches.

'Very well, so be it. But you and I have travelled too long and too far together to end our journey like this, so I will be at the hotel until noon tomorrow. But not an hour more, for I plan to take the first available crossing to Liverpool, then on to London.'

Outside the streets seemed as dark and forbidding as ever, and standing there I wondered how I might manage to find my way back to my lodging without the help of the man still lingering in that deserted place like some diehard disciple patiently waiting for Judgement Day itself.

Yet Providence seemed to be looking out for me, for after less than an hour I caught sight of the splendid new Assembly building where the linen merchants of the town conducted their business, lying only a short distance away from Waring Street and the Commercial Hotel.

When I got inside De Quincey was in the taproom, for I could see his tangle of grey hair above one of the snugs there, and he must have been staying up to waylay me before I got the chance to sneak upstairs.

As things stood there seemed no way of avoiding him, and I was greeted with, 'And how, may I enquire, did our little fishing expedition go this evening? Still, never mind, I can see from your expression the catch got away. By the by, where *is* your angling companion?'

'As you seem more than familiar with our movements, why don't you tell me?'

He looked at me for a moment before replying.

'While *you* were pursuing certain lines of investigation of your own, going to our preacher's tabernacle of redemption and repentance this evening, I found the place abandoned, congregation scattered to the four winds, and his famous disciple, having failed to show up and perform, our pastor was also preparing to decamp.'

'And did you get to speak with him? Had he anything to say?'

'Just that he, the pastor, had been betrayed by a Judas, a wolf in sheep's clothing, little knowing, of course, how close he was to the same gentleman's history. And not only had he abused the Christian sanctity of his home, he had corrupted his own stable boy to help him flee along with his young hussy.'

He paused, waiting for a response, but my head was still too full with what I had just heard.

'My dear chap, I am truly sorry the way this has turned out for you, finally denied a confrontation after all your immense efforts to achieve a resolution. But may I ask, do you intend still to soldier on, you and Mr Slack?'

'For me the case is closed.'

'Yet even if this old adversary appears to have won the battle, aren't you in the least bit curious regarding his present whereabouts?'

'No, for already I am pretty much certain of the location.'

On the instant his expression changed and he came forward in his chair.

'You are? How?'

Observing him at this instant, so convinced of his own powers of perception, yet so gullible, too, was something to relish, so I informed him, 'As far from here as it's possible to get on this island, and where someone like himself will never be found by people such as you and I.'

Sighing, eyes closed, he seemed to sink back in upon himself, his little dark-tinctured bottle to his lips, not caring whether I stayed or took my leave, and so I left him to his dreaming.

Yet though I felt a pressing need for my own bed, my brain was a great deal clearer now, much more so than Mr Thomas De Quincey's, readily swallowing, as he had done, what I had told him, when I was privately convinced William Hare was still somewhere here in the city, and with money in his pocket might be heading back across that same stretch of water he and I had first travelled together on this tangled journey of ours.

Safely settled in new lodgings, well away from our recent run of misadventures, I put it to the girl, 'Why don't I take a run outside and try and barter some of that stuff you laid your hands on back at the minister's place?'

But suspecting some ploy, keeping a tight hold on her bundle, she shook her head, and so I had to take her with me.

However, no such establishment of the sort we sought seemed to be at hand in such a stiff-necked, Protestant hole, not even near the docks where we were staying, so we turned back, having another good reason to lie low in Mrs Lawlor's kip of a boarding-house in Skipper Street, for, pushing through the crowds, while still looking high and low for the three golden globes, didn't I hear someone call out to me, and when I turned to see who it might be, I got an even bigger fright, for wasn't it the same rascal who had first set me on the missionary path, advising me how to get a free feed for myself. Yet, going by the current state of him, it would appear I was the one who had prospered, while he had not.

A second time he let this cry out of him, but having no wish to be seen next nor near him, pulling on the girl's sleeve, I raced her down the nearest entry, as others might recognise me in public as well, and so the plan was now to put this place and all my recent history far behind me and take the first cross-channel ferry.

But when I got to where the boats were lying moored, and saw the crowds waiting there for the start of an even longer journey by sea, Liverpool, then on beyond to the port of Boston, why not follow their example was what entered my head, for wasn't Amerikay the place we Irish usually ended up in when driven to the wall, and wasn't my own back as sore pressed as the next man's, maybe even more so?

So there all they were gathered in their near-naked desperation, men, women, children, babes in arms, huddled on the quayside with their bags and boxes, and by the look and sound of them from every part of the island itself and thus unlikely to have seen or heard of someone such as myself.

Nevertheless, I kept the brim of my hat pulled down over my brow and my ulster, as they call it here, buttoned to the throat, a garment his reverence had donated from his own wardrobe, even though a shade short for me, while from the same source the girl had found herself a sort of a dark woollen cloak to cover her condition.

Sailing tickets to hand, we joined the line waiting to climb the gangway to the steamship *Erin*, for I had heard the name from the people ordering the loading, as coarse and ill-mannered a crew as ever you'd care to come across, yelling and swearing as if we were little more than cattle to them, and when we got on board we might well have been, given the filthy state of the decks and quarters below where we were crammed in on top of one another, the noise and stink of it making a very hell of a place, with people already throwing up even before the ropes were cast off.

By the time we were under way well out into the Irish Sea, the land already starting to disappear, a mist having come up, so the weeping and wailing began. But not being sentimental over poor Oul' Ireland like the rest of her shipmates, my companion was more concerned about keeping her breakfast down, having found a corner near a family of five, and recognising how far gone she was, the mother offered her sisterly sympathy.

Leaving her in more capable hands than my own, I took myself up on deck, where cinders from the smokestack were raining down, so that between the wind and the gusts of soot those of us who had braved the weather were soon looking like blackamoors.

Sprawled in the lea of one of the great packing cases marked for England were three travellers with a bottle being passed around, and by the look and the noise of them already drunk, and had been before setting foot on board, one of them singing away regardless of the breeze and flying clinker.

Keeping my distance, I moved to another part of the deck, but one of them called out, 'Sure, don't be so stand-offish, your Honour. Come and join us and share some of our crack!' and hearing myself addressed in that manner, fulsome as it might be, yet with no malice or mockery intended, it seemed, I made my way to where they were stretched at their ease on the bare planks like it was some corner of a hayfield they had been toiling in scarce a day previous.

Making room for me, the man with the bottle greeted me with a, 'Have a drop of the hard stuff, and put a fresh lining on your insides,' and not having sampled a drop in an age I took a swallow of the stuff, as pure and clear a run of poteen as ever I tasted.

'Outward bound for the land of the free like ourselves, are you?' enquired another, and already starting to feel the benefit of the liquor, I told him indeed I was, and he said, 'But you'll not be getting your hands dirty like my brothers and me, for we're only poor labouring folk, while you're used to the easier life.'

Which was when it occurred to me, because of the clothes on my back and the regular use of a razor, I must present the appearance of someone greatly superior to the old William Hare who not so long since had been as rough as themselves, and the more I thought of it the more pleased with myself I grew.

'A medical gentleman, is it? Or a lawyer, would it be?'

To which I heard myself reply, 'More a humble follower of the Redeemer, and preacher of the Word,' and the instant I said it I saw them looking at the bottle still in my hand, and with a sarcastic ring to his voice the older one remarked, 'You've got yourself well shot of the clerical collar, so I see,' as in the heat of conversation I had let my coat flap open.

But as often the case when peril threatens, even with drink taken, tongue and brain can conspire together, and so I told him, 'Carrying the Gospel Message to our Red Indian brethren across the sea, it's more fitting to come amongst them dressed as an ordinary individual,' which seemed to satisfy them. But only till the drink curdled, souring their previous good humour, I told myself, the lesson being not to be quite so forward, or over-familiar with strangers, and so down I went below to where the girl was still being sick into a bucket, made worse by her delicate state and a swell at sea starting up.

What with the stench and the moaning and the children squealing, I was now feeling queasy myself, and so I set off to find some place else where there might be a respite from this hellish crossing. But the ticket I had was for steerage, while the next level up had cabins and something called staterooms where the better-off could take their ease. Bridging the two parts, a rope had been strung across, but as no one was on duty to keep the sheep from the goats, as it were, I ducked below, trusting a certain air of respectability would carry the day without me having to open my mouth, having the impression that first-class must be the preserve of toffs and others like them.

But when I got to the promised land, as I saw it, I realised I had been mistaken, for despite their attire and look of money the crowd there were as well on in drink as the three people I had parted with up on the open deck earlier.

Whiskey, wine, porter and ale were flowing freely, along with cards on the go, while a group of racing men were squandering their winnings on a parcel of trollops hanging on their necks at the bar, the same red-faced gents yelling the odds as if still on the course at Ferryhouse or Downpatrick or some of the other big horse meetings.

Now, it had been some considerable time since I had been at liberty to indulge myself, but the taste of mountain dew from up above still lingered, and so giving in to temptation, and him a man of God, says he, slipping through the throng, I purchased a dram, then another, swallowing them down like some thirsty traveller in the desert, and afterwards took a seat near the door where I could observe the proceedings without drawing attention to myself.

And so wasn't it the great change, me sitting there with an empty glass in my hand when once upon a time I would have enjoyed nothing better than being in the thick of things, for, as often is the case in drink, words lead to certain other words, and taking offence at something or other, one of the sporting types was now shouting and swearing he would see one of his companions in hell first. But as the noise was so general, no one else in the place seemed to be taking much notice, save a sober-looking gent across in a far corner sitting quietly on his own like myself.

The upset among the horsey lot with their whores guzzling champagne had now taken a turn for the worse, the one starting it off yelling, 'No one insults our king while there's a loyal breath in my body! Damn you, sir, and your treasonable remarks!', a glass being smashed, and someone on the far side of the room shouted, 'No politics, sir! Take your views some place else!'

'Aye, back to England, where they belong! We're still in Irish waters!'

'Not for much longer, thank God!'

With that the insults commenced flying thick and fast. But before bottles and glasses became the ammunition of choice, and my head was split open with Donnybrook confetti, as it's called, it was time for me to take my leave.

Rising to go, I saw that the shortish person in the corner in the dun overcoat and billycock hat, neat and contained in his person like some sort of tradesman or other professional, was himself on his feet, and catching his glance in my direction, sharp and piercing as an arrow, this bad feeling took a hold of me, and resolving to keep as far away from him as I could, I made my way below decks where I belonged, despite the decent suit of clothes on my back.

Yet coming down the companionway was like descending into a cesspit, and I very nearly turned about, ready to brave the weather a second time even though the seas by now were pounding the wooden walls on either side of us.

Threading a path through the mass of bodies stretched out and lying on the floor, I tried to recall where it was I had left the girl, searching for a familiar head of reddish hair among all the rest. But as more of that particular hue is common among my own people, the task seemed impossible, until, to my great relief, I caught sight of a mop of hair I *did* recognise, but pale as straw, belonging to one of the brats of the woman we had sat down alongside earlier. She was wailing and looking for her mother, who I knew could not be too far off, and so following the youngster I saw her push her way through the legs of a cluster of folk gathered around someone in their midst.

'What she needs is the attention of a physician,' one of the onlookers was saying, while another responded, 'But what are her chances of finding such a person in a floating hell-hole the like of this? God help the poor cratur, sure she's no better than some animal in a field. At least there she'd have solid ground under her.'

On hearing the words, this dark presentiment took hold of me and I hung back until I heard a woman cry out, 'Stand aside and give her room, for it's her time!' and coming over all queasy the men watching moved away.

Seeing me betwixt and between, as it were, a bearded old man, slow to leave, enquired if I was a doctor, and without giving me the chance to deny it, he called out, 'Make way, make way, a medical man is here!' and before I knew what was happening the crowd had parted and I was thrust forward to witness what was now upon me like a punishment, for on her back, barely decently covered, there she lay, with the same woman who had befriended her earlier kneeling alongside, urging her to help nature by bearing down and pushing hard, and looking up and catching sight of me standing there, the woman berated me.

'Bad cess to you for leaving her in her time of travail when she needs you most,' and another woman piped up, 'Is he not a doctor, after all? Is he the father?' and next minute they had rounded on me like a pack of harpies, while the girl strained and moaned, the sweat streaming off her like rain.

Now, if I was to swear, seeing her suffer thus, my heart went out to her, I would be a liar, being more concerned with my own welfare, so I said, 'No, no, she's my daughter.'

But far from helping my cause, didn't it make them all the more vengeful, calling me this filthy baste for abusing his own flesh and blood for his own unnatural ends, while the only person present there who could speak out in my cause was on her back powerless, even if she had been willing.

'Do you not even have a wish to see what you have brought into the world? Is there no human dacency in you at all?'

To be truthful, very little, I might have answered, that's if I'd wanted to make the situation any worse than it was, for already some were raising their fists, and it looked like I might be in for a right drubbing for all the woes they themselves had suffered at the hands of other brutes like myself. However, this was not the time for such dainty notions, flight being called for, and urgently, to where they couldn't follow.

Recalling what was inside it, I made a grab for the bundle lying alongside its owner on the floor, raising an even greater outcry, for not only was I this vile animal, but now a heartless thief to boot, and seeing what I was about one of the women pulled it from my hand.

'Shame on you, robbing the few duds put aside for herself and her poor wee wean. Is there no Christian pity in you whatsoever?'

And, again, none, I might well have replied, or barely any worth bothering about, and so with their screeches ringing in my ears I made for the sanctuary of the upper decks.

Halfway up the stairs, stopping, I listened for a moment. Yet even if the sound of some newborn could be heard above all that clamour, who could tell where such a cry came from anyway?

However, if I had hoped to find refuge in the open air, I was greatly mistaken, for tucked away safely out of sight, as I thought, behind some rigging, some while later I heard a voice call out, 'You're sure he came up here?' with another person answering, 'Where else, the dirty Protestant pig, turning his back on his leavings down below?'

'Anyway, one thing's for certain, he won't get far.'

'Not unless he can walk on water like the heavenly One he takes his orders from.'

'Sure, can't we always put him to the test.'

Knowing who they were by this time, I was in no mood to appreciate the jest, for it was the ones I had come across with the poteen earlier, and having got wind of my history below, were now intent on flushing me out.

Crouched there in as tight a spot as could be, open sea all around, and three against one, I searched about for something to defend myself with, but there was nothing to be seen, not even a bare stick. Yet, having no wish to be cornered like some trapped creature, rising to my feet, I waited for them to catch sight of their prey, and sure enough didn't there arise a sort of a hallooing like you might hear at a hunt in the country-side instead of on a steamship in the middle of the North Irish Channel.

As so often happens, the one leading the rush was the smallest of the lot, and so I had the advantage in height, as well as being sober, for he began slipping and sliding about on the wet planks before he could get a proper footing, and so I could have shortened the odds with a decent kick.

But resorting to bluff, I called out, 'If robbery is your intent, then I guarantee not a one of you will set foot ashore a free man.'

'Robbery, is it? More the pot callin' the kettle black.'

'Despite what others may have informed you, my name is Bernard Black on a Bible mission to convert the heathen tribes of America's far West,' which, curious as it might seem, I had even nearly started half-believing myself.

'Never mind that. To hell with you and your fine clothes and fancy airs. Prepare yourself for a long swim, we'll leave the direction up to you.'

By their tone and manner, drink or no drink, I could tell they were in deadly earnest, especially the short one, who by now had got his balance back.

'So, what's it to be? Lep, or be pushed?' and determined not to have to make the choice either way, I put it to them, 'Here, look, I have money. Take it, and that'll be the end of it,' pulling out what I had.

But despite his lack of inches, the one who seemed to be the ringleader was still frothing like a mad dog.

'Damn you to hell. Give it to the poor colleen you tried to rob below.'

So there I stood, William Hare, as once was, a good head and shoulders more than a match for this spitting little banty cock, yet unable to raise a hand in my own defence, when from behind me didn't another person speak out, but in an English accent.

'Have a care, sir, for I have prior business with this same gentleman,' and turning, I saw it was the person I had taken note of earlier in the stateroom, standing now by the mouth of the companionway.

As though taking offence at someone his own size daring to challenge him, the one all puffed up and eager to assert his meagre manhood rushed at me. But before he could land a blow, regaining my courage, I laid him flat on the deck, and before he could rise, fair play or no fair play, I dealt him an almighty kick in the knackers with the full force of my boot.

Enraged by this, the remaining two prepared themselves to make a run at me, but the stranger in brown called out, 'Take a step closer, either one of you, and you will deal with my barker here,' a most curious term, surely, yet nothing in the least doggy about it, being a small silver-plated pistol he had in his hand.

'This gentleman is my responsibility and I will conduct my dealings with him without interference or hindrance, so I caution you not to obstruct police business.'

Now, whether it was the sight of the 'barker' or the word 'police', or a combination of both, but our two brave Irish boyos retreated cursing, leaving their relative stretched on his back where I had felled him, and as my dander was now well and truly up, I drew back my boot to finish the job as was my wont before I took on the pretence of turning the other cheek.

'A return to your old habits, is it? Another dead man to add to the reckoning?'

And the instant I heard the words, pulling back, all the heat left me, and I said, 'May the Lord forgive me for letting my temper get the better of me instead of thanking you for your timely interference. These ruffians were out to rob me of what little I have. Permit me to introduce myself. Bernard Black.'

'Percival Speed, and still the one I was baptised with, unlike certain other people I could name.'

He still had the little pistol in his fist, and keeping my eye on it, I pondered where it was I had seen him before, not just in the ship's saloon below but somewhere else, on dry land.

'Sir, I have the feeling you might be confusing me with someone else with looks similar to my own.'

'God forbid,' says he, laughing. 'One villain in this world is more than enough to be going on with.'

And all of a sudden it was as if we were sharing this fine

joke, he and I, save for his 'barker', of course, small and deadly like himself.

However, so taken up with our conversation were we, the person laid out nearby had been forgotten, but raising himself up and glaring in our direction, he cried out, 'May you burn in hell, the pair of you, mistreating a poor defenceless man so,' before stumbling off in the direction his friends had taken earlier.

Watching him go, my companion remarked, 'Hades, says he? Well, he may have got the destination right in *your* particular case,' and when I still refused to rise to his bait, he went on, 'A long and clever race you've run, my friend, but unless you're a better swimmer than I give you credit for, here is where it ends.'

But I was happy for him to savour his moment of triumph, having waited so long for it, as it now came to me where our paths had nearly, but not quite, crossed, for this was the second man in the carriage from some nights previously, and now hearing his voice, the same person who had been asking after Bernard Black at the minister's house earlier that day.

'Come, we both know the game is up, why bother denying it?' and when I still played dumb, putting a hand inside his coat, he drew forth a sheet of paper.

'Look at this face, then tell me a picture lies, and I have been wasting my time in pursuit of someone else, and not the man in front of me, murderer, gallows-cheater, impostor, thief, with God only knows what other crimes outstanding.'

Pretending to take a long and careful look at the image, I said, 'Well, whoever he is, he has the look of a right black-guard, and no mistake. Still, whatever he may have done, past or present, he's nothing to do with me, and if you believe we're connected you're mistaken, and so must look some place else.'

Before I could return his precious evidence, as he saw it, a gust of wind carried it out of my hand, and away it went flying overboard. But watching it go, he said, 'No matter, for the face it bears has been with me since the day I first set out to hunt its owner down, and now I have him in my sights, he can run no further.'

Growing tired of this cat and mouse game, I said, 'What is it you want with me?' and fixing me with a look, he replied, 'The truth, and from your own lips, as all those who once might have spoken out against you are where you put them on a surgeon's slab as so much butcher's meat.'

'Well, if what you tell me is indeed fact, then it would seem you've already tried and convicted me a second time, so it makes no difference what I say, and so I will bid you good day and take my leave of you.'

But if I imagined that was to be the be all and end of it, I was sorely mistaken, for before I could reach the companionway and be shot of this Mr Percival Speed, as he called himself, I heard him call out, 'Take another step at your peril!' and when I turned, he had his little pistol out, aiming it in my direction.

'If you imagine I came all this way to resolve this matter in a polite and civilised manner, believe me, you are mistaken, for my particular calling is neither, and so, by God, sir, I will get an admission out of you by fair means or foul, the choice is yours.'

Now, a drowning man, they say, is supposed to see the events of his former life float past in front of him, and judging by what lay all around on either side of me, I wondered if I might get to find out the truth of it, for it seemed either that or a ball to the brain.

'Well? Speak up, damn you!'

All this time I hadn't moved an inch, while he kept coming on, until I could near see, as I thought, straight down the muzzle of his barker to what lay waiting primed there. Even more of a craziness, didn't I imagine I heard some other voice in my head making that same demand of me, and I was back in another place, facing someone else, an attorney's wig instead of a hat on his head, a writ in his hand instead of a cocked pistol aimed in my direction.

But all that was dead and gone, or so I believed until now, and so, pistol or no pistol, I took a step forward.

'Have a care what you are about, for no one will mourn you ending up like all those you once throttled.'

'And no one will miss some scurvy English dog joining the fishes, either,' making a rush at him, being more than a match, I reckoned, for this cockney sparrow of a policeman, never having much love for his profession, or his country, for that matter.

But, whether through intent or surprise, didn't the gun go off in his hand after all, followed by the ping of the bullet striking the smokestack, and before he could let loose another round, even if it had been his wish, I had him in my grip, the barker flying from his fist and into the scuppers, where it was of no use to either one of us.

Despite his age and softer way of life, he was far fitter than I gave him credit for, while I had said adieu to much of my old fighting skills, and so it was not long before the pair of us were rolling about the deck together, me on top one minute, then him, until it ended up where we could carry on no longer, panting, on our backs, our good clothes near ruined with the dirt and the wet, and after a time I heard him sigh, 'Percy, you have grown far too old for your former vocation, and a man should know when to leave it to others a lot younger than himself.'

Lying outstretched there, and catching my glance towards his little pocket weapon lying in the gutter, he said, 'Never fear, it was carried mainly for show. Still, grant me one final favour in return before we turn our backs on one another for good.'

But even though I had no need to enquire what that request might be, the words he wanted to hear still stuck in my throat, and after a time he gave another deep sigh.

'Very well, so be it, Hare by name as well as nature, sly and secretive to the very last. Still, no matter what label you take on for yourself, or wherever you end up, rest assured there will always be others like Percy Speed coming after you, never leaving you in peace.'

And as though all of it needed to come out, he continued talking, telling his side of this story of ours, whereas I was thinking all the while what I might do when I reached dry land, and if I would be on my own or not, depending on what I would find when it came time to rise up and go down below once more.

Enfield, Middlesex ✖ 21 October

SOME DAYS AGO, COMING ACROSS Lord Beckford's name in *The Times* newspaper, I read that the contents of his great country house were to be auctioned off, affording interested parties, so the piece said, a uniquely privileged opportunity to purchase certain items from his Lordship's private collection of rare and unusual artefacts.

The inventory ran to well near a column's length and, scanning the list, I searched in vain for one particular 'item', and the more I thought about it, the more that image took hold of me, until a week later I found myself drawn back to the place where I had first been commissioned to procure the object in question, then later seek out and find the person whose features were imprinted on it.

Travelling to Somerset was no easy matter, and on the journey I had ample time to reflect on what I was letting myself in for, even though on a Liverpool boat some few months previously I had convinced myself I had finally laid a certain 'ghost' to rest for good.

The night before the sale I stayed at an inn close by, and next morning set out for the house on foot, for it could plainly be seen among its encircling garland of trees, the sound of axe-men at work signifying not only were the contents of the house being disposed of, but the very timber on the estate itself. Still, never having much sympathy or regard for the owner, his present circumstances were of little concern to me, likewise the crowd of scavengers eagerly picking through his effects.

All the larger, more substantial pieces, chests, chairs,

sofas, mirrors, statuary, lay strewn about the lawn, and so I made my way through the confusion and up the marble steps to an even greater scene of bedlam, tradesmen carrying off crates of glass and china, buyers arguing over individual items like it was a Spitalfields market instead of some once great nobleman's residence.

More than a year had gone by since I had last set foot in these halls, and then they had been as lavishly furnished as some sultan's palace. Now they were hiving with strangers pawing over whatever scraps of grandeur remained, and recalling on that occasion being shown a chamber where Beckford kept some of his more private pieces, I made my way through the crush hoping to find it. But after entering several rooms and finding nothing save bare boards and stripped walls, I came close to giving up the search for something most probably now in some dealer's possession and who neither knew nor cared about its history.

However, if I thought to have been the only person present that day familiar with the object in question, I was mistaken, for glancing up to one of the galleries overhead I caught sight of a face I recognised, and when our eyes met, as if knowing what we were both there for, grinning, he held up a small leather valise, and determined not to indulge him I made off down the steps, putting the place and any memories it might hold behind me for good and where they belonged.

Yet being the persistent little piss-ant that he was, De Quincey came running out after me as fast as his puny legs could carry him, crying, 'Percy, Percy, stop, stop!' until the folk nearby turned their heads thinking I was making off with something without paying for it, and so not wishing for any further embarrassment I waited until he caught up with me, panting and holding on to a stone urn to get his breath back.

'God help us, Speed, have you no pity for a poor sedentary sluggard, near killing him like this? Even so, I'm more than pleased to renew our acquaintance, as we never managed to make our proper farewells back in that barbarous place across the water. Tell me, did you read my article on our fiendish friend and our dealings with him in *Blackwood's*?'

Unfortunately not, I told him, the journal scarcely one someone such as myself was likely to subscribe to, and even if I had, the subject of his piece no longer held the slightest interest for me.

'So what, may I be so bold to ask, draws you back to where your involvement with him first began?' and seeing me glance at the valise resting at his feet, smiling, he said, 'A memento, perhaps? Some souvenir to bear away with you?'

'Nothing other than the hope of recouping some of the monies owing me. But judging by what I see all around me, my journey's been a wasted one.'

'In that case come let us drown our sorrows, as both our missions would appear to have been fruitless,' and as he seemed determined to cling on to me there was nothing for it but accompany him back to The Bull, for that was where he, too, was staying, and so we walked together down the long gravelled drive, neither of us speaking until we reached the gates, where, looking back, De Quincey sighed and said, 'Alas, these once great households are vanishing one by one. All we can hope is that their treasures will not be lost along with their owners' patrician tastes. Before he fled his creditors my former friend and patron promised me one particular piece from his collection which I had always coveted. But like your good self, I, also, arrived too late to find our horde of human locusts had beaten us to it. But enough of that, let us commiserate over a glass or two.'

As there was no way of avoiding his company, we went on to the inn together, and when we were in its bar parlour and he had a glass of wine in front of him, says he, 'Just like old times, eh, my dear Speed? Although I have to confess I retain very little in the way of affection for that northern place where you and I spent so many long dark evenings together.'

He paused and, taking a sip from his claret, stared into the fire, until to break the sombre mood, I asked, 'And what of Jack Slack? I'd hoped he might have returned to his former duties and I would have met with him today. Still, I imagine any likelihood of that vanished along with his previous master and employer.'

He sighed.

'Ah, poor Slack indeed. Sadly, the last I heard tell, he had reverted to his former brutal calling.'

'Despite all those religious convictions of his?'

'Smiting the Pharisee in the grass ring instead of in the pulpit, you might say. *He*, at least, adhered to the precepts laid down in the Scriptures, unlike that other pair of whited sepulchres. Still, both received their just deserts, the wages of sin not such a biblical myth after all, it would appear.'

For an instant I stared at him.

'Dead? Dead, you say?'

'Well, one near as makes no difference, career and livelihood, dust and ashes, and if that is not sufficient, about to end up behind bars on a charge of false pretences and embezzlement of church funds.'

'And his accomplice?'

'With his Maker already, so I've been reliably informed.'

'By whom, may I ask?'

My sharpening tone must have betrayed me, for, leaning forward and fixing me with a beady eye, he said, 'So your interest in our former murderer and his fate hasn't been entirely dissipated after all.'

'Well, he and I did manage to come near enough within striking distance of one another.'

'Which must have been of little consolation to someone like yourself.'

'But not to you, it would appear.'

He laughed.

'My dear Speed, I am more than capable of filling in any

gaps in the story. That's what we journalistic folk do.'

No truer word was ever spoken, for in that famous article of his, which I *had* read, incidentally, there were almost as many 'gaps' and holes as in a sieve, nettling me at the time, knowing, as I did, that the individual concerned was as alive as we both were, and so pressing him, I enquired, 'Where, as a matter of curiosity, did he meet his end, as you say?'

'Oh, in some godforsaken spot in the wilds of Cork or Kerry, just as you predicted yourself, if you recall, the last time we spoke.'

'And the actual manner of it?'

'Done to death over some argument involving a young woman, so they say.'

'They?'

'Well, one, to be specific, Mulholland the coachman you employed. Having been impressed with his familiarity with everything and everyone worth knowing in the country, after you left for England I took the liberty of retaining his services, and having made his enquiries he supplied the information I have this moment passed on to you.'

Hard as it was for me not to laugh outright, along with the temptation to present him with the truth, I managed to repress both, telling him, 'In that case let you and I drink a toast to a fitting conclusion and final good riddance to Mr William Hare, now deceased.'

But instead of raising his glass, opening his valise, he produced his own miniature vial, raising it to his lips as I had seen him do on so many occasions before, and thus the mystery of what the valise contained was revealed, not the death mask, as I had supposed, but nothing other than that same familiar little brown apothecary's bottle.

That was the last time he and I were to meet. Next morning we went our separate ways, he to his family and friends in Edinburgh, and me to my well-deserved, retirement in Enfield in the English countryside.

However, I did happen to come across some other more recent writings of his, on 'the art of murder', of all things. But there was very little there to interest me, the author having nothing fresh or new to impart on the subject save what must have been inspired by the distilled essence of the poppy plant.

Left to themselves memories tend to fade, whereas a portrait on paper, or perhaps in some other more substantial material, does not. Like the object, in fact, I had an urge to see for myself one last time before vanishing for good like the person whose features it bore, and who himself stood facing me on a steamship taking both of us back to where our story first began. And sometimes, too, I think that was where it should have ended, not with talk, but a bullet, a quicker, more deserving end, surely, than the one he once handed out to others.

And here in the heart of Middlesex, I still recall how he and I stood those few paces apart on that bare wet wooden deck that day, with him unable or unwilling to utter a word in his defence. But then why should he? How could he? This, after all, was how it was always bound to end, no proper satisfaction gained, save Percy Speed finally getting to tell his own version of the story to someone with nowhere left to run save over a ship's rail and into the Irish Sea.

Lacking the kind of disposition usually described as fanciful or whimsical, such things I leave to the De Quinceys of this world and their laudanum dreams, yet once I remember seeing a handler of wild beasts perform in Coram Fields, and how he held his animal quiet and docile using nothing, it seemed, save the power of his words, whispering to it, a tiger, as I recall, that neither moved nor uttered a sound until he left its cage.

So in some strange fashion, had I become like that same handler myself, and the one now facing me, the beast? Certainly he had been likened to one in human form often enough. Yet even if I *had* managed to talk him into submission, not a word passed his lips, not even when I recounted how I had been employed to procure an image of him, and afterwards continue the search for the living original, until, as is the case with certain wealthy individuals of a fickle disposition, my patron lost interest in the project, whereas I, being of a stubborn, dogged, investigative nature, did not, carrying on until my quarry was standing, as he was, right now here in front of me.

And then there was no more to tell or be heard save the sound of the waves and the gulls overhead indicating the approach of land, when there came that same question, the one which I still couldn't answer properly.

'But what is it you *want* with me?'

So I told him, 'Nothing any more, for this matter between the two of us is finally settled, and I thank God this will be the first and last time our paths will ever need to cross.'

However, old habits being what they are, at Liverpool I watched from above, taking note of the passengers as they poured off the *Erin* on to the quayside where those onward bound for Boston and similar ports settled down to wait with their few pitiful belongings on the cold wet stones.

Scanning the crowds below, I searched for a glimpse of a solitary figure, one face out of all the rest, and only when the final ship's whistle had sounded was my patience rewarded, and I picked out my man standing near a pillar, coat collar pulled up against the chill, yet knowing him, as I did, to disguise and muffle his features.

'Sir, you have to leave, or go back the way you came.'

It was a sailor with a rope's end in his hand, and so I followed him to a lower deck where some of the sporting types I had seen earlier were refusing to disembark, and taking advantage of the melee I edged my way to the rail to observe my old enemy one last time.

It seemed to me, he, too, must be waiting to board the American boat, for he still hadn't moved, wary and watchful of everything around him, yet not knowing he had an observer high above.

But by now the sailors were threatening to raise the gangplank, so I joined the last drunken stragglers going ashore to whatever destination lay ahead of them. My own was the railway station, and making my way with my solitary piece of luggage in my hand through that huddled mass of patient humanity, I set out to catch a train south.

Where the quayside ended and the city's streets properly began, there stood a raised ramp with some steps, and bent on draining that last drop of intelligence from my quest, climbing up and looking back, I saw my man emerge from his pillar to ward off a young woman, a bundle of what looked like swaddling in her arms, running at him from the crowd, and on the instant the pair were surrounded by a swarm of old biddies swathed in shawls, raising their hands, upbraiding him, and despite my intention to concern myself no longer, I stood watching until some sort of calm was restored, and he and the young red-haired woman were swallowed up by the crowd, never to be seen again, at least for the purposes of this account, anyway.

And so concludes this final entry in Percival Speed's journal, setting down the events of his last case, that's if it ever could have been called such a thing, the quarry walking free, his pursuer not raising a hand to detain him, and at the finish of it, still being out of pocket, let it be said.

As to the future whereabouts of William Hare, or whatever name he might now be going under, nothing further was heard, America being as remote and mysterious a place as the moon is to the rest of us, the mask, too, disappearing, at least to this person's understanding, anyway, as though never created.

Yet, who knows, if ever it happens to end up in someone's cabinet, or on a mantelpiece, say, some careless servant girl one day might let fall that particular mould, and so with it would also perish the memory of someone who fled his rightful fate and destiny, fleet and artful as his own elusive namesake.

Acknowledgements

After Hare's last recorded sighting on the road to Carlisle, his subsequent whereabouts still remain a mystery, so anything later has to be speculation or, as in the foregoing, take the form of some kind of fictional reconstruction.

However, researching the earlier Scottish years I was greatly helped in the task by consulting certain historical records of the time, with an additional debt of gratitude going to Owen Dudley Edwards and his masterly and definitive *Burke and Hare*, incidentally, the work which first started me off on my own literary hunt for Mr Hare.